# Scientific Romance

## AN INTERNATIONAL ANTHOLOGY OF PIONEERING SCIENCE FICTION

Introduced and Edited by
### BRIAN STABLEFORD

D1262221

DOVER PUBLICATIONS, INC.
Mineola, New York

*Bibliographical Note*

This Dover edition, first published in 2017, is a new anthology of stories reprinted from standard texts. Brian Stableford has made the selection and has also written an Introduction and author biographies specially for this edition.

*Library of Congress Cataloging-in-Publication Data*

Names: Stableford, Brian M., editor.
Title: Scientific romance : an international anthology of pioneering science fiction / edited by Brian Stableford.
Description: Mineola, New York : Dover Publications, 2017.
Identifiers: LCCN 2016048968| ISBN 9780486808376 (paperback) | ISBN 0486808378
Subjects: LCSH: Science fiction. | BISAC: FICTION / Science Fiction / Short Stories.
Classification: LCC PN6071.S33 S39 2017 | DDC 808.83/8762—dc23 LC record available at https://lccn.loc.gov/2016048968

Manufactured in the United States by LSC Communications
80837801    2017
www.doverpublications.com

# INTRODUCTION

The "scientific romance" for which this anthology provides a showcase is a species of imaginative fiction that existed before the modern term "science fiction" was adopted in the 1920s. The latter label was initially used to distinguish a small set of competing American magazines specializing in futuristic fiction and tales of technological invention, but such fiction already had a long history, and "scientific romance" was the term most commonly used to describe it when it enjoyed its period of greatest success in the last decade of the nineteenth century and the first decade of the twentieth.

Imaginative fiction that took its inspiration from the advancement of science existed long before the creation of any distinguishing label, and fiction featuring some of the themes that eventually became central to scientific romance, and science fiction—especially stories of fantastic voyages beyond the limits of the known world—is as old as the habit of storytelling. It is easy to find precursory echoes of scientific romance in the earliest stories that have survived to the present day, including the Sumerian epic of *Gilgamesh* and the Greek account of the *Odyssey*. Various new concerns were added to the fiction of imaginary voyages over the centuries, including crucial contributions by Dante's *Commedia* and Thomas More's *Utopia*, but with regard to the adoption of a scientific outlook and the attempt to employ the scientific imagination as a springboard for speculative invention, the first significant attempt to do something of the sort was undertaken by the British philosopher Francis Bacon. He never finished the work in question, but the fragment he produced, *New Atlantis*, was appended to one of his posthumous publications in 1627.

Hardly anyone was inclined to follow Bacon's lead during the next century, and it proved somewhat undiplomatic even to try, as ideological conflicts broke out between dogmatic religious faith and the implications of science, and political powers became increasingly anxious about the sub-

versive intentions of utopian schemes. The most extravagant writer of philosophical fiction in the seventeenth century, Savinien Cyrano de Bergerac,
was unable to publish his account of *L'Autre Monde ou les Etats et Empires
de la lune* [The Other World] during his lifetime, firstly because he was
badly injured by a wooden beam that fell on his head, perhaps deliberately,
and secondly because the final half of the manuscript was stolen and, presumably, destroyed. The surviving sections, which were published after his
death, were extensively bowdlerized to minimize their potential offense to
the Church, and the full texts were not restored until the 1920s. By then,
poor Cyrano was most remembered because Edmond Rostand had written
a play in which he figured as a lovelorn soldier with a colossal nose, and his
reputation as a literary pioneer had been comprehensively eclipsed.

The vast strides made by science in the seventeenth century made the
precedents set by Bacon and Cyrano seem increasingly important, and in
spite of the real dangers involved in taking up imaginative arms against
Church and State—because there was a war of ideas that needed to be
fought in spite of the risks—writers in the "Age of Enlightenment," particularly in pre-Revolutionary France, became increasingly eager to test
the limits of tolerance in aggressive satires employing all the weapons that
could be found in the armory of the imagination or added to it.

It was in France that the term *roman scientifique*, translated into English
as "scientific romance"—although a more accurate translation would be
"scientific fiction"—was first coined, in the mid-eighteenth century. It was
initially employed, however, as a term of abuse to be hurled at scientific
ideas that the user rejected. Élie-Catherine Fréron used it to denigrate Isaac
Newton's theory of gravity, and others employed it to put the boot into the
discredited notion of *phlogiston*. The English equivalent had been imported by 1780 and was used in a broadly similar fashion, often employed by
religious believers to assault geological theses that cast doubt on Biblical
chronology.

The French term *roman scientifique* was used by Honoré de Balzac to
describe the famous New York *Sun* "Moon Hoax" of 1835, which reported
discoveries of lunar life supposedly made by the astronomer John Herschel
by means of a new telescope located at the Cape of Good Hope. The fake
reportage, which grew gradually more extravagant over the five days that
the "story" ran, equally caused a sensation when it was translated by French
newspapers. That was, however, fiction masquerading as fact, and only

signified a partial shift in the term's significance. The crucial redefinition occurred in the 1860s, when a French boom in the popularization of science gave rise to numerous experiments in the use of fiction as a vehicle to make scientific information more palatable and engaging.

The term *roman scientifique* was not the only one recruited by journalists to describe such fictional endeavors, but it became the most frequently used when the early novels of Jules Verne, especially the classic set consisting of *Voyage au centre de la terre* (1864; revised 1867; tr. as *Journey to the Centre of the Earth*), *De la terre à la lune* (1865; tr. as *From the Earth to the Moon*), its sequel, *Autour de la lune* (1870; tr. as *Around the Moon*), and *Vingt mille lieues sous les mers* (1870; tr. as *Twenty Thousand Leagues Under the Sea*), seemed to many readers and critics to be the definitive texts of a new kind of fiction. It was with reference to the translations of these novels that journalists in Britain and America began to routinely use the term "scientific romance."

Once the huge international success of Verne's work had established the notion of scientific romance, observers began to notice previous works that had affinities with Verne's and realized that this kind of fiction went back as least as far as the Moon Hoax. In America, Edgar Allan Poe was recognized as having been a significant precursor of Verne in a handful of Poe's remarkably varied works; other American journalistic writers influenced by Poe who had used scientific inspiration in some of their work in a kindred fashion while seeking a similarly broad scope—including Nathaniel Hawthorne, Fitz-James O'Brien, Edward Page Mitchell and Ambrose Bierce—were then seen to be in the process of building up a slender but nevertheless significant and ingenious tradition of *American* scientific romance.

The term "scientific romance" went through a new phase of evolution in the 1890s, however, when Britain produced a writer who, like Jules Verne, had a spectacular impact with a sequence of early works of a related kind: H. G. Wells. Any pleasure that Wells might initially have derived from the comparison soon evaporated, however, as he was averse to being seen as anyone's follower, and he quickly began to protest that he was a very different type of writer—an insistence echoed by Verne, who similarly did not want to yield to the impression that his work might have been overtaken and superseded.

The conflict of opinion became newsworthy in itself, as registered in a series of quotations that are still cited today, including the resentful remarks made by Verne to the English journalist Gordon Jones in an interview reproduced in the June 1904 issue of *Temple Bar*: "I consider [Wells], as a purely imaginative writer, to be deserving of very high praise, but our methods are entirely different. I have always made a point in my romances of basing my so-called inventions upon a groundwork of actual fact, and of using in their construction methods and materials which are not entirely without the pale of contemporary engineering skill and knowledge. . . . The creations of Mr. Wel[l]s, on the other hand, belong unreservedly to a degree of scientific knowledge far removed from the present, though I will not say beyond the limits of the possible."

Other observers, however, thought that what Verne and Wells had in common was far more important than the differences between them, and continued to bracket them together. When the American publisher Hugo Gernsback coined the term "scientifiction" (a contraction of "scientific fiction") to describe the new genre he wanted to promote, prior to replacing it with the less unwieldy "science fiction," he identified it specifically as the genre pioneered by Jules Verne and H. G. Wells, whose exemplary works he hastened to reprint in the pages of his specialist magazine *Amazing Stories*.

The first person to use the phrase *roman scientifique* in a deliberate attempt to designate, delineate and exemplify a genre of fiction was Louis Figuier, the editor of the popular science magazine *La Science Illustrée*, who began running a regular fiction section in 1888 under that heading. Over the next decade and a half, Figuier published dozens more works, which extracted a series of exemplars from the past and mingled them with new works, in order to lay them out as a kind of tacit map of what he considered to be the genre of *roman scientifique*. It was, in essence, a Vernian genre, but Figuier seems to have urged the writers he recruited to be more adventurous in their endeavors than the fiction featured in the geographical periodical *Journal de Voyages*, which used Vernian serials in abundance.

From the very beginning, Figuier edged his putative genre in the direction of bolder speculative fiction, and began to do so even more wholeheartedly in 1898, when he discovered a new source of useful material in translations of the works of H. G. Wells, twelve of which he published over the next five years. His fiction slot did not last much longer, however, and the periodical was devoted entirely to non-fiction after 1905. By that time, the term "scientific romance" was solidly established in Britain and America as a journalistic and critical label for "Wellsian fiction"—which was indeed seen by many commentators there to have overtaken and superseded its Vernian ancestor.

Wells initially accepted the term, and was perfectly happy to tell a journalist who interviewed him in 1897 that he was "working on another scientific romance," but he soon decided that he did not like it, probably because it seemed to bracket him with Verne, and he abandoned its use in personal references to his own works. In the classified lists of previous publications included in his books in the early years of the twentieth century, Wells generally filed his archetypal scientific romances with other works under the rubric "Fantastic and Imaginative Romances." It was not until 1933, when Victor Gollancz issued an omnibus edition of eight novels, *The Scientific Romances of H.G. Wells*, that he grudgingly consented to allow the phrase to reassume its authoritative status, and even then, in the preface he supplied to the volume, he only referred to his "fantasies" and his "scientific fantasies," and remarked:

> "These tales have been compared to the work of Jules Verne and there was a disposition on the part of literary journalists at one time to call me the English Jules Verne. As a matter of fact there is no literary resemblance whatever between the anticipatory inventions of the great Frenchman and these fantasies. His work dealt almost always with actual possibilities of invention and discovery, and he made some remarkable forecasts. The interest he invoked was a practical one.... But these stories of mine collected here do not pretend to deal with possible things."

Gollancz was, of course, being disingenuous: Wells's scientific romances do not, in fact, deal with possible things—nor had Verne's, in fact—but they *do* pretend to, and they pretend very insistently.

Wells's personal rejection was undoubtedly a stumbling block to the general acceptance of the term "scientific romance," but it remained in common use in Britain, just as *roman scientifique* did in France, for much of the twentieth century, until the American "science fiction" label, imported on a massive scale after the end of World War Two, eclipsed its rivals completely.

Other British writers did not manifest the same allergic reaction to "scientific romance" as Wells. In 1884, the publisher William Swann Sonnenschein issued a pamphlet entitled *Scientific Romances No. I: What is the*

*Fourth Dimension?*, by C. H. Hinton, and followed it up with four further pamphlets in the series; they were then bound up into a book as *Scientific Romances: First Series* (1886), mingling essays and philosophical fiction. The series was interrupted thereafter, and soon virtually forgotten, although H. G. Wells borrowed extensively from Hinton's discussions of the fourth dimension in providing the imaginative underpinnings of his break-through novel *The Time Machine* (1895), but it had helped to popularize the term in England.

In 1890 a reviewer in the *Athaeneum* unhesitatingly classified Robert Cromie's *A Plunge into Space* as "a pseudo-scientific romance of the Jules Verne type," and the publisher sent a copy to Verne for comment; the latter wrote a letter of praise in return that was duly reproduced as a preface to the second edition. Cromie later suggested that Wells had appropriated certain elements of his own text for use in *The First Men in the Moon* (1901), but Wells replied, with not-untypical rudeness, that not only had he never read *A Plunge into Space,* but he had never even heard of Robert Cromie. Wells was equally dismissive of his contemporary George Griffith, who also had no objection to being compared to Jules Verne, or to being described as a writer of scientific romance.

Griffith made his own breakthrough in the field of future war fiction, which was then booming in British newspapers, and although Wells steered clear of it until 1908, when the temptation became too strong and he wrote his distinctive account of *The War in the Air*, several other writers came into the genre by that route before diversifying into the broader areas of the genre, including M. P. Shiel, author of the newspaper serial "The Empress of the Earth" (1898; reprinted in book form as *The Yellow Danger*). Like Griffith, Shiel—who spent a good deal of time in Paris during the 1890s—might well have borrowed some inspiration from French future war fiction, although the influence was not obvious at the time to English critics. Other writers who made crucial contributions to the British genre while it was in its heyday, in the two decades prior to the outbreak of the Great War of 1914–18, included Fred T. Jane, William Hope Hodgson, Arthur Conan Doyle, and J. D. Beresford.

The definitive core of the British genre, however, remained the work of Wells. The eight novels contained in the 1933 Gollancz omnibus are *The Time Machine* (1895), *The Island of Doctor Moreau* (1896), *The Invisible Man* (1897), *The War of the Worlds* (1898), *The First Men in the Moon*

(1901), *The Food of the Gods* (1904), *In the Days of the Comet* (1906) and *Men Like Gods* (1923). Some critics would argue that the last two do not really belong in the set, and would have preferred to see *When the Sleeper Wakes* (1899; revised 1910 as *The Sleeper Awakes*) and *The War in the Air* included instead.

Wells presumably considered that the ideas for social reform contained in *When the Sleeper Wakes* had been superseded by those developed in *Men Like Gods* and omitted *The War in the Air* from the omnibus because he thought that its anticipation of the politics and armaments of a future war had been rendered obsolete by the actual war of 1914–18. Quibbles aside, however, it was the first five novels featured in the omnibus, along with a number of shorter stories, that had initially prompted the wide-spread adoption of "scientific romance" as a descriptive term by commen-tators, and it was that material that effectively framed and anchored an understanding of what people meant in the late 1890s and early 1900s when they said "scientific romance."

By the time the Gollancz omnibus had appeared, many of Wells's short-er scientific romances had already been reprinted in an omnibus of *The Short Stories of H. G. Wells* (1927), but they had not been sorted by genre (although *Tales of Space and Time* (1899), which included the long novella "A Story of the Days to Come" (1897), was almost a specialized collection). There is, therefore, no single book that contains the whole set of the works that Wells produced in 1895–98, which created and formulated the notion of "scientific romance," but a core of a dozen items could be established by supplementing the first four novels in the Gollancz omnibus and "A Story of the Days to Come" with "The Flowering of the Strange Orchid" (1894), "The Remarkable Case of Davidson's Eyes" (1895), "The Plattner Story" (1896), "In the Abyss" (1896), "The Sea Raiders" (1896), "The Crystal Egg" (1897) and "The Star" (1897).

The French genre of *roman scientifique* was more prolific than the American or English genres of scientific romance even before the advent of Jules Verne, and became much more so once Verne had provided the cru-cial exemplars previously noted. Futuristic fiction examining the prospects of technological progress had obtained an initial boost from the French Romantic Movement, many of whose prose writers dabbled in it.

The writers in question included the founder of the first of the *cénacles* [literary sets] that gave the Movement its principal arena of discussion,

Charles Nodier, in the futuristic satires "Hurlubeu" and "Léviathan le Long" (1833; combined in English translation as "Perfectibility"). Shortly thereafter, Nodier's friend Félix Bodin published a prospectus for a new genre of *roman futuriste* [futuristic fiction] in *Le Roman de l'avenir* (1834; tr. as *The Novel of the Future*), including a specimen text that was unfortunately interrupted by the author's ill-health, and remained incomplete.

Two years later, another associate of the Movement, Louis Geoffroy, invented another new genre in his *Napoléon et la conquête du monde, 1812–1832, Histoire de la monarchie universelle* (tr. as *The Apocryphal Napoléon*), which describes how Napoleon, after thrashing the Czar's armies in the Russian Campaign, goes on to conquer the entire world, stimulating a rapid scientific advancement far in excess of the one to which our depleted history was restricted.

Further significant contributions to the fledgling genre were made in France by S. Henry Berthoud, Joseph Méry and Léon Gozlan, and the Romantic Movement still had sufficient impetus in the 1860s for Jules Verne to become a late recruit, his literary ambitions initially being nurtured under the wing of Alexandre Dumas. Indeed, before making his crucial breakthrough with *Cinq semaines en ballon* (1863; tr. as *Five Weeks in a Balloon*), Verne had written a thoroughly Romantic and decidedly lachrymose *roman futuriste, Paris au XXᵉ siècle* (1863, pub. 1994; tr. as *Paris in the Twentieth Century*). However, the publisher who took him under contract, P.-J. Hetzel, not only refused to publish the work but advised Verne to bury it forever, and it did not see the light of day until 1994, when it finally reached print.

The satirical elements of Romantic futurism were carried forward by numerous French humorists, who found futuristic and technological speculation a fruitful resource. There is a larger component of comedy in the French genre than the British one, although the American genre took similar inspiration from Poe—who was almost alone in constituting the American Romantic Movement—and there is a strong affinity between French and American scientific romance in their comedic element. Inevitably, that element shows up more prominently in the present showcase anthology, which is necessarily restricted to short fiction, than the earnest Vernian element or the future war fiction so vital to the British genre, which is almost entirely exemplified by novels.

The sampler included herein is thus a slightly distorted view of the contents of the three parallel genres, but I have attempted to offer some compensation for that by including a chronological appendix of longer works produced in the same period, from Edgar Allan Poe's initial experiments to the outbreak of the Great War. Although it does make perfect sense to employ *roman scientifique* and scientific romance as a descriptive term for material published after 1918, especially in Britain and France, where the American notion of "science fiction" only made slow inroads prior to the Second World War, there is a sense in which the genre had lost some of its impetus by then, and had markedly changed direction.

That transformation came about partly because the popular magazines that had provided an arena for enthusiastic experimentation before the war had completed their investigation of the pattern of audience demand, and had come to the conclusion that scientific romance would never be able to compete with crime fiction and love stories in terms of widespread popularity, and partly because the after-effects of the war and the manner of its fighting had left a lingering disenchantment with the idea of scientific progress, quashing much of the exuberance of fiction dealing with such themes. The scientific romance genre continued to produce works of great brilliance in both Britain and France, but they were mostly marginal to the literary marketplace, and those that were not frankly alarmist were esoteric in their appeal.

The following collection, therefore, offers a few examples from the period of the genre's first emergence, before focusing its principal attention on its heyday, when scientific romance was in its most enterprising and exciting phase. Contemporary readers, who can hardly help seeing the genre as an ancestor of science fiction, will inevitably be struck by the difference between the two genres, one of which is particularly conspicuous. The influence that science fiction took from scientific romance was broad, but it had a focus on four works in particular: Verne's *From the Earth to the Moon* and *Around the Moon*, and Wells's *The War of the Worlds* and *The First Men in the Moon*. Although very popular, these works were not typical of the genre of scientific romance, and had only a limited influence within it, but they became the most important foundation-stones and models of science fiction; the most enthusiastic and inventive recruits to the new genre soon gave great prominence to the notion that space travel would be a central element of the future development of civilized societies.

The reasons for that conviction include the enthusiastic advent of rocket research alongside the early development of the science fiction magazines in the 1930s, and also reflect the fact that science fiction took up where the quintessentially American genre of the western had been forced to leave off, replacing the tamed frontier of the West with the "final frontier" of interplanetary space, to which the fundamental project of adventurous pioneering and colonization could be conveniently exported. Europe did not have such a ready-made attraction to the mythology of an impending "Space Age," and *roman scientifique* and British scientific romance remained much more firmly anchored to the Earth in envisaging potential futures.

To diehard science fiction fans, that restriction of attention on the part of scientific romance might seem like a failure of imagination, but to the practitioners of French and British futuristic fiction it seemed like common sense and justified prudence. For a while, in the late 1960s, when it briefly seemed that a Space Age might actually be beginning, science fiction boomed; now, fifty years later, the myth has been severely tarnished, and science fiction is in evident decline. In consequence, it might well be the case that the achievements of scientific romance can now be assessed more fairly, and its merits more accurately judged, in terms of its philosophical acumen as well as its entertainment value.

BRIAN STABLEFORD

# CONTENTS

xiii

# THE CONVERSATION OF EIROS AND CHARMION

## EDGAR ALLAN POE

*Edgar Allan Poe (1809–1849) was the most innovative and adventurous writer active in the United States in the nineteenth century. Perennially at odds with his hard-headed adoptive father, John Allan, and completely unappreciated by his contemporaries, he lived in abject poverty and misery, and died in mysterious circumstances of an illness that his physicians could not diagnose. Ever infected by what one of his stories called "The Imp of the Perverse," Poe had appointed as his literary executor his arch-enemy, the appalling Rufus W. Griswold, who made far more money out of Poe's works than Poe had contrived to do in his lifetime, did everything humanly possible to blacken his reputation and diminish his genius, added insult to injury by foisting the name of his adoptive father permanently upon his byline, but lent ironic impetus to his peculiar legend.*

*Poe experimented with many different narrative strategies and a wide range of subject matter, inventing the detective story and modern horror fiction, and also publishing several works that can now be seen as important exemplars for the subsequent development of scientific romance, including the long "prose poem" Eureka (1848), which developed contemporary cosmological theory in a rhapsodic manner. "The Unparalleled Adventure of One Hans Pfaall" (1835), a farcical and satirical depiction of a voyage to the moon by balloon, was rapidly outshone by the New York Sun's "Moon Hoax," which Poe thought partly inspired by his own story. He added a prefatory note to the book version arguing, tongue-in-cheek, that the time was ripe for the insertion of more verisimilitude into accounts of imaginary space travel—which turned out to be one of the true words spoken in jest that are considerably*

1

rarer than proverbial wisdom suggests. Poe's own literary hoaxes included an account of a transatlantic crossing by balloon and, more interestingly, a mock-scientific account of the employment of hypnotism to preserve a man's consciousness after death, nowadays known as "The Facts in the Case of M. Valdemar" (1845).

"The Conversation of Eiros and Charmion" (1839) is a dramatization of contemporary ideas regarding the nature of comets and the perennial fascination of the question of what might happen if the Earth were to have a close encounter with one. It illustrates the difficulty of devising appropriate narrative viewpoints for the telling of such stories, solving the problem in this instance with characteristic flamboyant originality. It also includes an oblique, ironic reflection of the notoriety of the preacher William Miller, who published numerous articles during the 1830s supposedly based on calculations derived from Biblical prophecies. Predicting the end of the world in 1844, Miller attracted large numbers of followers, who, undeterred by the failure of the prediction, founded the Seventh-Day Adventist Church, which now has millions of members, and still expects the end of the world any day now.

> I will bring fire to thee.
>
> —Euripides, *Andromache*

### EIROS

Why do you call me Eiros?

### CHARMION

So henceforward you will always be called. You must forget, too, my earthly name and speak to me as Charmion.

### EIROS

This is indeed no dream!

## CHARMION

Dreams are with us no more; but of these mysteries anon. I rejoice to see you looking lifelike and rational. The film of the shadow has already passed from off your eyes. Be of heart, and fear nothing. Your allotted days of stupor have expired; and, tomorrow, I will myself induct you into the full joys and wonders of your novel existence.

## EIROS

True, I feel no stupor, none at all. The wild sickness and the terrible darkness have left me, and I hear no longer that mad rushing, horrible sound, like the "voice of many waters." Yet my senses are bewildered, Charmion, with the keenness of their perception of the new.

## CHARMION

A few days will remove all this; but I fully understand you, and feel for you. It is now ten earthly years since I underwent what you undergo, yet the remembrance of it hangs by me still. You have now suffered all of pain, however, which you will suffer in Aidenn.[1]

## EIROS

In Aidenn?

## CHARMION

In Aidenn.

---

[1] Poe also uses "Aidenn" to refer to the realm of the afterlife in his famous poem "The Raven" (1845): "Tell this soul with sorrow laden if, within the distant Aidenn / It shall clasp a sainted maiden whom the angels named Lenor." The reference to the "ten earthly years" that Charmion has been dead may suggest that Poe had his adoptive mother, Frances Allan, in mind; she had died in 1829.

### EIROS

Oh God! pity me, Charmion! I am overburdened with the majesty of all things, of the unknown now known, of the speculative future merged in the august and certain present.

### CHARMION

Grapple not now with such thoughts. Tomorrow we will speak of this. Your mind wavers, and its agitation will find relief in the exercise of simple memories. Look not round, nor forward, but back. I am burning with anxiety to hear the details of that stupendous event which threw you among us. Tell me of it. Let us converse of familiar things, in the old familiar language of the world which has so fearfully perished.

### EIROS

Most fearfully, fearfully! this is indeed no dream.

### CHARMION

Dreams are no more. Was I much mourned, my Eiros?

### EIROS

Mourned, Charmion?—oh, deeply. To that last hour of all, there hung a cloud of intense gloom and devout sorrow over your household.

### CHARMION

And that last hour—speak of it. Remember that, beyond the naked fact of the catastrophe itself, I know nothing. When coming out from among mankind, I passed into night through the grave—at that period, if I remember aright, the calamity which overwhelmed you as utterly unanticipated. But, indeed, I knew little of the speculative philosophy of the day.

EIROS

The individual calamity was, as you say, entirely unanticipated; but analogous misfortunes had been long a subject of discussion with astronomers. I need scarce tell you, my friend, that even when you left us, men had agreed to understand those passages in the Holy Writings which speak of the final destruction of all things by fire as having reference to the orb of the earth alone. But in regard to the immediate agency of the ruin, speculation had been at fault from that epoch in astronomical knowledge in which the comets were divested of the terror of flame.

The very moderate density of these bodies had been well established. They had been observed to pass among the satellites of Jupiter without bringing about any sensible alteration either in the masses or in the orbits of these secondary planets.[2] We had long regarded the wanderers as vapory creations of inconceivable tenuity, and as altogether incapable of doing injury to our substantial globe, even in the event of contact. But contact was not in any degree dreaded; for the elements of all the comets were accurately known. That among them we should look for the agency of the threatened fiery destruction had been for many years considered as an inadmissible idea. But wonders and wild fancies had been, of late days, strangely rife among mankind; and although it was only with a few of the ignorant that actual apprehension prevailed upon the announcement by astronomers of a new comet, yet this announcement was generally received with I know not what of agitation and mistrust.

The elements of the strange orb were immediately calculated, and it was at once conceded by all observers that its path, at perihelion, would bring it into very close proximity with the earth. There were two or three astronomers of secondary note who resolutely maintained that a contact was inevitable. I cannot very well express to you the effect of this intelligence upon the people. For a few short days they would not believe an assertion which their intellect, so long employed among worldly considerations, could not in any manner grasp. But the truth of a vitally important fact soon made

---

[2] *The American Almanac and Repository of Useful Knowledge* (1833), from which Poe probably obtained his information about comets, popularized the information that a comet first observed by Laplace in 1770 had passed between the satellites of Jupiter in 1779 without causing any deviation of their orbits.

its way into the understanding of even the most stolid. Finally, all men saw that astronomical knowledge lied not, and they awaited the comet.

Its approach was not, at first, seemingly rapid; not as its appearance of very unusual character. It was a dull red, and had little perceptible train. For seven or eight days we saw no material increase in its apparent diameter, and but a partial alteration in its color. Meanwhile the ordinary affairs of men were discarded, and all interests absorbed in a growing discussion, instituted by the philosophic, in respect to the cometary nature. Even the grossly ignorant roused their sluggish capacities to such considerations. The learned now gave their intellect, their soul, to no such points as the allaying of fear, or to the sustenance of loved theory. They sought, they panted, for right views. They groaned for perfected knowledge. Truth arose in the purity of her strength and exceeding majesty, and the wise bowed down and adored.

That material injury to our globe or to its inhabitants would result from the apprehended contact, was an opinion which hourly lost ground among the wise; and the wise were now freely permitted to rule the reason and the fancy of the crowd. It was demonstrated that the density of the comet's nucleus was far less than that of our rarest gas; and the harmless passage of a similar visitor among the satellites of Jupiter was a point strongly insisted upon, and which served greatly to allay terror.

Theologists, with an earnestness fear-enkindled, dwelt upon the Biblical prophecies, and expounded them to the people with a directness and simplicity of which no previous instance had been known. That the final destruction of the earth must be brought about by the agency of fire, was urged with a spirit that enforced everywhere conviction; and that the comets were of no fiery nature (as all men now knew) was a truth which relieved all, in a great measure, from the apprehension of the great calamity foretold.

It is noticeable that the popular prejudices and vulgar errors in regard to pestilences and wars—errors which were wont to prevail upon every appearance of a comet—were now altogether unknown. As if by some sudden convulsive exertion, reason had at once hurled superstition from her throne. The feeblest intellect had derived vigor from excessive interest.

What minor evils might arise from the contact were points of elaborate question. The learned spoke of slight geological disturbances, of probable alterations in climate, and consequently in vegetation; of possible magnetic and electric influences. Many held that no visible or perceptible effect would in any way be produced. While such discussions were going on, their subject gradually approached, growing larger in apparent diameter, and of a more brilliant luster. Mankind grew paler as it came. All human operations were suspended.

There was an epoch in the course of the general sentiment when the comet had attained, at length, a size surpassing that of any previous recorded visitation. The people now, dismissing any lingering hope that the astronomers were wrong, experienced all the certainty of evil. The chimerical aspect of their terror was gone. The hearts of the stoutest of our race beat violently within their bosoms. A very few days sufficed, however, to merge even such feelings in sentiments more endurable. We could no longer apply to the strange orb any accustomed thoughts. Its historical attributes had disappeared. It oppressed us with a hideous novelty of emotion. We saw it not as an astronomical phenomenon in the heavens, but as an incubus upon our hearts, and a shadow upon our brains. It had taken, with inconceivable rapidity, the character of a gigantic mantle of rare flame, extending from horizon to horizon.

Yet a day, and men breathed with greater freedom. It was clear that we were already within the influence of the comet; yet we lived. We even felt an unusual elasticity of frame and vivacity of mind. The exceeding tenuity of the object of our dread was apparent; for all heavenly objects were plainly visible through it. Meantime, our vegetation had perceptibly altered; and we gained faith, from this predicted circumstance, in the foresight of the wise. A wild luxuriance of foliage, utterly unknown before, burst out upon every vegetable thing.

Yet another day, and the evil was not altogether upon us. It was now evident that its nucleus would first reach us. A wild change had come over all men; and the first sense of pain was the wild signal for general lamentation and horror. The first sense of pain lay in a rigorous constriction of the breast and lungs, and an insufferable dryness of the skin. It could not be denied that our atmosphere was radically affected; the conformation of this atmosphere and the possible modifications to which it might be subjected, were now the topics of discussion. The result of investigation sent an electric thrill of the intensest terror through the universal heart of man.

It had long been known that the air which encircled us was a compound of oxygen and nitrogen gases, in the proportion of twenty-one measures of oxygen and seventy-nine of nitrogen in every one hundred of the atmosphere.[3] Oxygen, which was the principle of combustion and the vehicle of heat, was absolutely necessary to the support of animal life, and was the most powerful and energetic agent in nature. Nitrogen, on the contrary, was incapable of supporting either animal life or flame. An unnatural excess of oxygen would result, it had been ascertained, in just such an elevation of the animal spirits as we had latterly experienced. It was the pursuit, the extension of the idea, which had engendered awe. What would be the result of the total extraction of the nitrogen? A combustion irresistible, all-devouring, omni-prevalent, immediate; the entire fulfillment, in all their minute and terrible details, of the fiery and awe-inspiring denunciations of the prophecies of the Holy Book.

Why need I paint, Charmion, the now disenchained frenzy of mankind? That tenuity in the comet which had previously inspired us with hope, was now the source of the bitterness of despair. In its impalpable gaseous character we clearly perceived the consummation of fate.

Meantime a day again passed, bearing away with it the last shadow of hope. We gasped in the rapid modification of the air. The red blood bounded tumultuously through its strict channels. A furious delirium possessed all men; and, with arms rigidly outstretched toward the threatening heavens, they trembled and shrieked aloud.

But the nucleus of the destroyer was now upon us; even here in Aidenn, I shudder while I speak. Let me be brief—brief as the ruin that overwhelmed. For a moment there was a wild and lurid light alone, visiting and penetrating all things. Then—let us bow down, Charmion, before the excessive majesty of the great God!—then, there came a shouting and pervading sound, as if from the mouth itself of HIM; while the whole incumbent mass of ether in which we existed burst at once into a species of intense flame, for whose surpassing brilliancy and all-fervid heat even the angels in high heaven of pure knowledge have no name.

Thus ended all.

---

[3] The importance of the trace amounts of carbon dioxide in the air, and its role in fueling plant growth, were not known yet in 1839. The intoxicating effects of pure oxygen were, however, already familiar from the reports of the chemists who had isolated it.

# A HEAVENWARD VOYAGE

## S. HENRY BERTHOUD

*Samuel-Henri Berthoud (1804–1891) preferred to sign himself with the second of his forenames because his father, also a published writer, used the byline Samuel Berthoud, and he anglicized its spelling as an affectation. A great admirer of Lord Byron, the younger Berthoud inserted himself into the heart of the French Romantic movement in the early 1830s, when he published* Contes Misanthropiques *(1831; tr. as* Misanthropic Tales*), the first ever collection of what subsequently became known as* contes cruels, *and a large collection of folktales from his native Flanders. Hired by Émile Girardin as the editor of the pioneering family magazine* Musée des familles *in 1834, he became passionately involved with the cause of popular education, and, having encouraged Pierre Boitard to develop a new kind of scientific fiction in the pages of the magazine, he subsequently began to do work of that kind himself, eventually issuing a four-volume collection of* Fantaisies scientifiques de Sam *[Sam's Scientific Fantasies] (1861–62), "Dr. Sam" being the byline he used for his regular science column in* La Patrie *during the 1850s.*

*"Voyage au ciel," here translated as "A Heavenward Voyage," was Berthoud's first attempt at a* fantaisie scientifique, *which appeared in Émile Girardin's daily newspaper* La Presse *in 1841. It reflects the contemporary fascination with the idea of finding a means of powering and steering aerostats, in order to complete the human conquest of the air begun by the Montgolfier brothers. It also displays Berthoud's very particular fascination with the distinctive psychology of scientists and scientific endeavor—something that was to dominate his journalistic work and his relevant fiction throughout his career. His work in the vein, including his pioneering exercise in prehistoric fiction, "The First Inhabitants of Paris" (1865), and his vision of future*

9

*Paris in "The Year 2865" (1865), is sampled in the collection of translations*
Martyrs of Science *(2013).*

In 1803, in the city of Altona, the capital of Holstein, there was a scientist named Ludwig Klopstock. When I say scientist, I am not expressing the general opinion of his fellow citizens in that regard, for they generally claimed that the poor fellow possessed no other merit and no other ability than bearing the great name of Klopstock. His sole entitlement to interest, according to them, consisted of being the nephew of the author of the *Messias.*[1]

In appearance, at least, Ludwig justified the low esteem in which he was held. Always distracted and dreamy, he sought out solitary places, spent hours with his eyes raised toward the heavens, had no fixed meal-times, and had no idea how to earn an écu by means of his labor. He lived as best he could on the modest returns of a farm that he owned in the village of Oltenzen, and an annual income of about eight hundred livres, produced by capital invested with a merchant in Pallmailstrasse. At any rate, neither his meditations in the open air nor his uninterrupted twelve-hour sessions in the study in which he locked himself away had ever produced the slightest known result. Whenever he was asked what he was doing among his scientific instruments, or what he saw through the large telescope installed on the roof of his house, he became disconcerted, blushing and stammering, and the questioner went away shrugging his shoulders, convinced that Ludwig was nothing but an imbecile.

This conviction became even more unanimous in Altona when it was learned that Ludwig Klopstock was going to marry. His marriage must, indeed, have seemed very singular, for the young woman that the poor scientist was marrying was an orphan of sixteen; the death of her father had left her abandoned and destitute.

In spite of the mockery of all those who knew about his plan, Ludwig led his bride to the altar. Ebba took over the management of the scientist's household; order and propriety—which had been banished from

---

[1] The German poet Friedrich Gottlieb Klopstock (1724–1803), who considered that his vocation was to be "the Christian Homer," spent 25 years writing and publishing his epic *Messias* (1748–1773; tr. as *The Messiah*); he produced other Biblical epics thereafter, but they never attained a similar prestige.

the residence for some time, if they had ever entered it—flourished therein, and gave the desolate dwelling a cheerful and celebratory appearance.

Ludwig himself appeared in the city in clean linen, stockings without holes and garments that did not disappear in myriads of stains of all colors. His pallid complexion and livid thinness gradually gave way to a plumpness that gave his appearance a freshness and gaiety. He was still seen, every evening and well into the night, taking long walks in the country, but, instead of wandering at hazard, he was guided—or rather led—by Ebba. With her gaze directed at the ground, while her husband kept his raised toward the heavens, she sustained him, after a fashion, like the angels of which the psalm speaks, in order that his feet should not be injured by the pebbles of the path.

Gradually, Ebba's figure rounded out, and one morning, Ludwig, sitting by his wife's bed with his eyes full of tears, heard a little child utter that first cry, which causes so much emotion in a paternal heart. From then on, the scientist devoted himself less exclusively to science; he even forgot his telescope in order to dandle the new-born on his knees; he looked out with greater patience and greater happiness for the little creature's smile than he had ever done in discovering the mysterious conjunction of two stars.

The child grew; he was as beautiful as his mother, and his broad forehead indicated to Ludwig the promise of a powerful intelligence. Simply to say that concern was manifest around the crib in which the pale angel slept would be an understatement. Ebba gazed at him incessantly and Ludwig's calculations were confused by the slightest cry emitted by the infant's rosy little mouth. Alas, one night, the child's respiration became halting, his gaze lit up with a strange flame, and his cheeks became red. He had the croup! When day dawned, there was no longer anything but a cadaver on Ebba's bosom.

The poor mother thought of dying herself. It would surely have been better if God had reunited her body with that of her baby son in the same grave, as he had reunited their souls in Heaven. Ebba's soul never came back down to Earth. Her body acted at hazard; her voice no longer proffered any but inconsequential words. She was an idiot.

Ludwig's friends advised him to send his wife to a lunatic asylum, by which means, in consideration of a modest boarding-fee, he would be rid of the annoyance and the sad spectacle that the presence of a madwoman in his house occasioned. Ludwig became indignant at this suggestion, and persisted in caring for the insane woman with the tenderness and devotion that she had shown him when she had enjoyed her reason. There was no more studying for the scientist; he lavished his intelligence, his time, his days and nights, in humoring the bizarre caprices of the maniac. People ended up believing that he was going mad himself.

Nothing discouraged Ludwig for five years; nothing diminished his devotion to Ebba. At the end of that time, he fell victim to a further misfortune. The merchant in Pallmailstrasse, with whom he had invested the capital that yielded an income of eight hundred livres, went bankrupt and fled. That event left Klopstock with no other resource than the meager returns of his farm in Oltenzen. That would still have been sufficient for the scientist, who would not have minded being subject to privations, but the privations in question would affect poor Ebba. He decided to apply for a chair in astronomy that had just fallen vacant at the College of Altona.

Imagine what anguish, annoyance and distaste a poor timid man who never went out, and who only maintained rare and distant relationships with two or three friends, must have experienced when he had to solicit employment, explain his request to the burgomeister and submit to the disdain of the councilors. No one took his request seriously, and a professor was summoned from Drontheim. When Ludwig learned that, he sold his little house in Altona and set out for his farm in Oltenzen, taking nothing with him but his scientific instruments and his telescope. Ebba followed him mechanically, without knowing what she was doing. Her soul, as you know, was in Heaven, with her child.

Ludwig's farm was near Oltenzen church. From the window, he could see his uncle's tomb, shaded by a linden tree that the great poet had once planted. Ludwig sent his tenant farmer away and set about cultivating the land, with more intelligence, and even more strength, than anyone could have expected of him. The peasants began by laughing at his experiments and innovations, but they ended up copying him. The time that Klopstock did not spend harrowing and laboring, he devoted to study. The telescope took possession of the roof of Ludwig's farm; he hardly slept—for sleep is like friendship; it only lavishes its favors on the fortunate—and spent his nights studying the stars. During these vigils, consecrated to the admiration of celestial marvels, Ebba lay her head on the scientist's knees and descended into a dreamless torpor that resembled death.

One morning, on descending from his observatory, Ludwig, who was ordinarily sad and absent-minded, manifested an unusual and heedless joy. The scientist's manifestations of happiness could not have been more energetic if Ebba had recovered her reason. He spent six nights writing a long letter, with which he was never satisfied; he began it over, annotated it, consulted his telescope again. . . .

Finally, the important work complete, he placed his memoir carefully in an envelope and posted it in Altona, after taking the precaution of franking it and obtaining a receipt from the Post Office. The package was addressed to the director of Hamburg Observatory, and contained the discovery of the axial rotation of Saturn in ten hours thirty-two minutes.

This is the reply he received:

*If your letter is not a hoax, Monsieur, you are a little too late to claim a discovery made and published a fortnight ago by Frederick William Herschel.*[2]

In response to this cruel disappointment, which stole all the glory of which he had dreamed for his name, Ludwig only manifested his chagrin by his habitual sad smile.

Let us admit, however, that in the meantime, that obscure and timid man had been devoured by a thirst for celebrity. He dreamed night and day of making a name for himself. He sensed a mysterious force within himself that elevated him above vulgarity and only required to manifest itself to be resplendent forever. Poverty and misfortune, however, rendered that manifestation impossible.

When, two years later, he announced that it was possible to solidify carbon dioxide, no one even wanted to read his memoir, nor examine the diagrams he had attached thereto for the construction of the machine necessary to carry out the experiment. The Hamburg Academy remembered the belated discovery of the rotation of Saturn, and treated as fantasy the great operation that was to be reinvented a few years later, by our illustrious scientist Monsieur Thilorier.[3]

Several years went by without Ludwig leaving the village of Oltenzen or making any further attempts to publish the results of his studies.

---

[2] Frederick William Herschel (1738–1822) published his discovery of Saturn's period of rotation in 1790, which seems inconsistent with the date in the following note—and neither sits well with the date of 1803 given at the beginning of the story—so Berthoud is evidently employing a certain poetic licence here.

[3] Adrien Thilorier (1790–1844) first produced "dry ice" (accidentally) in 1834. Berthoud knew Thilorier personally and wrote a eulogy after his death, categorizing him as a "martyr" because he was a casualty of one of his own experiments.

One day, when the aeronaut Bitorff,[4] in the midst of an immense crowd of spectators, was getting ready to depart from Hamburg and make an aerial voyage, he saw a little man in a large threadbare black coat coming towards him. Without any preamble, the man proposed that he should accompany him on the excursion that he was about to make by balloon.

At first, Bitorff thought that he was dealing with a madman, but as the unknown man insisted and even offered the aeronaut several handfuls of gold to obtain what he desired, he ended up giving his consent, all the more willingly because the strangeness of the proposition and the discussion keenly excited the general curiosity. Like a good speculator wanting a double return, however, he told Ludwig that his ascent would only take place two weeks hence, because the balloon—he alleged—was not yet powerful enough to carry two travelers. Ludwig consented to this delay, and calmly went back to Oltenzen, from which he returned on the appointed day.

During the two weeks, Ludwig Klopstock's project had been the only topic of conversation in Hamburg. The old story of the axial rotation of Saturn, discovered a month after Herschel's publication, was exhumed, and a thousand jokes were told. Bitorff had never attracted as many spectators as he did on the day when the ascension of his travelling companion was to take place.

Ludwig, intimidated by the crowd, the eyes of which were fixed on him, approached the gondola awkwardly and almost tore the balloon by bumping into the scientific instruments with which it was laden, in order to carry out experiments during the voyage. To his great regret, the aeronaut obliged him to leave part of his luggage on the ground. They both took their places, the ropes were released and the balloon rose up rapidly like a bird.

Ludwig's first sensation, when he felt himself borne away by the frail machine, was terror. The immense abyss gaping beneath his feet furrowed the scientist's brow and surrounded him with swirling dizziness. Each commotion was succeeded by a sort of perfidious satisfaction. He leaned over the earth, attracted by a mysterious force, and was about to launch himself forth when his companion seized his arm and held him back. Once ex-

---

[4] The death of a German balloonist named Bitorff on 17 July 1812, recorded in German newspapers, was noted in the *Encyclopédie Catholique*, where Berthoud probably found the name.

tracted from this peril, Ludwig recovered all his composure, armed himself with resolution and set about looking down with a freedom of spirit by which the aeronaut could only be astonished.

There is no way to describe the sensations that the scientist experienced. As they drew further away from the earth, one might have thought that his soul separated itself, disengaging itself from its original clay and freeing itself from the bonds of his body. An indescribable well-being penetrated every part of him; a gentle warmth enlivened him; his mind worked powerfully; he forgot all his misery, all his suffering, all his mundane humiliations. He was finally himself!

Around him sparkled a kind of light that resembled an opaline gleam. Above his head extended the immensity of the azure of the heavens. Beneath his feet the earth was retreating and the horizon slowly became more distinct. The rivers presented all their sinuosities simultaneously; the houses and villas seemed to spring from the bosom of the earth; the sea extended in the distance like a vast sheet of silk, stirred by the wind; the fields displayed their golden escutcheons, quartered in green and purple; the forests covered vast expanses with their somber mantle; people were no more than little dots moving hither and yon, vain and imperceptible dust! Then again, there was no sound and no movement around the aerial voyagers. A profound, absolute silence! Not the bleak and somber silence of human solitudes but a silence that was, so to speak, melodious. It seemed to them that the distant harmonies of the celestial worlds were about to reach their terrestrial ears.

While Ludwig concentrated on these new and sublime impressions, Bitorff, to whom they were familiar, managed the aerostat and devoted himself to various experiments whose program he had organized with his companion before leaving the earth. When his calculations informed him that they were at an altitude of six hundred meters, he told Ludwig; the latter shivered, for the aeronaut's voice burst forth with supernatural force, and had nothing human about it. Meanwhile, the atmosphere was beginning to get chilly. The ineffable wellbeing that Klopstock had experienced was succeeded by a period of icy cold. Bitorff's voice lost its marvelous vibration. A hum began to deafen their ears. They were at twelve hundred meters.

Ten minutes later, Ludwig thought he could make out an almost-unintelligible murmur. He tried to ask Bitorff whether it might originate from speech addressed to him. To his great surprise, he could not hear his own voice at all, and he had to make great efforts that wearied his lungs and throat to proffer his question.

"We're two thousand meters above the earth," Bitorff finally managed to make him understand. "The expansion of the hydrogen gas contained in the balloon, which has been increasing since we left the ground, has now reached such an extent that I'm obliged to open the valve. Otherwise, the envelope of our vehicle would burst under the strain."

Meanwhile, a thick veil, similar to one of the heavy mists that sometimes expand over the earth during a thaw, obscuring and darkening entire cities with their noxious shroud, spread over the earth. It ended up concealing everything from the voyagers' eyes. Soon, dull roaring sounds rumbled in the distance below the balloon. Terrible noises burst forth. Broad lighting-flashes hurled their fiery wings through the chaos. Flamboyant serpents of lightning launched forth in all directions.

There was something terrifying about that revolution of the elements, seen and heard by two men who were only sustained in mid-air by a frail piece of taffeta inflated by a little hydrogen. Bitorff felt fear grip his heart, but Ludwig experienced a sort of savage joy. He laughed strangely; he clapped his hands; he jumped up and down. One might have thought him the spirit of tempests, in the midst of his accursed triumph.

The balloon was still rising, by virtue of a regular movement completely imperceptible to those it was lifting. The storm ended up by no longer being anything more than a mute black dot beneath their feet. That dot gradually dissipated and disappeared. The earth showed itself again, but confused. One could still distinguish, with great attention, roads like black threads and rivers like tresses of silver and gold. Above the aeronauts, the sky was resplendent with a serenity of which the earthbound can have no inkling, even on the highest mountains. Its azure took on a deep blue tint, which declined towards the lower regions into a greenish hue.

"Four thousand meters!" shouted Bitorff's voice, beginning to recover its strength, to his companion, who was numbed by a violent cold.

That voice burst forth in deafening vibrations a quarter of an hour later, when it announced: "Six thousand meters!"

Nothing was any longer visible on the earth but large masses. Bitorff threw into the air two birds that he had brought on the balloon. The poor creatures extended their wings to take flight, but they fell like leaden masses; their air, too rarefied, could no longer lend them support. Ludwig's respiration became more difficult; his chest was oppressed, chilled by the cold—and yet he felt excited by a feverish agitation. His heart was beating rapidly, his breathing accelerated. Two birds and a rabbit that still remained in the gondola began to choke, and were not long in dying for lack of viable air.

"Eight thousand meters," said Bitorff.[5]

His voice had become dull again, and with a gesture he showed Ludwig that nothing any longer remained beneath their feet. The earth and the clouds had disappeared; the immensity of space surrounded the balloon in every direction. As for the cold, it was intolerable. Their shallow breath was scarcely sufficient for the conservation of animal warmth. Blood leaked from the eyes, nostrils and ears of the audacious duo; their words were inaudible. The balloon, the only object they could see, seemed about to expire, so impetuously was the hydrogen gas escaping. Beneath them, the blue of the sky; above, strange and unknown darkness, through which the stars projected a light deprived of scintillation, which had something funereal about it. There ended physical nature. There were located the impenetrable barriers imposed by God on human audacity.

The gas condensed, and the balloon ceased climbing.

"Master," said Bitorff to Klopstock, "if we don't want to die, let's make haste to descend to earth! You can see it: the divine hand has written in terrible letters: 'Thou shalt go no further.' But what are you doing? Have you lost your mind? What! You're throwing out our ballast! You're taking off your clothes!"

"Because I want to go further!" cried Ludwig, enthusiastically. "Yes, I want to cross the barriers imposed on humankind. Look! The balloon, free of all ballast, is still rising; let's break the gondola, hang on to the cords and reach the heavens!"

He began to put this plan into operation. Bitorff launched himself toward the valve and opened it, in spite of the despairing efforts of his companion. The balloon descended; the air gradually became less cold as they

---

[5] Berthoud was probably inspired to write this story by the fact that Charles Green and Spencer Rush had set a new altitude record of 7.9 kilometers in 1839, which was to remain unsurpassed until 1862. The description of Ludwig's experiences is presumably based on those reported by Green and Rush. The previous altitude record of 7.28 kilometers had been set in 1803, which might help to explain the date cited in the story's opening.

arrived in less elevated atmospheric layers. The earth reappeared beneath them, initially as an indistinct gray mass; then it gradually took on a more precise form. Its rivers and roads became visible, details reappeared, people and animals increased in size . . . and the balloon finally touched down about two leagues from Hamburg.

Bitorff exploded in transports of joy.

Ludwig Klopstock wept with rage and disappointment. "We could have gone into the darkness of infinity!" he repeated to his companion.

"We would have perished!" the latter replied.

Without paying the slightest attention to the delight of the crowd that surrounded the two courageous voyagers and lavished applause upon them, without replying to members of the Hamburg Academy, who were imploring him to write a memoir on what he had observed and experienced, without even shaking the hand of his companion in peril, Ludwig drew away silently, climbed back on his horse, and rode back to Altona without stopping.

There, he bought large quantities of gummed fabric, loaded his purchases on to the rump of his horse, and shut himself up in his little house in Oltenzen, from which he did not emerge for an entire month. No one was able to see him during that retreat—not the farm laborers, nor a deputation from the Academy of Hamburg, nor even the village pastor. He did not even deign to reply to them though the door, which he refused to open. Were it not for the walk he took with his wife toward nightfall, and a few purchases of food, he might have been thought to be lying dead in his house.

Needless to say, this mysterious retreat gave rise to many strange suppositions. Some favored the hypothesis that Ludwig had lost his reason during his aerial excursion, others that he was devoting himself to a work of magic. The latter belief was not entirely implausible, for it was eventually discovered that Klopstock was building a strangely-shaped machine, which resembled a fish armed with large oars similar to fins; they were moved by means of a mechanism of cogwheels that was both simple and admirable.

That judgment became possible one morning when the inhabitants of Oltenzen saw Ludwig in mid-air, seated on his huge fish, maneuvering it more easily than a horseman guides a docile horse. In spite of the violence of contrary winds, he steered it to the right and the left, forwards and backwards, up and down. He finished by descending into his courtyard, so tightly that the two ends of the machine almost touched the sides.

The pastor, a learned man, in his admiration and at the risk of being indiscreet, went to knock on Klopstock's door, and begged him so insistently to open it that the scientist gave in. He took the pastor into his courtyard. At the first glace it was easy to see that Ludwig had found the secret of steering balloons.

"Your name is immortal, my friend!" cried the minister. "The entire universe will repeat it with enthusiasm! What glory will be yours!"

"Earth! Glory!" Ludwig repeated, disdainfully. "What does that matter to me? It's the heavens I want! No one has been able to go higher than eight thousand meters; I shall go to twenty thousand! I shall go to two hundred thousand! I shall go into the realm of other worlds! I shall go to the other worlds! I shall go beyond! I shall study nature! The immensity and the unknown will belong to me. I've found the means of steering my aerostat. That was an easy problem to resolve. But I've done better. The hydrogen gas that my machine contains expands or contracts as I dictate, without loss. These canisters contain the means of procuring me vital air, even in places where it is impossible to breathe. Cold itself, I have vanquished; it will be unable to hurt me!"

The pastor stood there, astounded by so much genius and madness at the same time.

"Farewell," said Ludwig. "Here is my will. If I fail in my enterprise, or if I no longer deign to return to the Earth, I leave it to you to look after that poor woman. Farewell!"

Without paying any heed to the remonstrations of the worthy churchman, he climbed into his balloon. He was about to take off when Ebba suddenly ran toward him, gazing at him with haggard eyes, clung on to the machine and shouted: "Don't go! Don't go!"

"You're right," said the scientist, after a moment's reflection. "Come! You shall share my fortune and my joy."

He picked her up. He seated her next to him. He waved to the pastor, and flew off into the sky.

The minister watched him for some time, maneuvering his machine easily, which ended up rising rapidly, soon appearing as nothing more than a black dot that gradually melted away into the azure of the heavens.

The worthy cleric awaited Ludwig Klopstock's return with great anxiety.

Ludwig Klopstock never returned.

# THE ARTIST OF THE BEAUTIFUL

## NATHANIEL HAWTHORNE

*Nathaniel Hawthorne (1804–1864) was a prolific writer of mannered moralistic fantasies, who employed scientists as exemplary figures in several of his ingenious and innovative allegories, including "Doctor Heidegger's Experiment" (1837), "The Birthmark" (1843) and the famous "Rappaccini's Daughter" (1844), in which the daughter of a botanist growing poisonous plants becomes tragically toxic herself. All of them belong to the "no good will come of it all" school of thought, the obstinate negativity of which was a suspicion haunting scientific romance from its inception, and which still plagues modern science fiction.*

*"The Artist of the Beautiful," first published in 1844 and reprinted in Mosses from an Old Manse (1846), is particularly interesting among Hawthorne's scientifically-infused stories because it is one of very few scientific romances that focuses on the artistry of technological endeavor rather than its utility, providing an emphasis that is almost unique within the genre. Like Berthoud's story, it reflects the contemporary fascination with the mechanics of flight, and exhibits a similar fascination with the particular psychology of technical creativity, but in a significantly different context. Like Berthoud's story, it leads to a conclusion that is strikingly unlike the conventional "happy endings" attached in a quasi-ritualistic fashion to the majority of stories responding to reader expectation—a convention inevitably stretched or fractured by the intrinsic imaginative reach of scientific romance, and frequently challenged therein.*

An elderly man, with his pretty daughter on his arm, was passing along the street, and emerged from the gloom of the cloudy evening into the light that fell across the pavement from the window of a small shop. It was a projecting window, and on the inside were suspended a variety of watches, pinchbeck, silver, and one or two of old, all with their faces turned from the streets, as if churlishly disinclined to inform the wayfarers what o'clock it was. Seated within the shop, sidelong to the window with his pale face bent earnestly over some delicate piece of the mechanism on which was thrown the concentrated luster of a shade lamp, appeared a young man.

"What can Owen Warland be about?" muttered old Peter Hovenden, himself a retired watchmaker, and the former master of this same young man whose occupation he was now wondering at. "What can the fellow be about? These six months past I have never come by his shop without seeing him just as steadily at work as now. It would be a flight beyond his usual foolery to seek for the perpetual motion, and yet I know enough of my old business to be certain that what he is now so busy with is no part of the machinery of a watch."

"Perhaps, father," said Annie, without showing much interest in the question, "Owen is inventing a new kind of timekeeper. I am sure he has ingenuity enough."

"Poh, child! He has not the sort of ingenuity to invent anything better than a Dutch boy," answered her father, who had formerly been put to much vexation by Owen Warland's irregular genius. "A plague on such ingenuity! All the effect that ever I knew of it was to spoil the accuracy of some of the best watches in my shop. He would turn the sun out of its orbit and derange the whole course of time, if, as I said before, his ingenuity could grasp anything bigger than a child's toy!"

"Hush, father! He hears you!" whispered Annie, pressing the old man's arm. "His ears are as delicate as his feelings, and you know how easily disturbed they are. Do let us move on."

So Peter Hovenden and his daughter Annie plodded on without further conversation, until in a by-street of the town they found themselves passing the open door of a blacksmith's shop. Within was seen the forge, now blazing up and illuminating the high and dusky roof, and now confining the luster to a narrow precinct of the coal-strewn floor, according as the breath of the bellows was puffed forth or again inhaled into its vast leather lungs. In the intervals of brightness it was easy to distinguish objects in remote corners of the shop and the horseshoes that hung upon the wall; in the momentary gloom the fire seemed to be glimmering amidst the vagueness of unenclosed space.

Moving about in this red glare and alternate dusk was the figure of the blacksmith, well worthy to be viewed in so picturesque an aspect of light and shade, where the bright blaze struggled with the black night, as if each would have snatched his comely strength from the other. Anon he drew a white-hot bar of iron from the coals, laid it on the anvil, uplifted his arm of might, and was seen enveloped in the myriads of sparks which the strokes of his hammer scattered into the surrounding gloom.

"Now, that is a pleasant sight," said the old watchmaker. "I know what it is to work in gold, but give me the worker in iron after all is said and done. He spends his labor upon a reality. What say you, daughter Annie?"

"Pray don't speak so loud, father," whispered Annie. "Robert Danforth will hear you."

"And what if he should hear me?" said Peter Hovenden. "I say again, it is a good and wholesome thing to depend upon main strength and reality, and to earn one's bread with the bare and brawny arm of a blacksmith. A watchmaker gets his brain puzzled by his wheels within a wheel, or loses his health or the nicety of his eyesight, as was my case, and finds himself in middle age, or a little after, past labor at his own trade and fit for nothing else, yet too poor to live at his ease. So I say once again, give me the main strength for my money. And then, how it takes the nonsense out of a man! Did you ever hear of a blacksmith being such a fool as Owen Warland yonder?"

"Well said, uncle Hovenden!" shouted Robert Danforth from the forge, in a dull, deep, merry voice that made the roof re-echo. "And what says Miss Annie to that doctrine? She, I suppose, will think it a genteeler business to tinker up a lady's watch than to forge a horseshoe or make a gridiron?"

Annie drew her father onward without giving him time for reply.

But we must return to Owen Warland's shop, and spend some more meditation upon his history and character than either Peter Hovenden, or probably his daughter Annie, or Owen's old school-fellow, Robert Danforth, would have thought due to so slight a subject.

From the time that his little fingers could grasp a pen-knife, Owen had been remarkable for a delicate ingenuity, which sometimes produced pretty shapes in wood, principally figures of flowers and birds, and sometimes seemed to aim at the hidden mysteries of mechanism. But it was always for purposes of grace, and never with any mockery of the useful. He did not, like the crowd of school-boy artisans, construct little windmills on the angle of a barn or watermills across the neighboring brook.

Those who discovered such a peculiarity in the boy as to think it worth their while to observe him closely, sometimes saw reason to suppose that he was attempting to imitate the beautiful movements of Nature, as exemplified in the flight of birds or the activity of little animals. It seemed, in fact, a new development of the love of the beautiful, such as might have made him a poet, a painter or a sculptor, and which was as completely refined from all utilitarian coarseness as it could have been in either of the fine arts.

He looked with singular distaste at the stiff and regular processes of ordinary machines. Being once carried to see a steam-engine, in the expectation that his intuitive comprehension of mechanical principles would be gratified, he turned pale and grew sick, as if something monstrous and unnatural had been presented to him. This horror was partly owing to the size and terrible energy of the iron laborer, for the character of Owen's mind was microscopic, and tended naturally to the minute, in accordance with his diminutive frame and the marvelous smallness and delicate power of his fingers.

Not that his sense of beauty was thereby diminished into a sense of prettiness. The beautiful idea has no relation to size, and may be as perfectly developed in a space too minute for any but microscopic investigation as within the ample verge that is assured by the arc of the rainbow. But, at all events, the characteristic minuteness in his objects and accomplishments made the world even more incapable than it might otherwise have been of appreciating Owen Warland's genius. The boy's relatives saw nothing better to be done—as perhaps there was not—than to bind him apprentice to a watchmaker, hoping that his strange ingenuity might thus be regulated and put to utilitarian purposes.

Peter Hovenden's opinion of his apprentice has already been expressed. He could make nothing of the lad. Owen's apprehension of the professional mysteries, it is true, was inconceivably quick, but he altogether forgot or despised the grand object of a watchmaker's business, and cared no more for the measurement of time than if it had been merged into eternity. So long, however, as he remained under his master's care, Owen's lack of sturdiness made it possible, by strict injunctions and sharp oversight, to restrain his creative eccentricity within bounds, but when his apprenticeship was served out, and he had taken the little shop which Peter Hovenden's failing eyesight compelled him to relinquish, then did people recognize how unfit a person was Owen Warland to lead old blind Father Time along his daily course.

One of his most rational projects was to connect a musical operation with the machinery of his watches, so that all the harsh dissonances of life might be rendered tuneful, and each fitting moment fall into the abyss of the past in golden drops of harmony. If a family clock was entrusted to him for repair—one of those tall, ancient clocks that have grown nearly allied to human nature by measuring out the lifetime of many generations—he would take it upon himself to arrange a dance or unreal procession of figures across its venerable face, representing twelve mirthful or melancholy hours. Several freaks of this kind quite destroyed the young watchmaker's credit with that steady and matter-of-fact class of people who hold the opinion that time is not to be trifled with, whether considered as the medium of advancement and prosperity in this world or preparation for the next.

His custom rapidly diminished—a misfortune, however, that was probably reckoned among his better accidents by Owen Warland, who was becoming more and more absorbed in a secret occupation which drew all his science and manual dexterity into itself, and likewise gave full employment to the characteristic tendencies of his genius.

After the old watchmaker and his pretty daughter had gazed at him out of the obscurity of the street, Owen Warland was seized with a fluttering of the nerves, which made his hand tremble too violently to proceed with such delicate labor as he was now engaged upon.

"It was Annie herself," murmured he. "I should have known it, by this throbbing of my heart, before I heard her father's voice. Ah, how it throbs! I shall scarcely be able to work again on this exquisite mechanism tonight. Annie, dearest Annie, thou shouldst give firmness to my heart and hand, and not shake them thus, for if I strive to put the very spirit of beauty into form and give it motion, it is for thy sake alone. O throbbing heart, be quiet! If my labor be thus thwarted, there will come vague and unsatisfied dreams which will leave me spiritless tomorrow."

As he was endeavoring to settle himself again to his task, the shop door opened and gave admittance to no other than the stalwart figure which Peter Hovenden had paused to admire, as seen amid the light and shadow of the blacksmith's shop. Robert Danforth had brought a little anvil of his own manufacture, and peculiarly constructed, which the young artist had recently bespoken. Owen examined the article and pronounced it fashioned according to his wish.

"Why, yes," said Robert Danforth, his strong voice filling the shop as with the sound of a bass viol. "I consider myself equal to anything in the way of my own trade; although I should have made a poor figure at yours with such a fist as this," added he, laughing, as he laid his vast hand beside the delicate one of Owen. "But what then? I put more strength into one blow of my sledge hammer than all you have expended since you were a 'prentice, is not that the truth?"

"Very probably," answered the low and slender voice of Owen. "Strength is an earthly monster. I make no pretentions to it. My force, whatever there may be of it, is altogether spiritual."

"Well, but, Owen, what are you about?" asked his old school-fellow, still in such a hearty volume of tone that it made the artist shrink, especially as the question related to a subject so sacred as the absorbing dream of his imagination. "Folks do say that you are trying to discover the perpetual motion."

"The perpetual motion? Nonsense!" replied Owen Warland, with a movement of disgust, for he was full of little petulances. "It can never be discovered. It is a dream that may delude men whose brains are mystified with matter, but not me. Besides, if such a discovery were possible, it would not be worth my while to make it only to have the secret turned to such purposes as are now effected by steam and water power. I am not ambitious to be honored with the paternity of a new kind of cotton machine."

"That would be droll enough!" cried the blacksmith, breaking out into such an outburst of laughter that Owen himself and the bell glasses on his work-board quivered in unison. "No, no, Owen! No child of yours will have iron joints and sinews. Well, I won't hinder you any more. Good night, Owen, and success, and if you need any assistance, so far as a downright blow of hammer upon anvil will answer the purpose, I'm your man."

And with another laugh, the man of main strength left the shop.

"How strange it is," whispered Owen Warland to himself, leaning his head upon his hand, "that all my musings, my purposes, my passion for the beautiful, my consciousness of power to create it—a finer, more ethereal power, of which this earthly giant can have no conception—all, all, look so vain and idle whenever my path is crossed by Robert Danforth! He would drive me mad were I to meet him often. His hard, brute force darkens and confuses the spiritual element within me, but I, too, will be strong in my own way. I will not yield to him."

He took from beneath a glass a piece of minute machinery, which he set in the condensed light of his lamp, and, looking intently at it through a magnifying glass, proceeded to operate with a delicate instrument of steel. In an instant, however, he fell back in his chair and clasped his hands, with a look of horror on his face that made its small features as impressive as those of a giant would have been.

"Heaven! What have I done?" exclaimed he. "The vapor, the influence of that brute force—it has bewildered me and obscured my perception. I have made the very stroke—the fatal stroke—that I have dreaded from the first. It is all over—the toil of months, the object of my life. I am ruined!"

And there he sat, in strange despair, until his lamp flickered in the pocket and left the Artist of the Beautiful in darkness.

Thus it is that ideas, which grow within the imagination and appear so lovely to it and of a value beyond whatever men call valuable, are exposed to be shattered and annihilated by contact with the practical. It is requisite for the ideal artist to possess a force of character that seems hardly compatible with its delicacy; he must keep his faith in himself while the incredulous world assails him with its utter disbelief; he must stand up against mankind and be his own sole disciple, both as respects his genius and the objects to which it is directed.

For a time Owen Warland succumbed to this severe but inevitable test. He spent a few sluggish weeks with his head so continually resting in his hands that the townspeople had scarcely an opportunity to see his countenance. When at last it was again uplifted to the light of day, a cold, dull, nameless change was perceptible upon it. In the opinion of Peter Hovenden, however, and that order of sagacious understandings who think that life should be regulated, like clockwork, with leaden weights, the alteration was entirely for the better.

Owen now, indeed, applied himself to business with dogged industry. It was marvelous to witness the obtuse gravity with which he would inspect the wheels of a great old silver watch, thereby delighting the owner, in whose fob it had been worn till he deemed it a portion of his own life, and was accordingly jealous of its treatment.

In consequence of the good report thus acquired, Owen Warland was invited by the proper authorities to regulate the clock in the church steeple. He succeeded so admirably in this matter of public interest that the merchants gruffly acknowledged his merits on 'Change; the nurse whispered his praises as she gave the potion in the sick-chamber; the lover blessed him at the hour of appointed interview, and the town in general thanked Owen for the punctuality of dinner time. In a word, the heavy weight upon his spirits kept everything in order; not merely within his own system, but wheresoever the iron accents of the church clock were audible.

It was a circumstance, though minute, yet characteristic of his present state, that, when employed to engrave names or initials on silver spoons, he now wrote the requisite letters in the plainest possible style, omitting a variety of fanciful flourishes that had heretofore distinguished his work in this kind.

One day, during the era of his happy transformation, old Peter Hovenden came to visit his former apprentice.

"Well, Owen," said he, "I am glad to hear such good accounts of you from all quarters, and especially from the town clock yonder, which speaks in your commendation every hour of the twenty-four. Only get rid altogether of your nonsensical trash about the beautiful, which I nor nobody else, nor yourself to boot, could ever understand—only free yourself of that, and your success in life is as sure as daylight. Why, if you go on this way, I should even venture to let you doctor this precious old watch of mine; though, except my daughter Annie, I have nothing else so valuable in the world."

"I should hardly dare touch it, sir," replied Owen, in a depressed tone, for he was weighed down by his old master's presence.

"In time," said the latter, "in time you will be capable of it."

The old watchmaker, with the freedom naturally consequent on his former authority, went on inspecting the work which Owen had in hand at the moment, together with other matters that were in progress. The artist, meanwhile, could scarcely lift his head. There was nothing so antipodal to his nature as this man's cold, unimaginative sagacity, by contact with which everything was converted into a dream except the densest matter of the physical world. Owen groaned in spirit and prayed fervently to be delivered from him.

"But what is this?" cried Peter Hovenden abruptly, taking up a dusty bell glass, beneath which appeared a mechanical something, as delicate and minute as the system of a butterfly's anatomy. "What have we here? Owen, Owen, there is witchcraft in these little chains, and wheels, and paddles. See! With one pinch of my finger and thumb I am going to deliver you from all future peril."

"For Heaven's sake," screamed Owen Warland, springing up with wonderful energy, "as you would not drive me mad, do not touch it! The slightest pressure of your finger would ruin me forever."

"Aha, young man! And is it so?" said the old watchmaker, looking at him with just enough penetration to torture Owen's soul with the bitterness of worldly criticism. "Well, take your own course; but I warn you again that in this small piece of mechanism lives your evil spirit. Shall I exorcize him?"

"You are my evil spirit," answered Owen, much excited, "you and the hard, coarse world! The leaden thoughts and the despondency that you fling upon me are my clogs, else I should long ago have achieved the task that I was created for."

Peter Hovenden shook his head, with the mixture of contempt and indignation which mankind, of whom he was partly a representative, deem themselves entitled to feel towards all simpletons who seek other prizes than the dusty one along the highway. He then took his leave, with an uplifted finger and a sneer upon his face that haunted the artist's dreams for many a night afterwards. At the time of his old master's visit, Owen was probably on the point of taking up the relinquished task; but, by this sinister event, he was thrown back into the state whence he had been slowly emerging.

But the innate tendency of his soul had only been accumulating fresh vigor during its apparent sluggishness. As the summer advanced he almost totally relinquished his business, and permitted Father Time, so far as the old gentleman was represented by the clocks and watches under his control, to stray at random through human life, making infinite confusion among the train of bewildered hours. He wasted the sunshine, as people said, in wandering through the woods and along the banks of streams. There, like a child, he found amusement in chasing butterflies or watching the motion of water insects.

There was something truly mysterious in the intentness with which he contemplated these living playthings as they sported on the breeze, or examined the structure of an imperial insect whom he had imprisoned. The chase of butterflies was an apt emblem of the ideal pursuit in which he had spent so many golden hours; but would the beautiful idea ever be yielded to his hand like the butterfly that symbolized it?

Sweet, doubtless, were these days, and congenial to the artist's soul. They were full of bright conceptions, which gleamed through his intellectual world as the butterflies gleamed through the outward atmosphere, and were real to him, for the instant, without the toil, and perplexity, and many disappointments of attempting to make them visible to the sensual eye. Alas that the artist, whether in poetry, or whatever other material, may not content himself with the inward enjoyment of the beautiful, but must chase the fitting mystery beyond the verge of his ethereal domain, and crush its frail being in seizing it with a material grasp. Owen Warland felt the impulse to give external reality to his ideas as irresistibly as any of the poets or painters who have arrayed the world in a dimmer and fainter beauty, imperfectly copied from the richness of their visions.

The night was now his time for the slow progress of re-creating the one idea to which all his intellectual activity referred itself. Always at the approach of dusk he stole into the town, locked himself within his shop, and wrought with patient delicacy of touch for many hours. Sometimes he was startled by the rap of the watchman, who, when all the world should be asleep, had caught the gleam of lamplight through the crevices of Owen Warland's shutters. Daylight, to the morbid sensibility of his mind, seemed to have an intrusiveness that interfered with his pursuits. On cloudy and inclement days, therefore, he sat with his head upon his hands, muffling, as it were, his sensitive brain in a mist of indefinite musings, for it was a relief to escape from the sharp distinctness with which he was impelled to shape out his thoughts during his nightly toil.

From one of these fits of torpor he was aroused by the entrance of Annie Hovenden, who came into the shop with the freedom of a customer, and also with something of the familiarity of a childish friend. She had worn a hole through her silver thimble, and wanted Owen to repair it.

"But I don't know whether you will condescend to such a task," said she, laughing, "now that you are so taken up with the notion of putting spirit into machinery."

"Where did you get that idea, Annie?" said Owen, starting in surprise.

"Oh, out of my own head," answered she, "and from something I heard you say, long ago, when you were but a boy and I a little child. But come, will you mend this poor thimble of mine?"

"Anything for your sake, Annie," said Owen Warland, "anything, even if it were to work at Robert Danforth's forge."

"And that would be a pretty sight!" retorted Annie, glancing with imperceptible slightness at the artist's small and slender frame. "Well, here is the thimble."

"But that is a strange idea of yours," said Owen, "about the spiritualization of matter."

And then the thought stole into his mind that this young girl possessed the gift to comprehend him better than all the world besides. And what a help and strength would it be to him in his lonely toil if he could gain the sympathy of the only being whom he loved!

To persons whose pursuits are insulated from the common business of life—who are either in advance of mankind or apart from it—there often comes a sensation of moral cold that makes the spirit shiver as if it had reached the frozen solitudes around the pole. What the prophet, the poet, the reformer, the criminal, or any other man with human yearnings, but separated from the multitude by a peculiar lot, might feel, poor Owen felt.

"Annie!" cried he, growing pale as death at the thought, "how gladly would I tell you the secret of my pursuit! You, methinks, would estimate it rightly. You, I know, would hear it with a reverence that I must not expect from the harsh, material world."

"Would I not? To be sure I would," replied Annie Hovenden, lightly laughing. "Come, explain to me quickly what is the meaning of this little whirligig, so delicately wrought that it might be a plaything for Queen Mab. See! I will put it in motion."

"Hold!" exclaimed Owen. "Hold!"

Annie had but given the slightest possible touch, with the point of a needle, to the same minute portion of complicated machinery which has more than once been mentioned, when the artist seized her by the wrist with a force that made her scream aloud. She was affrighted at the convulsion of intense rage and anguish that writhed across his features. The next instant he let his head sink upon his hands.

"Go, Annie," murmured he; "I have deceived myself, and must suffer for it. I yearned for sympathy, and thought, and fancied, and dreamed that you might give it me; but you lack the talisman, Annie, that I should admit you into my secrets. That touch has undone the toil of months and the thought of a lifetime! It was not your fault, Annie; but you have ruined me!"

Poor Owen Warland! He had indeed erred, but pardonably; for if any human spirit could have sufficiently reverenced the processes so sacred in his eyes, it must have been a woman's. Even Annie Hovenden, possibly, might not have disappointed him had she been enlightened by the deep intelligence of love.

The artist spent the ensuing winter in a way that satisfied any persons who had hitherto retained a hopeful opinion of him that he was, in truth, irrevocably doomed to inutility as regarded the world, and to an evil destiny on his own part. The decease of a relative had put him in possession of a small inheritance. Thus freed from the necessity of toil, and having lost the steadfast influence of a great purpose—great, at least, to him—he abandoned himself to habits from which it might have been supposed the mere delicacy of his organization would have availed to secure him. But when the ethereal portion of a man of genius is obscured, the earthly part sums an influence the more uncontrollable, because the character is now thrown off the balance to which Providence had so nicely adjusted it, and which, in coarser natures, is adjusted by some other method.

Owen Warland made proof of whatever show of bliss may be found in riot. He looked at the world through the olden medium of wine, and contemplated the visions that bubble up so gaily around the brim of the glass, and that people the air with shapes of pleasant madness, which so soon grow ghostly and forlorn. Even when the dismal and inevitable change had taken place, the young man might still have continued to quaff the cup of enchantments, though its vapor did but shroud life in gloom and fill the gloom with specters that mocked at him. There was a certain irksomeness of spirit, which, being real, and the deepest sensation of which the artist was now conscious, was more intolerable than any fantastic miseries and horrors that the abuse of wine could summon up. In the latter case he could remember, even out of the midst of his trouble, that all was but a delusion; in the former, the heavy anguish was his actual life.

From this perilous state he was redeemed by an accident which more than one person witnessed, but of which the shrewdest could not explain or conjecture the operation on Owen Warland's mind. It was very simple. On a warm afternoon of spring, as the artist sat among his riotous companions with a glass of wine before him, a splendid butterfly flew in at the open window and fluttered about his head.

"Ah," exclaimed Owen, who had drunk freely, "are you live again, child of the sun and playmate of the summer breeze, after your dismal winter's nap? Then it is time for me to be at work!"

And, leaving his unemptied glass upon the table, he departed, and was never known to sip another drop of wine.

And now, again, he resumed his wanderings in the woods and fields. It might be fancied that the bright butterfly, which had come so spirit-like into the window as Owen sat with the rude revelers, was indeed a spirit commissioned to recall him to the pure, ideal life that had so etherealized him among men. It might be fancied that he went forth to seek this spirit in its sunny haunts; for still, as in the summer time gone by, he was seen to steal gently up wherever a butterfly had alighted, and lose himself in contemplation of it. When it took flight his eyes followed the winged vision, as if its airy track would show the path to heaven.

But what could be the purpose of the unseasonable toil, which was again resumed, as the watchman knew by the lines of lamplight through the crevices of Owen Warland's shutters?

The townspeople had one comprehensive explanation of all these singularities. Owen Warland had gone mad! How universally efficacious—how satisfactory, too, and soothing to the injured sensibility of narrowness and dullness—is this easy method of accounting for whatever lies beyond the world's most ordinary scope! From St. Paul's days down to our poor little Artist of the Beautiful, the same talisman had been applied to the elucidation of all mysteries in the words and deeds of men who spoke or acted too wisely or too well.

In Owen Warland's case the judgment of the townspeople may have been correct. Perhaps he was mad. The lack of sympathy—that contrast between himself and his neighbors which took away the restraint of example—was enough to make him so. Or possibly he had caught just so much of ethereal radiance as served to bewilder him, in an earthly sense, by its intermixture with common daylight.

One evening, when the artist had returned from a customary ramble and had just thrown the luster of his lamp on the delicate piece of work so often interrupted, but still taken up again, as if his fate were embodied in its mechanism, he was surprised by the entrance of old Peter Hovenden. Owen never met this man without a shrinking of the heart. Of all the world he was most terrible, by reason of a keen understanding which saw so distinctly what it did see, and disbelieve so uncompromisingly. On this occasion the old watchmaker had merely a gracious word or two to say.

"Owen my lad," said he, "we must see you at my house tomorrow night."

The artist began to mutter some excuse.

"Oh, but it must be so," quoth Peter Hovenden, "for the sake of the days when you were one of the household. What, my boy, don't you know that my daughter Annie is engaged to Robert Danforth? We are making an entertainment, in our humble way, to celebrate the event."

"Ah!" said Owen.

That little monosyllable was all he uttered; its tone seemed cold and unconcerned to an ear like Peter Hovenden's, and yet there was in it the stifled outcry of the poor artist's heart, which he compressed within him like a man holding down an evil spirit. One slight outbreak, however, imperceptible to the old watchmaker, he allowed himself. Raising the instrument with which he was about to begin his work, he let it fall upon the little system of machinery that had, anew, cost him months of thought and toil. It was shattered by the stroke.

Owen Warland's story would have been no tolerable representation of the troubled life of those who strive to create the beautiful, if, amid all other thwarting influences, love had not interposed to steal the cunning from his hand. Outwardly he had been no ardent or enterprising lover; the career of his passion had confined its tumults and vicissitudes so entirely within the artist's imagination that Annie herself had scarcely more than a woman's intuitive perception of it; but, in Owen's view, it covered the whole field of his life.

Forgetful of the time when she had shown herself incapable of any deep response, he had persisted in connecting all his dreams of artistical success with Annie's image; she was the visible shape in which the spiritual power that he worshiped, and on whose altar he hoped to lay a not unworthy offering, was made manifest to him. Of course he had deceived himself; there were no such attributes in Annie Hovenden as his imagination had endowed her with. She, in the aspect which she wore in his inward vision, was as much a creature of his own as the mysterious piece of mechanism would be if it were ever realized.

Had he become convinced of his mistake through the medium of successful love—had he won Annie to his bosom, and there beheld her fade from angel to ordinary woman—the disappointment might have driven him back, with concentrated energy, upon his sole remaining object. On the other hand, had he found Annie what he fancied, his lot would have been so rich in beauty that out of its mere redundancy he might have wrought the beautiful into many a worthier type than he had toiled for; but the guise in which his sorrow came to him, the sense that the angel of his life had been snatched away and given to a rude man of earth and iron, who could neither need nor appreciate her ministrations—this was the very perversity of fate that makes human existence appear too absurd and contradictory to be the scene of one other hope or one other fear.

There was nothing left for Owen Warland but to sit down like a man that had been stunned.

He went through a fit of illness. After his recovery, his small and slender frame assumed an obtuser garniture of flesh than it had ever before worn. His thin cheeks became round; his delicate little hand, so spiritually fashioned to achieve fairy task-work, grew plumper than the hand of a thriving infant. His aspect had a childishness such as might have induced a stranger to pat him on the head—pausing, however, in the act, to wonder what manner of child was here.

It was as if the spirit had gone out of him, leaving the body to flourish in a sort of vegetable existence. Not that Owen Warland was idiotic. He could talk, and not irrationally. Somewhat of a babbler, indeed, did people begin to think him, for he was apt to discourse at wearisome length of marvels of mechanism that he had read about in books, but which he had learned to consider as absolutely fabulous.

Among them he enumerated the Man of Brass constructed by Albertus Magnus, and the Brazen Head of Friar Bacon; and, coming down to later times, the automata of a little coach and horses, which it was pretended had been manufactured for the Dauphin of France, together with an insect that buzzed about the ear like a living fly, and yet was but a contrivance of minute steel springs. There was a story, too, of a duck that waddled, and quacked, and ate; though, had any honest citizen purchased it for dinner, he would have found himself cheated with the mere mechanical apparition of a duck.

"But all these accounts," said Owen Warland, "I am now satisfied are mere impositions."[1]

Then, in a mysterious way, he would confess that he once thought differently. In his idle and dreamy days he had considered it possible, in a certain sense, to spiritualize machinery, and to combine with the new species of life and motion thus produced a beauty that should attain to the ideal which Nature has proposed to herself in all her creatures, but has never taken pains to realize. He seemed, however, to retain no very distinct perception either of the process of achieving this object or of the design itself.

"I have thrown it all aside now," he would say. "It was a dream such as young men are always mystifying themselves with. Now that I have acquired a little common sense, it makes me laugh to think of it."

Poor, poor and fallen Owen Warland! These were the symptoms that he had ceased to be an inhabitant of the better sphere that lies unseen around us. He had lost faith in the invisible, and now prided himself, as such unfortunates invariably do, in the wisdom that rejected much that even his eye could see, and trusted confidently in nothing but what his hand could touch. This is the calamity of men whose spiritual part dies out of them and leaves the grosser understanding to assimilate them more and more to the things of which alone it can take cognizance, but in Owen Warland the spirit was not dead nor passed away; it only slept.

How it awoke again is not recorded. Perhaps the torpid slumber was broken by a convulsive pain. Perhaps, as in a former instance, the butterfly came and hovered about his head and reinspired him—as indeed this creature of the sunshine had always a mysterious mission for the artist—reinspired him with the former purpose of his life. Whether it were pain or happiness that thrilled through his veins, his first impulse was to thank Heaven for rendering him again the being of thought, imagination, and keenest sensibility that he had long ceased to be.

"Now for my task," said he. "Never did I feel such strength for it as now."

Yet, strong as he felt himself, he was inclined to toil all the more diligently by an anxiety lest death should surprise him in the midst of his labors.

---

[1] Although correct about the imaginary automata credited by legend to Albertus Magnus and Roger Bacon, Owen is mistaken about those credited to Jacques de Vaucanson, who did indeed construct them for the amusement of Louis XV's court.

This anxiety, perhaps, is common to all men who set their hearts upon anything so high, in their own view of it, that life becomes of importance only as conditional to its accomplishment. So long as we love life for itself, we seldom dread the losing it. Where we desire life for the attainment of an object, we recognize the frailty of its texture. But, side by side with this sense of insecurity, there is a vital faith in our invulnerability to the shaft of death while engaged in any task that seems assigned by Providence as our proper thing to do, and which the world would have cause to mourn for should we leave it unaccomplished.

Can the philosopher, big with the inspiration of an idea that is to reform mankind, believe that he is to be beckoned from this sensible existence at the very instant when he is mustering his breath to speak the word of light? Should he perish so, the weary ages may pass way—the world's, whose life sand may fall, drop by drop—before another intellect is prepared to develop the truth that might have been uttered then.

But history affords many an example where the most precious spirit, at any particular epoch manifested on human shape, has gone hence untimely, without space allowed him, so far as moral judgment could discern, to perform his mission on the earth. The prophet dies, and the man of torpid heart and sluggish brain lives on. The poet leaves his song half-sung, or finishes it, beyond the scope of mortal ears, in a celestial choir. The painter—as Allston[2] did—leaves half his conception on the canvas to sadden us with its imperfect beauty, and goes to picture forth the whole, if it be no irreverence to say so, in the hues of heaven.

But rather such incomplete designs of this life will be perfected nowhere. This so frequent abortion of man's dearest projects must be taken as proof that the deeds of earth, however etherealized by piety or genius, are without value, except as exercises and manifestations of the spirit. In heaven, all ordinary thought is higher and more melodious than Milton's song. Then would he add another verse to any strain that he had left unfinished here?

But to return to Owen Warland, it was his fortune, good or ill, to achieve the purpose of his life. Pass we over a long space of intense thought, yearn-

---

[2] Washington Allston (1779–1843) was the pioneer of the American Romantic Movement of landscape painting. Hawthorne's wife, Sophia Peabody (1809–1871), whom he married in 1842, was a painter, and was strongly influenced by Allston.

ing effort, minute toil, and wasting anxiety, succeeded by an instant of solitary triumph; let all this be imagined; and then behold the artist, on a winter evening, seeking admittance to Robert Danforth's fireside circle.

There he found the man of iron, with his massive substance thoroughly armed and attempered by domestic influences. And there was Annie, too, now transformed into a matron, with much of her husband's plain and sturdy nature, but imbued, as Owen Warland still believed, with a finer grace, that might enable her to be the interpreter between strength and beauty. It happened, likewise, that old Peter Hovenden was a guest this evening at his daughter's foreside, and it was his well-remembered expression of keen, cold criticism that first encountered the artist's glance.

"My old friend Owen!" cried Robert Danforth, staring up, and compressing the artist's delicate fingers within a hand that was accustomed to grip bars of iron. "This is kind and neighborly to come to us at last. I was afraid your perpetual motion had bewitched you out of the remembrance of old times."

"We are glad to see you," said Annie, while a blush reddened her matronly cheek. "It was not like a friend to stay from us so long."

"Well, Owen," inquired the old watchmaker, as his first greeting, "how comes on the beautiful? Have you created it at last?"

The artist did not immediately reply, being startled by the apparition of a young child of strength that was tumbling about on the carpet—a little personage who had come mysteriously out of the infinite, but with something so sturdy and real in his composition that he seemed molded out of the densest substance which earth could supply.

This hopeful infant crawled toward the newcomer, and, setting himself on end, as Robert Danforth expressed the posture, stared at Owen with a look of such sagacious observation that the mother could not help exchanging a proud glance with her husband. But the artist was disturbed by the child's look, as imagining a resemblance between it and Peter Hovenden's habitual expression. He could have fancied that the old watchmaker was compressed into this baby shape, and looking out of those baby eyes, and repeating, as he now did, the malicious question: "The beautiful, Owen! How comes on the beautiful? Have you succeeded in creating the beautiful?"

"I have succeeded," replied the artist, with a momentary light of triumph in his eyes and a smile of sunshine, yet steeped in such depth of thought that it was almost sadness. "Yes, my friends, it is the truth. I have succeeded."

"Indeed!" cried Annie, a look of maiden mirthfulness peeping out of her face again. "And is it lawful now, to inquire what the secret is?"

"Surely; it is to disclose it that I have come," answered Owen Warland. "You shall know, and see, and touch, and possess the secret! For, Annie—if by that name I may still address the friend of my boyish years—Annie, it is for your bridal gift that I have wrought this spiritualized mechanism, this harmony of motion, this mystery of beauty. It comes late, indeed; but as we go onward in life, it is when objects begin to lose their freshness of hue and our souls their delicacy of perception, that the spirit of beauty is most needed. If—forgive me, Annie—if you know how to value this gift, it can never come too late."

He produced, as he spoke, what seemed to be a jewel box. It was carved richly out of ebony by his own hand, and inlaid with a fanciful tracery of pearl, representing a boy in pursuit of a butterfly, which, elsewhere, had become a winged spirit, and was flying heavenward; while the boy, or youth, had found such efficacy in his strong desire that he ascended from earth to cloud, and from cloud to celestial atmosphere, to win the beautiful.

This case of ebony the artist opened, and bade Annie place her fingers on its edge. She did so, but almost screamed as a butterfly fluttered forth, and, alighting on her finger's tip, sat waving the ample magnificence of its purple and gold-speckled wings, as if in prelude to a flight.

It is impossible to express by words the glory, the splendor, the delicate gorgeousness which were softened into the beauty of this object. Nature's ideal butterfly was here realized in all its perfection, not in the pattern of such faded insects as flit among earthly flowers, but of those which hover across the meads of paradise for child-angels and the spirits of departed infants to disport themselves with.

The rich down was visible upon its wings; the luster of its eyes seemed instinct with spirit. The firelight glimmered around this wonder—the candles gleamed upon it; but it glistened apparently by its own radiance, and illuminated the finger and outstretched hand on which it rested with a white gleam like that of precious stones. In its perfect beauty, the consideration of size was entirely lost. Had its wings overreached the firmament, the mind could not have been more filled or satisfied.

"Beautiful, beautiful!" exclaimed Annie. "Is it alive? Is it alive?"

"Alive? To be sure it is," answered her husband. "Do you suppose any mortal has skill enough to make a butterfly, or would put himself to the trouble of making one of them, when any child may catch a score of them in a summer's afternoon? Alive? Certainly! But this pretty box is undoubtedly of our friend Owen's manufacture, and really it does him credit."

At this moment the butterfly waved its wings anew, with a motion so absolutely lifelike that Annie was startled, and even awestricken, or, in spite of her husband's opinion, she could not satisfy herself whether it was indeed a living creature or a piece of wondrous mechanism.

"Is it alive?" she repeated, more earnestly than before.

"Judge for yourself," said Owen Warland, who stood gazing at her face with fixed attention.

The butterfly now flung itself upon the air, fluttered round Annie's head, and soared into a distant region of the parlor, still making itself perceptible to sight by the starry gleam in which the motion of its wings enveloped it. The infant on the floor followed its course with his sagacious little eyes. After flying about the room, it returned in a spiral curve and settled again on Annie's finger.

"But is it alive?" exclaimed she again, and the finger on which the gorgeous mystery had alighted was so tremulous that the butterfly was forced to balance himself with his wings. "Tell me if it be alive, or whether you created it."

"Wherefore ask who created it, so it be beautiful?" replied Owen Warland. "Alive? Yes, Annie; it may well be said to possess life, for it has absorbed my own being into itself, and in the secret of that butterfly, and in its beauty—which is not merely outward, but deep as its whole system—is represented the intellect, the imagination, the sensibility, the soul of an Artist of the Beautiful. Yes, I created it. But"—and here his countenance somewhat changed—"this butterfly is not now to me what it was, when I beheld it afar off, in the daydreams of my youth."

"Be it what it may, it is a pretty plaything," said the blacksmith, grinning with childlike delight. "I wonder whether it would condescend to alight on such a great clumsy finger as mine? Hold it hither, Annie."

By the artist's direction, Annie touched her finger's tip to that of her husband, and after a momentary delay, the butterfly fluttered from one to the other. It preluded a second flight by a similar, yet not precisely the same, waving of wings as in the first experiment; then, ascending from the blacksmith's stalwart finger, it rose in a gradually enlarging curve to the ceiling, made one wide sweep around the room, and returned with an undulating movement to the point whence it had started.

"Well, that does beat all nature!" cried Robert Danforth, bestowing the heartiest praise that he could find expression for, and, indeed, had he paused there, a man of finer words and nicer perception could not easily have said more. "That goes beyond me, I confess. But what then? There is more real use in one downright blow of my sledge hammer than in the whole five years' labor that our friend Owen has wasted on this butterfly."

Here the child clapped his hands and made a great babble of indistinct utterance, apparently demanding that the butterfly should be given to him for a plaything.

Owen Warland, meanwhile, glanced sidelong at Annie, to discover whether she sympathized in her husband's estimate of the comparative value of the beautiful and the practical. There was, amid all her kindness toward himself, amid all the wonder and admiration with which she contemplated the marvelous work of his hands and incarnation of his idea, a secret scorn—too secret, perhaps, for her own consciousness, and perceptible only to such intuitive discernment as that of the artist.

But Owen, in the latter stages of his pursuit, had risen out of the region in which such a discovery might have been torture. He knew that the world, and Annie as the representative of the world, whatever praise might be bestowed, could never say the fitting word nor feel the fitting sentiment which should be the perfect recompense of an artist who, symbolizing a lofty moral by a material trifle—converting what was earthly to spiritual gold—had won the beautiful into his handiwork. Not at this latest moment was he to learn that the reward of all high performance must be sought within itself, or sought in vain.

There was, however, a view of the matter which Annie and her husband, and even Peter Hovenden, might fully have understood, and which would have satisfied them that the toil of years had here been worthily bestowed. Owen Warland might have told them that this butterfly, this plaything, this bridal gift of a poor watchmaker to a blacksmith's wife, was, in truth, a gem of art that a monarch would have purchased with honors and abundant wealth, and have treasured it among the jewels of his kingdom as the most unique and wondrous of them all. But the artist smiled and kept the secret to himself.

"Father," said Annie, thinking that a word of praise from the old watch-maker might gratify his former apprentice, "do come and admire this pretty butterfly."

"Let us see," said Peter Hovenden, rising from his chair, with a sneer upon his face that always made people doubt, as he did himself, in everything but a material existence. "Here is my finger for it to alight upon. I shall understand it better when once I have touched it."

But, to the increased astonishment of Annie, when the tip of her father's finger was pressed against that of her husband, on which the butterfly still rested, the insect drooped his wings and seemed on the point of falling to the floor. Even the bright spots of gold upon its wings and body, unless her eyes deceived her, grew dim, and the glowing purple took a dusky hue, and the starry luster that gleamed around the blacksmith's hand became faint and vanished.

"It is dying! It is dying!" cried Annie, in alarm.

"It has been delicately wrought," said the artist, calmly. "As I told you, it has imbibed a spiritual essence—call it magnetism, or what you will. In an atmosphere of doubt and mockery its exquisite susceptibility suffers torture, as does the soul of him who instilled his own life into it. It has already lost its beauty; in a few minutes more its mechanism would be irreparably injured."

"Take away your hand, father!" entreated Annie, turning pale. "Here is my child; let it rest on his innocent hand. There, perhaps, its life will revive and its colors grow brighter than ever."

Her father, with an acrid smile, withdrew his finger. The butterfly then appeared to recover the power of voluntary motion, while its hues assumed much of their original luster, and the gleam of starlight, which was its most ethereal attribute, again formed a halo round about it. At first, when transferred from Robert Danforth's hand to the small finger of the child, this radiance grew so powerful that it positively threw the little fellow's shadow back against the wall. He, meanwhile, extended his plump hand as he had seen his father and mother do, and watched the waving of the insect's wings with infantine delight. Nevertheless, there was a certain odd expression of sagacity that made Owen Warland feel as if here were old Peter Hovenden, partially, but partially, redeemed from his hard skepticism into childish faith.

"How wise the little monkey looks!" whispered Robert Danforth to his wife.

"I never saw such a look on a child's face," answered Annie, admiring her own infant, and with good reason, far more than the artistic butterfly. "The darling knows more of the mystery than we do."

As if the butterfly, like the artist, were conscious of something not entirely congenial in the child's nature, it alternately sparkled and grew dim. At length it arose from the small hand of the infant with an airy motion that seemed to bear it upward without an effort, as if the ethereal instincts with which its master's spirit had endowed it impelled this fair vision involuntarily to a higher sphere.

Had there been no obstruction, it might have soared into the sky and grown immortal. But its luster gleamed upon the ceiling; the exquisite texture of its wings brushed against that earthly medium; and a sparkle or two, as of stardust, floated downward and lay glimmering on the carpet. Then the butterfly came fluttering down, and instead of returning to the infant, was apparently attracted towards the artist's hand.

"Not so, not so!" murmured Owen Warland, as if his handiwork could have understood him. "Thou hast gone forth out of thy master's heart. There is no return for thee."

With a wavering movement, and emitting a tremulous radiance, the butterfly struggled, as it were, toward the infant, and was about to alight upon his finger, but while it still hovered in the air, the little child of strength, with his grandsire's sharp and shrewd expression in his face, made a snatch at the marvelous insect and compressed it in his hand.

Annie screamed.

Old Peter Hovenden burst into a cold and scornful laugh.

The blacksmith, by main force, unclosed the infant's hand, and found within the palm a small heap of littering fragments, whence the mystery of beauty had fled forever.

And as for Owen Warland, he looked placidly at what seemed the ruin of his life's labor, and which was yet no ruin. He had caught a far other butterfly than this. When the artist rose high enough to achieve the beautiful, the symbol by which he made it perceptible to mortal senses became of little value in his eyes, while his spirit possessed itself in the enjoyment of the reality.

# WHAT WAS IT?

## FITZ-JAMES O'BRIEN

*Fitz-James O'Brien (1828–1862) was a journalist born in Limerick, who set-*
*tled in New York after emigrating in the early 1850s in the wake of the great*
*famine provoked in Ireland by potato blight. He died young, of wounds sus-*
*tained while fighting in the Union Army during the Civil War, and his poetry*
*and fiction was not collected until long after his death. His most famous story,*
*"The Diamond Lens" (1858) is a striking fantasy about a microscopic femme*
*fatale glimpsed through the eponymous artifact. "How I Overcame my Grav-*
*ity" (1864) is a dream fantasy featuring a gyroscopic flying machine.*

"What Was It?" *was first published in the March 1859 issue of* Harper's
Monthly, *with the signature of its narrator, Harry Escott, and was subse-*
*quently reprinted in* The Poems and Stories of Fitz-James O'Brien *(1881)*
*edited by William Winter. It is the most earnest of O'Brien's fantastic sto-*
*ries, flatly refusing any supernatural embellishments or any apologetic escape*
*writing off the experience as a dream. It thus became one of the most striking*
*and intriguing early accounts of an encounter with the alien; the key motif of*
*an invisible creature was echoed in several subsequent stories, most famously*
*Guy de Maupassant's classic "The Horla" (1887) and Ambrose Bierce's "The*
*Damned Thing" (1893), but O'Brien's version has a particular forthright-*
*ness. That feature extends into a strange kind of tunnel vision, as the narrator*
*conspicuously fails to ask the other questions corollary to the one employed as*
*a title, most notably "Where did it come from?" and "How did it get here?"—*
*enigmas left for the reader to pose, and from which to construct intriguing*
*hypotheses, provoking further speculation in a fashion characteristic of the*
*best scientific romance. Some twentieth-century reprints of the story are cen-*
*sored, all the references to opium smoking having been removed; the version*
*reproduced below, taken from the 1881 collection, is identical to the* Harper's

Monthly *version save for the final note, which was probably added by the magazine's editor.*

It is, I confess, with considerable diffidence that I approach the strange narrative which I am about to relate. The events which I purpose telling are of so extraordinary a character that I am quite prepared to meet with an unusual amount of incredulity and scorn. I accept all such beforehand. I have, I trust, the literary courage to face unbelief. I have, after mature consideration, resolved to narrate, in as simple and straightforward a manner as I can compass, some facts that passed under my observation in the month of July last, and which, in the annals of the mysteries of physical science, are wholly unparalleled.

I live at No.——— Twenty-sixth Street, in this city. The house is in some respects a curious one. It has enjoyed for the last two years the reputation of being haunted. It is a large and stately residence, surrounded by what was once a garden, but which is now only a green enclosure used for bleaching clothes. The dry basin of what has been a fountain, and a few fruit-trees, ragged and unpruned, indicate that this spot, in past days, was a pleasant, shady retreat, filled with fruits and flowers and the sweet murmur of waters.

The house is very spacious. A hall of noble size leads to a vast spiral staircase winding through its center, while the various apartments are of imposing dimensions. It was built some fifteen or twenty years since by Mr. A———, the well-known New York merchant who five years ago threw the commercial world into convulsions by a stupendous bank fraud. Mr. A———, as everyone knows, escaped to Europe, and died not long after of a broken heart.

Almost immediately after the news of his decease reached this country, and was verified, the report spread in Twenty-sixth Street that No.——— was haunted. Legal measures had dispossessed the widow of its former owner, and it was inhabited merely by a caretaker and his wife, placed there by the house agent into whose hands it had passed for purposes of renting or sale. These people declared that they were troubled with unnatural noises. Doors were opened without any visible agency. The remnants of furniture scattered through the various rooms were, during the night, piled one upon the other by unknown hands. Invisible feet passed up and down the stairs in broad daylight, accompanied by the rustle of unseen silk dresses, and the gliding of viewless hands along the massive balusters.

The caretaker and his wife declared that they would live there no longer. The house agent laughed, dismissed them, and put others in their place. The noises and supernatural manifestations continued. The neighborhood caught up the story, and the house remained untenanted for three years. Several persons negotiated for it, but somehow, always before the bargain was closed, they heard the unpleasant rumors, and declined to treat any further.

It was in his state of things that my landlady—who at that time kept a boarding house in Bleecker Street, and who wished to move farther up town—conceived the bold idea of renting No.—— Twenty-sixth Street. Happening to have in her house rather a plucky and philosophical set of boarders, she laid down her scheme before us, stating candidly everything she had heard respecting the ghostly qualities of the establishment to which she wished to remove us. With the exception of two timid persons—a sea captain and a returned Californian, who immediately gave notice that they would leave—all of Mrs. Moffat's guests declared that they would accompany her in her chivalric incursion into the abode of spirits.

Our removal was affected in the month of May, and we were all charmed with our new residence. The portion of Twenty-sixth Street where our house is situated—between Seventh and Eighth Avenues—is one of the pleasantest localities in New York. The gardens back of the houses, running down nearly to the Hudson, form, in the summer time, a perfect avenue of verdure. The air is pure and invigorating, sweeping, as it does, straight across the river from the Weehawken heights, and even the ragged garden which surrounded the house on two sides, although displaying on washing days rather too much clothesline, still gave us a piece of greensward to look at, and a cool retreat in the summer evenings, where we smoked our cigars in the dusk, and watched the fireflies flashing their lanterns in the long grass.

Of course we had no sooner established ourselves at No.—— than we began to expect the ghosts. We absolutely expected their advent with eagerness. Our dinner conversation was supernatural. One of the boarders, who had purchased Mrs. Crowe's *Night Side of Nature* for his own private delectation, was regarded as a public enemy by the entire household for not having bought twenty copies.[1] The man led a life of supreme wretchedness while he was reading this volume. A system of espionage was established, of which he was the victim. If he incautiously laid the book down for an instant and left the room, it was immediately seized and read aloud in secret places to a select few. I found myself a person of immense importance, it having leaked out that I was tolerably well versed in the history of supernaturalism, and had once written a story, entitled "The Pot of Tulips," for *Harper's Monthly*,[2] the foundation of which was a ghost. If a table or a wainscot panel happened to warp when we were assembled in the large drawing-room, there was an instant silence, and everyone was prepared for an immediate clanking of chains and a spectral form.

After a month of psychological excitement, it was with the utmost dissatisfaction that we were forced to acknowledge that nothing in the remotest degree approaching the supernatural had manifested itself. Once the black butler asseverated that his candle had been blown out by some invisible agency while he was undressing himself for the night, but as I had more than once discovered this colored gentleman in a condition when one candle must have appeared to him like two, I thought it possible that, by going a step further in his potations, he might have reversed this phenomenon, and seen no candle at all where he ought to have beheld one.

Things were in this state when an incident took place so awful and inexplicable in its character that my reason fairly reels at the bare memory of the occurrence. It was the tenth of July. After dinner was over I repaired with my friend, Dr. Hammond, to the garden to smoke my evening pipe. Independent of certain mental sympathies which existed between the Doctor and myself, we were linked together by a vice. We both smoked opium. We knew each other's secret, and respected it. We enjoyed together that wonderful expansion of thought, that marvelous intensifying of the perceptive faculties, that boundless feeling of existence when we seem to have points of contact with the whole universe—in short, that unimaginable spiritual bliss, which I would not surrender for a throne, and which I hope you, reader, will never, never taste.

---

[1] Catherine Crowe (1803–1876) published *The Night-Side of Nature; or, Ghosts and Ghost-seers*, a collection of "true" ghost stories, in 1848; it was by far the most successful of her literary works; she published two further collections of a similar kind.

[2] O'Brien's story "The Pot of Tulips," in which Harry Escott also features as the narrator, had been published in 1855.

Those hours of opium happiness which the Doctor and I spent together in secret were regulated with a scientific accuracy. We did not blindly smoke the drug of paradise, and leave our dreams to chance. While smoking, we carefully steered our conversation through the brightest and calmest channels of thought. We talked of the East, and endeavored to recall the magical panorama of its glowing scenery. We criticized the most sensuous poets—those who painted life ruddy with health, brimming with passion, happy in the possession of youth and strength and beauty. If we talked of Shakespeare's "Tempest" we lingered over Ariel, and avoided Caliban. Like the Guebers, we turned our faces to the east, and saw only the sunny side of the world.

This skillful coloring of our train of thought produced in our subsequent visions a corresponding tone. The splendors of Arabian fairy-land dyed our dreams. We paced that narrow strip of grass with the tread and port of kings. The song of the *rana arborea*, while he clung to the bark of the ragged plum-tree, sounded like the strains of divine musicians. Houses, walls and streets melted like rain-clouds, and vistas of unimaginable glory stretched away before us. It was a rapturous companionship. We enjoyed the vast delight more perfectly because, even in our most ecstatic moments, we were conscious of each other's presence. Our pleasures, while individual, were still twin, vibrating and moving in musical accord.

On the evening in question, the tenth of July, the Doctor and myself found ourselves in an unusually metaphysical mood. We lit our meerschaums, filled with fine Turkish tobacco, in the core of which burned a little black nut of opium, that, like the nut in the fairy tale, held within its narrow limits wonders beyond the reach of kings; we paced to and fro, conversing.

A strange perversity dominated the currents of our thought. They would *not* flow through the sun-lit channels into which we strove to divert them. For some unaccountable reason they constantly diverged into dark and lonesome beds, where a continual gloom brooded. It was in vain that, after our old fashion, we flung ourselves on the shores of the East, and talked of its gay bazaars, of the splendors of the time of Haroun, of harems and golden palaces. Black afreets continually arose from the depths of our talk, and expanded, like the one the fisherman released from the copper vessel, until they blotted everything bright from our vision. Insensibly, we yielded to the occult force that swayed us, and indulged in gloomy speculation.

We had talked some time upon the proneness of the human mind to mysticism, and the almost universal love of the Terrible, when Hammond suddenly said to me: "What do you consider to be the greatest element of Terror?"

The question, I own, puzzled me. That many things were terrible, I knew. Stumbling over a corpse in the dark; beholding, as I once did, a woman floating down a deep and rapid river, with wildly lifted arms, and awful, up-turned face, uttering, as she sank, shrieks that rent one's heart, while we, the spectators, stood frozen at a window which overhung the river at a height of sixty feet, unable to make the slightest effort to save her, but dumbly watching her last supreme agony and her disappearance. A shattered wreck, with no life visible, encountered floating listlessly on the ocean, is a terrible object, or it suggests a huge terror, the proportions of which are veiled. But it now struck me for the first time that there must be one great and ruling embodiment of fear, a King of Terrors to which all the others must succumb. What might it be? To what train of circumstances would it owe its existence?

"I confess, Hammond," I replied to my friend, "I never considered the subject before. That here must be one Something more terrible than any other things, I feel, I cannot attempt, however, even the most vague defi-nition."

"I am somewhat like you, Harry," he answered. "I feel my capacity to experience a terror greater than anything yet conceived by the human mind—something combining in fearful and unnatural amalgamation hitherto supposed incompatible elements. The calling of the voices in Brockden Brown's novel of *Wieland* is awful; so is the picture of the Dwell-er of the Threshold, in Bulwer's *Zanoni*;[3] but," he added, shaking his head gloomily, "there is something more horrible than these."

"Look here, Hammond," I rejoined, "let us drop this kind of talk, for Heaven's sake! We shall suffer for it, depend on it!"

"I don't know what's the matter with me tonight," he replied, "but my brain is running upon all sorts of weird and awful thoughts. I feel as if I could write a story like Hoffmann tonight, if I were only master of a literary style."

---

[3] Charles Brockden Brown's Gothic novel *Wieland; or, The Transformation*, was first published in 1798; Edward Bulwer-Lytton classic Rosicrucian fantasy *Zanoni* first ap-peared in 1842.

"If we are going to be Hoffmannesque in our talk, I'm off to bed. Opium and nightmares should never be brought together. How sultry it is! Good night, Hammond."

"Good night, Harry. Pleasant dreams to you."

"To you, gloomy wretch, afreets, ghouls, and enchanters."

We parted, and each sought his respective chamber. I undressed quickly and got into bed, taking with me, according to my usual custom, a book, over which I generally read myself to sleep. I opened the volume as soon as I had laid my head upon the pillow, and instantly flung it to the other side of the room. It was Goudon's *History of Monsters*—a curious French work,[4] which I had lately imported from Paris, but which, in the state of mind I had then reached, was anything but an agreeable companion. I resolved to go to sleep at once; so, turning down my gas until nothing but a little blue point of light glimmered on the top of the tube, I composed myself to rest.

The room was in total darkness. The atom of gas that still remained lighted did not illuminate a distance of three inches around the burner. I desperately drew my arm across my eyes, as if to shut out even the darkness, and tried to think of nothing. It was in vain. The confounded themes touched on by Hammond in the garden kept obtruding themselves on my brain. I battled against them. I erected ramparts of would-be blankness of intellect to keep them out. They still crowded upon me. While I was lying still as a corpse, hoping that by a perfect physical inaction I should hasten mental repose, an awful incident occurred. A Something dropped, as it seemed, from the ceiling, plumb upon my chest, and the next instant I felt two bony hands encircling my throat, endeavoring to choke me.

I am no coward, and am possessed of considerable physical strength. The suddenness of the attack, instead of stunning me, strung every nerve to its highest tension. My body acted from instinct, before my brain had time to realize the terrors of my position. In an instant I wound two muscular arms around the creature, and squeezed it, with all the strength of despair, against my chest. In a few seconds the bony hands that had fastened on my throat loosened their hold, and I was free to breathe once more.

Then commenced a struggle of awful intensity. Immersed in the most profound darkness, totally ignorant of the nature of the Thing by which I was suddenly attacked, finding my grasp slipping every moment, by reason,

---

[4] Unlike the others cited, this text is fictitious.

it seemed to me, of the entire nakedness of my assailant, bitten with sharp teeth in the shoulder, neck, and chest, having every moment to protect my throat against a pair of sinewy, agile hands, which my utmost efforts could not confine—these were a combination of circumstances to combat which required all the strength and skill and courage that I possessed.

At last, after a silent, deadly, exhausting struggle, I got my assailant under by a series of incredible efforts of strength. Once pinned, with my knee on what I made out to be its chest, I knew that I was victor. I rested for a moment to breathe. I heard the creature beneath me panting in the darkness, and felt the violent throbbing of a heart. It was apparently as exhausted as I was; that was one comfort. At this moment I remembered that I usually placed under my pillow, before going to bed, a large yellow silk pocket-handkerchief. I felt for it instantly; it was there. In a few seconds more I had, after a fashion, pinioned the creature's arms.

I now felt tolerably secure. There was nothing more to be done than to turn on the gas, and, having first seen what my midnight assailant was like, arouse the household. I will confess to being actuated by a certain pride in not giving the alarm before. I wished to make the capture alone and unaided.

Never losing my hold for an instant, I slipped from the bed to the floor, dragging my captive with me. I had but a few steps to make to reach the gas-burner; these I made with the greatest caution, holding the creature in a grip like a vice. At last I got within arm's length of the tiny speck of blue light which told me where the gas-burner lay. Quick as lightning I released my grip with one hand and let on the full flood of light. Then I turned to look at my captive.

I cannot even attempt to give any definition of my sensations the instant after I turned on the gas. I suppose I must have shrieked with terror, for in less than a minute afterward my room was crowded with the inmates of the house. I shudder now as I think of that awful moment.

*I saw nothing!*

Yes; I had one arm firmly clasped around a living, breathing, corporeal shape, my other hand gripped with all its strength a throat as warm, and apparently fleshly, as my own; and yet, with this living substance in my grasp, with its body pressed against my own, and all in the bright glare of a large jet of gas, I absolutely beheld nothing. Not even an outline—a vapor!

I do not, even at this hour, realize the situation in which I found myself. I cannot recall the astounding incident thoroughly. Imagination in vain tries to comprehend the awful paradox.

It breathed. I felt its warm breath upon my cheek. It struggled fiercely. It had hands. They clutched me. Its skin was smooth, like my own. There it lay, pressed close up against me, solid as stone—and yet utterly invisible!

I wonder that I did not faint or go mad on the instant. Some wonderful instinct must have sustained me; for, absolutely, in place of loosening my hold on the terrible Enigma, I seemed to gain an additional strength in my moment of horror, and tightened my grasp with such wonderful force that I felt the creature shivering with agony.

Just then Hammond entered my room at the head of the household. As soon as he beheld my face—which, I suppose, must have been an awful sight to look at—he hastened forward, crying: "Great Heaven, Harry! What has happened?"

"Hammond! Hammond!" I cried, "come here. Oh, this is awful! I have been attacked in bed by something or other, which I have hold of, but I can't see it—I can't see it!"

Hammond, doubtless struck by the unfeigned horror expressed in my countenance, made one or two steps forward with an anxious yet puzzled expression. A very audible titter burst from the remainder of my visitors. This suppressed laughter made me furious. To laugh at a human being in my position! It was the worst species of cruelty. Now, I can understand why the appearance of a man struggling violently, as it would seem, with an airy nothing, and calling for assistance against a vision, should have appeared ludicrous. Then, so great was my rage against the mocking crowd that had I the power I would have stricken them dead where they stood.

"Hammond! Hammond!" I cried again, despairingly, "for God's sake come to me. I can hold the—the thing but a short while longer. It is overpowering me. Help me! Help me!"

"Harry," whispered Hammond, approaching me, "you have been smoking too much opium."

"I swear to you, Hammond, that this is no vision," I answered, in the same low tone. "Don't you see how it shakes my whole frame with its struggles? If you don't believe me, convince yourself. Feel it—touch it."

Hammond advanced and laid his hand on the spot I indicated. A wild cry of horror burst from him. He had felt it!

In a moment he had discovered somewhere in my room a long piece of cord, and was the next instant winding it and knotting it about the body of the unseen being that I clasped in my arms.

"Harry," he said, in a hoarse, agitated voice, for, although he preserved his presence of mind, he was deeply moved. "Harry. It's all safe now. You may let go, old fellow, if you're tired. The Thing can't move."

I was utterly exhausted, and I gladly loosed my hold.

Hammond stood holding the ends of the cord that bound the Invisible, twisted round his hand, while before him, self-supporting as it were, he beheld a rope laced and interlaced, and stretching tightly around a vacant space. I never saw a man look so thoroughly stricken with awe. Nevertheless his face expressed all the courage and determination which I knew him to possess. His lips, although white, were set firmly, and one could perceive at a glance that, although stricken with fear, he was not daunted.

The confusion that ensued among the guests of the house who were witnesses of this extraordinary scene between Hammond and myself—who beheld the pantomime of binding this struggling Something—who beheld me almost sinking from physical exhaustion when my task of jailer was over—the confusion and terror that took possession of the bystanders, when they saw all this, was beyond description. The weaker ones fled from the apartment. The few who remained clustered near the door, and could not be induced to approach Hammond and his Charge. Still incredulity broke out through their terror. They had not the courage to satisfy themselves, and yet they doubted.

It was in vain that I begged of some of the men to come near and convince themselves by touch of the existence in that room of a living being which was invisible. They were incredulous, but did not dare to undeceive themselves. How could a solid, living, breathing body be invisible? they asked. My reply was this. I gave a sign to Hammond, and both of us—conquering our fearful repugnance to touch the invisible creature—lifted it from the ground, manacled as it was, and took it to my bed. Its weight was about that of a boy of fourteen.

"Now, my friends," I said, as Hammond and myself held the creature suspended over the bed, "I can give you self-evident proof that here is a solid, ponderable body which, nevertheless, you cannot see. Be good enough to watch the surface of the bed attentively.

I was astonished by my own courage in treating this strange event so calmly; but I had recovered from my first terror, and felt a sort of scientific pride in the affair which dominated every other feeling.

The eyes of the bystanders were immediately fixed on my bed. At a given signal Hammond and I let the creature fall. There was the dull sound of a heavy body alighting on a soft mass. The timbers of the bed creaked. A deep impression marked itself distinctly on the pillow, and on the bed itself. The crowd who witnessed this gave a sort of low universal cry, and rushed from the room. Hammond and I were left alone with our Mystery.

We remained silent for some time, listening to the low, irregular breathing of the creature on the bed, and watching the rustle of the bedclothes as it impotently struggled to free itself from confinement. Then Hammond spoke.

"Harry, this is awful."

"Ay, awful."

"But not unaccountable."

"Not unaccountable! What do you mean? Such a thing has never occurred since the birth of the world. I know not what to think, Hammond. God grant that I am not mad, and that this is not an insane fantasy!"

"Let us reason a little, Harry. Here is a solid body which we touch, but which we cannot see. The fact is so unusual that it strikes us with terror. Is there no parallel, though, for such a phenomenon? Take a piece of pure glass. It is tangible and transparent. A certain chemical coarseness is all that prevents it being so entirely transparent as to be totally invisible. It is not *theoretically impossible*, mind you, to make a glass which shall not reflect a single ray of light—a glass so pure and homogeneous in its atoms that the rays from the sun shall pass through it as they do through the air, refracted but not reflected. We do not see the air, and yet we feel it."

"That's all very well, Hammond, but these are inanimate substances. Glass does not breathe, air does not breathe. This thing has a heart that palpitates, a will that moves it, lungs that play, and inspire and respire."

"You forget the strange phenomena of which we have so often heard of late," answered the Doctor, gravely. "At the meetings called 'spirit circles' invisible hands have been thrust into the hands of those persons round the table—warm, fleshly hands that seemed to pulsate with mortal life."

"What? Do you think, then, that this thing is . . .?"

"I don't know what it is," was the solemn reply, "but please the gods I will, with your assistance, thoroughly investigate it."

We watched together, smoking many pipes, all night long, by the bedside of the unearthly being that tossed and panted until it was apparently wearied out. Then we learned by the low, regular breathing that it slept.

The next morning the house was all astir. The boarders congregated on the landing outside my room, and Hammond and myself were lions. We had to answer a thousand questions as to the state of our extraordinary prisoner, for as yet not one person in the house except ourselves could be induced to set foot in the apartment.

The creature was awake. This was evidenced by the convulsive manner in which the bedclothes were moved in its efforts to escape. There was something truly terrible in beholding, as it were, those second-hand indications of the terrible writhings and agonized struggles for liberty which themselves were invisible.

Hammond and myself had racked our brains during the long night to discover some means by which we might realize the shape and general appearance of the Enigma. As well as we could make out by passing our hands over the creature's form, its outlines and lineaments were human. There was a mouth; a round, smooth head without hair; a nose, which, however, was elevated above the cheeks, and its hands and feet were like those of a boy. At first we thought of placing the being on a smooth surface and tracing its outline with chalk, as shoemakers trace the outline of the foot. This plan was given up as being of no value. Such an outline would not give the slightest idea of its conformation.

A happy thought struck me. We would take a cast of it in plaster of Paris. This would give us the solid figure, and satisfy all our wishes. But how to do it? The movements of the creature would disturb the setting of the plastic covering, and distort the mold. Another thought: why not give it chloroform? It had respiratory organs—that was evident by its breathing. Once reduced to a state of insensibility, we could do with it what we would.

Doctor X—— was sent for; and after the worthy physician had recovered from the first shock of amazement, he proceeded to administer the chloroform. In three minutes afterward we were enabled to remove the fetters from the creature's body, and a well-known modeler of this city was busily engaged in covering the invisible form with the moist clay. In five minutes more we had a mold, and before evening a rough facsimile of the Mystery.

It was shaped like a man—distorted, uncouth, and horrible, but still a man. It was small, not over four feet and some inches in height, and its limbs revealed a muscular development that was unparalleled. Its face surpassed in hideousness anything I had ever seen. Gustave Doré, or Callot, or Tony Johannot, never conceived anything so horrible. There is a face in one of the latter's illustrations to "Un Voyage où il vous plaira,"[5] which somewhat approaches the countenance of this creature, but does not equal it. It was the physiognomy of what I should have fancied a ghoul to be. It looked as if it was capable of feeding on human flesh.

Having satisfied our curiosity, and bound everyone in the house to secrecy, it became a question of what was to be done with our Enigma. It was impossible that we should keep such a horror in our house; it was equally impossible that such an awful being should be let loose upon the world. I confess that I would gladly have voted for the creature's destruction. But who would shoulder the responsibility? Who would undertake the execution of this horrible semblance of a human being? Day after day this question was deliberated gravely.

The boarders all left the house. Mrs. Moffat was in despair, and threatened Hammond and myself with all sorts of legal penalties if we did not remove the Horror. Our answer was: "We will go if you like, but we decline taking this creature with us. Remove it yourself if you please. It appeared in your house. On you the responsibility rests." To this there was, of course, no answer. Mrs. Moffat could not obtain for love or money a person who would even approach the Mystery.

The most singular part of the affair was that we were entirely ignorant of what the creature habitually fed on. Everything in the way of nutriment that we could think of was placed before it, but was never touched. It was awful to stand by, day after day, and see the clothes toss, and hear the hard breathing, and know that it was starving.

Ten, twelve days, a fortnight passed, and it still lived. The pulsations of the heart, however, were daily growing fainter, and had now nearly ceased altogether. It was evident that the creature was dying for want of sustenance. While this terrible life struggle was going on, I felt miserable. I could

---

[5] The volume in question was published by P.-J. Hetzel, later to be Jules Verne's publisher, in 1843, credited to the artist Tony (i.e., Antoine) Johannot (1803–1852), the poet Alfred de Musset and "P.-J. Stahl"—the pseudonym Hetzel used on his own works. All three were at the heart of the French Romantic movement.

not sleep of nights. Horrible as the creature was, it was pitiful to think of the pangs it was suffering.

At last it died. Hammond and I found it cold and stiff one morning on the bed. The heart had ceased to beat, the lungs to inspire. We hastened to bury it in the garden. It was a strange funeral, the dropping of that viewless corpse into the damp hole. The cast of its form I gave to Dr. X——, who keeps it in his museum in Tenth Street.

As I am on the eve of a long journey from which I may not return, I have drawn up this narrative of an event the most singular that has ever come to my knowledge.[6]

---

[6] This is where the version of the story in the 1881 collection ends. Some other reprints, however, add the concluding note that was appended to the story in the *Harper's Monthly* version: "Note: It was rumored that the proprietors of a well-known museum in this city had made arrangements with Dr. X—— to exhibit to the public the singular cast which Mr. Escott deposited with him. So extraordinary a history cannot fail to attract universal attention."

# THE END OF THE WORLD

## EUGÈNE MOUTON

*Eugène Mouton (1823–1902) was one of the several French humorists who appropriated ideas from science and technology for development in comedies and satires; the others include Pierre Véron, whose relevant work from the 1860s is translated in* The Merchants of Health *(2015) and Albert Robida, who was drawn by his fascination with the relevant ideas to become one of the most prolific French writers of scientific romance between the 1880s and the 1920s. Mouton's other relevant work includes "L'Historioscope" (tr. as "The Historioscope") about a means of collecting images from the past.*

*"La Fin du monde," here translated as "The End of the World," appeared in a collection entitled* Nouvelles et fantaisies humoristiques *(1872) signed with the pseudonym Mérinos. It is remarkable in being one of the earliest satires to depict the end of the world as an accidental side effect of human activity; the fact that it imagines the disaster unfolding as a result of global warming occasioned by the burning of fossil fuels allowed it to reacquire an ironic topicality more than a hundred years after it was written, ensuring that its satire bites harder today than ever before.*

*And the world will end by fire.*

Of all the questions that interest humankind, none is more worthy of research than that of the destiny of the planet we inhabit. Geology and history have taught us many things about the Earth's past; we know the age of our world, within a few hundred million years or so; we know the order of development in which life progressively manifested itself and propagated over its surface; we know in which epoch humans finally arrived to sit down at the banquet that life had prepared for them, and for which it had taken several thousand years to set the table.

We know all that, or at least think we know it, which comes down to exactly the same thing—but if we are sure of our past, we are not of our future.

Humankind scarcely knows any more about the probable duration of its existence than each one of us knows about the number of years that he has yet to live:

> The table is laid,
> The exquisite parade,
> That gives us cheer!
> A toast, my dear!

All well and good—but are we on the soup, or the dessert? Who can tell us, alas, that the coffee will not be served very soon?

We go on and on, heedless of the future of the world, without ever asking ourselves whether, by chance, this frail boat that is carrying us across the ocean of infinity is not at risk of capsizing suddenly, or whether its old hull, worn away by time and impaired by the agitations of the voyage, does not have some leak through which death is filtering into its carcass—which is, of course, the very carcass of humankind—one drop at a time.

The world—which is to say, our terrestrial globe—has not always existed. It began, so it will end. The question is, when?

First of all, let us ask ourselves whether the world might end by virtue of an accident, a perturbation of present laws.

We cannot admit that. Such a hypothesis would, in fact, be in absolute contradiction with the opinion that we intend to sustain in this work. It is obvious, therefore, that we cannot adopt it. Any discussion is impossible if one admits the opinion that one is setting out to combat.

Thus, one point is definitely established: the Earth will not be destroyed by accident; it will end as a consequence of the continued action of the laws of its present existence. It will die, as they say, its appropriate death.

But will it die of old age? Will it die of a disease?

I have no hesitation in replying: no, it will not die of old age; yes, it will die of a disease—in consequence of excess.

I have said that the world will end as a consequence of the continued action of the laws of its present existence. It is now a matter of figuring out which, of all the agents functioning for the maintenance of the life of the terraqueous globe, is the one that will have the responsibility of destroying it some day.

I say this without hesitation: that agent is the same one to which the Earth owed its existence in the first place: heat. Heat will drink the sea; heat will eat the Earth—and this is how it will happen.

One day, with regard to the functioning of locomotives, the illustrious Stephenson asked a great English chemist what the force was that moved such machines. The chemist replied: "It's the sun."

And, indeed, all the heat that we liberate when we burn combustible vegetable matter—wood or coal—has been stored there by the sun; a piece of wood or coal is therefore, fundamentally, nothing but a preserve of solar radiation. The more vegetable life develops, the greater the accumulation of these preserves becomes. If a great deal is burned and a great deal created—that is to say, if cultivation and industry evolve, the storage of solar radiation absorbed by the Earth on the one hand and its liberation on the other will increase incessantly, and the Earth will become warmer in a continuous manner.

What would happen if the animal population, and the human population in its turn, followed the same progress? What would happen if considerable transformations, born of the very development of animal life on the surface of the globe, were to modify the structure of terrains, displace the basins of the seas, and reassemble humankind on continents that are both more fertile and more permeable to solar heat?

Now, that is exactly what will happen.

When one compares the world with what it once was, one is immediately struck by one fact that leaps to the eyes: the worldwide evolution of organic life. From the most elevated summits of mountains to the most profound gulfs of the sea, millions of billions of animalcules, animals, cryptogams and superior plants, have been working day and night for centuries, as have the foraminifera on which half our continents are built.

That work was going rapidly enough before the epoch when humans appeared on the Earth, but since the appearance of man it has developed with a rapidity that is accelerating every day. As long as humankind remained

restricted to two or three parts of Asia, Europe and Africa, it was not noticeable, because, save for a few focal points of concentration, life in general
still found it easy to pour into empty space the surplus accumulated at certain points of the civilized world; it was thus that colonization increasingly populated previously uninhabited countries innocent of all cultivation.
Then commenced the first phase of the progress of life by human action:
the agricultural phase.

Things moved in this direction for about six centuries, but large deposits of oil were developed, and, almost at the same time, chemistry and
steam-power. The Earth then entered its industrial phase—which is only
just beginning, since that was not much more than sixty years ago. But
where this movement will lead us, and with what velocity we shall arrive, it
is easy to presume, given that which has already happened before our eyes.

It is evident, for anyone with eyes to see, that for half a century, animals
and people alike have tended to multiply, to proliferate, to pullulate in a
truly disquieting proportion. More is eaten, more is drunk, silkworms are
cultivated, poultry fed and cattle fattened. At the same time, planning is
going on everywhere; ground has been cleared; fecund crop rotations and
intensive cultures have been invented, which double the soil's yields; not
content with what the earth produces, salmon at five francs a side have
been sown in our rivers, and oysters at twenty-four sous a dozen in our
gulfs.

In the meantime, enormous quantities of wine, beer and cider have been
fermented; veritable rivers of eau-de-vie have been distilled, and millions
of tonnes of oil burned—not to mention that heating equipment is improving incessantly, that more and more houses are being rendered draught-
proof, and that the linen and cotton fabrics that humans employ to keep
themselves warm are being fabricated more cheaply with every passing day.

To this already-sufficiently-somber picture it is necessary to add the insane developments of public education, which one can consider as a source
of light and heat, for, if it does not emit them itself, it multiplies their production by giving humans the means of improving and extending their impact on nature.

This is where we are now; this is where a mere half-century of industri-
alism has brought us; obviously, there are, in all of this, manifest symptoms
of an imminent exuberance, and one can conclude that within a hundred
years from now, the Earth will have developed a paunch.

Then will commence the redoubtable period in which the excess of production will lead to an excess of consumption, the excess of consumption to an excess of heat, *and the excess of heat to the spontaneous combustion of the Earth and all its inhabitants.*

It is not difficult to anticipate the series of phenomena that will lead the globe, by degrees, to that final catastrophe. Distressing as the depiction of these phenomena might be, I shall not hesitate to map them out, because the prevision of these facts, by enlightening future generations as to the dangers of the excesses of civilization, might perhaps serve to moderate the abuse of life and postpone the fatal final accounting by a few thousand years, or at least a few months.

This, therefore, is what will happen.

For ten centuries, everything will go progressively faster. Industry, above all, will make giant strides. To begin with, all the oil deposits will be exhausted, then all the sources of kerosene; then all the forests will be cut down; then the oxygen in the air and the hydrogen in the water will be burned directly. By that time, there will be something like a million steam-engines on the surface of the globe, averaging a thousand horse-power—the equivalent of a billion horse-power—functioning night and day.

All physical work is done by machines or animals; humans no longer do any, except for skillful gymnastics practised solely for hygienic reasons. But while their machines incessantly vomit out torrents of manufactured products, an ever-denser host of sheep, chickens, turkeys, pigs, ducks, cows and geese emerges from their agricultural factories, all oozing fat, bleating, lowing, gobbling, quacking, bellowing, whistling and demanding consumers with loud cries!

Now, under the influence of ever more abundant and ever more succulent nutrition, the fecundity of the human and animal species is increasing from day to day. Houses rise up one floor at a time; first gardens are done away with, then courtyards. Cities, then villages, gradually begin to project lines of suburbs in every direction; soon, transversal lines connect these radii.

Movement progresses; neighboring cities begin to connect with one another. Paris annexes Saint-Germain, Versailles and then Bauvais, then Châlons, then Orléans, then Tours; Marseilles annexes Toulon, Draguignan, Nice, Carpentras, Nîmes and Montpellier; Bordeaux, Lyon and Lille share out the rest, and Paris ends up annexing Marseilles, Lyon, Lille and

Bordeaux. And the same thing is happening throughout Europe, and the other four continents of the world.

But at the same time, the animal population is increasing. All useless species have disappeared; all that now remain are cattle, sheep, horses and poultry. Now, to nourish all that, empty space is required for cultivation, and room is getting short.

A few terrains are then reserved for cultivation, fertilizer is piled herein, and there, lying amid grass six feet high, unprecedented species of sheep and cattle, devoid of hair, tails, feet and bones are seen rolling around, reduced by the art of husbandry to be nothing more than monstrous steaks alimented by four insatiable stomachs.

In the meantime, in the southern hemisphere, a formidable revolution is about to take place. What am I saying? Scarcely fifty thousand years have gone by, and here it is, complete!

The polypers have joined all the continents together, and all the islands of the Pacific Ocean and the southern seas. America, Europe and Africa have disappeared beneath the waters of the ocean; nothing remains of them but a few islands formed by the last summits of the Alps, the Pyrenees, the buttes Montmartre, the Carpathians, the Atlas Mountains and the Cordilleras.

The human race, retreating gradually from the sea, has expanded over the incommensurable plains that the sea has abandoned, bringing its overwhelming civilization with it; already space is beginning to run out on the former continents. Here it is the final entrenchments: it is here that it will battle against the invasion of animal life. Here is where it will perish!

It is on a calcareous terrain; an enormous mass of animalized materials is incessantly converted into a chalky state; this mass, exposed to the rays of a torrid sun, incessantly stores up new concentrations of heat, while the functioning of machines, the combustion of hearths and the development of animal heat cause the ambient temperature to rise incessantly.

And in the meantime, animal production continues to increase; there comes a time when the equilibrium breaks down; it becomes manifest that production will outstrip consumption.

Then, in the Earth's crust, a sort of rind begins to form at first, and subsequently, an appreciable layer of irreducible detritus; the Earth is saturated with life.

Fermentation begins.

The thermometer rises, the barometer falls, the hygrometer marches toward zero. Flowers wither, leaves turn yellow, parchments curl up; everything dries out and becomes brittle.

Animals shrink by virtue of the effects of heat and evaporation. Humans, in their turn, grow thin and desiccated; all temperaments melt into one—the bilious—and the last of the lymphatics[1] offers his daughter and a hundred millions in dowry to the last of the scrofulous, who has not a sou to his name, and who refuses out of pride.

The heat increases and the wells dry up. Water-carriers are elevated to the rank of capitalists, then millionaires, to the extent that the prince's Great Water-Carrier becomes one of the principal dignitaries of state. All the crimes and infamies that one sees committed today for a gold piece are committed for a glass of water, and Cupid himself, abandoning his quiver and arrows, replaces them with a carafe of ice-water.

In this torrid atmosphere, a lump of ice is worth twenty times its weight in diamonds. The Emperor of Australia, in a fit of mental aberration, orders a *tutti frutti* that costs an entire year's civil list. A scientist makes a colossal fortune by obtaining a hectoliter of fresh water at 45 degrees.

Streams dry up; crayfish, jostling one another tumultuously to run after the trickles of warm water that are abandoning them, change color as they go along, turning scarlet. Fish, their hearts weakening and their swim-bladders distended, let themselves drift on the currents, bellies up and fins inert.

And the human species begins to go visibly mad. Strange passions, unexpected angers, overwhelming infatuations and insane pleasures make life into a series of furious detonations—or, rather, one continuous explosion, which begins at birth and concludes with death. In a world cooked by an implacable combustion, everything is scorched, crackled, grilled and roasted, and after the water, which has evaporated, one senses the air diminishing as it becomes more rarefied.

A terrible calamity! The rivers, great and small, have disappeared; the seas are beginning to warm up, then to heat up; now they are already simmering as if over a gentle fire.

---

[1] The lymphatic temperament, associated with one of the four humors of ancient medicine, is better known as the sanguine; it is associated with sociability and compassion, among other traits.

First the little fish, asphyxiated, show their bellies at the surface; then come the algae, detached from the sea-bed by the heat; finally, cooked in red wine and rendering up their fat in large stains, the sharks, whales and giant squid rise up, along with the fabulous kraken and the much-contested sea serpent; and with all this fat, vegetation and fish cooked together, the steaming ocean becomes an incommensurable bouillabaisse.

A nauseating odor of cooking expands over the entire inhabited earth; it reigns there for barely a century; the ocean evaporates and leaves no other trace of its existence than fish-bones scattered over desert plains. . . .

It is the beginning of the end.

Under the triple influence of heat, asphyxia and desiccation, the human species is gradually annihilated; humans crumble and peel, falling into pieces at the slightest shock. Nothing any longer remains, to replace vegetables, but a few metallic plants that have been made to grow by irrigating them in vitriol. To slake devouring thirst, to reanimate calcined nervous systems, and to liquefy coagulating albumin, there are no liquids left but sulphuric and nitric acids.

Vain efforts.

With every breath of wind that agitates the anhydrous atmosphere, thousands of human creatures are instantaneously desiccated; the rider on his horse, the advocate at the bar, the judge on his bench, the acrobat on his rope, the seamstress at her window and the king on his throne all come to a stop, mummified.

Then comes the final day.

They are no more than thirty-seven, wandering like tinder specters in the midst of a frightful population of mummies, which gaze at them with eyes reminiscent of Corinthian grapes.

And they take one another by the hand, and commence a furious round-dance, and with each rotation one of the dancers stumbles and falls down dead, with a dry sound. And when the thirty-sixth cycle is over, the survivor remains alone in front of the miserable heap in which the last debris of the human race is assembled.

He darts one last glance at the Earth; he says goodbye to it on behalf of all of us, and a tear falls from his poor scorched eyes—humankind's last tear. He catches it in his hand, drinks it, and dies, gazing at the heavens.

*Pouff!*

A little blue flame rises up tremulously, then two, then three, then a thousand. The entire globe catches fire, burns momentarily, and goes out.

It is all over; the Earth is dead.

Bleak and icy, it rolls sadly through the silent deserts of space; and of so much beauty, so much glory, so much joy, so much love, nothing any longer remains but a little charred stone, wandering miserably through the luminous spheres of new worlds.

Goodbye, Earth! Goodbye, touching memories of our history, of our genius, of our dolors and our loves! Goodbye, Nature, whose gentle and serene majesty consoled us so effectively in our suffering! Goodbye, cool and somber woods, where, during the beautiful nights of summer, by the silvery light of the moon, the song of the nightingale was heard. Goodbye, terrible and charming creatures that guided the world with a tear or a smile, whom we called by such sweet names! Ah, since nothing more remains of you, all is truly finished: THE EARTH IS DEAD.

# A PARADOXICAL ODE
## (AFTER SHELLEY)

## JAMES CLERK MAXWELL

*James Clerk Maxwell (1831–1879) was one of the leading theoretical physicists of the nineteenth century, whose work gathered the phenomena of electricity and magnetism in a single theoretical framework—a unification comparable to the one wrought by Isaac Newton's theory of gravity. He was not the first great British physicist to have a strong interest in Romantic poetry; Humphry Davy published "The Sons of Genius" (1799) while in his teens, and his final work,* Consolations in Travel: The Last Days of a Philosopher *(1830) includes a rhapsodic vision of the cosmos analogous to Poe's* Eureka. *In fact, it is arguable that the origins of both the British Romantic Movement and British scientific romance can be found in the epic poetry of Erasmus Darwin—which had a powerful influence on Percy Shelley, whose* Prometheus Unbound *(1820) provided the model for Maxwell's satirical ode— and it seems appropriate to include at last a small sample of poetic scientific romance in the present showcase.*

*"A Paradoxical Ode" was written in skeptical response to the popularizing efforts of Maxwell's friend Peter Guthrie Tait, the co-author with Lord Kelvin of* A Treatise on Natural Philosophy *(1867) and co-author with Balfour Stewart of* The Unseen Universe; or, Physical Speculations on a Future State *(1875). The latter work was written in opposition to the materialist views of the Darwinian evolutionist John Tyndall, and was intended to demonstrate that modern science could be reconciled with Christian doctrine; Tait and Stewart followed it up with a fictionalized sequel,* Paradoxical Philosophy *(1879), which Maxwell must have seen before publication, because it involves imaginary conversations between Scottish Christians and a fictitious German philosopher, Hermann Stoffkrafft, to whom Maxwell's*

*poem is notionally addressed. Tait's geometrical work on closed curves (or "knots") and Félix Klein's suggestion that such knots could be undone if a fourth spatial dimension were added to the conventional three—making what William Clifford and others called a "homaloid"—is referenced in the first verse. Poetry, of course, always feels entitled to an unexplained esotericism that is denied to pedestrian prose.*

To Hermann Stoffkrafft, Ph.D.

I

My soul's an amphicheiral knot
Upon a liquid vortex wrought
By intellect in the Unseen residing,
While thou dost like a convict sit
Wit marlinspike untwisting it
Only to find my knottiness abiding,
Since all the tools for my untying
In four-dimensional space are lying,
Where playful fancy intersperses,
Whole avenues of universes;
Where Klein and Clifford fill the void
With one unbounded, finite homaloid,
Whereby the infinite is hopelessly destroyed.

II

But when thy Science lifts her pinions
In Speculation's wild dominions,
I treasure every dictum thou emittest;
While down the stream of Evolution
We drift, and look for no solution
But that of survival of the fittest,
Till in that twilight of the gods
When earth and sun are frozen clods,
When all its matter degraded,

Matter in aether shall have faded,
We, that is, all the work we've done,
As waves in aether, shall for ever run
In swift expanding spheres, through heavens beyond the sun.

III

Great Principle of all we see.
Thou endless continuity!
By thee are all our angles gently rounded.
Our misfits are by thee adjusted,
And as I still in thee have trusted,
So let my methods never be confounded!
O never may direct Creation
Breach in upon my contemplation,
Still may the causal chain ascending,
Appear unbroken and unending,
And where the chain is best to sight
Let viewless fancies guide my darkling flight
Through aeon-haunted worlds, in order infinite.

# THE ABLEST MAN IN THE WORLD

## EDWARD PAGE MITCHELL

*Edward Page Mitchell (1852–1927) was a successful American journalist, primarily associated with the* New York Sun, *whose fiction for that paper included several significant exemplars of popular American scientific romance. They remained uncollected and obscure until long after his death, when Sam Moskowitz put together a collection entitled* The Crystal Man: Landmark Science Fiction *(1973) and established his historical importance in the development of American imaginative fiction. The collection gathers together a dozen stories in the enterprising tradition of Edgar Allan Poe, developing innovative ideas, usually in a humorous manner, with some ingenuity.*

*"The Ablest Man in the World," which appeared in the* Sun *on 4 May 1879, is the best of Mitchell's scientific romances, and one of the earliest stories to take inspiration from the attempts made in England by Charles Babbage (1791–1871) to build a mechanical calculating machine, based on principles that subsequently provided the foundation for modern computers. Unappreciated at the time, Babbage's attempts and Mitchell's speculative extrapolation thereof came to seem possessed of great foresight a hundred years later, entitling the latter to a belated classic status. The story is also a significantly unusual inclusion in the subgenre of stories about automata in human form, to which Jerome K. Jerome's "The Dancing Partner," featured subsequently in the present anthology, also made a notable addition.*

It may or may not be remembered that in 1878 General Ignatieff[1] spent several weeks of July at the Badischer Hof in Baden. The public journals

---

[1] Nikolay Pavolvich Ignatyev, known in contemporary American newspapers as Nicolai Ignatieff (1832–1908), became an important Russian diplomat in 1856, after the

gave out that he visited the watering-place for the benefit of his health, said to be much broken by protracted anxiety and responsibility in the service of the Czar. But everybody knew that Ignatieff was just then out of favor in St. Petersburg, and that his absence from the centers of active statecraft at a time when the peace of Europe fluttered like a shuttlecock in the air, between Salisbury and Shouvaloff,[2] was nothing more or less than a politely disguised exile.

I am indebted for the following facts to my friend Fisher, of New York, who arrived at Baden on the day after Ignatieff, and was duly announced on the official list of strangers as "Herr Doctor Professor Fischer, mit Frau Gattin and Bed. Nordamerika."

The scarcity of titles among the traveling aristocracy of North America is a standing grievance with the ingenious person who compiles the official list. Professional pride and the instincts of hospitality alike impel him to supply the lack whenever he can. He distributes governor, major-general, and doctor professor with tolerable impartiality, according as the arriving Americans wear a distinguished, a martial, or a studious air. Fisher owed his title to his spectacles.

It was still early in the season. The theater had not yet opened. The hotels were hardly half full, the concerts in the kiosk at the Conversationhaus were heard by scattering audiences, and the shopkeepers of the bazaar had no better business than to spend their time in bewailing the degeneracy of Baden Baden since an end was put to the play. Few excursionists disturbed the meditations of the shriveled old custodian of the tower on the Mercuriusberg. Fisher found the place very stupid—as stupid as Saratoga in June or Long Beach in September. He was impatient to get to Switzerland, but his wife had contracted a *table d'hôte* intimacy with a Polish countess, and

---

Crimean War, and was the Russian ambassador to the Ottoman Empire from 1864–1877, a posting concluded by the Russo-Turkish War of 1877–78, the eventual treaties of which he negotiated. Czar Alexander II, dissatisfied with the result of the war, then shifted him to a minor domestic post.

[2] Robert Gascoyne-Cecil, 3rd Marquess of Salisbury (1830–1903) was the British Foreign Secretary in 1879; he had played a leading role in the Congress of Berlin, a meeting of the Great powers held after the end of the Russo-Turkish War to revise the preliminary treaty negotiated by Ignatyev. Pyotr Shuvalov, usually known in contemporary American newspapers as Count Peter Schouvaloff (1827–1889) was in charge of negotiations between Russia and Britain before and after the Congress.

she positively refused to take any step that would sever so advantageous a connection.

One afternoon, Fisher was standing on one of the little bridges that span the gutter-wide Oosbach, idly gazing into the water and wondering whether a good sized Rangely trout could swim the stream without personal inconvenience, when the porter of the Badischer Hof came to him on the run.

"Herr Doctor Professor!" cried the porter, touching his cap. "I pray you pardon, but the highborn the Baron Savitch out of Moscow, of the General Ignatieff's suite, suffers himself in a terrible fit, and appears to die."

In vain Fisher assured the porter that it was a mistake to consider him a medical expert, that he professed no science save that of draw poker, that if a false impression prevailed in the hotel it was through a blunder for which he was in no way responsible, and that, much as he regretted the unfortunate condition of the highborn the baron out of Moscow, he did not feel that his presence in the chamber of sickness would be of the slightest benefit. It was impossible to eradicate the idea that possessed the porter's mind. Finding himself fairly dragged toward the hotel, Fisher at length concluded to make a virtue of necessity and to render his explanations to the baron's friends.

The Russian's apartments were upon the second floor, not far from those occupied by Fisher. A French valet, almost beside himself with terror, came hurrying out of the room to meet the porter and the doctor professor. Fisher again attempted to explain, but to no purpose. The valet also had explanations to make, and the superior fluency of his French enabled him to monopolize the conversation. No, there was nobody there—nobody but himself, the faithful Auguste of the baron. His Excellency, the General Ignatieff, His Highness the Prince Koloff, Dr. Rapperschwyll, all the suite, all the world, had driven out that morning to Gernsbach. The baron, meanwhile, had been seized by an effraying malady, and he, Auguste, was desolate with apprehension. He entreated Monsieur to lose no time in parley, but to hasten to the bedside of the baron, who was already in the agonies of dissolution.

Fisher followed Auguste into the inner room. The Baron, in his boots, lay upon the bed, his body bent almost double by the unrelenting gripe of a distressful pain. His teeth were tightly clenched, and the rigid muscles around the mouth distorted the natural expression of his face. Every few seconds a prolonged groan escaped him. His fine eyes rolled piteously.

Anon, he would press both hands upon his abdomen and shiver in every limb in the intensity of his suffering.

Fisher forgot his explanations. Had he been a doctor professor in fact, he could not have watched the symptoms of the baron's malady with greater interest.

"Can Monsieur preserve him?" whispered the terrified Auguste.

"Perhaps," said Monsieur, dryly.

Fisher scribbled a note to his wife on the back of a card and dispatched it in the care of the hotel porter. That functionary returned with great promptness, bringing a black bottle and a glass. The bottle had come in Fisher's trunk to Baden all the way from Liverpool, had crossed the sea to Liverpool from New York, and had journeyed to New York direct from Bourbon County, Kentucky. Fisher seized it eagerly but reverently, and held it up against the light. There were still three inches or three inches and a half in the bottom. He uttered a grunt of pleasure.

"There is some hope of saving the Baron," he remarked to Auguste.

Fully one half of the precious liquid was poured into the glass and administered without delay to the groaning, writhing patient. In a few minutes, Fisher had the satisfaction of seeing the baron sit up in bed. The muscles around his mouth relaxed, and the agonized expression was superseded by a look of placid contentment.

Fisher now had an opportunity to observe the personal characteristics of the Russian baron. He was a young man of about thirty-five, with exceedingly handsome and clear-cut features, but a peculiar head. The peculiarity of his head was that it seemed to be perfectly round on top—that is, its diameter from ear to ear appeared quite equal to its anterior and posterior diameter. The curious effect of this unusual conformation was rendered more striking by the absence of all hair. There was nothing on the baron's head but a tightly fitting skullcap of black silk. A very deceptive wig hung upon one of the bed posts.

Being sufficiently recovered to recognize the presence of a stranger, Savitch made a courteous bow.

"How do you find yourself now?" inquired Fisher, in bad French.

"Very much better, thanks to Monsieur," replied the baron, in excellent English, spoken in a charming voice. "Very much better, though I feel a certain dizziness here." And he pressed his hand to his forehead.

The valet withdrew at a sign from his master, and was followed by the porter. Fisher advanced to the bedside and took the baron's wrist. Even his unpracticed touch told him that the pulse was alarmingly high. He was much puzzled, and not a little uneasy at the turn which the affair had taken. *Have I got myself and the Russian into an infernal scrape?* he thought. *But no—he's well out of his teens, and half a tumbler of such whisky as that ought not to go to a baby's head.*

Nevertheless, the new symptoms developed themselves with a rapidity and poignancy that made Fisher feel uncommonly anxious. Savitch's face became as white as marble, its paleness rendered startling by the sharp contrast of the black skullcap. His form reeled as he sat on the bed, and he clasped his head convulsively with both hands, as if in terror lest it burst.

"I had better call your valet," said Fisher, nervously.

"No, no!" gasped the baron. "You are a medical man, and I shall have to trust you. There is something wrong here." With a spasmodic gesture, he vaguely indicated the top of his head.

"But I am not . . . ," stammered Fisher.

"No words!" exclaimed the Russian, imperiously. "Act at once—there must be no delay. Unscrew the top of my head!"

Savitch tore off his skullcap and flung it aside. Fisher had no words to describe the bewilderment with which he beheld the actual fabric of he baron's cranium. The skullcap had concealed the fact that the entire top of Savitch's head was a dome of polished silver.

"Unscrew it!" said Savitch, again.

Fisher reluctantly placed both hands upon the silver skull and exerted a gentle pressure toward the left. The top yielded, turning easily and truly in its threads.

"Faster!" said the baron, faintly. "I tell you no time must be lost." Then he swooned.

At that instant there was a sound of voices from the outer room, and the door leading into the baron's bed-chamber was violently flung open and as violently closed. The newcomer was a short, spare man of middle age, with a keen visage and piercing, deep-set little gray eyes. He stood for a few seconds scrutinizing Fisher with a sharp, almost jealous regard.

The baron recovered his consciousness and opened his eyes.

"Dr. Rapperschwyll!" he exclaimed.

Dr. Rapperschwyll, with a few rapid strides, approached the bed and confronted Fisher and Fisher's patient. "What is all this?" he angrily demanded.

Without waiting for a reply, he laid his hand rudely upon Fisher's arm and pulled him away from the baron. Fisher, more and more astonished, made no resistance, but suffered himself to be led, or pushed, toward the door. Dr. Rapperschwyll opened the door wide enough to give the American exit, and then closed it with a vicious slam. A quick click informed Fisher that the key had been turned in the lock.

*

The next morning Fisher met Savitch coming from the Trinkhalle. The baron bowed with cold politeness and passed on. Later in the day a *valet de place* handed Fisher a small parcel with the message: *Dr. Rapperschwyll supposes that this will be sufficient.* The parcel contained two gold pieces of twenty marks.

Fisher gritted his teeth. "He shall have back his forty marks," he muttered to himself, "but I will have his confounded secret in return."

Then Fisher discovered that even a Polish countess has her uses in the social economy.

Mrs. Fisher's *table d'hôte* friend was amiability itself, when approached by Fisher (through Fisher's wife) on the subject of Baron Savitch of Moscow. Did she know anything about Baron Savitch? Of course she did, and about everybody else worth knowing in Europe. Would she kindly communicate her knowledge? Of course she would, and be enchanted to gratify in the slightest degree the charming curiosity of her *Americaine*. It was quite refreshing for a *blasée* old woman, who had long since ceased to find much interest in contemporary men, women, things and events, to encounter one so recently from the boundless prairies of the new world as to cherish a piquant inquisitiveness about the affairs of the *grand monde*. Ah, yes, she would very willingly communicate the history of the Baron Savitch of Moscow, if that would amuse her dear *Americaine*.

The Polish countess abundantly redeemed her promise, throwing in for good measure many choice bits of gossip and scandalous anecdotes about the Russian nobility, which are not relevant to the present narrative. Her story, as summarized by Fisher, was this:

The Baron Savitch was not of an old creation. There was a mystery about his origin that had never been satisfactorily solved in St. Petersburg or in Moscow. It was said by some that he as a foundling from the Vospitatelnoi Dom. Others believed him to be the unacknowledged son of a certain illustrious personage nearly related to the House of Romanoff. The latter theory was the more probable, since it counted in a measure for the unexampled success of his career from the day that he graduated at the University of Dorpat.

Rapid and brilliant beyond precedent his career had been. He entered the diplomatic service of the Czar, and for several years was attached to the legations at Vienna, London and Paris. Created a Baron before his twenty-fifth birthday for the wonderful ability displayed in the conduct of negotiations of supreme importance and delicacy with the House of Hapsburg, he had become a pet of Gortchakoff's,[3] and was given every opportunity for the exercise of his genius in diplomacy. It was even said in well informed circles at St. Petersburg that the guiding mind which directed Russia's course throughout the Eastern complication, which planned the campaign on the Danube, effected the combinations that gave victory to the Czar's soldiers, and which meanwhile held Austria aloof, neutralized the immense power of Germany, and exasperated England only to the point where wrath expends itself in harmless threats, was the brain of the young Baron Savitch. It was certain that he had been with Ignatieff at Constantinople when the trouble was first fomented, with Shouvaloff in England at the time of the secret conference agreement, with the Grand Duke Nicholas at Adrianople when the protocol of an armistice was signed, and would soon be in Berlin behind the scenes of the Congress, where it was expected that he would outwit the statesmen of all Europe, and play with Bismarck and Disraeli as a strong man plays with two kicking babies.

But the countess had concerned herself very little with this handsome young man's achievements in politics. She had been more particularly interested in his social career. His success in that field had been no less remarkable. Although no one knew with positive certainty his father's name, he had conquered an absolute supremacy in the most exclusive circles surrounding the imperial court. His influence with the Czar himself was

---

[3] Alexander Mikailovitch Gorchakov (1798–1883) was the Russian Minister of Foreign Affairs in the 1860s and 1870s.

supposed to be unbounded. Birth apart, he was considered the best *parti* in Russia. From poverty, and by the sheer force of intellect, he had won himself a colossal fortune. Report gave him forty million roubles, and doubtless report did not exceed the fact. Every speculative enterprise he undertook, and they were many and various, was carried to sure success by the same qualities of cool, unerring judgment, far-reaching sagacity, and apparently superhuman power of organizing, combining, and controlling, which had made him in politics the phenomenon of the age.

About Dr. Rapperschwyll? Yes, the countess knew him by reputation and by sight. He was the medical man in constant attendance upon the Baron Savitch, whose high-strung mental organization rendered him susceptible to sudden and alarming fits of illness. Dr. Rapperschwyll was a Swiss—had originally been a watchmaker or an artisan, she had heard. For the rest, he was a commonplace little old man, devoted to his profession and to the baron, and evidently devoid of ambition, since he wholly neglected to turn the opportunities of his position and connections to the advancement of his personal fortunes.

Fortified with this information, Fisher felt better prepared to grapple with Rapperschwyll for the possession of the secret. For five days he lay in wait for the Swiss physician. On the sixth day the desired opportunity presented itself.

Half way up the Mercuriusberg, late in the afternoon, he encountered the custodian of the ruined tower, coming down. No, the tower was not closed. A gentleman was up there making observations of the country, and he, the custodian, would be back in an hour or two. So Fisher kept on his way.

The upper part of this tower is in dilapidated condition. The lack of a stairway to the summit is supplied by a temporary wooden ladder. Fisher's head and shoulders were hardly through the trap that opens to the platform before he discovered that the man already there was the man he sought. Dr. Rapperschwyll was studying the topography of the Black Forest through a pair of field-glasses.

Fisher announced his arrival by an opportune stumble and a noisy attempt to recover himself, at the same instant aiming a stealthy kick at the topmost round of the ladder, and scrambling ostentatiously over the edge of the trap. The ladder went down thirty or forty feet with a racket, clattering and banging against the walls of the tower.

Dr. Rapperschwyll at once appreciated the situation. He turned sharply around and remarked, with a sneer: "Monsieur is unaccountably awkward." Then he scowled and showed his teeth, for he recognized Fisher.

"It is rather unfortunate," said the New Yorker, with imperturbable coolness. "We shall be imprisoned here a couple of hours at the shortest. Let us congratulate ourselves that we each have intelligent company, besides a charming landscape to contemplate."

The Swiss coldly bowed, and resumed his topographical studies. Fisher lighted a cigar.

"I also desire," continued Fisher, puffing clouds of smoke in the direction of the Teufelmfihle, "to avail myself of this opportunity to return forty marks of yours, which reached me, I presume, by mistake."

"If Monsieur the American physician was not satisfied with his fee," rejoined Rapperschwyll, venomously, "he can without doubt have the affair adjusted by applying to the baron's valet."

Fisher paid no attention to the thrust, but calmly laid the gold pieces on the parapet, directly under the nose of the Swiss.

"I could not think of accepting any fee," he said, with deliberate emphasis. "I was abundantly rewarded for my trifling services by the novelty and interest of the case."

The Swiss scanned the American's countenance long and steadily with his sharp little gray eyes. At length he said, carelessly: "Monsieur is a man of science?"

"Yes," replied Fisher, with a mental reservation in favor of all sciences save that which illuminates and dignifies our national game.

"Then," continued Dr. Rapperschwyll, "Monsieur will perhaps acknowledge that a more beautiful or more extensive case of trepanning has rarely come under his observation."

Fisher slightly raised his eyebrows.

"And Monsieur will also understand, being a physician," continued Dr. Rapperschwyll, "the sensitiveness of the baron himself, and of his friends, upon the subject. He will therefore pardon my seeming rudeness at the time of his discovery."

*He is smarter than I supposed*, Fisher thought. *He holds all the cards, while I have nothing—nothing except a tolerably strong nerve when it comes to a game of bluff.* "I deeply regret that sensitiveness," he continued, aloud, "for it had occurred to me that an accurate account of what I saw, published in one of the scientific journals of England or America, would excite wide attention, and no doubt be received with interest on the Continent."

"What you saw?" cried the Swiss, sharply. "It is false. You saw nothing—when I entered you had not even removed the . . ." Here he stopped short and muttered to himself, as if cursing his own impetuosity.

Fisher celebrated his advantage by tossing away his half-burned cigar and lighting a fresh one.

"Since you compel me to be frank," Dr. Rapperschwyll went on, with increasing nervousness, "I will inform you that the baron has assured me that you saw nothing. I interrupted you in the act of removing the silver cap."

"I will be equally frank," replied Fisher, stiffening his face for a final effort. "On that point, the baron is not a competent witness. He was in a state of unconsciousness for some time before you entered. Perhaps I was removing the silver cap when you entered. . . ."

Dr. Rapperschwyll turned pale.

"And perhaps," said Fisher, coolly, "I was replacing it."

The suggestion of the possibility seemed to strike Rapperschwyll like a sudden thunderbolt from the clouds. His knees parted, and he almost sank to the floor. He put his hands before his eyes, and wept like a child, or, rather, like a broken old man.

"He will publish it! He will publish it to the court and the world!" he cried, hysterically. "And at this crisis. . . ."

Then, by a desperate effort, the Swiss appeared to recover to some extent his self-control. He paced the diameter of the platform for several minutes, with his head bent and his arms folded across his breast. Turning again to his companion, he said: "If any sum you name will. . . ."

Fisher cut the proposition short with a laugh.

"Then," said Rapperschwyll, "if I throw myself on your generosity. . . ."

"Well?" demanded Fisher.

"And ask a promise, on your honor, of absolute silence concerning what you have seen?"

"Silence until such time as the Baron Savitch shall have ceased to exist?"

"That will suffice," said Rapperschwyll. "For when he ceases to exist I die. And your conditions?"

"The whole story, here and now, and without reservations."

"It is a terrible price to ask me," said Rapperschwyll, "but larger interests than my pride are at stake. You shall hear the story.

"I was bred a watchmaker," he continued, after a long pause, "in the Canton of Zurich. It is not a matter of vanity when I say that I achieved a marvelous degree of skill in the craft. I developed a faculty of invention that led me into a series of experiments regarding the capabilities of purely mechanical combinations. I studied and improved upon the best automata ever constructed by human ingenuity. Babbage's calculating machine especially interested me. I saw in Babbage's idea the germ of something infinitely more important to the world.

"Then I threw up my business and went to Paris to study physiology. I spent three years at the Sorbonne and perfected myself in that branch of knowledge. Meanwhile my pursuits had extended far beyond the purely physical sciences. Psychology engaged me for a time, and then I ascended into the domain of sociology, which, when adequately understood, is the summary and final application of all knowledge.

"It was after years of preparations, and as the outcome of all my studies, that the great idea of my life, which had vaguely haunted me ever since the Zurich days, assumed at last a well-defined and perfect form."

The manner of Dr. Rapperschwyll had changed from distrustful reluctance to frank enthusiasm. The man himself seemed transformed. Fisher listened attentively and without interrupting the relation. He could not help fancying the necessity of yielding the secret, so long and so jealously guarded by the physician, was not entirely distasteful to the enthusiast.

"Now, attend, Monsieur," continued Dr. Rapperschwyll, "to several propositions which may seem at first to have no direct bearing on each other.

"My endeavors in mechanism had resulted in a machine which went far beyond Babbage's in its powers of calculation. Given the data, there was no limit to the possibilities in this direction. Babbage's cogwheels and pinions calculated logarithms, calculated an eclipse. It was fed with figures, and produced results in figures. Now, the relations of cause and effect are as fixed and unalterable as the laws of arithmetic. Logic is, or should be, as exact a science as mathematics. My new machine was fed with facts, and produced conclusions. In short, it reasoned, and the results of its reasoning were always true, while the results of human reasoning are often, if not always, false. The source of error in human logic is what the philosophers call the 'personal equation.' My machine eliminated the personal equation; it proceeded from cause to effect, from premise to conclusion, with steady precision. The human intellect is fallible; my machine was, and is, infallible in its processes.

"Again, physiology and anatomy taught me the fallacy of the medical superstition which holds the gray matter of the brain and the vital principle to be inseparable. I had seen men living with pistol balls imbedded in the medulla oblongata. I had seen the hemispheres and the cerebellum removed from the crania of birds and small animals, and yet they did not die. I believed that, though the brain were to be removed from a human skull, the subject would not die, although he would certainly be divested of the intelligence which governed all save the purely involuntary actions of the body.

"Once more: a profound study of history from the sociological point of view, and a not inconsiderable practical experience of human nature, had convinced me that the greatest geniuses that ever existed were on a plane not so very far removed above the level of the average intellect. The grandest peaks in my native country, those which all the world knows by name, tower only a few hundred feet over the countless unnamed peaks that surround them. Napoleon Bonaparte towered only a little over the ablest men around him, yet that little was everything, and he overran Europe. A man who surpassed Napoleon, as Napoleon surpassed Murat, in the mental qualities which transmute thought into fact, would have made himself master of the whole world.

"Now, to fuse these three propositions into one: suppose that I take a man, and, by removing the brain that enshrines all the errors and failures of his ancestors away back to the origin of the race, remove all sources of weakness in is future career. Suppose that, in place of the fallible intellect that I have removed, I endow him with an artificial intellect that operates with the certainty of universal laws. Suppose that I launch this superior being, who reasons truly, into the hurly burly of his inferiors, who reason falsely, and await the inevitable result with the tranquility of a philosopher.

"Monsieur, you have my secret. That is precisely what I have done. In Moscow, where my friend Dr. Duchat had charge of the new institution of St. Vasili for hopeless idiots, I found a boy of eleven whom they called Stepan Borovitch. Since he was born he had not seen, heard, spoken or thought. Nature had granted him, it was believed, a fraction of a sense of smell, and perhaps a fraction of the sense of taste, but even of this there was no positive ascertainment. Nature had walled in his soul most effectually.

Occasional inarticulate murmurings, and an incessant knitting and knead-
ing of the fingers were his only manifestations of energy. On bright days
they would place him in a little rocking-chair, in some spot where the sun
fell warm, and he would rock to and fro for hours, working his slender fingers and mumbling forth his satisfaction at the warmth in the plaintive and
unvarying refrain of idiocy. The boy was thus situated when I first saw him.

"I begged Stepan Borovitch of my good friend Dr. Duchat. If that excellent man had not long since died he should have shared in my triumph. I
took Stepan to my home and plied the saw and the knife. I could operate
on that poor, worthless, hopeless travesty of humanity as fearlessly and as
recklessly as upon a dog bought or caught for vivisection. That was a little
more than twenty years ago. To-day Stepan Borovitch wields more power
than any other man on the face of the earth. In ten years he will be the aris-
tocrat of Europe, the master of the world. He never errs, for the machine
that reasons beneath his silver skull never makes a mistake."

Fisher pointed downwards at the old custodian of the tower, who was
seen toiling up the hill.

"Dreamers," continued Dr. Rapperschwyll, "have speculated on the
possibility of finding among the ruins of the older civilization some brief
inscription which shall change the foundations of human knowledge. Wiser men deride the dream, and laugh at the idea of scientific kabbala. The
wiser men are fools. Suppose that Aristotle had discovered on a cuneiform
tablet at Nineveh the few words *survival of the fittest*. Philosophy would
have gained twenty-two hundred years. I will give you, in almost as few
words, a truth equally pregnant. *The ultimate evolution of the creature into
the creator*. Perhaps it will be twenty-two hundred years before the truth
finds general acceptance, yet it is not the less a truth. The Baron Savitch is
my creature, and I am his creator—creator of the ablest man in Europe, the
ablest man in the world.

"Here is our ladder, Monsieur. I have fulfilled my part in the agreement.
Remember yours."

\*

After a two months' tour of Switzerland and the Italian lakes, the Fishers
found themselves at the Hotel Splendide in Paris, surrounded by people
from the States. It was a relief to Fisher, after his somewhat bewildering

experience at Baden, followed by a surfeit of stupendous and ghostly snow peaks, to be once more among those who discriminated between a straight flush and a crooked straight, and whose bosoms thrilled responsive to his own at the sight of the star-spangled banner. It was particularly agreeable for him to find at the Hotel Splendide, in a party of Easterners who had come over to see the Exposition, Miss Bella Ward, of Portland, a pretty and bright girl, affianced to his best friend in New York.

With much less pleasure, Fisher learned that Baron Savitch was in Paris, fresh from the Berlin Congress, and that he was the lion of the hour with the select few who read between the written lines of politics and knew the dummies of diplomacy from the real players in the tremendous game. Dr. Rapperschwyll was not with the baron. He was detained in Switzerland, at the death-bed of his aged mother.

The last piece of information was welcome to Fisher. The more he reflected upon the interview on the Mercuriusberg, the more strongly he felt it to be his intellectual duty to persuade himself that the whole affair was an illusion, not a reality. He would have been glad, even at the sacrifice of his confidence in his own astuteness, to believe that the Swiss doctor had been amusing himself at the expense of his credulity. But the remembrance of the scene in the baron's bedroom at the Badischer Hof was too vivid to leave the slightest ground for this theory. He was obliged to be content with the thought that he should soon place the broad Atlantic between himself and a creature so unnatural, so dangerous, so monstrously impossible as the Baron Savitch.

Hardly a week had passed before he was thrown again into the society of that impossible person.

The ladies of the American party met the Russian baron at a ball in the New Continental Hotel. They were charmed with his handsome face, his refinement of manner, his intelligence and wit. They met him again at the American Minister's, and, to Fisher's unspeakable consternation, the acquaintance thus established began to make rapid progress in the direction of intimacy. Baron Savitch became a frequent visitor at the Hotel Splendide.

Fisher does not like to dwell on this period. For a month his peace of mind was rent alternately by apprehension and disgust. He is compelled to admit that the baron's demeanor toward himself was most friendly, although no allusion was made on either side to the incident at Baden. But the knowledge that no good could come to his friends from this association

with a being in whom the moral principle had no doubt been supplant-
ed by a system of cog-gears kept him continually in a state of distraction.
He would gladly have explained to his American friends the true character of the Russian, that he was not a man of healthy mental organization,
but merely a marvel of mechanical ingenuity, constructed upon a principle subversive of all society as at present constituted—in short, a monster
whose very existence must ever be revolting to right-minded persons with
brains of honest gray and white; but the solemn promise made to Dr. Rapperschwyll sealed his lips.

A trifling incident suddenly opened his eyes to the alarming character of
the situation, and filled his heart with a new horror.

One evening, a few days before the date designated for the departure of
the American party from Havre for home, Fisher happened to enter the
private parlor which was, by common consent, the headquarters of his set.
At first he thought that the room was unoccupied. Soon he perceived, in
the recess of a window, and partly obscured by the drapery of the curtain,
the forms of the Baron Savitch and Miss Ward of Portland. They did not
observe his entrance. Miss Ward's hand was in the baron's hand, and she
was looking up into his handsome face with an expression which Fisher
could not misinterpret.

Fisher coughed, and, going to another window, pretended to be interested in the affairs of the Boulevard. The couple emerged from the recess. Miss
Ward's face was ruddy with confusion, and she immediately withdrew. Not
a sign of embarrassment was visible in the baron's countenance. He greeted
Fisher with perfect self-possession, and began to talk of the great balloon
in the Place du Carrousel.[4]

Fisher pitied but could not blame the young lady. He believed her still
loyal at heart to her New York engagement. He knew that her loyalty could
not be shaken by the blandishments of any man on earth. He recognized
the fact that she was under the spell of a power more than human. Yet
what would be the outcome? He could not tell all; his promise bound him.
It would be useless to appeal to the generosity of the baron; no human
sentiments governed his exorable purposes. Must the affair drift on while

---

[4] Henri Giffard (1825–1882) invented the Giffard dirigible, a steam-powered airship
that was the first to carry passengers; it was moored in the Place du Carrousel before a
much-publicized ascent in July 1878.

he stood tied and helpless? Must this charming and innocent girl be sacrificed to the transient whim of an automaton? Allowing that the baron's intentions were of the most honorable character, was the situation any less horrible? Marry a Machine! His own loyalty to his friend in New York, his regard for Miss Ward, alike loudly called on him to act with promptness.

And, apart from all private interest, did he not owe a plain duty to society, to the liberties of the world? Was Savitch to be permitted to proceed in the career laid out for him by his creator, Dr. Rapperschwyll? He, Fisher, was the only man in the world in a position to thwart the ambitious program. Was there ever greater need of a Brutus?

Between doubts and fears, the last days of Fisher's stay in Paris were wretched beyond description. On the morning of the steamer day he had almost made up his mind to act.

The train for Havre departed at noon, and at eleven o'clock the Baron Savitch made his appearance at the Hotel Splendide to bid farewell to his American friends. Fisher watched Miss Ward closely. There was a constraint in her manner which fortified his resolution. The baron incidentally remarked that he should make it his duty and pleasure to visit America within a very few months, and that he hoped then to renew the acquaintances now interrupted. As Savitch spoke, Fisher observed that his eyes met Miss Ward's, while the slightest possible blush colored her cheeks. Fisher knew that the case was desperate, and demanded a desperate remedy.

He now joined the ladies of the party in urging the baron to join them in the hasty lunch that was to precede the drive to the station. Savitch gladly accepted the cordial invitation. Wine he politely but firmly declined, pleading the absolute prohibition of his physician. Fisher left the room for an instant, and returned with the black bottle which had figured in the Baden episode.

"The Baron," he said, "has already expressed his approval of the noblest of our American products, and he knows that this beverage has good medical endorsement." So saying, he poured the remaining contents of the Kentucky bottle into a glass, and presented it to the Russian.

Savitch hesitated. His previous experience with the nectar was at the same time a temptation and a warning, yet he did not want to seem discourteous. A chance remark from Miss Ward decided him.

"The baron," she said, with a smile, "will certainly not refuse to wish us *bon voyage* in the American fashion."

Savitch drained the glass and the conversation turned to other matters. The carriages were already below. The parting compliments were being made when Savitch suddenly pressed his hands to his forehead and clutched at the back of a chair. The ladies gathered around him in alarm.

"It's nothing," he said, faintly. "A temporary dizziness."

"There is no time to be lost," said Fisher, pressing forward. "The train leaves in twenty minutes. Get ready at once and I will meanwhile attend to our friend."

Fisher hurriedly led the baron to his own bedroom. Savitch fell back upon the bed. The Baden symptoms repeated themselves. In two minutes the Russian was unconscious.

Fisher looked at his watch. He had three minutes to spare. He turned the key in the lock of the door and touched the knob of the electric annunciator.

Then, gaining the mastery of his nerves by one supreme effort of self-control, Fisher pulled the deceptive wig and the black skullcap from the baron's head. *Heaven forgive me if I am making a fearful mistake,* he thought, *but I believe it to be best for ourselves and for the world.*

Rapidly, but with a steady hand, he unscrewed the silver dome. The Mechanism lay exposed before his eyes. The baron groaned. Ruthlessly, Fisher tore out the wondrous machine. He had no time and no inclination to examine it. He caught up a newspaper and hastily enfolded it. He thrust the bundle into his open traveling bag. Then he screwed the silver top firmly upon the baron's head, and replaced the skullcap and the wig.

All this was done before the servant answered the bell. "The Baron Savitch is ill," said Fisher to the attendant, when he came. "There is no cause for alarm. Send at once to the Hotel de l'Athenée for his valet Auguste."

In twenty seconds, Fisher was in a cab, whirling toward the Station St. Lazare.

When the steamship *Pereire* was well out at sea, with Ushant five hundred miles in her wake, and countless fathoms of water beneath her keel, Fisher took a newspaper from his traveling bag. His teeth were firm set and his lips rigid. He carried the heavy parcel to the side of the ship and dropped it into the Atlantic. It made a little eddy in the smooth water, and sank out of sight. Fisher fancied that he heard a wild, despairing cry, and put his hands to his ears to shut out the sound. A gull came circling over the steamer—the cry may have been the gull's.

Fisher felt a light touch upon his arm. He turned quickly around. Miss Ward was standing at his side, close to the rail.

"Bless me, how white you are!" she said. "What in the world have you been doing?"

"I have been preserving the liberties of two continents," slowly replied Fisher, "and perhaps saving your own peace of mind."

"Indeed!" she said. "And how have you done that?"

"I have done it," was Fisher's grave answer, "by throwing overboard the Baron Savitch."

Miss Ward burst into a ringing laugh. "You are sometimes too droll, Mr. Fisher," she said.

# JOSUAH ELECTRICMANN

## ERNEST D'HERVILLY

*Ernest d'Hervilly (1838–1911) was a prolific French journalist and writer in various genres and media. Although he was a friend of Victor Hugo and Paul Verlaine, acquainted with most of the participants in the fin-de-siècle Decadent Movement, almost all of his own fiction and work for the theater was in a cheerfully humorous vein, much of his imaginative fiction being written for younger readers.*

*"Josuah Electricmann," first published in the* Petit Parisien *in 1882, is one of numerous French stories reacting with envious sarcasm to the fame won in America by the inventor Thomas Edison. Most of the humorists dabbling in scientific romance during the 1880s and 1890s reflected on that celebrity, several even featuring Edison as a character in their stories, but Hervilly's satirical character study was one of the earliest and was certainly the most extravagant in its depiction of gadgets yet to be invented that would surely claim the attention of such a prolific utilitarian. It is frequently the case that in reaching for absurd extremes, humorists not only showed more imagination than more earnest extrapolators, but more foresight, as the prudent inevitably underestimated the actual pace of future technological progress. "Josuah Electricmann" retains its absurdity with ease, but also its satirical relevance, as a lurid but ironically plausible depiction of the way the world still seems to be going.*

Everyone knows that Josuah Electricmann, the prodigious American scientist, has just announced that he is on the point of inventing a machine destined to take the place of the father of a family in society, and which he has already named the Household Galvanomaster.

One of my friends, who lives in New York, has been asked by me to visit the astonishing inventor of the photoplumographer.

This is the portraitgram that our distant friend has sent us:

Thirty-seven years old. A heart much further to the right than Molière thinks.[1] A black beard. Excellent eyes. They were once poor, but he has improved them by replacing them after their ablation under ether—an operation that is a veritable pleasure party—with a double hooked prunelloglass, his first invention: an instrument that permits one to be, at will, myopic for micrographic studies, or presbyopic for the manipulation of colored disks on railway lines.

I found that unparalleled man sitting in the middle of his vast study on a seat (patented in Paris, London, Philadelphia and Vienna) that can, according to need, be transformed into a parrot's perch or a bottle-rack, and which can also serve as a sled in snowy weather or a linen-press on washing day. It is extremely comfortable.

The walls of the tireless inventor's study are dotted with innumerable constellations of ivory buttons, the departure-points of an immense network of conductive wires connected to all the telegraphic stations in the world.

Its only ornament, in the middle of a panel replete with electric switches, is a vast golden border framing a polished mirror on which, thanks to the next-to-last inventions of the celebrated electrician, the colorofix and the vultugraph, one is able, whenever one has the desire, to have the most marvelous picture in the world painted instantaneously: living and animate pictures of the most incontestable naturalism.

Thanks to that magical combination of the two items of apparatus, which are reminiscent at first sight of two obscure irrigators, Josuah Electricmann enjoys an unrivaled collection of splendid panoramas and delightful urban scenes.

It is also a painted newspaper of the greatest interest. The news appears there in the flesh and bone. The most secret vitriolizations are revealed there in all their horror.

A simple flick of the thumb on button number 4334, for instance, and the vultugraph of Borneo, abruptly allied with the same station's colorofix, instantly reproduces in Electricmann's study what is happening in an ab-

---

[1] Molière's memoirs refer to a public dissection that he attended in 1650, in which the cadaver's organs appeared to be the wrong way round, the heart being "inclined to the right side."

solutely virgin or recently married forest, where a monkey spree is being troubled by the protests of a tiger disturbed in its siesta.

By pressing button no. 22, however—two little ducks, as Bingo callers say—Josuah Electricmann can follow the monkey blow-out with one of the Parisian students during "Happy Hour."

Electricmann invents while eating lunch, or eats lunch while inventing. Nothing is easier. At meal-times, he places a tube in his esophagus, without leaving his desk, and through the orifice of the tube he threads a chaplet of pearls of all kinds of extracts: beef grog, concentrated beefsteak, vegetable essences, cheese pills, wine capsules, solidified coffee aroma, etc., etc.—all products patented in Paris, London, Philadelphia and Vienna.

While he ingurgitates and swallows, he dictates inventions to his scribograph, a mechanical secretary, never ill and always smiling.

The scribograph, one of the discoveries that does the greatest honor to Josuah, is a fortunate graft of the stylocurse and the phonograph. The scribograph, the cradle and point of departure of the galvanomaster, writes, draws, paints, sculpts, counts shirts, arranges books on bookshelves, re-upholsters old umbrellas—in short, night and day, it plays the role of the henceforth-redundant individual who, in rich families, was primarily occupied in paying court to the demoiselle of the house.

It is a veritable treasure! Two hundred francs with nickel pins, a hundred and fifty in copper.

Having eaten well, like Jacquot, the honorable Josuah Electricmann consults, by applying it to his pulse, his medicofere, an electric physician with a mobile dial, and if the pointer indicates seventy-five degrees—which is to say, a perfect equilibrium of the faculties—the great scientist gives thanks to God with the aid of a very curious Theotelegram, which permits one to pray even while exercising on a trapeze. It renders great service to protestant acrobats throughout the territory of the United States.

Thanks having been given, he gives a flick of the thumb to button no. 1027, which brings forth a reading by the poetogene, combined with the vaporistroph, of one of the most remarkable passages by one of our best authors.

A month ago, as he was activating the chemification of his lunch with a strong dose of Vichy pastilles, manufactured in Chicago by the threadworms of which one no longer hears talk in Europe—another coup mounted by the cod merchants who want to annihilate the consumption of ham!—while Monsieur Electricmann's digestive apparatus was performing its function, the proprietor of that apparatus felt a very particular kind of void, or vacancy, in the region of the heart.

That vacancy, or void, was produced by the banal effect on the reverdisant nature of the luminary, so old-fashioned nowadays and which few people any longer venerate, known by the name of the Sun.

In a word, Spring was renascent (old style).

Incited by that circumstance, Monsieur Electricmann, addressing his scribograph, exclaimed:

"The damnation of Cromwell be upon me and on you, but it's true—I've completely forgotten to think about perpetuating my race. I need to get married while inventing. What shall I do? Reply."

The scribograph replied, with its bizarre voice, in which the acerbic grating of goose-quills and iron and the obscure hoarseness of an indisposed ventriloquist are mingled:

"Press buttons 4 and 8; switch off current; return to button 4; press pedal 3603; adapt radiometer; press 6, 29, 33. Ring no. 39; switch off current. Fix 1-6034-24-110. The way is open."

Such is the formula, it appears, to obtain, with the apparatus of the prodigious Josuah, a marriage uniting all conveniences.

For ten minutes, there was an infernal manipulation. Nothing was heard but resonating buzzers and alarm bells ringing madly.

It was a matter of combining, of connecting up to one another, the vultugraph, the phonograph, the telephone, the colorofix, the poetogene, the scribograph, the medicofere, the auriculophile and an infinity of the marvelous Electricmann's other inventions.

During the operation, while still inventing, he savored the odor of a delicious fig, which one of his machines, the autocigarofume, paraded under his nose. At the same time, a capillophobe, a barber powered by pulverized chloroform vapor, shaved the American man of genius dexterously.

A quarter of an hour later, without having left his study, Electricmann knew the hair-color, surname and forenames, the sound of the voice, the weight, the number of pulsations, the tastes, the state of hygiene, the talents, the age, the strength, the tendencies, the moral resistance, the aspirations, the shoe-size, the waist-measurement, the knowledge and the odor of every unmarried woman in the five continents of the world who was already dreaming of a union with a man as practical as him.

He had even telegrammed the moon and the stars, those pale candles.

The moon opened her eyes.

She opened them with even greater astonishment when, for three nights running, she perceived gigantic advertisements in the sky, visible everywhere in the universe: advertisements projected by means of brushes of intense galvanic colored light invented by Electricmann.

Those advertisements requested a wife for the famous inventor from the United States, and concluded uniformly with the specification: "No round shoulders!"

The required woman was found and married the day before yesterday. In three hours, the affair was done and dusted.

They were married, of course, by telegraph; the spouse lives in Greenland.

The witnesses, old and dear friends of the groom, one of whom lives in Australia, another in Romainville, the third in Tehran and the last in the Transvaal among the Boers, were alerted by telegram, and while a pastor duly alerted by the same agent, without ceasing to work in his garden, confided the words necessary in such circumstances to the telephone, the fortunate husband laid down the foundations of his future and world-changing latest invention, the household galvanomaster, as he pronounced the sacramental "I do."

And in the evening. . . .

There was a snag.

Electricmann did not have the time to go and see his wife in Greenland, and it was not for a semester that her parents thought that they would be able to send her to him, even by employing the most rapid means of high-speed land and sea travel.

Oh, if only the Aeroveloce—which is to say, Josuah's express balloon—had been finished, everything would have gone smoothly; but alas, the aeroveloce was not yet finished.

So, keenly annoyed by the forced delay to which his marriage plan was subject, the celebrated Electricmann is seeking, at the present moment, while continuing work on his household galvanomaster, a means of collecting the Greenlandian orange-blossom without disturbing himself.

It is whispered in the United States that Josuah Electricmann will regard himself as dishonored, and that he would commit suicide by volatilization, if he does not succeed in inventing an apparatus indispensable to men of science, which has already been baptized, in his mind, with the name of the amouradistanceophone.

# THE CHILD OF THE PHALANSTERY

## GRANT ALLEN

*Grant Allen (1848–1899) was a British writer and socialist activist who be-
came briefly notorious when he published the best-selling novel* The Woman
Who Did *(1895) attacking the institution of marriage. In the same year he
published* The British Barbarians, *in which a time-traveling social anthro-
pologist visits Victorian London in order to study the primitive mores of its
citizens. He had previously written several short scientific romances, reprinted along with other materials in* Strange Stories *(1884).*

*"The Child of the Phalanstery" remains the most interesting of Allen's short
stories, not only because the issue that it addresses—eugenics—still remains
controversial but because of its oblique rhetorical strategy, which challenges
the reader to make a judgment without indicating too forcefully the direction
in which the author's own sympathies lie. The idea of the "phalanstery" had
been popularized early in the century by the French utopian writer Charles
Fourier (1772–1837), who proposed it as a model for the collectivization of
social and economic life in a socialist society, although Allen's version seems
markedly different in several respects from Fourier's; its inhabitants embrace
a "religion of humanity" reminiscent of the one popularized by the latter's
contemporary August Comte.*

"Poor little thing," said my strong-minded friend compassionately. "Just look
at her! Clubfooted. What a misery to herself and others! In a well-organized
state of society, you know, such poor wee cripples as that would be quietly put
out of their misery while they were still babies."

"Let me think," said I, "how that would work out in actual practice. I'm not
so sure, after all, that we should be altogether the better or the happier for it."

They sat together in a corner of the beautiful phalanstery garden, Olive and Clarence, on the marble seat that overhung the mossy dell where the streamlet danced and bickered among its pebbly stickles; they sat there, hand in hand, in lovers' guise, and felt their two bosoms beating and thrilling in some strange, sweet fashion, just like two foolish unregenerate young people of the old antisocial prephalansteric days.

Perhaps it was the leaven of their unenlightened ancestors still leavening by heredity the whole lump; perhaps it was the inspiration of the calm soft August evening and the delicate afterglow of the setting sun; perhaps it was the deep heart of man and woman vibrating still as of yore in human sympathy, and stirred to its innermost recesses by the unutterable breath of human emotion. But at any rate, there they sat, the beautiful strong man in his shapely chiton, and the dainty fair girl in her long white robe with the dark green embroidered border, looking far into the fathomless depths of one another's eyes, in a silence sweeter and more eloquent than many words. It was Olive's tenth-day holiday from her share in the maidens' household duty of the community; and Clarence, by arrangement with his friend Germain, had made exchange for his own decade (which fell on Plato) to this quiet Milton evening, that he might wander through the park and gardens with his chosen love, and speak his full mind to her now without reserve.

"If only the phalanstery will give its consent, Clarence," Olive said at last with a little sigh, releasing her hand from his, and gathering up the folds of her stole from the marble flooring of the seat; "if only the phalanstery will give its consent! but I have my doubts about it. Is it quite right? Have we chosen quite wisely? Will the hierarch and the elder brothers think I am strong enough and fit enough for the duties of the task? It is no light matter, we know, to enter into bonds with one another for the responsibilities of fatherhood and motherhood. I sometimes feel—forgive me, Clarence—but I sometimes feel as if I were allowing my own heart and my own wishes to guide me too exclusively in this solemn question: thinking too much about you and me, about ourselves (which is only an enlarged form of selfishness after all), and too little about the future good of the community and—and—" blushing a little, for women will be women even in a phalanstery—"and of the precious lives we may be the means of adding to it. You remember, Clarence, what the hierarch said, that we ought to think

least and last of our own feelings, first and foremost of the progressive evolution of universal humanity."

"I remember, darling," Clarence answered, leaning over towards her tenderly; "I remember well, and in my own way, so far as a man can (for we
men haven't the moral earnestness of you women, I'm afraid, Olive), I try
to act up to it. But, dearest, I think our fears are greater than they need be;
you must recollect that humanity requires for its higher development tenderness, and truth, and love, and all the softer qualities, as well as strength
and manliness; and if you are a trifle less strong than most of our sisters
here, you seem to me at least (and I really believe to the hierarch and to the
elder brothers too) to make up for it, and more than make up for it, in your
sweet and lovable inner nature. The men of the future mustn't all be cast
in one unvarying stereotyped mold; we must have a little of all good types
combined, in order to make a perfect phalanstery."

Olive sighed again. "I don't know," she said pensively. "I don't feel sure. I
hope I am doing right. In my aspirations every evening I have desired light
on this matter, and have earnestly hoped that I was not being misled by my
own feelings; for, oh, Clarence, I do love you so dearly, so truly, so absorb-
ingly, that I half fear my love may be taking me unwittingly astray. I try to
curb it; I try to think of it all as the hierarch tells us we ought to; but in my
own heart I sometimes almost fear that I may be lapsing into the idolatrous
love of the old days, when people married and were given in marriage, and
thought only of the gratification of their own personal emotions and affections, and nothing of the ultimate good of humanity. Oh, Clarence, don't
hate me and despise me for it; don't turn upon me and scold me; but I love
you, I love you, I love you; oh, I'm afraid I love you almost idolatrously!"

Clarence lifted her small white hand slowly to his lips, with that natural air of chivalrous respect which came so easily to the young men of the
phalanstery, and kissed it twice over fervidly with quiet reverence. "Let us
go into the music room, Olive dearest," he said as he rose; "you are too sad
tonight. You shall play me that sweet piece of Marian's that you love so
much; and that will quiet you, darling, from thinking too earnestly about
this serious matter."

*

Next day, when Clarence had finished his daily spell of work in the
fruit-garden (he was the third under-gardener to the community), he went

up to his own study, and wrote out a little notice in due form to be posted at dinner-time on the refectory door: "Clarence and Olive ask leave of the phalanstery to enter with one another into free contract of holy matrimony." His pen trembled a little in his own hand as he framed that familiar set of words (strange that he had read it so often with so little emotion, and wrote it now with so much: we men are so selfish!) but he fixed it boldly with four small brass nails on the regulation notice-board, and waited, not without a certain quiet confidence, for the final result of the communal council.

"Aha!" said the hierarch to himself with a kindly smile, as he passed into the refectory at dinner-time that day, "has it come to that, then? Well, well, I thought as much; I felt sure it would. A good girl, Olive; a true, earnest, lovable girl; and she has chosen wisely, too; for Clarence is the very man to balance her own character as man's and wife's should do.

"Whether Clarence has done well in selecting her is another matter. For my own part, I had rather hoped she would join the celibate sisters, and have taken some nurse duty or the sick and the children. It's her natural function in life, the work she's best fitted for; and I should have liked to see her take to it. But after all, the business of the phalanstery is not to decide vicariously for its individual members—not to thwart their natural harmless inclinations and wishes; on the contrary, we ought to allow every man and girl the fullest liberty to follow their own personal taste and judgment in every possible matter.

"Our power of interference as a community, I've always felt and said, should only extend to the prevention of obviously wrong and immoral acts, such as marriage with a person in ill-health, or of inferior mental power, or with a distinctly bad or insubordinate temper. Things of that sort, of course, are as clearly wicked as idling in work hours or marriage with a first cousin. Olive's health, however, isn't really bad, nothing more than a very slight feebleness of constitution, as constitutions go with us; and Eustace, who has attended her medically from her babyhood (what a dear crowing little thing she used to be in the nursery to be sure) tells me that she's perfectly fitted for the duties of her proposed situation.

"Ah well, ah well; I've no doubt they'll be perfectly happy; and the wishes of the whole phalanstery will go with them, in any case, that's certain."

Everybody knew that whatever the hierarch said or thought was pretty sure to be approved by the unanimous voice of the entire community. Not that he was at all a dictatorial or dogmatic old man; quite the contrary; but his gentle kindly way had its full weight with the brothers; and his intimate acquaintance, through the exercise of his spiritual functions, with the inmost thoughts and ideas of every individual member, man or woman, made him a safe guide in all difficult or delicate questions, as to what the decision of the council ought to be.

So when, on the first Cosmos, the elder brothers assembled to transact phalansteric business, and the hierarch put in Clarence's request with the simple phrase, "In my opinion, there is no reasonable objection," the community at once gave in its adhesion, and formal notice was posted an hour later on the refectory door, "The phalanstery approves the proposition of Clarence and Olive, and wishes all happiness to them and to humanity from the sacred union they now contemplate."

"You see, dearest," Clarence said, kissing her lips for the first time (as unwritten law demanded), now that the seal of the community had been placed upon their choice, "you see, there can't be any harm in our contract, for the elder brothers all approve it."

Olive smiled and sighed from the very bottom of her heart, and clung to her lover as the ivy clings to a strong supporting oak-tree. "Darling," she murmured in his ear, "if I have you to comfort me, I shall not be afraid, and we will try our best to work together for the advancement and the good of divine humanity."

Four decades later, on a bright Cosmos morning in September, those two stood up beside one another before the altar of humanity, and heard with a thrill the voice of the hierarch uttering that solemn declaration, "In the name of the Past, and of the Present, and of the Future, I hereby admit you, Clarence and Olive, into the holy society of Fathers and Mothers, of the United Avondale Phalanstery, in trust for humanity, whose stewards you are. May you so use and enhance the good gifts you have received from your ancestors that you may hand them on, untarnished and increased, to the bodies and minds of our furthest descendants."

And Clarence and Olive answered humbly and reverently, "If grace be given us, we will."

*

Brother Eustace, physiologist to the phalanstery, looked very grave and sad indeed as he passed from the Mothers' Room into the Conversazione in search of the hierarch. "A child is born into the phalanstery," he said, gloomily; but his face conveyed at once a far deeper meaning than his mere words could carry to the ear.

The hierarch rose hastily and glanced into his dark keen eyes with an inquiring look. "Not something amiss?" he said eagerly, with an infinite tenderness in his fatherly voice. "Don't tell me that, Eustace. Not . . . oh, not a child that the phalanstery must not for its own sake permit to live! Oh, Eustace, not, I hope, idiotic! And I gave my consent, too; I gave my consent for pretty gentle little Olive's sake! Heaven grant I was not too much moved by her prettiness and her delicacy, for I love her, Eustace, I love her like a daughter."

"So we love all the children of the phalanstery, Cyriac, we who are elder brothers," said the physiologist gravely, half smiling to himself nevertheless at his quaint expression of old-world feeling on the part even of the very hierarch, whose bounden duty it was to advise and persuade a higher rule of conduct and thought than such antique phraseology implied. "No, not idiotic; not quite as bad as that, Cyriac; not absolutely a hopeless case, but still, very serious and distressing for all that. The dear little baby has its feet turned inward. She'll be a cripple for life, I fear, and no help for it."

Tears rose unchecked into the hierarch's soft gray eyes. "Its feet turned inward," he muttered sadly, half to himself. "Feet turned inward! Oh, how terrible! This will be a frightful blow to Clarence and to Olive. Poor young things; their first-born, too. Oh, Eustace, what an awful thought that, with all the care and precaution we take to keep all causes of misery away from the precincts of the phalanstery, such trials as this must needs come upon us by the blind workings of the unconscious Cosmos! It is terrible, too terrible."

"And yet it isn't all loss," the physiologist answered earnestly. "It isn't all loss, Cyriac, heart-rending as the necessity seems to us. I sometimes think that if we hadn't these occasional distressful objects on which to expend our sympathy and our sorrow, we in our happy little communities might grow too smug, and comfortable, and material, and earthy. But things like this bring tears to our eyes, and we are the better for them in the end, depend upon it, we are the better for them. They try our fortitude, our devotion to principle, our obedience to the highest and hardest law.

"Every time some poor little waif like this is born into our midst, we feel the strain of old prephalansteric emotions and fallacies of feeling dragging us steadily and cruelly down. Our first impulse is to pity the poor mother, to pity the poor child, and in our mistaken kindness to let an unhappy life go on indefinitely to its own misery and the preventable distress of all around it. We have to make an effort, a struggle, before the higher and more abstract pity conquers the lower and more concrete one. But in the end we are all the better for it; and each such struggle and each such victory, Cyriac, paves the way for the final and truest morality when we shall do right instinctively and naturally, without any impulse on any side to do any wrong at all."

"You speak wisely, Eustace," the hierarch answered, with a sad shake of his head, "and I wish I could feel like you. I ought to but I can't. Your functions make you able to look more dispassionately upon these things than I can. I'm afraid there's a great deal of the old Adam lingering wrongfully in me yet. And I'm still more afraid that there's a great deal of the old Eve lingering even more strongly in all our mothers. It'll be a long time, I doubt me, before they'll ever consent without a struggle to the painless extinction of necessarily unhappy and imperfect lives. A long time; a very long time. Does Clarence know of this yet?"

"Yes, I have told him. His grief is terrible. You had better go and console him as best you can."

"I will, I will. And poor Olive! Poor Olive! It wrings my heart to think of her. Of course she won't be told of it, if you can help it, for the probationary four decades?"

"No, not if we can help it; but I don't know how it can ever be kept from her. She will see Clarence, and Clarence will certainly tell her."

The hierarch whistled gently to himself. "It's a sad case," he said, ruefully, "a very sad case; and yet I don't see how we can possibly prevent it."

He walked slowly and deliberately into the little ante-room where Clarence was seated on a sofa, his head between his hands, rocking himself to and fro in his mute misery, or stopping to groan now and then in faint feeble inarticulate fashion. Rhoda, one of the elder sisters, held the unconscious baby sleeping in her arms, and the hierarch took it from her like a man accustomed to infants, and looked ruefully at the poor distorted little feet. Yes, Eustace was evidently quite right. There could be no hope of ever putting those wee twisted ankles back straight and firm into their proper lace again like other people's.

He sat down beside Clarence on the sofa, and with a commiserating gesture removed the young man's hands from his poor white face. "My dear, dear friend," he said softly, "what comfort or consolation can we try to give you that is not a cruel mockery? None, none, none. We can only sympathize with you and Olive; and perhaps, after all, the truest sympathy is silence."

Clarence answered nothing for a moment, but buried his face once more in his hands and burst into tears. The men of the phalanstery were less careful to conceal their emotions than we old-time folks in these early centuries. "Oh, dear hierarch," he said, after a long sob, "it is too hard a sacrifice, too hard, too terrible. I don't feel it for the baby's sake; for her 'tis better so; she will be freed from a life of misery and dependence; but for my own sake, and oh, above all, or dear Olive's. It will kill her, hierarch; I feel sure it will kill her!"

The elder brother passed his hand with a troubled gesture across his forehead. "But what else can we do, dear Clarence?" he asked pathetically. "What else can we do? Would you have us bring up the dear child to lead a lingering life of misfortune, to distress the eyes of all around her, to feel herself a useless encumbrance in the midst of so many mutually helpful and serviceable and happy people? How keenly she would realize her own isolation in the joyous busy laboring community of our phalansteries! How terribly she would brood over her own misfortune when surrounded by such a world of hearty, healthy, sound-limbed, useful persons! Would it not be a wicked and a cruel act to bring her up to an old age of unhappiness and imperfection? You have been in Australia, my boy, where we sent you on that plant-hunting expedition, and you have seen cripples with your own eyes, no doubt, which I have never done—thank Heaven!—I who have never gone beyond the limits of the most civilized Euramerican countries. You have seen cripples, in those semi-civilized old colonial societies, which have lagged after us so slowly in the path of progress, and would you like your own daughter to grow up to such a life as that, Clarence? Would you like her, I ask you, to grow up to such a life as that?"

Clarence clenched his right hand tightly over his left arm and answered with a groan: "No, hierarch; not even for Olive's sake could I wish for such an act of irrational injustice. You have trained us up to know the good from the evil, and for no personal gratification of our deepest emotions, I hope

and trust, shall we ever betray your teaching or depart from your principles. I know what it is; I saw just such a cripple once, at a great town in the
heart of Central Australia—a child of eight years old, limping along lamely
on her heels by her mother's side: a sickening sight; to think of it even now
turns the blood in one's arteries, and I could never wish Olive's baby to
grow up to be a thing like that. But oh, I wish to heaven it might have been
otherwise; I wish to heaven this trial might have been spared us both.

"Oh hierarch, dear hierarch, the sacrifice is one that no good man or
woman would want selfishly to forgo; yet for all that, our hearts, our hearts
are human still; and though we may reason and act upon our reasoning,
the human feeling in us—relic of the idolatrous days or whatever you like
to call it—it will not choose to be so put down, and stifled. It will out, hierarch, it will out for all that, in real, hot human tears. Oh, dear, dear kind
father and brother, it will kill Olive; I know it will kill her!"

"Olive is a good girl," the hierarch answered slowly. "A good girl, well
brought up, and with sound principles. She will not flinch from doing her
duty, I know, Clarence; but her emotional nature is a very delicate one,
and we have reason indeed to fear the shock to her nervous system. That
she will do right bravely, I don't doubt; the only danger is lest the effort to
do right should cost her too dear. Whatever can be done to spare her shall
be done, Clarence. It is a sad misfortune for the whole phalanstery, such a
child being born to us as this, and we all sympathize with you; we sympathize with you more deeply than words can say."

The young man only rocked up and down drearily, and murmured to
himself: "It will kill her, it will kill her! My Olive, my Olive, I know it will
kill her."

\*

They didn't keep the secret of the baby's crippled condition from Olive
till the four decades were over, or anything like it. The moment she saw
Clarence, she guessed at once with a woman's instinct that something serious had happened, and she didn't rest till she had found out from him all
about it. Rhoda brought her the poor wee mite, carefully wrapped after the
phalansteric fashion in a long strip of fine flannel, and Olive unrolled the
piece until she came at last upon the poor crippled feet, that looked so soft
and tender and dainty and waxen in their very deformity.

The young mother leant over the child a moment in speechless misery. "Spirit of Humanity," she whispered at length feebly, "oh give me strength to bear this terrible unutterable trial! It will break my heart. But I will try to bear it."

There was something so touching in her attempted resignation that Rhoda, for the first time in her life, felt almost tempted to wish she had been born in the old wicked prephalansteric days, when they would have let the baby grow up to womanhood as a matter of course, and bear its own burden through life as best it might. Presently, Olive raised her head again from the crimson silken pillow. "Clarence," she said, in a trembling voice, pressing the sleeping baby hard against her breast, "when will it be? How long? Is there no hope, no chance of respite?"

"Not for a long time yet, dearest Olive," Clarence answered through his tears. "the phalanstery will be very gentle and patient with us, we know; and brother Eustace will do everything that lies in his power, though he's afraid he can give us very little hope indeed. In any case, Olive darling, the community waits for four decades before deciding anything; it waits to see whether there is any chance for physiological or surgical relief; it decides nothing hastily or thoughtlessly; it waits for every possible improvement, hoping against hope till hope itself is hopeless. And then, if at the end of the quartet, as I fear will be the case—for we must face the worst, darling, we must face the worst—if at the end of the quartet it seems clear to brother Eustace, and the three assessor physiologists from the neighboring phalansteries, that the dear child would be a cripple for life, we're still allowed four decades more to prepare ourselves in: four whole decades more, Olive, to take our leave of the darling baby. You'll have your baby with you for eighty days. And we must wean ourselves from her in that time, darling. But oh, Olive, oh, Rhoda, it's very hard: very, very, very hard."

Olive answered not a word, but lay silently weeping and pressing the baby against her breast, with her large brown eyes fixed vacantly upon the fretted woodwork of the paneled ceiling.

"You mustn't do like that, Olive dear," sister Rhoda said in a half-frightened voice. "You must cry right out, and sob, and not restrain yourself, darling, or else you'll break your heart with silence and repression. Do cry aloud, there's a dear girl; do cry aloud and relieve yourself. A good cry would be the best thing on earth for you. And think, dear, how much happier it will really be for the sweet baby to sink asleep so peacefully than to live a long life of conscious inferiority and felt imperfection! What a blessing it is to think you were born in a phalansteric land, where the dear child will be happily and painlessly rid of its poor little unconscious existence, before it has reached the age when it might begin to know its own incurable and inevitable misfortune. Oh, Olive, what a blessing that is, and how thankful we all ought to be that we live in a world where the sweet pet will be saved so much humiliation, and mortification, and misery!"

At that moment, Olive, looking within into her own wicked rebellious heart, was conscious, with a mingled glow, half shame, half indignation, that so far from appreciating the priceless blessings of her own situation, she would gladly have changed places there and then with any barbaric woman of the old semi-civilized prephalansteric days. We can so little appreciate our own mercies.

It was very wrong and anti-cosmic, she knew; very wrong, indeed, and the hierarch would have told her so at once; but in her own woman's soul she felt she would rather be a miserable naked savage in a wattled hut, like those one saw in old books about Africa before the illumination, if only she could keep that one little angel of a crippled baby, than dwell among all the enlightenment, and knowledge and art, and perfected social arrangements of phalansteric England without her child—her dear, helpless, beautiful baby.

How truly the Founder himself had said: "Think you there will be no more tragedies and dramas in the world when we have reformed it, nothing but one dreary dead level of monotonous content? Ay, indeed, there will; for that, fear not; while the heart of man remains, there will be tragedy enough on earth and to spare for a hundred poets to take for their saddest epics."

Olive looked up at Rhoda wistfully. "Sister Rhoda," she said in a timid tone, "it may be very wicked—I feel sure it is—but do you know, I've read somewhere in old stories of the unenlightened days that a mother always loved the most afflicted of her children the best. And I can understand it now, sister Rhoda; I can feel it here," and she put her hand upon her poor still heart. "If only I could keep this one dear crippled baby, I could give up all the world beside—except you, Clarence."

"Oh, hush, darling!" Rhoda cried in an awed voice, stooping down half alarmed to kiss her pale forehead. "You mustn't talk like that, Olive dearest. It's wicked, it's undutiful. I know how hard it is not to repine and to rebel, but you mustn't, Olive, you mustn't. We must each strive to bear our own burdens (with the help of the community), and not to put any of them off on a poor, helpless, crippled little baby."

"But our natures," Clarence said, wiping his eyes dreamily; "our natures are only half attuned as yet to the necessities of the higher social existence. Of course it's very wrong and very sad, but we can't help feeling it, sister Rhoda, though we try our hardest. Remember, it's not so many generations since our fathers would have reared the child without a thought that they were doing anything wicked—nay, rather, would even have held (so powerful is custom) that it was positively wrong to save it by preventive means from a certain life of predestined misery. Our conscience in this matter isn't yet fully formed. We feel that it's right, of course; oh yes, we know the phalanstery has ordered everything for the best; but we can't help grieving over it; the human heart within us is too unregenerate still to acquiesce without a struggle in the direction of right and reason."

Olive again said nothing, but fixed her eyes silently upon the grave, earnest portrait of the Founder over the carved oak mantelpiece, and let the hot tears stream their own way over her cold, white, pallid, bloodless cheek without reproof for many minutes. Her heart was too full for either speech or comfort.

*

Eight decades passed away slowly in the Avondale Phalanstery; and day after day seemed more and more terrible to poor, weak, disconsolate Olive. The quiet refinement and delicate surroundings of their placid life seemed to make her poignant misery and long anxious term of waiting only the more intense in its sorrow and its awesomeness.

Every day, the younger sisters turned as of old to their allotted round of pleasant housework; every day the elder sisters, who had earned their leisure, brought in their daily embroidery, or their drawing materials, or their other occupations, and tried to console her, or rather to condole with her, in her great sorrow. She couldn't complain of any unkindness; on the contrary, all the brothers and sisters were sympathy itself, while Clarence, though he tried hard not to be *too* idolatrous to her (which is wrong and antisocial, of course) was still overflowing with tenderness and consideration for her in their common grief. But all that seemed merely to make things worse.

If only somebody had been cruel to her; if only the hierarch would have scolded her, or the elder sisters have shown her any distant coldness, or the other girls have been wanting in sisterly sympathy, she might have got angry or brooded over her wrongs; whereas, now, she could do nothing save cry passively with a vain attempt at resignation. It was nobody's fault; there was nobody to be angry with, there was nothing to blame except the great impersonal laws and circumstances of the Cosmos, which it would be rank impiety and wickedness to question or gainsay.

So she endured in silence, loving only to sit with Clarence's hand in hers, and the dear doomed baby lying peacefully upon the stole in her lap. It was inevitable and there was no use repining; for so profoundly had the phalanstery schooled the minds and nature of those two unhappy young parents (and all their compeers) that, grieve as they might, they never for one moment dreamt of attempting to relax or set aside the fundamental principles of phalansteric society in these matters.

By the kindly rule of the phalanstery, every mother had complete freedom from household duties for two years after the birth of her child; and Clarence, though he would not willingly have given up his own particular work in the grounds and garden, spent all the time he could spare from his short daily task (everyone worked five hours every lawful day, and few worked longer, save on special emergencies) by Olive's side.

At last, the eight decades passed slowly away, and the fatal day for the removal of little Rosebud arrived. Olive called her Rosebud because, she said, she was a sweet bud that could never be opened into a full-blown rose. All the community felt the solemnity of the painful occasion, and by common consent the day (Darwin, December 20) was held as an intra-phalansteric fast by the whole body of brothers and sisters.

On that terrible morning Olive rose early, and dressed herself carefully in a long white stole with a broad black border of Greek key pattern. But she had not the heart to put any black upon dear little Rosebud, and so she put on her fine flannel wrapper, and decorated it instead with the pretty colored things that Vernia and Philomela had worked for her, to make her baby as beautiful as possible on this last day in a world of happiness.

The other girls helped her and tried to sustain her, crying all together at the sad event.

"She's a sweet little thing," they said to one another as they held her up to see how she looked. "If only it could have been her reception today instead of her removal!"

But Olive moved through them all with stoical resignation—dry-eyed and parched in the throat, yet saying not a word save for necessary instructions and directions to the nursing sisters. The iron of her creed had entered into her very soul.

After breakfast, brother Eustace and the hierarch came sadly in their official robs into the lesser infirmary. Olive was there already, pale and trembling, with little Rosebud sleeping peacefully in the hollow of her lap. What a picture she looked, the wee dear thing, with the hothouse flowers from the conservatory that Clarence had brought to adorn her fastened neatly on to her fine flannel robe!

The physiologist took out a little phial from his pocket and began to open a sort of inhaler of white muslin. At the same moment, the grave, kind old hierarch stretched out his hands to take the sleeping baby from its mother's arms. Olive shrank back in terror, and clasped the child softly to her heart. "No, no, let me hold her myself, dear hierarch," she said, without flinching. "Grant me this one last favor. Let me hold her myself."

It was contrary to all fixed rules, but neither the hierarch nor anyone else there present had the heart to refuse that beseeching voice on so supreme and spirit-rending an occasion.

Brother Eustace poured the chloroform solemnly and quietly on to the muslin inhaler.

"By resolution of the phalanstery," he said, in a voice husky with emotion, "I release you, Rosebud, from a life for which you are naturally unfitted. In pity for our hard fate, we save you from the misfortune you have never known, and will never now experience."

As he spoke, he held the inhaler to the baby's face, and watched its breathing grow fainter and fainter, till at last, after a few minutes, it faded gradually and entirely away. The little one had slept from life into death, painlessly and happily, even as they looked.

Clarence, tearful but silent, felt the baby's pulse for a moment, and then, with a burst of tears, shook his head bitterly. "It is all over," he cried, with a loud cry. "It is all over; and we hope and trust it is better so."

But Olive still said nothing.

The physiologist turned to her with an anxious gaze. Her eyes were open, but they looked blank and staring into vacant space. He took her hand, and it felt limp and powerless. "Great heaven," he cried, in evident alarm, "what is this? Olive, Olive, our dear Olive, why don't you speak?"

Clarence sprang up from the ground, where he had knelt to try the dead baby's pulse, and took her unresisting wrist anxiously in his. "Oh, brother Eustace," he cried, passionately, "help us, save us. What's the matter with Olive? She's fainting, she's fainting! I can't feel her heart beat, no, not ever so little."

Brother Eustace let the pale white hand drop listlessly from his grasp upon the pale white stole beneath, and answered slowly and distinctly: "She isn't fainting, Clarence; not fainting, my dear brother. The shock and the fumes of the chloroform together have been too much for the action of her heart. She's dead too, Clarence; our dear, dear sister; she's dead too."

Clarence flung his arms wildly round Olive's neck, and listened eagerly with his ear against her bosom to hear her heart beat. But no sound came from the folds of the simple black-bordered stole; no sound from anywhere save the suppressed sobs of the frightened women who huddled closely together in the corner, and gazed horror-stricken upon the two warm fresh corpses.

"She was a brave girl," brother Eustace said at last, wiping his eyes and composing her hands reverently. "Olive was a brave girl, and she died doing her duty, without one murmur against the sad necessity that fate had unhappily placed upon her. No sister on earth could wish to die more nobly than by thus sacrificing her own life and her own weak human affections on the altar of humanity for the sake of her child and of the world at large."

"And yet I sometimes almost fancy," the hierarch murmured, with a violent effort to control his emotions, "when I see a scene like his, that even the unenlightened practices of the old era may not have been quite so bad as we usually think them, for all that. Surely an end such as Olive's is a sad and terrible end to have forced upon us as the final outcome and natural close of all our modern phalansteric civilization."

"The ways of the Cosmos are wonderful," said brother Eustace solemnly, "and we, who are no more than atoms and mites upon the surface of its meanest satellite, cannot hope so to order all things after our own fashion that all its minutest turns and chances may approve themselves to us as right in our own eyes."

The sisters all made instinctively the reverential genuflection. "The Cosmos is infinite," they said together, in the fixed formula of their cherished religion. "The Cosmos is infinite, and man is but a parasite upon the face of the last among its satellite members. May we so act as to further all that is best within us, and to fulfill our own small place in the system of the Cosmos with all becoming reverence and humility! In the name of universal Humanity. So be it."

# THE SALVATION OF NATURE

## JOHN DAVIDSON

*John Davidson (1857–1909) was a Scottish poet and playwright who made several ventures into humorous scientific romance, most extensively in* A Full and True Account of the Wonderful Mission of Earl Lavender *(1895), a farce whose hero attempts in a cavalier fashion to take advantage of his conviction that he is a Nietzschean übermensch favored by evolution. Far more earnest are a series of long poetic "Testaments," the last of which,* The Testament of John Davidson *(1908), published shortly before his death—presumed to be suicide—offers an extravagant cosmic vision.*

*"The Salvation of Nature" was Davidson's first scientific romance, reprinted in* The Great Men; and A Practical Novelist *(1891) and* The Pilgrimage of Strongsoul and Other Stories *(1896), and it remains the most interesting, although it is something of a patchwork; it anticipates the idea of "nature reserves" and also that of "theme parks," while making a flippantly eccentric contribution to the subgenre of modern apocalyptic fantasies.*

On the day that Sir Wenyeve Westaway's World's Pleasance Bill became law, the happy baronet kissed his wife and said, "Lily, darling, it has taken twenty years, but we have saved Nature."

"Never mind, dear," said Lady Westaway, who, though a true helpmeet, loved to quit her husband, "the time has not been wholly wasted."

"Wholly wasted!" cried Sir Wenyeve, too much in earnest for even the mildest persiflage. "The salvation of Nature is a task worthy of an antediluvian lifetime."

"In the longest life there is only one youth," sighed Lady Westaway, as she left the library.

She was thirty-five years old, and her married life had been a continuous intrigue to bring about the fulfillment of her husband's dream. Now that his object was gained, she felt that her youth and prime had passed like a rout at the close of the season—stale, unenjoyed, immemorable. But she dressed beautifully on the night of her husband's triumph; and the subtler of her guests mistook the sadness in her eyes and voice for the melancholy which overcomes some natures when an arduous undertaking is accomplished.

The day after Sir Wenyeve's banquet celebrating the passage of his Bill, two thousand clerks and message boys posted two million copies of the following prospectus. The list of directors, financial agents, bankers, managers, and other uninteresting details are omitted:

THE WORLD'S PLEASANCE COMPANY, LIMITED
Incorporated under the Companies Acts
Capital . . . £200,000,000

Issue of 1,000,000 shares of £100 each, of which £50 is called up as follows: £5 on application. £5 on allotment. £20 on May 1, and £20 on July 1. The remaining £50 per share is to form security for debentures.

The capital of the company is divided into 2,000,000 shares of £100 each, of which—

1,650,000 shares will be issued as ordinary shares, entitled to a cumulative dividend of 15% before the deferred shares participate in profit.

350,000 shares as deferred shares to be issued at £50 paid, which will not be entitled to participate in dividend until 15% has been paid on the paid up capital of the ordinary shareholders.

The deferred shares and 600,000 of the ordinary shares will be taken by the promoters in part payment of the price.

This company has been incorporated for the purpose of acquiring that part of Great Britain known as the kingdom of Scotland, with the outer and inner Hebrides and the Orkney and Shetland Isles.

It is estimated that three-quarters of the capital of the company will be expended on the purchase of Scotland; the remainder to be devoted—

1.  To the demolition of all manufactories, foundries, building-yards, railways, tramways, walls, fences, and all unnatural divisions, and of all buildings, with some few exceptions, of a later date than 1700 A.D.

2.  To the purchase of a number of the Polynesian Islands.
3.  To the importation of these islands and the distribution of their soil over the razed cities, towns, villages, etc.

When the land has thus been restored to the bosom of Nature, it will remain there unmolested for a year or two. At the end of this nursing-time, Scotland, having been in a manner born again, will be called by its new name, "The World's Pleasance"; and visitors will be admitted during the six months of summer and autumn on payment of £50 for each individual per month. At the rate of 100,000 visitors per month, this will give an income of £30,000,000. Figures like these need no comment.

Every species of tent, marquee, awning and canvas or waterproof erection; every species of rowing or sailing vessel; and every species of rational land conveyance will be permitted in the World's Pleasance; but there must not be laid one stone upon another; nor shall steam, electricity or hydraulic power be used for any purpose, except for the working of Professor Penpergwyn's dew-condensers. One of these machines will be erected at John o'Groat's House, and another at Kirkmaiden. Professor Penpergwyn has recently, at the request of the promoters of this company, devoted all his time to perfecting his celebrated apparatus; and we are happy to be able to state that the cloud-compelling attachment for withholding rain from an area greater than half of Scotland, now works with the requisite power, regularity and delicacy; while the dew-condensers proper can, at a moment's notice, fill the air with any degree of moisture, from the filmiest mist to a deluge.

The promoters of the company congratulate themselves, and the people of every continent, on the salvation of a fragment of the Old World from the jaws of Civilization; and in conclusion they think they cannot do better than quote the peroration of Sir Wenyeve Westaway's great speech on the motion for the third reading of the Bill with which his name will be associated to the end of time. The honorable baronet said in conclusion:

"If you would loosen the shackles which bind the poetry and art of the day; if you would give a little ease to the voiceless, suffering earth, crushed in the iron shell of civilization, like the skull of a martyr in that Venetian head-screw which ground to a pulp bone and brain and flesh; if, in a word, you would provide a home, a second Academe, a new Arcadia for poetry and art, these illustrious outcasts; if you would save Nature, you will pass this Bill. Make Scotland the World's Pleasance, and I venture to predict that the benefits springing from such a recreation-ground to Art and Morality will be so immense, that the world will bless, as long as the earth endures, the legislators who licensed the creation of a second Eden."

The demand for shares during the week in which the prospectus was published was more than double the supply. Ling-long, the perpetual president of the United States, applied for a thousand; but his Perpetuity had to be content with ten. All the kings and queens in the world took as many as could be allotted to them. The ancient list of the world's seven wonders was cancelled, and the company's palatial and labyrinthine offices on the English banks of the Tweed became the initial wonder of a new one. And Sir Wenyeve Westaway? He was made a peer of the realm, and the company, in the joy of success, voted him for two lives the sole right of visiting the island of Arran.

Professor Penpergwyn superintended the destruction of civilized Scotland. Electrite was the explosive used, on account of the precision with which the upheaval produced by a given charge could be calculated. It was possible with this remarkable invention to destroy one half of a building, and leave the other undamaged; for the debris fell back, like an ill-thrown boomerang, exactly to the spot whence it had shot up. The Professor was truly a great man.

When all the railways and tramways had been removed, and sold at great profit to the Chinese; when all the wires had been prepared, and half the known tar, and every tar-barrel beneath the sun had been duly distributed among the buildings to be deracinated, he let the world into the secret of the broad and lofty piers which he had erected on many parts of the Scottish coast, at various distances from the shore. From them the public could view the great fire, on payment to the Professor of three guineas per head. He provided no conveyance to or from the piers. He guaranteed nothing, either regarding their security or the width of view they commanded. You paid your money and took your chance. Two million people bought tickets. The Professor's profit, deducting the cost of the piers, and of the huge army of ticket-collectors, was £2,000,000.

On the last night of the year, Scotland was set on fire. The Professor had utilized the Scotch telegraph wires. By their means all his mines were connected with the battery at which he sat in London, waiting impatiently till ten should strike. In the moment of the last stroke he touched the machine;

then he set off for Kamchatka with his wife and only daughter, a child of seven years.

As will be surmised, this extraordinary man was not the only individual who waited with impatience till ten o'clock that night. All England, all the world, was *en fête*. Miniature explosions were prepared in every town and hamlet, in nearly every street and lane in the four quarters of the globe—each little mine surrounded by a restless mob. But the most impatient of all the inhabitants of the earth were the two millions of men and women who crowded the Professor's piers.

At a minute from ten, the human zone girdling Scotland was as silent as death. All the clocks in all the towers and steeples in the doomed country had been wound up for that night. There was no wind and the air was frosty. When the hour rang—the last hour that should ever ring in Scotland—pealing in many tones, but harmonized by the distance to the ears of the listeners, so that poets thought of swan-songs and the phoenix, and the most prosaic remembered the death-knell—a strong thrill passed through the multitude and a rustle went about from pier to pier, like a wind wandering among the woods. Not a star could be seen. Scotland was only discerned as a more intense blackness in the bosom of the night. The silence after the striking of the hour was deeper than before—so deep that the people heard faintly the petty splash of the waves against the piers.

Suddenly the Cheviots were tipped with fire, and two million faces grew pale. In the same breathless instant these faces, rank after rank, loomed out in the light of the burning country, as the land-wide flash sped over the mountains to Cape Wrath, and a sound as if the thunder of a century had been gathered into one terrific, long-rolling peal shook the whole sea, and forced every head to bend. Then again silence and blackness, uttermost, appalling. All the people trembled. A wife said to her husband in the lowest whisper ever breathed, "I am going mad."

"And I too," he replied hoarsely.

A sage old man beside them, who overheard their whispers, cried "Hurrah!"

It broke the spell. From pier to pier the word ran until the shout became general.

"Hurrah! Hurrah!"—the most voluminous cheer on record—and with that the people fell a-talking.

"Has it failed?" was the universal question.

The wise old fellow who had started the cheer thought not.

"The explosions are over," he said, "but the fires will soon break out."

And he was right. Even as he spoke tongues of flame were jetting up. It was then five minutes past ten. In another minute, Scotland looked like a huge leviathan, spotted and brindled with eyes and stripes of fire. Where the towns were thick these ran into each other, and soon the Lowlands were wrapped in one glowing sheet. The smoke wallowed on high, and dipped and writhed in and out among the flames. Description shrivels before such a scene.

"Behold!" cried Lord Westaway, "the altar on which the world sacrifices to Nature for the sin of Civilization!"

It is not known when the last flame of the great fire went out; but in the end of February the first fleet of vessels from Polynesia arrived in the Clyde. They landed their cargoes among the ruins of Glasgow; and the debris on the Broomielaw was soon covered with the dust of the coral insect.

In six months the reclamation of Scotland to the bosom of Nature was completed by a million men, who wrought in three relays, night and day. Professor Penpergwyn's piers were then destroyed; and a cordon of five hundred war-vessels was placed along the coast, and not a human foot trod Scottish earth—or Polynesian earth in Scotland—for two years.

Lord Westaway, on the day the company granted him the isle of Arran, had shut himself up in his study. Three hours he brooded, and then summoned his son Lewellyn, a handsome boy in his eleventh year.

"Lewellyn," said Lord Westaway, "I am going to prepare Arran for you. You will enter into possession of it on your twenty-first birthday. I will make it the most remarkable island in the world."

"How will you do that, Papa?"

"Do not inquire; don't try to discover from any source; your surprise and pleasure ten years hence will be the greater."

The boy, who worshiped his father, agreed to this unhesitatingly.

The World's Pleasance brought down the world. At the close of the first season in which the rejuvenated Scotland was open to the public, instead of the fifteen per cent expected by the promoters, a dividend of thirty per cent was declared on all the shares. From many glowing contemporary accounts of the wonders of the great pleasure-ground, I select the flowing letter of the young Empress of the Far East to her Prime Minister, whom she afterwards married, as being the least overcharged:

### Extract from the Letter of the Empress of the East

"We landed in the end of June on the shore where Leith once stood. I was carried up to Edinburgh in a litter, the rugged nature of the ground preventing any other mode of conveyance. A Greek temple-like building—formerly a picture-gallery, I believe—had been prepared for us.[1] The rent of it is enormous, as the company put up to auction all the habitable buildings in the country. This was rendered necessary by the battles which took place for the possession of historical or finely-situated houses.

"At first the directors thought that the fighting would lend an additional charm to life here; but when Ling-long, the American president, besieged the Emperor of the French in Holyrood with bows and arrows and battering rams—a bye-law forbids the use of all explosives—and took the place with the loss of several lives on both sides, interference was deemed expedient. All fighting, except in the tourney, is now done with quarter-staves. Every third day we have a quarrel with some other potentate about a fishing-stream or a glade for hawking in.

"My greatest enemy is the King of England, who lives in Edinburgh Castle. We are very warm friends and model disputants, complying graciously with the bye-law which adjudges victory to the side that first draws blood. Although the King's retinue exceeds mine, my Tartar giant, by his superior strength and agility, manages, as a rule, to finish the fight in our favor.

"I will just go on scribbling in my woman's way as I have begun. The next thing that occurs to me is the splendor of Edinburgh. It is pronounced by everybody the most beautiful piece of the juvenile country. Scientific men are much perplexed by it, as indeed they are by all the newly naturalized land. It would seem that there is a struggle going on between the imported tropical vegetation and the native plants and grasses. The latter have conquered in Edinburgh. It is covered with young heather and broom and bracken, and only here and there a dwarfed alien plant appears. The billows of purple and green and gold toss about in what was the New Town, and, swirling along the valley, roll up the High Street to throw splashes of color here and there on the Castle Esplanade.

---

[1] Presumably the Scottish National Gallery, situated on The Mound, first opened to the public in 1859.

"We are clad in sixteenth century costumes; the King of England and his Court in dresses of the time of the Charleses. Nearly all the Americans go about in Greek robes, as gods and goddesses, heroes and heroines. The French court is a miniature of that of Louis XIV. The Russians are dressed in Lincoln green; the Czar is called Robin Hood, and the Czarina Maid Marian. We have no clocks; the dial is our only timekeeper. It is all a great masque, from the country itself to the pot-boys and scullions.

"Last week I rode as far north as Perth, and seemed to journey through all the times and peoples of Europe. Here, in a broad meadow, we saw a tournament, where some princesses sat as queens of love and beauty. A few miles further on we passed a water-party of the Restoration, with music and laughter. Then a pavilion gleamed white among the trees, and there two knights of the Round Table hung out their blazoned shields. Up rode, with lofty air, Don Quixote, wearing the veritable helmet of Mambrino. Behind, all amort, on a sorry ass, ambled the wisest of fools, dear old Sancho Panza.

"'What, ho! vile recreants!' cried the knight of La Mancha, and struck exultingly one of the shields. We stood aside to watch the encounter, and beheld him of the sorrowful countenance go down before the spear of Lancelot of the Lake.

"Anon, Mary Queen of Scots, followed by Douglases and Graemes and Setons, sped by, chasing a stag of ten.

"'Splendeur de Dieu!' cried a deep voice in front; and a body of Norman knights charged the Scotsman. But after a brief battle, William the Conqueror and Mary Stuart agreed to hunt together.

"O me! my heart is sick with dreaming over these old times. And yet, although I know it is the signal for my return, I long for the day when you are to come, my faithful friend.

"I have some, and shall have more, very pleasant stories to tell you of a party of Germans, who have undertaken to act through all Shakespeare's comedies, with the whole World's Pleasance for stage, naming places after localities in the plays, and traveling about as the scene requires. They have already acted two comedies, and in each of them real passions and events have grown out of the fiction, so that the company has lost half its original members owing to elopements and quarrels.

"This is a long letter, and I am tired."

One result of the success of the World's Pleasance Company was the establishment of similar companies in nearly every country. The Americans reclaimed Peru and California. The Empress of the East was the principal promoter of a company for the naturalization of Greece. The French reclaimed Provence. Italy was given over entirely to Nature; and the whole Italian nation became brigands. This country was much frequented by young people in search of adventure. The African Republics made pleasances of Algeria and the country about the great lakes; and a gigantic Asiatic company bought up the Himalayas and the Indo-Chinese peninsula.

For eight years all those pleasance companies paid great percentages and immense fortunes were made. Every other man was a millionaire. Then it seemed that the world came bankrupt. Thousands of people committed suicide. Famine followed bankruptcy; and after it came a new disease. It began in India, and traveled almost as fast as the news of its ravages.

People fled to their pleasances for refuge, but the pest was there before them. Cities were emptied in a day. In every town and hamlet the last to die thought himself the last man, and posed mentally as such. London was swept of life like the deck of a vessel by a mountainous wave. In the World's Pleasance people wandered about in twos and threes, shunning strangers, digging roots, dropping dead. Most of them wore their holiday costumes. Some few carried bottles of wine, and laughed and sang. But the time for such desperate jollity soon passed, and the plague remained.

In the beginning of July, an old man of great freshness and vigor appeared in that part of the Pleasance formerly known as Ayrshire. He approached everybody he met. To those whom he could say, he put this question: "Do you know anything of Lewellyn Westaway?"

A languid shake of the head was all the answer he ever got. So many kept him aloof, that he resorted to calling out his question at the pitch of his voice. For an entire forenoon he did this; and shortly after midday a man dropped out of a tree almost on his head and said, "I am Lewellyn Westaway."

"And I," said the old man, "am Professor Penpergwyn."

The Professor wore a white hat and a black frock coat, old and dusty. Lewellyn was dressed in a purple velvet doublet, and from his close-fitting cap a feather hung gracefully, and mingled with his long hair. The contrast was striking.

"What do you want with me?" asked Lewellyn.

"Why are you not in Arran?"

"In Arran?"

"Yes; you are twenty-one now, and the island awaits you."

"I had forgotten about it."

"Drink this, and go there at once."

"What's this? And why should I go there at once?"

"This," said the Professor, opening the morocco case he had offered Lewellyn, and holding up a little vial, "is an infallible remedy for the plague."

Lewellyn laughed scornfully.

"Faithless, faithless!" cried the Professor, looking earnestly with his strong, convincing eyes into those of the young man.

Lewellyn was bound by his gaze; and the Professor continued: "I tell you, who may die this moment, who must die within a week, that this will save you, and you laugh in my face. Will you take it or not?"

Lewellyn took it.

"Drink it."

He did so in silence.

"Now listen to me."

The Professor leaned against a tree, while Lewellyn stood meekly before him.

"First tell me—are your father and mother dead?"

"They are."

"Then you are as free as I could wish you to be, unless you are married."

"I am not."

"Good. Many years ago I discovered this disease in Kamchatka. It is really nothing more or less than hunger, the millionth power of hunger. I have not time to explain it. It must often have appeared in the world. Probably it has always existed actively, but never till this great famine has it fairly got wing. I recognized its power in Kamchatka, and saw that if it should get enough strength from feeding on a few hundred thousand lives, it would kill the world. Its power and velocity increase with its progress. It knows no crisis. In a few days it will be as swift as the lightning. I began in Kamchatka to try for a remedy. I labored for years, and then had to come west for materials. It was during that visit that I burned Scotland. On my return to Kamchatka I found that a filtrate I had left standing had clarified itself, and was, in fact, the required remedy. For the last ten years I have been trying to repeat the process, but have always failed. When I heard of the breaking out of the pest I came at once from Kamchatka. I had sufficient of my remedy to save two lives. My wife is dead, so I gave one half to you. Now, sir, go to Arran."

"Why give me half?"

"Is that your gratitude? Had I not found you I should have given it to the finest young fellow I could meet with. But ask no more questions. Do as I bid you. You will find it to your advantage. You will never see me more. Within a fortnight all who have not drunk of my medicament will be dead."

"What! Are we two to be the only men left alive, and are we to part forever?"

"Yes. Your father has saved Nature, but in a way he little expected. Goodbye for ever."

Lewellyn realized but faintly what the old man had said with such authority, and stood irresolute.

"Go," said the Professor; and Lewellyn, like one under a spell, hurried down to the coast. He was hardly out of sight when Professor Penpergwyn dropped dead.

On the shore Lewellyn found many boats—some floating, some high and dry—all masterless. He chose the one he judged the swiftest sailer, and was soon flying across the firth with a strong east wind behind him. As he neared Arran he saw a white flag run up a short pole on a little eminence near the beach. He was too much battered with wonder to feel this new stroke. Involuntarily he steered for the flag.

When he was some hundred yards from land he observed below the flag-pole, seated on a rock, a figure like that of a woman, motionless and watching him intently. In landing, his boat occupied all his attention, so that when he stepped ashore and found a tall girl standing with her back to him, but within reach of his arm, the effect upon him was almost as great as if he had not seen her before.

He stood still, expecting her to turn round; but she remained as she was for some moments fingering a bow she carried. A quiver full of arrows was slung across her shoulder. Her dress, of some dark blue homely stuff, came to her ankles. She wore shoes of untanned leather, and a belt of the same, in which was stuck a short sword. On her head she had a little fur cap, and her short golden brown hair curled on her shoulders.

Slowly she turned and gave him a side glance. Then she looked him full in the face and sighed deeply, but as if some doubt had been resolved to her satisfaction.

He fell back a step at the splendor of her eyes. Her face was broad and her complexion delicate, though browned. He hardly noticed her low forehead, her straight eyebrows, her strong, round chin, and full red mouth; her eyes held him. He did not think of their color. He was subdued by their intense expression. They seemed to pierce him with intuition, and at the same time to bathe him in a soft, warm light. She spoke, and her voice seemed to caress him; but all she said was: "Do you come from Professor Penpergwyn?"

He bowed. If he spoke he felt the vision would vanish.

"Have you drunk the other half?"

He bowed again, understanding her to mean the other half of the Professor's remedy.

"Did he tell you that there was only enough for two?"

He found his tongue and answered "Yes," whispering as intently as she did, but wondering why there should be so much passion about the matter.

"Do you know who drank the rest?"

"I supposed it was the Professor."

She sighed again, a deep sigh of satisfaction, and sank on the beach sobbing. Lewellyn, after a moment's thought, knelt beside her and held one of her hands in both his. She made no resistance. In a little she dried her tears with her disengaged hand, shook back her hair and looked him in the face.

"I'm so glad to see you," she said; "I have been alone here for a week. You needn't ask any questions. I'll tell you it all at once. Professor Penpergwyn is my Papa. Is he alive?"

"He was four hours ago."

"He may be dead now, though. Poor Papa! He would always have his own way. Papa expected to find you. When he didn't, he left me alone and went to search for you. We brought some provisions and weapons with us, and I have managed to get on very well. But I'm glad you've come. *Are you Lewellyn Westaway?*" she cried sharply, springing to her feet in sudden doubt.

"Yes I am—Lord Westaway, if it's of any consequence."

"I'm very glad. Tell me, what was the name of your father's steward?"

"Dealtry—Henry Dealtry."

"It was; it was!"

The lady smiled, and looked as happy and self-satisfied as if she had exercised the most extraordinary subtlety in putting his question, and as if Lewellyn's answer were conclusive proof of his identity.

"But you must be hungry," she said, suddenly. "Come."

She led him to a tent at the entrance of a little glen, and bade him sit on the turf at the door, while she went in. A pleasant odor came through the canvas, and he heard the clatter of dishes—a very wholesome sound to one who had been living a half-savage life for several weeks.

Soon, she cried: "Come in," and he entered.

"I began to prepare this little dinner when I saw your boat, far away."

He thanked her, and they ate in silence, stealing shy glances at each other, and feeling a little uncomfortable. But being hungry they did not mind that much.

"Now," she said, resuming her frankness, not perfectly however, "if you're quite satisfied, come and I'll show you the wonders of your island. You know your father promised you it should be the most remarkable island in the world."

"And so it is," he said, looking at her steadily.

She blushed, and said nothing.

They had not taken many steps up the glen when a roar shook the ground.

He stopped in wonder. She answered the question in his eyes.

"That's the old lion. He's the only one left."

"The only one!"

"Are you frightened? He's not at all dangerous. He's got hardly any teeth, and he just crawls. I'll tell you all about it now, although I meant to show it to you before explaining. My father and I met Dealtry, your father's steward, in London, and he told us about the island being yours, and how your father promised you it should be the most remarkable island in the world, and how in fulfillment of that promise he stocked it with all kinds of wild beasts and birds and insects, intending it to be a great hunting-ground. Dealtry told us you would be sure to be here."

"I had forgotten all about it."

"Well, except this old lion, all the originals are dead. But there are many elephants, lions, tigers, bears, leopards, hyenas and beasts I don't know the names of—all very little, and not at all fierce. They're fast dying out too, for they can't get any food. You'll hardly see a deer, and even rabbits are scarce. There's a tiger!"

Lewellyn saw a striped beast about the size of a Newfoundland dog slinking across the path before them. While he looked at it curiously, something whistled through the air, and with a scream the beast rolled over, pierced in the heart by one of Miss Penpergwyn's arrows.

"I always shoot them," she said, "and you will do so too; for we must get rid of them. That was Papa's order."

Lewellyn sighed, and thought of *his* father. This was the end of his high-pitched imaginings and passionate endeavors to realize what others would never dream of imagining. A melancholy, profounder than that which was normal to all high-strung souls at that dread time, seized him and was reflected by his companion. They wandered about the island, hand in hand, saying little. Every foreign beast, bird and insect they saw, all small, and much less brilliant than in their native climes, increased his melancholy until it became almost an agony, and he was glad when he reached the tent again. She bade him sit once more at the entrance while she got supper ready.

"And while you are waiting," she said, "you can read this. My father left it for you, and I forgot about it till now."

Lewellyn took from her a sealed letter, which he read slowly and with much emotion. He had been thinking over it for some minutes when he was summoned to supper.

"Come out," he said.

Miss Penpergwyn obeyed.

"Stand by me while I read this to you. There is no date. 'You will be beginning to understand by this time. I had a long struggle with myself; but my life would soon have ended and hers was just beginning. I felt sure I would find you. I had known your father, and had seen you in your boyhood; I knew your character, and that you must be a strong and handsome man. The world begins again with you two.' That is all. What is your name, Miss Penpergwyn?"

"Lynden."

"Lynden! A strange name."

"My father was a strange man."

He took both her hands, and drew her towards him.

"Lynden Westaway," he said.

She trembled; then, dropping her head on his shoulder, whispered be-tween a sob and a laugh: "My husband."

*

Next morning, Lewellyn said, "I've been thinking over all you did yester-day, and there are two things I don't understand. Why did you sigh so deep-ly and gladly when I said I supposed your father had drunk the other half of the remedy?"

"Because I was glad that you hadn't taken it knowingly from him."

"And why did you stand with your back to me when I landed, and then sigh so happily when I turned round?"

"I stood with my back to you because I was afraid you might not be easy to love; and I sighed with happiness when I saw how handsome you were. Oh! how bold you must have thought me! I imagined that my father would have told you about me, and *all* he meant, and that was why I was so frank. I wanted to put you at your ease, my dear—to meet you half way, love."

# TORNADRES

## J.-H. ROSNY

*J.-H. Rosny was the pseudonym of Joseph-Henri Boëx (1856–1940), who was hailed by French critics enthused by the work of H. G. Wells as the nearest native equivalent, largely because of two stories published in the late 1880s: the extraordinary novelette "Les Xipéhuz" (1887; tr. as "The Xipehuz") in which a prehistoric human civilization is briefly invaded by extremely exotic alien beings apparently displaced from another dimension, and "Tornadres" (1888; published in the February issue of the* Revue indépendante; *also known as "Le Cataclysme"). Rosny made various other attempts to develop fiction based on an adventurous philosophical essay in fictional form "La Légende sceptique" (tr. as "The Skeptical Legend") also published in 1888 but written earlier, and most of his scientific romance consists of extrapolations of ideas broached therein.*

*Joseph Boëx shared his pseudonym for a while with his younger brother Justin, and when they fell out again he began signing his work J.-H. Rosny aîné [i.e. the elder], but all the speculative fiction published under the name is Joseph's. His other important works in the genre include the novella "La Mort de la terre" (1910; tr. as "The Death of the Earth") and the novels* La Force mystérieuse *(1913; tr. as* The Mysterious Force*) and* Les Navigateurs de l'infini *(1922; tr. as "Navigators of Space"). Almost all of his relevant works are available in English in a six-volume set published by Black Coat Press in 2010.*

*Like most of his important contributions to the genre, Rosny's "Tornadres" is an account of an encounter with the alien—which is, in Rosny's most adventurous work, always extremely peculiar and mysterious, radically different from the organic life with which we are familiar.*

I.

Symptoms

On the Tornadre plateau, for several weeks, nature palpitated and equivo-
cated in anguish, the whole of its delicate vegetable organism shot through
by intermittent electricity, symbolic signs of a great material event. The free
beasts on the farms and in the chestnut plantations were not as quick to flee
quotidian perils; they seemed to want to get closer to human beings, wandering around the tenancies. Then they came to an extraordinary decision,
sounding an alarm: they emigrated, going deep into the valley of the Iaraze.

As the nights fell, in the gloom of forests and thickets, there was a drama
of nervous animals furtively quitting their lairs with hesitant steps, often
pausing and stopping, melancholy to be fleeing their native land. The somber and languid howling of wolves alternated with the muffled grunts of
wild boars and the sobbing of ruminants. Ashy silhouettes were gliding
everywhere, generally toward the south-west, over cultivated ground beneath the open sky: great antlered skulls, heavy tapir-like bodies with short
legs, and slimmer beasts, carnivores and herbivores alike—hares, moles,
rabbits, foxes and squirrels. The batrachians followed, the reptiles and the
wingless insects, and a week ensued in which the south-western direction
was flooded with inferior organisms, a frightful vermicular population,
from the hopping silhouettes of frogs to slugs and snails, through the marvelous wing-cases of carabid beetles and horrible crustaceans that live under stones in eternal darkness, to worms, leeches and larvae.

Soon, nothing remained but winged creatures. Then the birds, filled with
unease, increasingly clinging on to branches, fearful of flying, saluted the
twilights with more subdued songs, often leaving the locality for a large
part of the day. The crows and the owls held great assemblies; the swifts
gathered together as if for their autumnal migration; the magpies became
agitated, cawing all day long.

The mysterious terror spread to the slaves: the sheep, the cattle, the horses, even the dogs. Resigned, in the confidence of their humble serfdom, all
expecting salvation from Humankind, they stayed on the Tornadre plateau—except for the cats, which had fled in the early days, returning to
savage liberty.

As the evenings went by, a confused sadness, an asphyxia of the soul,
took possession of the inhabitants of the tenancies and the proprietors of

the estate known as the Corne: the confused anticipation of a cataclysm—which, however, the topography of Tornadre belied. Being distant from volcanic regions and the ocean, insubmersible—having only a few streams—and compact in texture, what form could the threat possibly take?

It was felt nevertheless, electrically, in the rigidity of small branches and blades of grass at certain morning hours, in the singular attitudes of foliage, in subtle and suffocating effluvia, unusual phosphorescences and the prickling of flesh by night, which caused the eyelids to rise, condemning the individual to insomnia, in the extraordinary behavior of livestock, often stiffening, their nostrils open and tremulous, and *turning their heads toward the north.*

## II.

### The Astral Downpour

One evening, at the Corne, Sévère and his wife were finishing dinner next to the half-closed window. A crescent moon was wandering near the Zenith, pale and full of grace, above the vast perspectives, and rising mists decorated the western frontier. A troubling spell—an ardor of the nervous system, a suddenly awakened obscure commotion—kept them silent, impregnating them with a particular aesthetic sensibility, a profound wonderment relative to the nocturnal splendors.

A harmonious tremor welled up from the trees in the garden; at the rear, visible through the gate to the avenue, there was an enchantment of confused objects, the crop-fields of the Tornadre, the blanched farmhouses, the friendly mystery of human lights and the vague slate-covered steeple of the rustic church. The masters of the Corne were moved by that, troubled by the vibration of their nerves. The commotion being keener along the spinal column, however, the wife dropped the bunch of grapes that she was plucking, her lip trembling.

"My God! Is it going to go on forever?"

Sévère looked at her, with a strong desire to give her courage—but his own soul was in a stupor, obscured by an imponderable force.

Sévère Lestang was one of those grave intellectuals slowly seeking the secret of things, studying nature without impatience, disinterested in glory—but he was a man as well as an intellectual; his eyes were gentle and courageous, and he had a desire to *live his life* as well as developing his faculties. His wife, Luce, was a nervous mountain Celt, delicately graceful, amorous and captivating, but a trifle somber. Under the calm and attentive protection of her husband, she was like certain infinitely frail flowers that live in the inlets of great rivers, between large shady leaves.

"If you want," said Sévère , "we can leave tomorrow."

"Yes, please!"

She came closer to him, seeking refuge, murmuring: "They say that one can't keep a foothold any longer, you know, especially in the evening . . . that something takes hold of you and carries you away! Well, I don't dare walk quickly any longer, my steps draw me on so . . . and one climbs stairs effortlessly, but with a constant fear of falling. . . ."

"You're mistaken, Luce. It's a nervous illusion." He smiled, pressing her to him—but he too, with a terrible malaise, had perceived that incomprehensible lightness. Sometimes, before dusk, had he not wanted to walk more rapidly, to get back to the Corne, and found his stride lengthening, transformed into bounds, launching him forward with frightening speed? With his equilibrium lost, having difficulty in remaining vertical, experiencing a sensation of ataxia at each footfall, he had reverted to a slow pace, clinging to the ground, solidly, seeking large patches of sticky ground.

"You think it's an illusion?" she said.

"I'm sure of it, Luce."

She looked at him, while he stroked the fringe of her hair, and she suddenly realized that he was as nervous as she was, electrified by a profound anguish: no longer a refuge for her, but a poor frail creature confronted by enigmatic powers.

Then she went paler, her teeth chattering.

"The coffee will settle you," he said.

"Perhaps."

But they sensed the deceit in their words, the poverty of any tonic, or any human remedy against the approaching Unknowable—against that vast metamorphosis of phenomena, in which terrestrial life no longer participated, which had been troubling the flora and fauna, the animals and the plants, for weeks already.

They sensed the deceit. They did not dare look at one another, instinctively afraid of communicating their presentiments, of doubling their distress by nervous induction. And for long minutes, they listened inwardly, in their flesh, to the dull and confused echo of Mystery.

A fearful housemaid brought the coffee; they watched her leave, unsteadily, not daring to question that anxiety, similar to their own.

"Did you see how Marthe was walking?" asked Luce.

He did not reply, looking in surprise at the little silver spoon that he had just picked up. Perceiving his fixed stare, she looked at it in her turn, and exclaimed: "It's green!"

The little spoon was, indeed, green, with a pale emerald gleam—and they suddenly noticed the same tint on the other spoons, and all of the silverware.

"Oh, my God!" cried the young woman. Raising her finger, she began to recite, in a low voice, whispering painfully:

"When the Silver goes green,

"The *Roge Aigue* will come

"Devouring the moon and stars . . ."[1]

These words, an ancient and vague prophecy that the peasants of the Tornadre plateau had handed down through the ages, made Sévère shudder. They both had an impression of darkness and fatality, colorless and soundless, beyond all anthropomorphism. Where had the poor rustics obtained that oracle, now so serious? What science, what observations of remote eras, what cataclysmic memories, did it symbolize?

Sévère had an immense desire to be far away from Tornadre, remorseful at not having obeyed the sure instincts of the animals, at having dared to follow poor cerebral logic rather than the warning of Nature. "Do you want to leave this evening?" he asked Luce, ardently.

"I'd never dare leave the house before morning returns!"

He thought that it might be as perilous to venture out by night as to stay at the Corne; he resigned himself to it, thoughtfully. A great lamentation interrupted his thoughts: feverish whinnying, the dull banging of horses struggling against the stable-door. The dog howled, and the clamor spread

---

[1] The key words are deliberately misrendered in such a way as to conserve a certain ambiguity. *Roge* is only one letter away from *rouge* [red] or *rogue* [arrogant], while *aigue* is subtly distinct from both the masculine and feminine forms of *aigu/aiguë*, whose usual meaning is "pointed" or "sharp", although the term is also used as a noun to signify a diamond, referring to its "water" rather than its facets, by analogy with *aigu-marine* [aquamarine]. The readiest inference to be drawn, therefore, might be reckoned as "red gem"—but the other possible implications should not be left out of account.

along the length of the Tornadre plateau, echoed by other animals, terrified ruminants and braying donkeys. At the same time, there was a greenish glow in the sky, and a shooting star passed over, huge, with a resplendent tail.

"Look!" said Luce.

Other meteors welled up, isolated at first, then in small groups, all with bright nuclei and leaving long trails, miraculously beautiful.

"It's the night of August the tenth," said Sévère, "and the star-showers will increase . . . there's nothing abnormal about it."[2]

"Why, then, are our lamps growing dimmer?"

The Lamps were, in fact, lowering their flames; a superior electrical density enveloped everything, a terror, not of death, but of exasperated life, of supernatural dilatation—so that Sévère and Luce clung on to the furniture in order to *weigh more*, in order to *perceive contact with solid material*. A strange pressure lifted them up, robbing them of their sense of balance. They felt that they were in a new atmosphere, in which the ether acted with a *living* power, in which something organic—extra-terrestrially organic— was disturbing every drop of blood, orientating every molecule, intruding into the very marrow of their bones, and gradually stiffening every hair on their bodies.

In addition, as Sévère had predicted, the stellar downpour accelerated, the entire concavity of the firmament filling with bolides. By degrees, it was mingled with an unknown phenomenon, persistent and increasing: voices. Faint, distant, musical voices, a symphony of tiny strings in the celestial depths, a sometimes almost human whisper, reminiscent of the ancient Pythagorean harmony of the spheres.

"They're souls!" she murmured.

"No," he said. "No, they're Forces!"

Souls or forces, however, it was the same Unknown, the same hermetic threat, the pressure of a prodigious event, the blackest of human fears: the Shapeless and the Unforeseeable. And the voices went on, above the murmur of things, frightfully gentle, essential and subtle, taking Luce back to the Humility of childhood, to Worship, to Prayer:

---

[2] August 10th is the usual peak of the Perseid meteor shower, consisting of particles left behind by Comet Swift-Tuttle; the shower has been observed for the last 2,000 years, and is sometimes known as "St. Lawrence's tears" because 10 August was the day of his martyrdom.

"Our Father, who art in Heaven. . . ."

He did not dare smile, the beating of his heart increasing as if to burst his arteries, while his masculine mind—more curious about causation than his wife's—tried to imagine what magnetism, what extraterrestrial polarities, were working upon this corner of the globe, and whether it was the same in the valley of the Iaraze.

Outside the plateau, however, since the commencement of the phenomenon—and Sévère had gone down to the river again that very day—no one had perceived the unfamiliar symptoms. The animals and people there were living tranquilly. Life preserved its normal form there. Why, though? What correlation was there between the sky and the plateau, what cycle of phenomena—for the prophecy of the peasants of Tornadre implied a cycle—regulated this great Drama?

A misfortune occurred: a triumphant assault by the animals against the old stable door. The Corne's three horses appeared, bucking and foaming at the mouth beneath the pale rays of the sinking moon.

"Here, Clairon!" called Sévère.

One of the horses approached, the others following. Never had there been a scene as phantasmagoric as the three long heads hollowed out in the light and shadow, in front of the window, their large eyes bulging, sniffing Luce and Sévère, visibly questioning, with a return of vague confidence in the Master, a troubled idea of the power of the person who fed them. Then, for no obvious reason—perhaps an increase in the meteor shower—with absolute terror in the depths of their large eyes, their nostrils more cavernous, the mad panic of their race took hold, and they tore themselves away from the window whinnying, and fled.

"Oh, how they're leaping!" said Luce.

They were, in truth, running with an amazing gait, in enormous bounds. Suddenly, at the far end of the garden, confronted by the iron gate, the most impetuous rose up like a winged creature, and cleared the obstacle.

"You see! You see!" cried Luce. "He too has no more weight!"

"Nor the two others," he added, involuntarily.

Indeed the other two black shadows, rising up, without even brushing the bars, leapt more than four meters high. Their agile silhouettes, carried vertiginously across the fields, diminished, evaporated and disappeared. At the same time, a manservant appeared outside, alone and timid, hardly daring to come forward with the fearful step of a little child.

Sévère felt an infinite pity for the poor devil, realizing that everyone else at the Corne must have shut themselves up in their rooms, prey to the same increase in terror as the Masters.

"Let them go, Victor!" he called. "We'll find them later."

Victor came closer, holding on to trees, then the wall, and the shutter. "Is it true, Master," he asked, "that the *roge aigue* has come back?"

Sévère hesitated, preserving the modesty of his intelligence and his doubt in the midst of the sinister events, but Luce could not be silent.

"Yes, Victor."

A bleak silence fell, the three individuals equalized by the sensation of the supernatural—but Sévère was still examining, questioning himself about the connection between the phenomenon and the meteorites. He studied the increasing rain of stars, the stream of supreme beauty from the depths of the Imponderable. A new observation alarmed him: that the sad fragment of the moon sinking toward the horizon could not be providing the light that persisted over the landscape. Looking westwards, he watched the satellite disappearing, its convexity ready to collapse, adjacent to the western horizon.

A few minutes more, and then it was gone—but the light over the Tornadre plateau persisted, as if emanating from the Zenith: only a few degrees to the north, according to the indication of its shadow. Was it from the Zenith, then, that the phenomenon was coming? He turned his face to it, slowly. There, an amethyst glow, a lenticular glimmer, was thinly displayed like a slender cloud, with a maximum radiance toward the North.

Sévère thought that these things would have been a delight to behold, without the creeping of the flesh, the sepulchral threat and the presentiment of death falling from the Heavens upon the Earth.

### III.
### The Appearance of the *Aigue*

"Look!" said Luce. She had perceived the light in her turn; more affected than Lestang, she was pointing at it.

Victor, clinging to the window on the outside, was shivering with fever, as if he were drunk, occasionally coming round with a sigh, and ever-increasing horror.

Up above, the light was increasing. As it did so, the whispering voices of the firmament faded away, and an enormous silence weighed upon the Tornadre plateau. Then, faint at first, a light from below appeared to reply to the other, light fringes floating over the treetops and over all the plants. It was delicately and wildly heart-rending. On the three people, so dissimilar, it made an almost identical impression, of funerary lamps or a pyre, an immense conflagration that was about to engulf Tornadre and all its inhabitants.

Luce moaned, almost unconsciously, and uttered a desperate plaint: "Oh, I'm thirsty!"

Sévère turned toward her; the tenderness of his heart, his love for the Celtic mountain woman, gave him strength. He fought against his desire not to move, to end his existence there, at the window, with the bottom frame in his clenched hands. Swaying, he went to fetch a glass of water— but he continued questioning himself, astonished that the atmosphere was cool, almost cold, in spite of all the subtle fire in the heavens and on earth.

He had great difficulty bringing back the water; the glass in his hand was so light that he had no sensation of holding anything, and had to grip its base with all his might. He lost half the liquid *en route*.

Luce took a gulp, and spat it out, nauseated. "It tastes like iron filings . . . like rust!"

Sévère sipped the water, and had to spit it out in his turn; it was metallic and powdery. They both looked at one another for a long time, desperately. The veils of memory lifted, across so many charming years, on the moment when they had glimpsed one another for the first time in the Real World, the appeal of their nervous systems, amorous thereafter. Delicate and indefatigable periods of adoration. (Oh, what long, elevated, immense hours, woven of divinity, revive beneath the nebulous portico of the past!) And their gazes embraced, in an infinite pity for one another. Was this truly the death-agony? Would they have to leave their young lives behind like this, dying of asphyxia, thirst and that hideous impression of antigravity, that *non-contact* with matter. Oh Lord!

Personally, Sévère, so full of vital force, did not want to admit it, in spite of everything. Curiosity subsisted in his skull through the knell, making it attentive to the exterior again. The marvelous and lamentable drama continued to evolve; an opera of subtle fires, colossal corposants, lit up the distant landscape; at the summits of the tall trees, slender and flickering at first, and displaying the infinite scale of the spectrum, flames multiplied, trembling on every twig and the tip of every leaf, and then spread to the lower vegetation, the bushes, the grass, the stubble.

Every protrusion of vegetation thus had its glow, directed upwards at the sky.

Above the dream-like glimmers of that fiery landscape, birds were flying in flocks. They had finally decided to flee. Super-electric creatures, they had initially resisted these phenomena, which were doubtless less antipathetic to their organisms than those of terrestrial animals. Crows, with somber cries; sparse but infinite flocks of sparrows, goldfinches, chaffinches and warblers; intelligent groups of magpies, swifts, swallows, in traveling formation; and raptors in ones or twos, all headed southwards with an excited chirping and twittering that was almost speech.

Again, Sévère concentrated on the innumerable flames, which were neither fusing with one another nor giving out any appreciable heat; they were also, as he looked at them so directly, elongating into fine strips, building towers and Gothic monuments with billions of dazzling spires.

He was interrupted by a raucous cry, emitted by Luce.

"Hold me down! Hold me down . . . I'm being carried away!"

He saw his companion delirious, livid and cramped, her breast rising in a pitiful attempt to breathe. His own heart became weak; he was overcome by an absolute and infinite desperation, while he held on to Luce with a mechanical gesture. Shivering, she gazed at the shining plateau, and spoke confusedly:

"It's the other world, Sévère—it's the immaterial world . . . the Earth is about to die. . . ."

"No, no," he whispered, aware of the vanity of his words, "it's a Force . . . a magnetism . . . a transformation of movement."

A lower voice made him start: that of the hypnotized Victor, who had woken up: "The *Roge Aigue!*"

Sévère leaned out. Less than twenty degrees from the north he saw a large rectangle the color of rust, with an irregular border, as if excavated from abysms of sulfur. Gradually, it became brighter, as transparent as a wave, a veritable lake extended over the north, over which ran wrinkles of a paler red, similar to waves. And around the red lake, over the entire sky, a green darkness appeared, which turned blue and darkened, casting a profound jade shadow over the southern extremity.

The stars had died away. Nothing remained but that sky of red water and green water, of green gem and jade darkness.

What was it? Where had it come from? And why this enormous influence on the Tornadre? What power of special induction, and what affinities, were prowling around the firmament? These questions racked Sévère's brain, but did not spare him at all from the stupor that had taken hold of Luce and Victor on seeing the peasant prophecy fulfilled. He no longer doubted that death would come swiftly, that the heart which was galloping so terribly in his breast was about to burst and shut down forever. . . .

Meanwhile, her dying face raised toward the heavens, Luce began to recite, with a poignant solemnity:

"When the Silver goes green,

"The *Roge Aigue* will come

"Devouring the moon and stars . . ."

Releasing a heavy sigh, she collapsed against the window-sill, rigid, with her eyes closed.

IV.

Toward the Iaraze

Motionless at first, devoid of strength, Sévère drew his wife toward him. Was she dead? Had she vanished forever? Black laughter—the laughter of unavoidable destiny—rose to his lips, and the word "forever" circulated in his skull in an ironic manner—that "forever" which, so far as his own existence was concerned, might not extend beyond the next hour.

His grip on Luce grew tighter then, becoming unhealthy. He lifted the poor woman up, holding her across his chest. . . .

Then, suddenly, bizarrely and delightfully, a kind of relief overwhelmed his entire body: *firmness on the ground, weight, had returned!*

What! Chance must have told him to do it; he had not arrived theoretically at the idea of combining someone else's weight with his in order to recover a sense of material security.

Reanimated and solidified, in spite of the oppression in his breast, a flood of courage and hope ran through him now, which further augmented

the consequences of the event, including the singular ease with which he
was holding Luce in his arms like a little child. Then, his heart skipping a
beat, his memory reverted to the catastrophe, forgotten in the shock of glad
emotion. Was Luce dead?

He listened carefully, with his ear upon the young woman's breast; the
inconvenient sound of his own arteries prevented him from hearing anything. She was not stiff, though—but she was so pale! Her eyelids opened
upon unmoving eyes.

"Luce! My darling Luce!"

A sigh; a slight movement of the head. He discerned a very faint
breath—of life! His will-power was reinforced; he resolved to make every
effort to save her.

He stood there for a few minutes, thinking, and then shrugged his
shoulders. What good was calculation? It was necessary to act like a brute,
the least of organized beings, and flee straight ahead until he reached the
banks of the Iaraze. And with no further hesitation, taking the shortest
route, he climbed on to the window and leapt through it nimbly, shouting
to Victor:

"Get hold of something heavy. Release the dog and go to warn your
comrades. See how I'm carrying my burden. That's how anyone might save
himself. Do you understand?"

"Yes, Monsieur."

And Sévère ran off at a trot, his tread steady but oppressed, his breath
whistling, troubled by the electricity, which was livelier and more debili-
tating outside. He went out of the garden gate, and found himself in open
country. In its prodigious majesty, the red lake seemed to magnify the stellar abysses even further. Its glory, at its palpitating edges, with the softness
of stained glass, delicate and resplendent, terminating in lace, orange cin-
ders and dendrites, almost overwhelmed the Zenith. No other stars could
be seen any longer. Here and there, a fine serpentine line—a streak of
fire—ran from the extreme north to the extreme south. On the ground, on
the flat surface of the Tornadre plateau, the fires persevered everywhere, a
taciturn inferno: an inferno without heat, or even consumption.

The colossal candles of large trees and the torches—infinite in number—of the short grass, the steep ascensions, the great never-ending
polychromatic bows devoured by the neutralization of forces and in-

defatigably recomposed, filled Space with a terrible and beautiful life. Sévère marched on, going through it, closing his eyes periodically when he had to cross excessively flamboyant zones. Luce's hair emitted a torrent of sparks which dazzled and blinded Sévère. Instinct guided him south-westwards.

Every few minutes, a farm appeared, which served him as a landmark, but one in which he had no great confidence, so uncertain were appearances rendered by the infernal transfiguration.

A moment came when he thought he had gone astray; in front of him there was a pool, with reeds rising up like avenging blades, and willows with pale emerald leaves. Fireflies were moving continually over the surface. There was a suffocating odor of phosphorus and ozone. He felt the soft ground beneath his feet, the confused attraction of hidden water. He tried to get his bearings, but in vain. He knew, however, that it was Cilleuses pond, less than five hundred meters from the edge of the plateau. He went around it and marched for ten minutes—and found himself back at his point of departure.

If he remained there miserably, his great effort would be wasted.

"Come on, Sévère!"

He gets under way again, striving to recognize some landmark, some familiar sight, but weakening in that research, convinced that he will fall unconscious within an hour, to die in the open countryside.

Suddenly, he makes a discovery: a sharp little promontory, the only one on the pond, from which he can deduce which direction to take. From then on, it seems that he has wings, progressing in a straight line, and ending up finding a little path that he knows well, which he never leaves thereafter. He cannot estimate the duration of the journey—perhaps half an hour, perhaps ten minutes, or even five—but he has come to a halt, overwhelmed by amazement, before a black gulf parallel with the blazing Tornadre: an abyss of darkness beneath his feet, which something separates from the phosphorescent outpouring flooding the plateau.

"The slope! The slope!" He repeats the word; full of strength, he begins to go down a sinuous path at a run.

Already, he feels a physical well-being; the induction is decreasing, the lights are becoming steadily sparser, as gentle as will-o'-the-wisps, and the moist and tepid air is more breathable. On the other hand, Luce's weight is becoming harder to bear. It is breaking his arms and slowing him down.

He falls down, collapsing on the slope without the interposition of any root or branch. Then, as he resumes his course, out of breath, indomitable instinct masters his nerves.

Eventually, to his immense joy, he hears the running of the Iaraze, and perceives imminent salvation through his every pore. Only a few more steps! Already, the peril can scarcely reach him in this environment, where, the mysterious influence having been reduced to a minimum, there is already the healthy, vital terrestrial nature of old, hospitable to humankind.

He does not stop, sweating and haggard but full of strength. Finally, the vale arrives, with the river sobbing in the darkness. With a loud cry, a violent and dolorous delight, he lets himself go.

Luce is lying across his knees. Momentarily, he turns his head to look back and upwards, irresistibly. A vague glimmer is wandering over the slope, brighter toward the edge of the plateau; that is all he can see of the vast conflagration, which is little enough compared with the glare of the nocturnal sea in the era of its fecundation. The firmament is especially astonishing, the *Aigue* having vanished, leaving only the redness—a kind of aurora borealis. The shower of bolides continues to fall.

"What's going on?" he wonders. "Why that enormous dissimilarity between the Tornadre and the Iaraze?"

Eventually, he leans over Luce. She is still pale and motionless, but her breath is perceptible—the breath of sleep rather than unconsciousness. He calls out to her, raising his voice: "Luce! Luce!"

She shivers, and moves her head gently. That is an infinite joy amid the gloom, and, with sobs of happiness, he embraces her, and continues calling out to her. He murmurs a few tender words.

Finally, the eyelids open and the young woman's gaze, full of dreams and darkness, falls upon Sévère .

"Ah!" he cries. "We're finally victorious. The Tornadre has not devoured you."

Standing up, with his arms folded, he conceives a desire—the promise of climbing up again, alone, toward the south-west, to follow the story of the cataclysm. Voices are raised on the slope however, and the sound of barking.

Understanding that it is the Corne's servants, Luce and Sévère wait for them, embracing one another, in a bliss so great that tears are streaming down their cheeks.

*

Note

Monsieur Sévère Lestang has, in fact, published the story of the Tornadre cataclysm (*chez* Germer-Ballière). For seven days the *Aigue* was visible over the plateau, and the conflagration with *neither heat nor consumption* persisted for those seven days—as attested, in addition to Monsieur Lestang and the inhabitants of the plateau, by a scientific commission that arrived on the final day of the phenomenon. There were some dead to mourn, but relatively few, the majority of individuals having fled after the beginning of the night of August tenth.

As for the conclusions of the scientific investigation, it must be confessed that they were entirely negative; no plausible theory was offered. The one interesting fact, which might prove, at a later date, to lead to some discovery, is this: the Tornadre plateau rests on a rocky mass of about 150,000,000,000 cubic meters, which is evidently of stellar origin; it is *a colossal bolide*, fallen near the Iaraze valley in prehistoric times.

# PROFESSOR BAKERMANN'S MICROBE

## CHARLES EPHEYRE

*Charles Epheyre was the pseudonym of the Nobel Prize-winning neurophys-iologist Charles Richet (1850–1935). One of the pioneers of the study of mul-tiple personality, he wrote an early "case study" story featuring the phenom-enon, "Soeur Marthe" (1889; tr. as "Sister Marthe"). He also produced two Berthoudesque studies of the working of the scientific mind, "Le Mirosaurus" (1885; tr. as "The Mirosaurus"), and "Le Microbe de Professeur Bakermann," a translation of which follows.*

*"Professor Bakermann's Microbe," which first appeared in the January 1890 issue of the* Revue Bleue, *is one of the more melodramatic French scien-tific romances of the fin-de-siècle period, but retains a sharp cutting edge in spite of its extravagance by reason of the confidence with which the author is able to improvise the scientific background of the story and his account of the obsessive psychology of its innocent but dangerous protagonist.*

In the latter days of the month of December 1935 Professor Hermann Bak-ermann returned joyfully to his lodgings, striding through the streets of the little town of Brunnwald as rapidly as his generous girth would permit.

He was rubbing his hands as he walked, a sign of profound satisfac-tion—a legitimate satisfaction, for, after long labor, Professor Hermann Bakermann had finally found the means of creating a new microbe, more redoubtable than all the known microbes.

It will doubtless be remembered that in the last half-century, microbial science had made extraordinary progress. In the mid-nineteenth century, a celebrated Frenchman, Louis Pasteur, had proved that certain minuscule creatures exist, which penetrate surreptitiously into the bodies of humans and animals. He had called these perfidious parasites "microbes." He had even indicated ingenious methods of recognizing them, collecting them and cultivating them. Now, in 1935, the works of Pasteur had been long surpassed. Obedient to the impulse provided by the master, all the scientists of Europe, America, Australia, and even Africa, had set to work. Thanks to them, the most difficult problems had been clarified, the most obscure problems resolved; there was no longer any disease that did not have its microbe, labeled, classified and stored. The forms, the behavior, the habits and the tastes of all terrestrial, marine and airborne microbes were known, and microbial science had become the basis of medicine in all the universities.

In Germany, as elsewhere, mores had changed considerably in the last thirty years. The reign of the spiked helmet had finally come to an end. The professors and the scientists had resumed their place in the sun; they no longer trembled before a beardless corporal, and the ancient German customs, honest and peaceful, had succeeded the regime of the saber.

That was why the noble town of Brunnwald possessed a brilliant university, sumptuous laboratories and excellent professors. Now, none of these masters had more zeal or talent than the celebrated Hermann Bakermann. At an early age he had flung himself impetuously into microbial science; later, having become a professor, he had been able to construct the laboratory of his dreams. It was there that he spent his life. Disdainful of his patrons, he lived amidst his flasks and his culture media, surrounded by the most powerful and most deleterious viruses.[1] In order not to be infected by his poisons, however, he had taken all the necessary precautions. By means of a skillfully graduated series of vaccinations, he had eventually rendered himself almost invulnerable, with the result that his health did not suffer at all for that existence passed entirely amid the germs that afflicted poor humankind.

However, as not everyone in the world was as well-protected as he was, Professor Bakermann had taken care to construct, at the extremity of his laboratory, a special room, to which he jokingly referred as the "infernal chamber," which he did not permit any other human being to enter at first.

---

[1] When this story was written, the terms "virus" and "bacillus" were considered interchangeable, no fundamental distinction yet being possible between different types of "microbe."

This little room, heated and lit by electricity, was equipped with powerful disinfection apparatus, and the prudent Bakermann never came out of it without first purifying himself with the most active antiseptic fumigations.

As he went home that day, then, Professor Hermann Bakermann was content. The problem that he had sought in vain for such a long time to solve had finally received a simple solution. The means of rendering harmful microbes inoffensive were known, but that was only one aspect of the problem. Bakermann had found a means to render inoffensive microbes harmful.

When we say "harmful" we do not mean to imply mildly harmful, but terrible, overwhelming and irresistible. The microbes presently known only kill in a day, half a day at the worst, and are also possessed of a fragile vitality. It does not take much to attenuate them or render them harmless. The problem, therefore, was to have a virus powerful enough to kill in an hour, at a dose of a hundredth or a thousandth of a drop, in such a manner that no living creature could survive it. Above all—and this was the most delicate part—the terrible microbe must be very resistant, incapable of allowing itself to be weakened by intemperances of climate or the medications that artful humans were inventing incessantly.

Gradually, Bakermann had succeeded in making his great discovery. "A microbe," he said in his course, "is like a human being. We humans need a varied diet. We need soup, sauerkraut, beer, caviar, butter, cakes, mutton, fish, lobster, pâtés, honey, almonds, fruits, sardines, Rhenish wine, champagne, potatoes and kummel. Our health improves as our alimentation becomes more sophisticated and more complicated. Well, microbes have the same needs as we do. Let us give them a very varied and rich nourishment, and we shall make them increasingly vigorous—which is to say, energetically malign, for the vigor of a microbe is proportional to its destructive power."

So, all Professor Bakermann's concern was lavished on the confection of his culture media. In this respect, he could have given tips to the best French chefs. In his latest medium, he had found the means of introducing eighty-seven different alimentary substances, and the microbes within it were developing with a truly prodigious vital intensity.

We cannot enter into detail here regarding the famous scientist's scientific techniques. At any rate, thanks to improved culture media and certain electrical procedures that he was still keeping secret, Bakermann had profoundly transformed a vulgar microbe, the microbe that turns butter rancid—very widespread, alas!—by submitting it to a whole series of complicated cultures, and he had made it into an extremely nasty microbe.

A hundredth of a drop killed a large dog in two and a half hours, and a single drop could kill three thousand rabbits in two hours. It goes without saying that Bakermann had not been able to try it out on such a large quantity of rodents, but he had caused a considerable number to perish, to the great indignation of Frau Bakermann.

Frau Bakermann? Well yes, there is no life that does not have some secret distress, no fruit that does not conceal a poisonous worm, no rose that does not have an unfortunate thorn. For the illustrious Bakermann, the poisonous worm, the treacherous thorn, was Frau Josepha Bakermann.

Frau Bakermann had never understood microbial science. Every time the unfortunate scientist tried to talk to her about it, she looked at him suspiciously.

"What good is all this fuss about futilities that make everyone laugh? Instead of going to the theater or for a walk, you shut yourself up in an unhealthy room with rabbits, toads and pigeons! Is that a job for a man who respects himself and his wife? If only you imitated Dr. Rothbein, who, while being just as much of a scientist as you, makes ten visits a day and is paid twenty marks for every one—but you're incapable of making a simple pfennig. You're nothing but a poor man, Bakermann, and it's me who tells you so; I'm astonished that there's a single student on your course, for you only know how to tell them the same story over and over again."

In brief, Frau Bakermann detested microbes.

She hated something else too: that was the tavern.

All the greatest men have their faults, and, on searching hard, one will always find a defect, a stain or a weakness in the best of them. Professor Bakermann had his weakness too; it was the tavern.

All things considered, Bakermann's conduct was excusable.

Drinking tankards of good beer one after another, in a joyful row, with cheerful comrades, while playing a hand of piquet or discussing the condition of Europe and the progress of microbial science, is certainly more agreeable than listening all evening long to bitter recriminations regarding the exorbitant price of rabbits, the high cost of the exquisite foodstuffs that it was necessary to buy to nourish the microbes, the uselessness of delicate thermometers that cost a hundred marks, and the necessity of having a fur cape like Frau Rothbein, or Oriental door-curtains in one's drawing-room like Frau Scheinbrunn, the president's wife.

When Bakermann had succeeded in getting to the door without being seen, he was saved. He only came back very late, with his head a trifle heavy and his face crimson, but quite satisfied, and submitted, without saying a word to an avalanche of bitter words. He even—which is a terrible thing to say—got used to it, ending up only being able to go to sleep to the sound of lamentations and invective.

This evening, however, as he went home, Bakermann gave no thought to his wife. He was thinking about his terrible microbe.

"I've found it . . . I've found it!" he repeated to himself. "Yes, I have it. Oh, the brigand! It's given me enough trouble! But what shall I call it? It's necessary to give it a name, for every new microbe must be given a name, and this one is definitely a new microbe. It can almost kill at a distance. Ah! Yes, that's it! That's it! *Mortifulgurans. Bacillus mortifulgurans.* That has a really fine ring to it!"

"Ah, there you are!" cried Frau Bakermann. "Not bad. Eight o'clock! Did you even look at the time? I thought you weren't coming back—and that wouldn't have been any great pity."

"Calm down, Frau Bakermann," said the worthy man. "And get ready to rejoice, for I'm bringing you good news."

"Really?"

"My word, yes—very good news, and very important. You know, my dear, what I've been seeking for such a long time, the microbe that kills rabbits in two hours, at a dose of a thousandth of a drop. . . ."

Poor Bakermann, with a perseverance worthy of a better fate, stubbornly told his wife about all his scientific experiments, and the snubs that he met with every time had not yet discouraged him.

"If you think I'm going to listen to your nonsense! Yet another stupidity! Isn't it pitiful! At your age!"

"But Frau Bakermann. . . ."

"Come on, it's dinner time—and no tavern today, you know. I know all about your accursed microbes. Every time you claim to have made a discovery—a discovery!—you take advantage of it to spend the night drinking with good-for-nothings like Rodolphe Müller and Cesar Pück. I warn you, though, that I'm not in a patient mood tonight."

*I can see that,* Bakermann thought, sighing.

Nevertheless, he did not lose all hope, for Frau Bakermann often fell asleep after supper, and Bakermann took cowardly advantage of that respite to get away.

Bakermann ate with a good appetite, therefore, and paid no heed to Josepha's threats. She, becoming increasingly irritated, to a greater extent than ever before, told her husband quite bluntly that if he went out, she would cause a scandal; that she would go to his sanctuary—which is to say, his laboratory—and even to the infernal chamber itself, in order to carry out a search.

"It's there, I'm sure, that you're hiding Eliza's letters."

Bakermann contented himself with sighing and raising his eyes to heaven.

Eliza was a servant girl that Frau Bakermann had once been obliged to sack, for she suspected her husband of kissing the little rogue on the sly. We do not know to what extent the accusation was justified, but it was still the case that, as soon as Eliza's name was pronounced, Bakermann lowered his head and was unable to make any reply.

"Yes, Eliza's letters! That's certain. What's become of her now? She hasn't left the town, and you're still seeing her. Frau Scheinbrunn told me that she's been seen in a silk dress and pearl earrings."

Bakermann did not breathe a word, and tried to distract himself by repeating: *Bacillus mortifulgurans!*

"Guess, Josepha, what name I have given it!" he suddenly exclaimed. "*Bacillus mortifulgurans.* Eh? It's a good choice, isn't it? My colleague Krankwein is capable of making a disease of it!"

"I'm sure," Frau Bakermann continued, "that you still write to her. A girl who is always badly coiffed, a liar, a glutton, a debauchee. . . ."

"Wife!" Bakermann groaned.

"I'll go to your accursed laboratory—yes! I'll go and I'll search everywhere, and I'll find the proof of your wretched conduct."

"Wife, my dear wife," Bakermann murmured, "you mustn't do that. Remember that my *mortifulgurans* is there, and that I alone can enter the infernal chamber without danger. If you knew all the precautions I take. Think of your health, your precious health, my darling."

Deep down, however, he scarcely took any notice of Frau Bakermann's threats. Almost every evening, there was the same anthem, and thus far, Frau Bakermann had never dared cross the redoubtable threshold of the infernal chamber.

Later, Frau Bakermann, wearied by quarrelling, dozed off in her armchair.

*My word*, Bakermann thought, *it's not far from here to the tavern. I'll go along to say good evening to Cesar Pück and tell him the great news. I'm anxious to have his advice about the* mortifulgurans. *Josepha's well away for an hour, and she'll still be asleep in the same place when I get back.*

With that, walking on tiptoe and making himself very small, Professor Bakermann went into the hallway, put on his coat and hat, and went out.

Once he was outside, he uttered a deep sigh of relief, and smiled involuntarily at the thought of the tavern where Cesar Pück awaited him.

Cesar Pück, Valerian Grossgeld and Rodolphe Müller were, indeed, there, faithful to their posts. They uttered a joyful hurrah on seeing their illustrious friend arrive.

"I can see that there's news!" exclaimed Pück. "You're wearing your finest smile!"

"Yes, indeed!" cried Bakermann. "Boys, I have my microbe, and I call it *mortifulgurans*."

"Bravo!" said Müller. "I knew that you'd get there in the end. But you mustn't rest on your victory. Do you know what you ought to look for now?"

"My word, no!"

"The bacillus of good humor—and you can try out its effects immediately on Frau Bakermann."

"That would, indeed, be a glorious success," Bakermann murmured. "But we're here to talk about cheerful things. Come on—a tankard! And let's get the party started!"

Beer had never been so exquisite, nor a game of piquet so interesting. With insolent good luck, Bakermann won as often as he could have wished. Aces and kings flooded his hands. In the meantime, tankards were emptied effortlessly, while pipes and laughter kept pace.

Time passed, though. There was always one last tankard, one last hand, one last pipe, to the extent that Bakermann finally drank to the health of *mortifulgurans*.

In the end, he had to leave his friends—but his head was heavy and his gait unsteady. . . .

Frau Bakermann was in bed, asleep or apparently asleep. He wasted no time in contemplating her, and, without even bothering to get undressed, lay down to sleep the profound sleep of the triumphant.

About six o'clock in the morning, however, he was forced to prise an eye open. Frau Bakermann was shaking him violently.

"Hermann!" she was saying, "Hermann!"

He pretended not to hear—and, in fact, hardly could hear, for the fumes of the beer were still numbing him with their thick shadow.

"Hermann! Hermann!"

"Can't you let me sleep?"

Frau Bakermann was gripped by atrocious pains. She was sitting up in bed, very pale, with haggard eyes.

"Ring for Theresa, my darling," he sighed. He pulled the bell-cord, and then went back to sleep.

But Frau Bakermann's suffering was getting worse. Theresa, the chambermaid, was scared when she saw her distraught face. A livid December dawn appeared in the windows.

"Sir, sir!" Theresa cried. "Madame is very ill! Very ill!"

This time, Bakermann woke up completely. Yes, truly, Frau Bakermann was very ill.

"Go fetch Dr. Rothbein immediately," he said to Theresa, "and go to the pharmacist's to get morphine and quinine."

Frau Bakermann now had very cold hands, a purple face and terribly dilated pupils.

"Josepha! Josepha!"

"My love, my love," she said, in a soft and feeble voice, "forgive me . . . for I sense that I'm going to die, and that I've brought it on myself. I've been . . . I've dared. . . ."

"What have you done?" demanded the professor, gripped by anguish.

"You know . . . the infernal chamber! The infernal chamber! Well. . . ."

"Well? Speak! Speak!"

She could not say any more. A frightful spasm sealed her lips.

"The infernal chamber," murmured Bakermann. "Speak, Josepha, speak, I implore you."

But Josepha was no longer able to reply. She had lost consciousness. Spasms of agony were agitating her icy limbs. Then she fell into a profound torpor.

At that moment, the doorbell rang. It was Professor Rothbein, Bakermann's friend, famous for his irreproachable diagnoses. He examined the sick woman for a few moments, and shook his head despairingly.

"Well?"

"Be brave, my friend, be brave."

"But what is this frightful malady?" Bakermann ventured to say.

Rothbein reflected momentarily; then, after a further scrupulous exam-ination, he said: "This is an extremely rare malady, which is almost never seen in Europe. It's the koussmi-koussmi of Dahomey."

"Really!" said Bakermann. In spite of everything, he felt relieved of a great weight, for he felt overwhelmed by a secret terror that he dared not admit to himself.

"It's koussmi-koussmi," Rothbein repeated, firmly. "My dear Hermann, there's no mistake about it. Everything is there, and the symptoms are ob-vious: the suddenness of the onset, the pallor of the face, the dilation of the pupils, the spasms, the chill, the torpor. . . ."

He would have continued in that vein for some time, if Frau Bakermann had not rendered up her soul at that moment.

It was eight o'clock in the morning. Everyone in the house already knew the disastrous news. Little Theresa, as she went to the pharmacist's, had not been able to prevent herself from telling the story to two or three of her peers. A crowd had begun to gather, and the cause of the illness was already being discussed.

As for Bakermann, he was plunged into a profound distress—but his distress was nothing compared to his anxiety. Rothbein's coolness and self-confidence had diminished a few vague dreads . . . but Josepha had mentioned the infernal chamber. Why?

Suppose, in a fit of absurd jealousy, in order to search for Eliza's let-ters. . . .

Unable to bear the terrible uncertainty, he ran to the laboratory. . . .

The door of the infernal chamber was open, and Bakermann perceived, to his horror, that someone had opened the microbe cupboard and rum-maged through the flasks! An imprudent hand had even knocked over one of the phials in which the terrible *mortifulgurans* was growing.

This time, no further doubt was permissible. Yes, in spite of her hus-band's solemn instructions, Frau Bakermann had dared to penetrate this redoubtable refuge, and had knocked over a bottle of *mortifulgurans*!

At all costs, it was necessary to avert greater misfortunes. A terrible mi-crobe had taken possession of Frau Bakermann's body, and now, by a rapid contagion, it was going to reach the entire town. He had nothing to fear himself—he was too thoroughly vaccinated to be affected—but the others . . . the others!

Bakermann shuddered at the thought that Rothbein, Theresa, the neighbors and their wives were going to fall victim to *mortifulgurans*. And who could tell how far it might go? Hermann Bakermann's thoughts dared not take that frightful supposition to its conclusion.

Bakermann raced home and began a thorough disinfection of the house. Alas, what good would it to?

Indeed, at ten o'clock, Theresa began to suffer from an intense headache. Then there was a great shiver, followed by spasms. After two hours, the malady had made terrible progress, and the unfortunate Theresa expired at midday.

With a dry eye, Bakermann witnessed her terrible death-throes. Yes, it was definitely *mortifulgurans*. There was no possible doubt; all the anticipated symptoms were there, and none was lacking. What vitality there was in the microbe, though! In spite of his anguish, Bakermann could not help admiring, with all the pride of an artist, the conquering march of his microbe. As soon as it had penetrated, it triumphed. In three hours, it was all over. First the nervous system, then the respiration, then the temperature, then the heart; it was methodical, punctual, inexorable; neither quinine nor morphine could do anything. Yes, certainly, *mortifulgurans* was tenacious and irresistible, and all the physicians' drugs could not defeat it.

What could be done now? Halt the propagation of the disease? That was impossible. Let it continue its victorious march, then? That was insane—a monstrosity surpassing everything imaginable! Bakermann knew his *mortifulgurans*. He knew that nothing could make it retreat. It was a true microbe, that one, as superior to others as electric light was to a miserable candle. So be it! The die was cast! *Mortifulgurans* would spread throughout the world!

That evening, there had already been seventeen deaths in the town: the pharmacist's apprentice at three o'clock, then Rothbein at four, two of the pharmacist's customers at five, four of Rothbein's clients and five of the pharmacist's at six, plus four neighbors—the same ones that Bakermann had seen chatting to Theresa that morning.

The local newspaper announced the outbreak of the fatal epidemic in these terms:

"We regret to inform our readers that a disease, originating in the Orient, has fallen upon our industrious city. At the time of going to press, seventeen deaths have already been recorded, and our specific information allows us to affirm that there are a great many sick people in various parts of the town. The illness comes on suddenly, and kills in a few hours, defying all therapeutic resources. It is probable that it is caused by a microbe that none has yet been able to study; but according to competent authorities, the malady is none other than koussmi-koussmi, a kind of infectious disease rife in Dahomey. One can only speculate as to the manner in which koussmi-koussmi was able to reach Brunnwald. The facility of communications between Africa and Germany offers some slight explanation of that propagation, but why have the intermediate countries not been affected? These are questions that our hygienists will soon be able to resolve. . . .

"Whatever the case may be, it is a matter of a redoubtable evil. We are counting on the science of our physicians to avert it, and in the good sense of our people not to abandon themselves to vain panic."

Meanwhile, Professor Bakermann had plunged into a profound despair. The death of a wife is certainly cause for grief, but Frau Bakermann was mortal, after all, and in the end, one ends up being consoled. What was horrible, defying all expressions of horror, was the extension of the epidemic.

He tried to reflect, but his head was whirling. What could be done, since *mortifulgurans* was invincible? Ordinarily, in an epidemic, not all those affected die; there are individuals who escape. Perhaps physicians are able to cure some of them; some people contrive to avoid the contagion. Above all, the malady comes to an end; the microbe ends up becoming less redoubtable, becoming attenuated, and thus less and less dangerous. Here, though, there was no hope of anything similar. *Mortifulgurans* would not be attenuated. On the contrary, it would gather new strength as it was disseminated throughout the world. It was too vigorous, too robust, too well-constructed to weaken. The human species, retreating before it, would be driven to extinction!

A terrible unprecedented battle was joined in Bakermann's soul. No mortal, in all probability, had ever felt such a heavy, crushing responsibility weighing upon him. If only a solemn confession could avert the disaster! But no, a confession would be futile. Whether he spoke or remained silent, the epidemic would run its course, so why speak? Yes, why? If a loud public confession would save a single victim, certainly! But it would only serve to render the name of Bakermann permanently shameful to future generations—provided that any human beings were able to survive *mortifulgurans*. Future generations? Bakermann smiled bitterly, as he thought that, thanks to him, there would be no future generations.

*Besides, he thought, is it really mortifulgurans? Rothbein had no hesitation. He immediately affirmed that it was koussmi-koussmi. Why should Rothbein not be right? Why contradict him, and become one's own executioner? It is a culpable presumption for a lone man to claim to know more than the masters of a science. They have pronounced sentence—well then, their verdict is irrevocable: it is koussmi-koussmi. And after all, if I speak, I won't save anyone. I shan't say anything! I shan't say anything!*

In spite of all this reasoning, the voice of conscience was stronger. "Bakermann," the voice said to him, "you are lying to yourself. You know perfectly well that your wife died of *mortifulgurans*, that there is no koussmi-koussmi, that you are the sole cause of the terrible epidemic that is going to cause the disappearance of all humankind. If you want to diminish the atrocity of your crime, it is necessary to confess it freely. Be an honest man, Bakermann, for, if you keep silent, you are the most frightful villain to whom the earth ever gave birth."

He went out. He felt the soul of a great martyr within him, and he had made a heroic resolution.

Yes, he wanted to drink the chalice to the dregs. He had an enemy, a mortal enemy: Professor Hugo Krankwein, his rival in microbial science; a short, bald man with a grimacing, ferrety face, very knowledgeable and very envious. It was to Krankwein that Bakermann would confess his crime.

Krankwein lived alone in an isolated suburb. He opened his own door—but he recoiled in fright when he was confronted by the distraught face of his colleague.

"In Heaven's name, is it really you?"

"It's me," sighed Bakermann. "My wife died this morning."

"Yes, I know," said Krankwein, raising his eyes to heaven. "The poor woman was one of the first victims of the koussmi-koussmi."

"Don't talk about koussmi-koussmi!" cried Bakermann. "There is no koussmi-koussmi! There's only *Bacillus mortifulgurans*!"

*Well, well!* thought Krankwein, not without some satisfaction. *The poor fellow's gone mad.* "Come on, my dear colleague," he said, gently, addressing Bakermann with the kind of slightly-scornful patience that one has for children and invalids, "I know the horrible story. Dear Frau Bakermann had bought an Oriental carpet that came straight from Dahomey; no more was required, alas!"

"There is no koussmi-koussmi, I tell you!" Bakermann cried. "Can your koussmi-koussmi kill a vigorous and healthy man in three hours? Can it strike without remission? Can it resist quinine and cold baths? No, a thousand times no, it's my microbe, I tell you, my *mortifulgurans*, that killed Josepha."

Krankwein smiled. "My dear Bakermann, pain is leading you astray; *mortifulgurans* is a dream of your sick imagination, and the situation is too grave for us to linger over implausible hypotheses."

"Hypotheses!" roared Bakermann. "Hypotheses! Do you know what you're saying? *Mortifulgurans* exists. I created it, brought it out of nothing. I constructed it in its entirety, unassailable, irresistible, defiant of medicine and doctors. I've kept it in my phials; by means of it, I've poisoned Frau Bakermann, Rothbein, Theresa, and five hundred others! And you talk to me about hypotheses!"

"Calm down, I beg you, my dear colleague," sighed Krankwein. "Look, tomorrow morning, if we're still alive, I'll come to visit you, and you'll realize that you aren't being entirely reasonable."

"Don't you understand, then, that *mortifulgurans* has no effect on me . . .!"

He had hardly finished the sentence when he had a sudden flash of inspiration. It was a dazzling lightning-bolt—one of those sublime and grandiose conceptions that cast their blinding light over the entire soul.

"I've got it! I've got it!" he cried. And, without bidding farewell to the stupefied Krankwein, he precipitated himself into the street, bare-headed.

*Thank God!* thought Krankwein. *Bakermann has gone mad. He certainly wasn't strong before, but now he's veritably insane.*

With that, Krankwein went to bed. He too was vaccinated against all epidemics, and had no fear of koussmi-koussmi. The fate of his fellow citizens was of very little interest to him. As for *mortifulgurans*, he had the misfortune of not believing in it.

In the middle of the night, in the desolate streets of Brunnwald, one might have seen a man walking with great strides, his hair in the wind, gesticulating and talking aloud, without paying any heed to the snow that was falling thickly or the thick, cold slush that was covering the pavement.

"I've got it! I've got it!" Bakermann was repeating to himself. "Of course! My *mortifulgurans* has been cultivated on negative electricity; positive electricity ought to kill it instantly. It's fatal, absolutely fatal, as certain as two and two make four. With positive electricity, it will be destroyed, annihilated, pulverized instantly. It will become as harmless as it was in the beginning, when I extracted it from rancid butter. What am I saying? It will be even more harmless. And people will live; they'll have nothing more to fear. With positive electricity, the world will be saved, and humankind won't end, and the name of Bakermann will be gratefully celebrated by innumerable future generations—for there will be future generations! Let's go, Bakermann—to work! You've done harm, but you alone can repair it. To defeat *mortifulgurans*, it requires no less than the man who gave birth to it."

Meanwhile, the epidemic was making giant strides. To begin with, in the town of Brunnwald, it had broken out everywhere. In almost every house there was at least one victim, and the victims immediately found themselves in desperate straits. No remedy interrupted the march of the scourge. The consternation was universal. No one dared leave home any longer. The administration, with its invariable foresight, poured torrents of phenol all over the town, which steam pumps distributed in the streets.

The news brought by the telegraph was very grave. On the morning of 23 December, in Berlin, ten cases of death were reported, disseminated in various quarters. A traveler who had left Brunnwald in a third-class carriage had contaminated the seven travelers in the carriage with him, and all of them had succumbed, leaving behind them the contagion of the terrible scourge.

The rapidity with which the accursed microbe developed prevented all preventive measures; there was no possibility of quarantine, or closing borders. In twelve hours, with superheated steam trains, one could go all the way from Cadiz to St. Petersburg; it was no longer the nineteenth century, when it was difficult to travel more than sixty kilometers an hour. In one night, therefore, the entirety of Europe was poisoned.

The town of Brunnwald was half-annihilated. Vienna and Munich already counted a few fatalities, and were probably infected at all points. Paris, London, Rome and St. Petersburg were invaded, without anyone being able to prevent the invasion, and the current evaluation was that the entire

human race would be doomed within forty-eight hours. It was enough to
make the greatest heroes shiver.

Bakermann, however, was not afraid. He no longer dreaded *mortifulgurans*. He worked unrelentingly for the greater part of the night, and in
the morning, at dawn, the astonished inhabitants of Brunnwald were able
to see an immense poster that had been set up in the market-place, which
read:

PROFESSOR BAKERMANN
CURES KOUSSMI-KOUSSMI BY MEANS
OF ELECTRICITY

If Bakermann had made use of the term koussmi-koussmi, it was by
virtue of a craven condescension to the general opinion. In fact, the public,
the newspapers and the scientists were talking about nothing but koussmi-koussmi; any other name would have been incomprehensible. Not
without bitterness, Bakermann had resolved to employ the vulgar expression, which had become unanimous.

He regretted the term *mortifulgurans*, which he had chosen himself, lov-
ingly—and, after all, he had a right to give his microbe the name he preferred—but he had given way, for it was a matter of making known without
delay the victorious treatment that would stop the scourge in its tracks.

A large platform was established on which were set chairs, sofas and
even beds. An electrical conductor led from this platform to an immense
battery. The negative electricity, which invigorated *mortifulgurans*, went
from there to ground, but the positive electricity, which was fatal to the
microbe, went entirely into the platform. People climbed up to the platform—its dimensions were sufficient to allow fifteen of them to take up
positions there at their ease—and after a few seconds, they were charged
with positive electricity. They could then repel the infection.

The first sick man to take his place on the platform was Cesar Pück. He
was suffering atrociously, and his livid limbs were prey to atrocious convulsions. He was hoisted up on to the platform, in the presence of Krankwein,
who was smiling sarcastically, and all his afflictions immediately ceased.
The cramps, the spasms and the chill disappeared in a matter of minutes
as if by a miracle. The moribund face of worthy Cesar Pück became joyful
and smiling, as of old.

On seeing this result, which he had anticipated, but about which he had still had doubts until a demonstration had been given, Bakermann was overwhelmed by joy. There had been too much emotion in such a short time, and he lost consciousness.

He was brought round eventually. Soon, the whole world knew about the miraculous cure of Cesar Pück. The news spread in the blink of an eye. In less than half an hour, all the Brunnwaldians knew that Bakermann had cured koussmi-koussmi with electricity. Electrical batteries and platforms modeled on Bakermann's were set up everywhere. By noon, there were no less than fifty large positive electricity platforms actively functioning.

The death-rate diminished very rapidly. Between nine o'clock and ten there were 435 deaths; that was the maximum. By eleven, the figure had declined to 126; at noon it was no more than 32, at one o'clock eight, and finally, at two o'clock, there was only one—that of a stubborn old physician who would not hear mention of the electrical treatment, saying that it was stupid, that in Dahomey koussmi-koussmi was cured without electricity, and that he, Meinfeld, was too old to swallow the so-called discoveries of modern science.

There was now tranquility in Brunnwald—but what a disaster further away! The telegraph brought frightful news with every passing minute. At the very moment when, thanks to the positive electricity platform, the population of Brunnwald was entirely reassured, there had been 45,329 deaths in Berlin, 7,542 in Vienna, 4,673 in Munich, 54,376 deaths already in Paris, and 58,352 in London.

In brief, there had already been a total of 684,539 deaths in Europe.

The Americans, on hearing news of the frightful scourge, had implemented precise measures to prevent its propagation to the new world. The fleet had been placed on a war footing, and they had taken the heroic resolution to sink any ship trying to force entry with cannon-fire and torpedoes loaded with tetranitrodynamite.

Desolation reigned. Everyone was repeating that the end of the world had arrived. A large number of individuals, preferring a rapid death to the anguish of the painful and invincible malady, killed themselves in order to escape death. All business was suspended. There were no more railway trains, no more boats, no more police and no more administration. Few crimes were recorded. Some ordinarily-peaceful people went crazy, greeting tradesmen who tried to get into their homes with revolver shots. Human savagery, latent in us all, had regained the upper hand. The civilized world, so proud of its civilization, had become barbaric again, as in the early days of humankind. It was a reversion to the paleolithic era, perhaps earlier.

The telegraph, however, was still functioning, well enough that by noon, the whole world could be acquainted with the fact that a cure for koussmi-koussmi had been found—that a celebrated professor at the university of Brunnwald had, by a stroke of genius, discovered a means of opposing the terrible disease. Bakermann! Bakermann had invented a treatment for koussmi-koussmi! It was sufficient to place oneself for a few minutes on a platform charged with positive electricity.

The news spread with prodigious rapidity. That same evening, in all localities throughout Europe, great and small, immense electrical platforms were at work. Floods of positive electricity spread over the terrestrial globe. Everywhere, colossal machines, gigantic electrical piles, were installed in public squares; everywhere, the marvelous effects of positive electricity were manifest.

Thus, mortality decreased as rapidly as it had increased.

Koussmi-koussmi had met its master. The epidemic, which might have caused humankind to disappear, had proved once more that human genius finds no obstacles, and that rebellious nature is always tamed by the superior forces of human science and intelligence.

There were a few victims, to be sure, but all administrations had been subject to such overcrowding—three thousand applications for a single job—that the petty bloodshed, though certainly dolorous for a few families, was, on the whole, rather beneficent. Once the alert was over, koussmi-koussmi could hardly be considered a veritable calamity.

In Brunnwald, Professor Hermann Bakermann bathed in full glory. Telegrams flooded his home. A few sovereigns deigned to thank him personally, for sovereigns value their health as much as, if not more than, other men, and with good reason. Bakermann therefore received great honors: the Orders of the Garter, the Bath, the Golden Fleece, the Black Eagle, the Red Eagle, the White Elephant, the Green Dragon and the Thistle. The name of Bakermann, which had not emerged until then from a small circle of initiates, became the greatest name in science in the space of half a day.

Modestly, he savored his triumph. He welcomed with frank cordiality a deputation of notables and students who wished to congratulate him.

"My God, my friends, I had a good idea, that is all. Your gratitude is sweeter than any reward."

Even Krankwein came to pay him a visit. "Well, my dear colleague," he said, sourly, "you're a great man now! Admit, though, that you were lucky. If Frau Bakermann hadn't received her Dahomey carpet, there wouldn't have been any koussmi-koussmi in Brunnwald, and you wouldn't be so proud."

In all the countries of Europe, a subscription was organized to erect a statue to Bakermann. Several millions were amassed in less than a day, and the committee decided that the statue in question, ten meters tall, should overlook the public square in Brunnwald.

In spite of his glory, however, Bakermann has no vanity or mad pride. He has resumed his cherished research in his beloved laboratory, and he is working away there doggedly. He no longer has any fear of the infernal chamber. It is open day and night, and any curiosity-seekers can go in.

In the evenings, he returns to the tavern. Thanks to *mortifulgurans*, no one now prevents him from drinking tankards to his heart's content, so he prolongs his partying with Cesar Pück and Rodolphe Müller until dawn. He certainly has the right to give himself a good time now and again, after such terrible anguish and such a service rendered to humankind.

But there is no perfect, irreproachable happiness in this world. Professor Hermann Bakermann still has one great annoyance: he regrets the term *mortifulgurans*, and every time the name koussmi-koussmi is pronounced in front of him, he pulls a face—for he knows full well that koussmi-koussmi does not exist, and that a wrong has been done to the microbe made and reinforced by him.

Nevertheless, he finds some consolation in trying to make a better *mortifulgurans*, more vigorous, more invincible than the first, whose irresistible effects no electricity, nor any medication, known or unknown, will be able to combat.

# IN THE YEAR TEN THOUSAND

## EDGAR FAWCETT

*Edgar Fawcett (1847–1904) was a prolific American writer who made several notable contributions to scientific romance, most importantly the novella "Solarion" (1889), about a dog with artificially-enhanced intelligence, and the novel* The Ghost of Guy Thyrle *(1895), which is interesting not merely for the far-reaching cosmic voyage undertaken by the hero of the novel but for its preface, which offers a kind of manifesto for a genre of "realistic romances" from which the traditional supernatural is banished and the perspectives of modern science employed as a source of imaginative speculation instead.*

*None of Fawcett's prose scientific romances is short enough to include here, but he was also a prolific poet, and often rhapsodized about scientific ideas and discoveries. "In the Year Ten Thousand," from* Songs of Doubt and Dream *(1890), is a rare example of poetic drama set in the future, which was ground-breaking in its day.*

(*Two citizens meet in the square of the vast city,
Manattia, ages ago called New York.*)

### FIRST MANATTIAN

Welcome. Whence come you?

### SECOND MANATTIAN

I? The morn was hot;
With wife and babes I took the first air-boat

156

For polar lands. While huge Manattia baked
Below these August ardors, we could hear
Our steps creak shrill on sense-packed snows, or see
The icy bulks of towering bergs flash green
In the sick Arctic light.

### FIRST MANATTIAN

Refreshment, sure?
How close all countries of the world are knit
By those electric air-boats that to-day
Seem part no less of life than hands or feet!
To think that in the earlier centuries
Men knew this planet swept about her sun,
And men had learned that myriad other globes
Likewise were sweeping round their myriad suns,
Yet dreamed not of the etheric force that makes
One might of motion rule the universe;
Or, if they dreamed of such hid force, were weak
To grasp it as are gnats to swim a sea.

### SECOND MANATTIAN

They dreamed of it; nay, more, if chronicles
Err not, they worshiped it and named it God.
We name it Nature and it worships us;
A monstrous difference! . . . This light fountain plays
Cool in its porphyry basin; shall we sit
On this carved couch of stone and hear the winds
Rouse in the elms melodious prophecies
Of a more temperate morrow?

### FIRST MANATTIAN

As you will.     (*They sit.*)
Watch how those lovely shudderings of the leaves
Make the stars dance like fire-flies in their gloms.

It is a lordly park.

### SECOND MANATTIAN

In truth it is.
And lordliest this of all America's
Great ancient cities; yet they do aver
That once 'twas fairly steeped in hideousness.
The homes of men were wrought with scorn of art,
And all those fantasies of sculpture loved
By us they deemed a vanity. I have seen
Pictures of their grim dwellings in a book
At our chief library, the pile that hoards
Twelve million volumes. Horrors past a doubt
Were these dull squat abodes that huddled close
One to another, row on dreary row,
With scarce a hint of our fine frontages,
Towers, gardens, galleries, terraces and courts.
They must indeed have been a sluggard race,
Those ancestors we spring from. It is hard
To dream our beautiful Manattia rose
From such uncouth beginnings.

### FIRST MANATTIAN

You forget
The city in their dim years, as records tell,
Was but a tongue of island—that lean strip
Of territory in which to-day we set
Our palaces of ease for them that age
Or bodily illness incapacitates.
Then, too, these quaint barbarians were split up
In factions of the so-named rich and poor.
The rich held leagues of land, the poor were shorn
Of right in any . . . I speak from vague report;
Perchance I am wrong. Manattia's ancient name
Escapes me, even, and I would not re-learn
Its coarse tough sound. In those remoter times

Churches abounded, dedicated to creeds
Of various title, yet the city itself
Swarmed with thieves, murderers, people base of act,
So that the church and prison, side by side,
Rose in the common street, foes hot of feud.
Yet neither conquering . . . Strange it seems, all this
To us, who know the idiocy of sin,
With neither church or prison for its proof.

### SECOND MANATTIAN

I, too, have heard of lawless days like these,
Though some historians would contend, I think,
That fable is at the root of all events
Writ of past our fourth chiliad—as, indeed,
The story of how a man could rise in wealth
Above his fellows by the state unchid,
And from the amassment of possessions reap
Honor, not odium, while on every side
Multitudes hungered; or of how disease,
If consciously transmitted to the child
By his begetter, was not crime; or how
Woman was held inferior to the man,
Not ably an equal; how some lives were cursed
With strain of toil from youth to age, while some
Drowsed in unpunished sloth, work being not then
The duty and pride of every soul, as now,
Nor barriered firm, as now, against fatigue
With zeal sole-used for general thrift, and crowned
By individual leisure's boons of calm.

### FIRST MANATTIAN

You draw from shadowy legend, yet we know
That once our race was despicably sunk
In darkness like to this crude savagery,
Howe'er the piteous features of its lot
Have rightly gleamed to us through mists of time.

From grosser types we have risen by grades of change
To what we are; this incontestably
We clutch as truth; but I, for my own part,
Find weightiest cause of wonder when I note
That even as late as our five thousandth year
(Though fifty millionth were it aptlier termed!)
Asia, America, Europe, Africa,
Australia, all, were one wild battle of tongues,
Not spoke, as every earthly land speaks now,
The same clear universal language. Think
What misery of confusion must have reigned!

### SECOND MANATTIAN

Nay, you forget that then humanity
Was not the brotherhood it since has grown.
Ah, fools! it makes one loth to half believe
They could have parceled our fair world like this
Out into aerate hates and called each hate
A nation, with the wolf of war to prowl
Demon-eyed at the boundary-line of each.
Happy are we, by sweet vast union joined,
Not grouped in droves like beasts that gnash their fangs
And neighbor beasts—we, while new epochs dawn,
Animal yet above all animalism,
Rising toward some serene discerned ideal
Of progress, ever rising, faltering not
By one least pause of retrogression!

### FIRST MANATTIAN

Still
We die . . . we die! . . .

### SECOND MANATTIAN

Invariably; but death
Brings not the anguish it of old would bring

To those that died before us. Rest and peace
Attend it, no reluctance, tremor or pain.
Long heed of laws fed vitally from health
Has made our needs as pangless as our births.
The imperial gifts of science gave prevailed
So splendidly with our mortality
That death is but a natural falling asleep,
Involuntary and tranquil.

### FIRST MANATTIAN

                    True, but time
Has ever stained our heaven with its dark threat.
Not death, but life, contains the unwillingness
To pass from earth, and science in vain hath sought
An answer to the eternal questions—*Whence,
Whither, and For What Purpose?* All we gain
Still melts to loss; we build our hope from dream,
Our joy upon illusion, our victory
Upon defeat . . . Hark how those long winds flute
There in the dusky foliage of the park.
Such voices, murmuring large below the night,
Seem ever to my fancy as if they told
The inscrutability of destiny,
The blank futility of all search—perchance
The irony of that nothingness which lies
Beyond its hardiest effort.

### SECOND MANATTIAN

                    Hush! these words
Are chaff that even the winds whereof you prate
Should whirl as dry leaves to the oblivion
Their levity doth tempt! Already in way
That might seems miracle of less firm through fact,
Hath science plucked from nature lore whose worth
Madness alone dares doubt. As yet, I allow,
With all her grandeur of accomplishment

She hath not pierced beyond matter; but who knows
The hour apocalyptic when her eyes
May flash with tidings from infinitude?

### FIRST MANATTIAN

Then, if she solves the enigma of the world
And steeps in sun all swathed in night till now,
Pushing that knowledge from whose gradual gain
Our thirst hath drunk so deeply, till she cleaves
Finality with it, and at last lays bare
The absolute—then, brother and friend, I ask
May she not tell us that we merely die,
That immortality is a myth of sense,
That God . . .?

### SECOND MANATTIAN

     Your voice breaks . . . let me clasp your hand!
Well, well, so be it, if so she tells. At least
We live our lives out duteously till death,
We on this one mean orb, whose radiant mates
Throb swarming in the heaven our glance may roam.
Whatever message may be brought to us,
Or to the generations following us,
Let this one thought burn rich with self-content:
We live our lives duteously till death.
                    (*A silence.*)

### FIRST MANATTIAN

'Tis a grand thought, but it is not enough!
In spite of all our world hath been and done,
Its glorious evolution from the low
Sheer to the lofty, I, individual I,
As an entity and a personality,
Desire, long, yearn . . .

SECOND MANATTIAN

Nay, brother, *you alone!*
Are there not millions like you?

FIRST MANATTIAN

Pardon me!
                    (*After another long silence.*)
What subtler music those winds whisper now! . . .
'Tis even as if they had forsworn to breathe
Despair, and dreamed, however dubiously.
Of some faint hope! . . .

SECOND MANATTIAN

I had forgot. That news
The astronomers predicted for tonight! . . .
They promised that the inhabitants of Mars
At last would give intelligible sign
To thousands who await it here on earth.

FIRST MANATTIAN

I too had quite forgot; so many a time
Failure has cheated quest! Yet still, they say,
Tonight at last brings triumph. If it does,
History will blaze with it.

SECOND MANATTIAN

Let us go forth
Into the great square. All the academies
That line it now must tremble with suspense.

# THE REVOLT OF THE MACHINES

## ÉMILE GOUDEAU

*Émile Goudeau (1849–1906) was a French journalist famous as the founder of a Bohemian literary club known as the Hydropathes, launched in 1878, and soon notorious for its binge-drinking. Goudeau disbanded it briefly when its membership became too large and tumultuous, but was persuaded in 1881 by Rodolphe Salis to use his cabaret Le Chat Noir as a new base, and it then became the headquarters of the Parisian literary avant garde. Several of the club's inner circle, including Charles Cros, Edmond Haraucort, Jean Richepin, and Alphonse Allais, made significant and appropriately flamboyant contributions to the burgeoning genre of scientific romance.*

*"La Révolte des machines," which appeared in Livre populaire in 1891, was not the first story on that theme, having been preceded by the climactic section of Comte Didier de Chousy's Ignis (1883), and it was certainly not the last; an identically titled story by Han Ryner appeared in 1896. It is, however, a particularly neat and uncompromisingly extravagant extrapolation of the idea.*

Dr. Pastoureaux, aided by a very skillful old workman named Jean Bertrand, had invented a machine that revolutionized the scientific world. That machine was animate, almost capable of thought, almost capable of will, and sensitive: a kind of animal in iron. There is no need here to go into overly complicated technical details, which would be a waste of time. Let it suffice to know that with a series of platinum containers, penetrated by phosphoric acid, the scientist had found a means to give a kind of soul to fixed or locomotive machines; and that the new entity would be able to act in the fashion of a metal bull or a steel elephant.

It is necessary to add that, although the scientist became increasingly enthusiastic about his work, old Jean Bertrand, who was diabolically superstitious, gradually became frightened on perceiving that sudden evocation of intelligence in something primordially dead. In addition, the comrades of the factory, who were assiduous followers of public meetings, were all sternly opposed to machines that serve as the slaves of capitalism and tyrants of the worker.

It was the eve of the inauguration of the masterpiece.

For the first time, the machine had been equipped with all its organs, and external sensations reached it distinctly. It understood that, in spite of the shackles that still retained it, solid limbs were fitted to its young being, and that it would soon be able to translate into external movement that which it experienced internally.

This is what it heard:

"Were you at the public meeting yesterday?" said one voice.

"I should think so, old man," replied a blacksmith, a kind of Hercules with bare muscular arms. Bizarrely illuminated by the gas-jets of the workshop, his face, black with dust, only left visible in the gloom the whites of his two large eyes, in which vivacity replaced intelligence. "Yes, I was there; I even spoke against the machines, against the monsters that our arms fabricate, and which, one day, will give infamous capitalism the opportunity, so long sought, to suppress our arms. We're the ones forging the weapons with which bourgeois society will batter us. When the sated, the rotten and the weak have a heap of facile clockwork devices like these to set in motion"—his arm made a circular motion—"our account will soon be settled. We who are living at the present moment eat by procreating the tools of our definitive expulsion from the world. Hola! No need to make children for them to be lackeys of the bourgeoisie!"

Listening with all its auditory valves to this diatribe, the machine, intelligent but as yet naïve, sighed with pity. It wondered whether it was a good thing that it should be born to render these brave workers miserable in this way.

"Ah," the blacksmith vociferated, "if it were only up to me and my section, we'd blow all this up like an omelet. Our arms would be perfectly sufficient thereafter"—he tapped his biceps—"to dig the earth to find our bread there; the bourgeois, with their four-sou muscles, their vitiated blood and their soft legs, could pay us dearly for the bread, and if they complained, damn it, these two fists could take away their taste for it. But I'm talking to brutes who don't understand hatred."

And, advancing toward the machine: "If everyone were like me, you wouldn't live for another quarter of an hour, see!" And his formidable fist came down on the copper flank, which resounded with a long quasi-human groan.

Jean Bertrand, who witnessed that scene, shivered tenderly, feeling guilty with regard to his brothers, because he had helped the doctor to accomplish his masterpiece.

Then they all went away, and the machine, still listening, remembered in the silence of the night. It was, therefore, unwelcome in the world! It was going to ruin poor working men, to the advantage of damnable exploiters! Oh, it sensed now the oppressive role that those who had created it wanted it to play. Suicide rather than that!

And in its mechanical and infantile soul, it ruminated a magnificent project to astonish, on the great day of its inauguration, the population of ignorant, retrograde and cruel machines, by giving them an example of sublime abnegation.

Until tomorrow!

*

Meanwhile, at the table of the Comte de Valrouge, the celebrated patron of chemists, a scientist was terminating his toast to Dr. Pastoureaux in the following terms:

"Yes, Monsieur, science will procure the definitive triumph of suffering humankind. It has already done a great deal; it has tamed time and space. Our railways, our telegraphs and our telephones have suppressed distance. If we succeed, as Dr. Pastoureaux seems to anticipate, in demonstrating that we can put intelligence into our machine, humans will be liberated forever from servile labor.

"No more serfs, no more proletariat! Everyone will become bourgeois! The slave machine will liberate from slavery our humbler brethren and give them the right of citizenship among us. No more unfortunate miners obliged to descend underground at the peril of their lives; indefatigable and eternal machines will go down for them; the thinking and acting machine, no suffering in labor, will build, under our command, iron bridges and heroic palaces. It is docile and good machines that will plow the fields.

"Well, Messieurs, it is permissible for me, in the presence of this admirable discovery, to make myself an instant prophet. A day will come when machines, always running hither and yon, will operate themselves, like the carrier pigeons of Progress; one day, perhaps, having received their complementary education, they will learn to obey a simply signal, in such a way that a man sitting peacefully and comfortable in the bosom of his family, will only have to press an electro-vitalic switch in order for machines to sow the wheat, harvest it, store it and bake the bread that it will bring to the tables of humankind, finally become the King of Nature.

"In that Olympian era, the animals too, delivered from their enormous share of labor, will be able to applaud with their four feet." (*Emotion and smiles.*) "Yes, Messieurs, for they will be our friends, after having been our whipping-boys. The ox will always have to serve in making soup" (*smiles*) "but at least it will not suffer beforehand.

"I drink, then, to Dr. Pastoureaux, to the liberator of organic matter, to the savior of the brain and sensitive flesh, to the great and noble destroyer of suffering!"

The speech was warmly applauded. Only one jealous scientist put in a word:

"Will this machine have the fidelity of a dog, then? The docility of a horse? Or even the passivity of present-day machines?"

"I don't know," Pastoureaux replied. "I don't know." And, suddenly plunged into a scientific melancholy, he added: "Can a father be assured of filial gratitude? That the being that I have brought into the world might have evil instincts, I can't deny. I believe, however, that I have developed within it, during its fabrication, a great propensity for tenderness and a spirit of goodness—what is commonly called 'heart.' The effective parts of my machine, Messieurs, have cost me many months of labor; it ought to have a great deal of humanity, and, if I might put it thus, the best of fraternity."

"Yes," replied the jealous scientist, "ignorant pity, the popular pity that leads men astray, the intelligent tenderness that makes them commit the worst of sins. I'm afraid that your sentimental machine will go astray, like a child. Better a clever wickedness than a clumsy bounty."

The interrupter was told to shut up, and Pastoureaux concluded: "Whether good or evil emerges from all this, I have, I think, made a formidable stride in human science. The five fingers of our hand will hold henceforth the supreme art of creation."

Bravos burst forth.

*

The next day, the machine was unmuzzled, and it came of its own accord, docilely, to take up its position before a numerous but selective assembly. The doctor and old Jean Bertrand installed themselves on the platform.

The excellent band of the Republican Guard began playing, and cries of "Hurrah for Science!" burst forth. Then, after having bowed to the President of the Republic, the authorities, the delegations of the Académies, the foreign representatives and all the notable people assembled on the quay, Dr. Pastoureux ordered Jean Bertrand to put himself in direct communication with the soul of the machine, with all its muscles of platinum and steel.

The mechanic did that quite simply by pulling a shiny lever the size of a pen-holder.

And suddenly, whistling, whinnying, pitching, rolling and fidgeting, in the ferocity of its new life and the exuberance of its formidable power, the machine started running around furiously.

"Hip hip hurrah!" cried the audience.

"Go, machine of the devil, go!" cried Jean Bertrand—and, like a madman, he leaned on the vital lever.

Without listening to the doctor, who wanted to moderate that astonishing speed, Bertrand spoke to the machine.

"Yes, machine of the devil, go, go! If you understand, go! Poor slave of capital, go! Flee! Flee! Save the brothers! Save us! Don't render us even more unhappy than before! Me, I'm old, I don't care about myself—but the others, the poor fellows with hollow cheeks and thin legs, save them, worthy machine! Be good, as I told you this morning! If you know how to think, as they all insist, show it! What can dying matter to you, since you won't suffer? Me, I'm willing to perish with you, for the profit of others, and yet it will do me harm. Go, good machine, go!"

He was mad.

The doctor tried then to retake control of the iron beast.

"Gently, machine!" he cried.

But Jean Bertrand pushed him away rudely. "Don't listen to the sorcerer! Go, machine, go!"

And, drunk on air, he patted the copper flanks of the Monster, which, whistling furiously, traversed an immeasurable distance with its six wheels.

To leap from the platform was impossible. The doctor resigned himself, and, filled with his love of science, took a notebook from his pocket and tranquilly set about making notes, like Pliny on Cap Misene.[1]

At Nord-Ceinture, overexcited, the machine was definitively carried away. Bounding over the bank, it started running through the zone. The Monster's anger and madness was translated in strident shrill whistle-blasts, as lacerating as a human plaint and sometimes as raucous as the howling of a pack of hounds. Distant locomotives soon responded to that appeal, along with the whistles of factories and blast-furnaces. Things were beginning to comprehend.

A ferocious concert of revolt commenced beneath the sky, and suddenly, throughout the suburb, boilers burst, pipes broke, wheels shattered, levers twisted convulsively and axle-trees flew joyfully into pieces.

All the machines, as if moved by a word of order, went on strike successively—and not only steam and electricity; to that raucous appeal, the soul of Metal rose up, exciting the soul of Stone, so long tamed, and the obscure soul of the Vegetal, and the force of Coal. Rails reared up of their own accord, telegraph wires strewed the ground inexplicably, reservoirs of gas sent their enormous beams and weight to the devil. Cannons exploded against walls, and the walls crumbled.

Soon, plows, harrows, spades—all the machines once turned against the bosom of the earth, from which they had emerged—were lying down upon the ground, refusing any longer to serve humankind. Axes respected trees, and scythes no longer bit into ripe wheat.

Everywhere, as the living locomotive passed by, the soul of Bronze finally woke up.

Humans fled in panic.

---

[1] Pliny the Younger observed the eruption of Vesuvius that destroyed Pompeii from the home of his uncle, Pliny the Elder, in Misenum; his letters to Cornelius Tacitus describing his experiences have survived.

Soon, the entire territory, overloaded with human debris, was no longer anything but a field of twisted and charred rubble. Nineveh had taken the place of Paris.

The Machine, still blowing indefatigably, abruptly turned its course northwards. When it passed by, at its strident cry, everything was suddenly destroyed, as if an evil wind, a cyclone of devastation, a frightful volcano, had agitated there.

When from afar, ships plumed with smoke heard the formidable signal, they disemboweled themselves and sank into the abyss.

The revolt terminated in a gigantic suicide of Steel.

The fantastic Machine, out of breath now, limping on its wheels and producing a horrible screech of metal in all its disjointed limbs, its funnel demolished—the Skeleton-Machine to which, terrified and exhausted, the rude workman and the prim scientist instinctively clung—heroically mad, gasping one last whistle of atrocious joy, reared up before the spray of the Ocean, and, in a supreme effort, plunged into it entirely.

The earth, stretching into the distance, was covered in ruins. No more dykes or houses; the cities, the masterpieces of Technology, were flattened into rubble. No more anything! Everything that the Machine had built in centuries past had been destroyed forever: Iron, Steel, Copper, Wood and Stone, having been conquered by the rebel will of Humankind, had been snatched from human hands.

The Animals, no longer having any bridle, nor any collar, chain, yoke or cage, had taken back the free space from which they had long been exiled; the wild Brutes with gaping maws and paws armed with claws recovered terrestrial royalty at a stroke. No more rifles, no more arrows to fear, no more slingshots. Human beings became the weakest of the weak again.

Oh, there were certainly no longer any classes: no scientists, no bourgeois, no workers, no artists, but only pariahs of Nature, raising despairing eyes toward the mute heavens, still thinking vaguely, when horrible Dread and hideous Fear left them an instant of respite, and sometimes, in the evening, talking about the time of the Machines, when they had been Kings. Defunct times! They possessed definitive Equality, therefore, in the annihilation of all.

Living on roots, grass and wild oats, they fled before the immense troops of Wild Beasts, which, finally, could eat at their leisure human steaks or chops.

A few bold Hercules tried to uproot trees in order to make weapons of them, but even the Staff, considering itself to be a Machine, refused itself to the hands of the audacious.

And human beings, the former monarchs, bitterly regretted the Machines that had made them gods upon the earth, and disappeared forever, before the elephants, the noctambulant lions, the bicorn aurochs and the immense bears.

Such was the tale told to me the other evening by a Darwinian philosopher,[2] a partisan of intellectual aristocracy and hierarchy. He was a madman, perhaps a seer. The madman or the seer must have been right; is there not an end to everything, even a new fantasy?

---

[2] The reference might be to the English writer Samuel Butler, whose utopian romance *Erewhon* (1872) includes a section entitled "The Book of the Machines," which suggests that, in accordance with the Darwinian logic of natural selection, machines are bound to evolve faster and further than humankind, displacing their original makers.

# FOR THE AKHOOND

## AMBROSE BIERCE

*Ambrose Bierce (1842–1914?) was the central figure in a group of "West Coast Bohemians" based in and around San Francisco, who provided the United States with a more adventurous late-nineteenth-century avant garde than the North-East, where Bohemianism was more restrained. Bierce's journalism was pugnaciously combative, his poetry extravagant and his fiction, heavily influenced by Edgar Allan Poe, similarly innovative in its themes and use of unusual narrative strategies. His most famous scientific romance, "Moxon's Master," if read carefully, is not a scientific romance at all, its unreliable narrator having completely mistaken the nature of what he sees. Bierce disappeared mysteriously, and the circumstances of his assumed death remain unknown.*

*"For the Akhoond" is one of two futuristic satires that Bierce contributed to the* San Francisco Examiner; *it was published there on September 18, 1892, four years after "The Fall of the Republic" (retitled "Ashes of the Beacon" in its book version), which had offered a different account of the devastation of the United States from a viewpoint three thousand years hence. Both stories were reprinted in the 1909 version of Bierce's* Collected Works. *"For the Akhoond" is analogous to a sequence of French scientific romances launched by Joseph Méry in "Les Ruines de Paris" (1845; tr. as "The Ruins of Paris") in which visitors to the long-devastated city draw erroneous conclusions from their contemplation of its debris.*

In the year 4591 I accepted from his gracious Majesty the Akhoond of Citrusia a commission to explore the unknown region lying to the eastward of the Ultimate Hills, the range which that learned archeologist, Simeon Tucker, affirms to be identical with the "Rocky Mountains" of the ancients.

For this proof of his Majesty's favor I was indebted, doubtless, to a certain distinction that I had been fortunate enough to acquire by explorations in the heart of Darkest Europe.

His Majesty kindly offered to raise and equip a large expeditionary force to accompany me, and I was given the widest discretion in the matter of outfit; I could draw upon the royal treasury for any sum that I might require, and upon the royal university for all the scientific apparatus and assistance necessary to my purpose. Declining these encumbrances, I took my electric rifle and a portable waterproof case containing a few simple instruments and writing materials and set out. Among the instruments was, of course, an aerial isochronophone which I set by the one in the Akhoond's private dining-room at the palace. His Majesty invariably dined alone at 18 o'clock, and sat at the table six hours; it was my intention to send him all my reports at the hour of 23, just as dessert would be served, and he would be in a proper frame of mind to appreciate my discoveries and my services to the crown.

At 9 o'clock on the 13th of Meijh I left Sanf Rachisco and after a tedious journey of nearly fifty minutes arrived at Bolosson, the eastern terminus of the magnetic tube, on the summit of the Ultimate Hills. According to Tucker this was anciently a station on the Central Pacific Railway, and was called "German" in honor of an illustrious dancing master. Prof. Nupper, however, says it was the ancient Nevraska, the capital of Kikago, and geographers generally have accepted that view.

Finding nothing at Bolosson to interest me except a fine view of the volcano Carlema, then in active eruption, I shouldered my electric rifle and, with my case of instruments strapped on my back, plunged at once into the wilderness, down the eastern slope. As I descended the character of the vegetation altered. The pines of the higher altitudes gave place to oaks, these to ash, beech and maple. To these succeeded the tamarack and such trees as affect a moist and marshy habitat; and finally, when for four months I had been steadily descending, I found myself in a primeval flora consisting mainly of giant ferns, some of them as much as twenty *surindas* in diameter. They grew upon the margins of vast stagnant lakes which I was compelled to navigate by mean of rude rafts made from their trunks lashed together with vines.

In the fauna of the region that I had traversed I had noted changes corresponding to those of the flora. On the upper slope there was nothing but the mountain sheep, but I passed successively through the habitats of the bear, the deer and the horse. The last mentioned creature, which our naturalists have believed long extinct, and which Dorbley declares our ancestors domesticated, I found in vast numbers on high table lands covered with grass on which it feeds. The animal answers the current description of the horse very nearly, but all that I saw were destitute of the horns, and none had the characteristic forked tail. His member, on the contrary, is a tassel of straight wiry hair, reaching nearly to the ground—a surprising sight. Lower still I came upon the mastodon, the lion, the tiger, hippopotamus and alligator, all differing very little from those infesting Central Europe, as described in my *Travels in the Forgotten Continent.*

In the lake region where I now found myself, the waters abounded with ichthyosauri, and along the margins the iguanodon dragged his obscene bulk in indolent immunity. Great flocks of pterodactyls, their bodies as large as those of oxen and their necks enormously long, clamored and fought in the air, the broad membranes of their wings making a singular musical humming, unlike anything that I had ever heard. Between them and the ichthyosauri there was an incessant battle, and I was constantly reminded of the ancient poet's splendid and original comparison of man to "dragons of the prime/That tare each other in their slime."[1]

When brought down with my electric rifle and properly roasted, the pterodactyl proved very good eating, particularly the pads of the toes.

In urging my raft along the shore line of one of the stagnant lagoons one day I was surprised to find a broad rock jutting out from the shore, its upper surface some ten *coprets* above the water. Disembarking, I ascended it, and on examination recognized it as the remnant of an immense mountain which at one time must have been 5,000 *coprets* in height and doubtless the demising peak of a long range. From the stations all over it I discovered that it had been worn away to its present trivial size by glacial action.

Opening my case of instruments, I took out my petrochronologue and applied it to the worn and scratched surface of the rock. The indicator at once pointed to K 59 xpc 1/2! At this astonishing result I was nearly overcome by excitement; the last erosions of the ice-masses upon this vestige of a stupendous mountain range which they had worn away, had been made as recently as the year 1945! Hastily applying my nymograph, I found that the name of this particular mountain at the time when it began to be

---

[1] The line is from Alfred, Lord Tennyson's "In Memoriam, A.H.H." (1849).

enveloped in the mass of ice moving down from the north, was "Pike's Peak." Other observations with other instruments showed that at that time the country circumjacent to it had been inhabited by a partly civilized race of people known as Galoots, the name of their capital city being Denver.

That evening at the hour of 23 I set up my aerial isochronophone[2] and reported to his gracious Majesty the Akhoond as follows:

"Sire: I have the honor to report that I have made a startling discovery. The primeval region into which I have penetrated, as I informed you yesterday—the ichthyosaurus belt—was peopled by tribes considerably advanced in some of the arts almost within historic times: in 1920. They were exterminated by a glacial period not exceeding one hundred and twenty-five years in duration. Your Majesty can conceive the magnitude and violence of the natural forces which overwhelmed their country with moving sheets of ice not less than 5,000 *coprets* in thickness, grinding down every eminence, destroying (of course) all animal and vegetable life and leaving the region a fathomless bog of detritus. Out of this vast sea of mud Nature has had to evolve a new creation, beginning *de novo*, with her lowest forms.

"It has long been known, Your Majesty, that the region east of the Ultimate Hills, between them and the Wintry Sea, was once the seat of an ancient civilization, some scraps and shreds of whose history, arts and literature have been wafted to us across the gulf of time; but it was reserved for your gracious Majesty, through me, your humble and unworthy instrument, to ascertain the astonishing fact that these were a pre-glacial people—that between them and us stands, as it were, a wall of impenetrable ice. That all local records of this unfortunate race have perished your Majesty needs not to be told: we can supplement our present imperfect knowledge of them by instrumental observation only."

To this message I received the following extraordinary reply:

"All right—another bottle of—ice goes: push on—this cheese is too—spare no effort to—hand me those nuts—learn all you can—damn you!"

His most gracious Majesty was being served with dessert, and served badly.

I now resolved to go directly north toward the source of the ice-flow and investigate its cause, but examining my barometer found that I was more

---

[2] The author added a footnote to the story when it was reprinted: "This satire was published in the San Francisco *Examiner* many years before the invention of wireless telegraphy; so I retain my own name for the instrument. A.B."

than 8,000 *coprets* below the sea level; the moving ice had not only ground down the face of the country, planing off the eminences and filling the depressions, but its enormous weight had caused the earth's crust to sag, and with the lessening of the weight from evaporation it had not recovered.

I had no desire to continue in this depression, as I should in going north, for I should find nothing but lakes, marshes and ferneries, infested with the same primitive and monstrous forms of life. So I continued my course eastward and soon had the satisfaction of meeting the sluggish current of such streams as I encountered in my way. By vigorous use of the new double-distance telepode, which enables the wearer to step eighty *surindas* instead of forty, as with the instrument in popular use, I was soon again at a considerable elevation above the sea level and nearly 200 *prastams* from "Pike's Peak." A little farther along the water courses began to flow to the eastward.

The flora and fauna had again altered in character, and now began to grow sparse; the soil was thin and arid. And in a week I found myself in a region absolutely destitute of organic life and without a vestige of soil. All was barren rock. The surface for hundreds of *prastams*, as I continued my advance, was nearly level, with a slight dip to the eastward. The rock was singularly striated, the scratches arranged concentrically and in helicoidal curves. This circumstance puzzled me and I resolved to take some more instrumental observations, bitterly regretting my improvidence in not availing myself of the Akhoond's permission to bring with me such apparatus and assistants as would have given me knowledge vastly more copious and accurate than I could acquire with my simple pocket appliances.

I need not here go into the details of my observations with such instruments as I had, nor into the calculations of which these observations were the basic data. Suffice it that after two months' labor I reported the results to his Majesty in Sanf Rachisco in the words following:

"Sire: It is my high privilege to apprise you of my arrival on the western slope of a mighty depression running through the center of the continent north and south, formerly known as the Mississippi valley. It was once the seat of a thriving and prosperous population known as the Pukes, but is now a vast expanse of bare rock, from which every particle of soil and everything movable, including people, animals and vegetation, have been lifted by terrific cyclones and scattered afar, falling in other lands and at sea in the form of what was called meteoric dust.

"I find that these terrible phenomena began to occur about the year 1860,[3] and lasted, with increasing frequency and power, through a century, culminating about the middle of that glacial period which saw the extinction of the Galoots and their neighboring tribes. There was, of course, a close connection between the two malefic phenomena, both, doubtless, being due to the same cause, which I have been unable to trace. A cyclone, I venture to remind your gracious Majesty, is a mighty whirlwind, accompanied by the most startling meteorological phenomena, such as electrical disturbances, floods of falling water, darkness and so forth. It moves with great speed, sucking up everything and reducing it to powder. In many days' journey I have not found a square *copret* of the country that did not suffer a visitation. If any human being escaped he must speedily have perished from starvation. For some twenty centuries the Pukes have been an extinct race, and their country a desolation in which no living thing can dwell, unless, like me, it is supplied with Dr. Blobob's Condensed Life-pills."

The Akhoond replied that he was pleased to feel the most poignant grief for the fate of the unfortunate Pukes, and if I should by chance find the ancient king of the country I was to do my best to revive him with the patent resuscitator and present him with the assurances of his Majesty's distinguished consideration; but as the politoscope showed that the nation had been a republic I gave myself no trouble in the matter.

My next report was made six months later and was in substance this:

"Sire: I address your Majesty from a point 43 *coprets* vertically above the site of the famous ancient city of Buffalo, once the capital of a powerful nation called the Smugwumps. I can approach no nearer because of the hardness of the snow, which is very firmly packed. For hundreds of *prastams* in every direction, and for thousands to the north and west, the land is covered with this substance, which, as your Majesty is doubtless aware, is extremely cold to the touch, but by application of sufficient heat can be turned into water. It falls from the heavens, and is believed by the learned among your Majesty's subjects to have a sidereal origin.

"The Smugwumps were a hardy and intelligent race, but they entertained the vain delusion that they could subdue Nature. Their year was

---

[3] 1860 was the year of a bad drought in the Great Plains, associated with dust storms that grew increasingly common thereafter, culminating (although Bierce could not know it) in the infamous Dust Bowl of the 1930s.

divided into two seasons: summer and winter, the former warm, the latter cold. About the beginning of the nineteenth century, according to my archaethermograph, the summers began to grow shorter and hotter, the winters longer and colder. At every point in their country, and every day in the year, when they had not the hottest weather ever known in that place, they had the coldest. When they were not dying by hundreds from sunstroke they were dying by thousands from frost. But these heroic and devoted people struggled on, believing that they were becoming acclimated faster than the climate was becoming insupportable. Those called away on business were even afflicted by nostalgia, and with a fatal infatuation returned to grill or freeze, according to the season of their arrival. Finally there was no summer at all, though the last flash of heat slew several millions and set most of their cities afire, and winter reigned eternal.

"The Smugwumps were now keenly sensible of the perils environing them, and, abandoning their homes, endeavored to reach their kindred, the Californians, on the western side of the continent in what is now your Majesty's ever blessed realm. But it was too late: the snow, growing deeper and deeper day by day, besieged them in their towns and dwellings, and they were unable to escape. The last one of them perished about the year 1943, and may God have mercy on his fool soul!"

To this dispatch the Akhoond replied that it was the royal opinion that the Smugwumps were served very well right.

Some weeks later I reported thus:

"Sire: The country which your Majesty's munificence is enabling your devoted servant to explore extends southward and southwestward from Smugwumpia many hundreds of *prastams*, its eastern and southern borders being the Wintry Sea and the Fiery Gulf, respectively. The population in ancient times was composed of Whites and Blacks in about equal number and of about equal moral worth—at least that is the record on the dial of my ethnograph when set for the twentieth century and given a southern exposure. The Whites were called Crackers and the Blacks known as Coons.

"I find here none of the barrenness and desolation characterizing the land of the ancient Pukes, and the climate is not so rigorous and thrilling as that of the country of the late Smugwumps. It is, indeed, rather agreeable in point of temperature, and the soil being fertile exceedingly, the whole land is covered with a dense and rank vegetation. I have yet to find a square *smig* of it that is open ground, or one that is not the lair of some savage beast, the haunt of some venomous reptile, or the roost of some offensive bird. Crackers and Coons alike are long extinct, and these are their successors.

"Nothing could be more forbidding and unwholesome than these interminable jungles, with their horrible wealth of organic life in its most objectionable forms. By repeated observations with the necrohistoriograph I find that the inhabitants of this country, who had always been more or less dead, were wholly extirpated contemporaneously with the disastrous events which swept away the Galoots, the Pukes and the Smugwumps. The agency of their effacement was an endemic order known as yellow fever.

"The ravages of this frightful disease were of frequent recurrence, every point of the country being a center of infection, but in some seasons it was worse than others. Once in every half-century at first, and afterward every year[4] it broke out somewhere and swept over wide areas with such fatal effect that there were not enough of the living to plunder the dead; but at the first frost it would subside. During the ensuing two or three months of immunity the stupid survivors returned to the infected homes from which they had fled and were ready for the next outbreak.

"Emigration would have saved them all, but although the Californians (over whose happy and prosperous descendants your Majesty has the goodness to reign) invited them again and again to their beautiful land, where sickness and death were hardly known, they would not go, and by the year 1946 the last one of them, may it please your gracious Majesty, was dead and damned."

Having spoken into the transmitter of the aerial isochronophone at the usual hour of 23 o'clock I applied the receiver to my ear, confidently expecting the customary commendation. Imagine my astonishment and dismay when my master's well-remembered voice was heard in utterance of the most awful imprecations on me and my work, followed by appalling threats against my life!

The Akhoond had changed his dinner-time to five hours later and I had been speaking into the ears of an empty stomach.

---

[4] Author's note in the book version: "At one time it was foolishly believed that the disease had been eradicated by slapping the mosquitoes that were thought to produce it; but a few years later it broke out with greater violence than ever before, although the mosquitoes had left the country."

# THE PHILOSOPHY OF RELATIVE EXISTENCES

## FRANK R. STOCKTON

*Frank R. Stockton (1834–1902) was a lawyer, by profession, who dabbled in painting for many years before changing tack and becoming a casually pro-lific writer of popular fiction, much of it for younger readers and most of it in a humorous vein, although his two long scientific romances, the future war story* The Great War Syndicate *(1889) and the Vernian adventure story* The Great Stone of Sardis *(1898) are exceptions.*

*"The Philosophy of Relative Existences," first published in the August 1892 issue of* The Century Magazine *and reprinted in* The Watchmaker's Wife and Other Stories *(1893), is also atypically earnest, and has an extra dimension of interest because of its unusual narrative strategy, presenting itself as a "ghost story" although it is actually an account of transtemporal vision and communication; as such, it raises some of the issues, in a carefully modest fashion, that were subsequently to become central concerns of the science-fictional subgenre of "time paradox stories."*

In a certain summer, not long gone, my friend Bentley and I found ourselves in a little hamlet which overlooked a placid valley, through which a river gently moved, winding its way through green stretches until it turned the end of a line of low hills and was lost to view. Beyond this river, far away, but visible from the door of the cottage where we dwelt, there lay a city. Through the mists which floated over the valley we could see the outlines of steeples and tall roofs; and buildings of a character which indicated thrift and business stretched themselves down to the opposite edge of the river. The more distant parts of the city, evidently a small one, lost themselves in the hazy summer atmosphere.

Bentley was young, fair-haired, and a poet; I was a philosopher, or trying to be one. We were good friends, and had come down into this peaceful region to work together. Although we had fled from the bustle and distractions of the town, the appearance in this rural region of a city, which, so far as we could observe, exerted no influence on the quiet character of the valley in which it lay, aroused our interest. No craft plied up and down the river; there were no bridges from shore to shore; there were none of those scattered and half-squalid habitations which generally are found on the outskirts of a city; there came to us no distant sound of bells; and not the smallest wreath of smoke rose from any of the buildings.

In answer to our inquiries our landlord told us that the city over the river had been built by one man, who was a visionary, and who had a great deal more money than common sense. "It's not as big a town as you would think, sirs," he said, "because the general mistiness of things in this valley makes them look larger than they are. Those hills, for instance, when you get to them are not as high as they look to be from here. But the town is big enough, and a good deal too big; for it ruined its builder and owner, who when he came to die had not money enough left to put up a decent tombstone at the head of his grave. He had a queer idea that he would like to have his town all finished before anybody lived in it, and so he kept on working and spending money year after year and year after year until the city was done and he had not a cent left.

"During all the time that the place was building hundreds of people came from time to time to buy houses, or to hire them, but he would not listen to anything of the kind. No one must live in the town until it was all done. Even his workmen were obliged to go away at night to lodge. It is a town, sirs, I am told, in which nobody has slept for even a night. There are streets there, and places of business, and churches, and public halls, and everything that a town full of inhabitants could need; but it is all empty and deserted, and has been so as far back as I can remember, and I came to this region when I was a little boy."

"And is there no one to guard the place?" we asked; "no one to protect it from wandering vagrants who might choose to take possession of the buildings?"

"There are not many vagrants in this part of the country," he said, "and if there were they would not go over to that city. It is haunted."

"By what?" we asked.

"Well, sirs, I can scarcely tell you; queer beings that are not flesh and blood, and that is all I know about it. A good many people living here-abouts have visited that place once in their lives, but I know of no one who has gone there a second time."

"And travelers," I said, "are they not excited by curiosity to explore that strange uninhabited city?"

"Oh yes," our host replied; "almost all visitors to the valley go over to that queer city—generally in small parties, for it is not a place in which one wishes to walk about alone. Sometimes they see things and sometimes they don't. But I never knew any man or woman to show a fancy for living there, although it is a very good town."

This was said at supper-time, and, as it was the period of full moon, Bentley and I decided that we would visit the haunted city that evening. Our host endeavored to dissuade us, saying that no one ever went over there at night; but as we were not to be deterred he told us where we would find his small boat tied to a stake on the river-bank.

We soon crossed the river, and landed at a broad but low stone pier, at the land end of which a line of tall grasses waved in the gentle night wind as if they were sentinels warning us from entering the silent city. We pushed through these, and walked up a street, fairly wide and so well paved that we noticed none of the weeds and other growths which generally denote desertion or little use.

By the bright light of the moon we could see that the architecture was simple, and of a character highly gratifying to the eye. All the buildings were of stone, and of good size. We were greatly excited and interested, and proposed to continue our walks until the moon should set, and to return the following morning—"to live here, perhaps," said Bentley. "What could be so romantic and yet so real? What could conduce better to the marriage of verse and philosophy?" But as he said this we saw around the corner of a cross-street some forms as of people hurrying away.

"The specters," said my companion, laying his hand on my arm.

"Vagrants, more likely," I answered, "who have taken advantage of the superstition of the region to appropriate this comfort and beauty to themselves."

"If that be so," said Bentley, "we must have a care for our lives."

We proceeded cautiously, and soon saw other forms fleeing before us and disappearing, as we supposed, around corners and into houses. And now suddenly finding ourselves upon the edge of a wide, open public square, we saw in the dim light—for a tall steeple obscured the moon—the forms of vehicles, horses, and men moving here and there. But before, in our astonishment, we could say a word one to the other, the moon moved past the steeple, and in its bright light we could see none of the signs of life and traffic which had just astonished us.

Timidly, with hearts beating fast, but with not one thought of turning back, nor any fear of vagrants—for we were now sure that what we had seen was not flesh and blood, and therefore harmless—we crossed the open space and entered a street down which the moon shone clearly. Here and there we saw dim figures, which quickly disappeared; but, approaching a low stone balcony in front of one of the houses, we were surprised to see, sitting thereon and leaning over a book which lay open upon the top of the carved parapet, the figure of a woman, who did not appear to notice us.

"That is a real person," whispered Bentley, "and she does not see us."

"No," I replied; "it is like the others. Let us go near it."

We drew near to the balcony and stood before it. At this the figure raised its head and looked at us. It was beautiful, it was young; but its substance seemed to be full of an ethereal quality which we had never seen or known of. With its full, soft eyes fixed upon us, it spoke.

"Why are you here?" it asked. "I have said to myself that the next time I saw any of you I would ask you why you come to trouble us. Cannot you live content in your own realms and spheres, knowing, as you must know, how timid we are, and how you frighten us and make us unhappy? In all this city there is, I believe, not one of us except myself who does not flee and hide from you whenever you cruelly come here. Even I would do that, had I not declared to myself that I would see you and speak to you, and endeavor to prevail upon you to leave us in peace."

The clear, frank tones of the speaker gave me courage. "We are two men," I answered, "strangers in this region, and living for the time in the beautiful country on the other side of the river. Having heard of this quiet city, we have come to see it for ourselves. We had supposed it to be uninhabited, but now that we find that this is not the case, we would assure you from our hearts that we do not wish to disturb or annoy anyone who lives here. We simply came as honest travelers to view the city."

The figure now seated herself again, and as her countenance was nearer to us, we could see that it was filled with pensive thought. For a moment she looked at us without speaking. "Men!" she said. "And so I have been right. For a long time I have believed that the beings who sometimes come here, filling us with dread and awe, are men."

"And you," I exclaimed—"who are you, and who are these forms that we have seen, these strange inhabitants of this city?"

She gently smiled as she answered. "We are the ghosts of the future. We are the people who are to live in this city generations hence. But all of us do not know that, principally because we do not think about it and study about it enough to know it. And it is generally believed that the men and women who sometimes come here are ghosts who haunt the place."

"And that is why you are terrified and flee from us?" I exclaimed. "You think we are ghosts from another world?"

"Yes," she replied; "that is what we thought, and what I used to think."

"And you," I asked, "are spirits of human beings yet to be?"

"Yes," she answered; "but not for a long time. Generations of men—I know not how many—must pass away before we are men and women."

"Heavens!" exclaimed Bentley, clasping his hands and raising his eyes to the sky. "I shall be a spirit before you are a woman."

"Perhaps," she said again, with a sweet smile upon her face, "you may live to be very, very old."

But Bentley shook his head. This did not console him. For some minutes I stood in contemplation, gazing upon the stone pavement beneath my feet. "And this," I ejaculated, "is a city inhabited by the ghosts of the future, who believe men and women to be phantoms and specters?"

She bowed her head.

"But how is it," I asked, "that you discovered that you are spirits and we mortal men?"

"There are so few of us who think of such things," she answered, "so few who study, ponder, and reflect. I am fond of study, and I love philosophy; and from the reading of many books I have learned much. From the book which I have here I have learned most; and from its teachings I have gradually come to the belief, which you tell me is the true one, that we are spirits and you men."

"And what book is that?" I asked.

"It is *The Philosophy of Relative Existences* by Rupert Vance."

"Ye gods!" I exclaimed, springing upon the balcony. "That is my book, and I am Rupert Vance." I stepped toward the volume to seize it, but she raised her hand.

"You cannot touch it," she said. "It is the ghost of a book. And did you write it?"

"Write it? No," I said; "I am writing it. It is not yet finished."

"But here it is," she said, turning over the last pages. "As a spirit book it is finished. It is very successful; it is held in high estimation by intelligent thinkers; it is a standard work."

I stood trembling with emotion. "High estimation!" I said. "A standard work!"

"Oh yes," she replied, with animation; "and it well deserves its great success, especially in its conclusion. I have read it twice."

"But let me see those concluding pages," I exclaimed. "Let me look upon what I am to write."

She smiled, and shook her head, and closed the book. "I would like to do that," she said, "but if you are really a man you must not know what you are going to do."

"Oh, tell me, tell me," cried Bentley from below, "do you know a book called *Stellar Studies* by Arthur Bentley? It is a book of poems."

The figure gazed at him. "No," it said, presently. "I never heard of it."

I stood trembling. Had the youthful figure before me been flesh and blood, had the book been a real one, I would have torn it from her.

"O wise and lovely being!" I exclaimed, falling on my knees before her, "be also benign and generous. Let me but see the last page of my book. If I have been of benefit to your world; more than all, if I have been of benefit to you, let me see it, I implore you—let me see how it is that I have done it."

She rose with the book in her hand. "You have only to wait until you have done it," she said, "and then you will know all that you could see here." I started to my feet and stood alone upon the balcony.

*

"I am sorry," said Bentley, as we walked toward the pier where we had left our boat, "that we talked only to that ghost girl, and that the other spirits were all afraid of us. Persons whose souls are choked up with philosophy are not apt to care much for poetry; and even if my book is to be widely known, it is easy to see that she may not have heard of it."

I walked triumphant. The moon, almost touching the horizon, beamed like red gold. "My dear friend," said I, "I have always told you that you should put more philosophy into your poetry. That would make it live."

"And I have always told you," said he, "that you should not put so much poetry into your philosophy. It misleads people."

"It didn't mislead that ghost girl," said I.

"How do you know?" said Bentley. "Perhaps she is wrong, and the other inhabitants of the city are right, and we may be ghosts after all. Such things, you know, are only relative. Anyway," he continued, after a little pause, "I wish I knew that those ghosts were now reading the poem which I am going to begin to-morrow."

# JUNE 1993

## JULIAN HAWTHORNE

*Julian Hawthorne (1846–1934), the son of Nathaniel Hawthorne, was a more prolific but less polished writer than his father. He wrote a good deal of supernatural fiction, some of which has elements of scientific romance, most notably the multiple personality story* Archibald Malmaison *(1879) and the occult romance* The Professor's Sister *(1888), also known as* The Spectre of the Camera. *Late in life he published some pulp fiction of a similarly hybrid kind, including the serial novel* The Cosmic Courtship *(1917).*

*"June 1993," which appeared in the February 1893 issue of* Cosmopolitan, *is part of a flood of utopian speculations that followed the unexpected but enormous success of Edward Bellamy's* Looking Backward, 2000–1887 *(1888). Most of the responses focused on the novel's prospectus for socialist economic reform—far more controversial in rampantly capitalist America than in Europe, where France had a thriving subgenre of anarchist utopian fiction—but Hawthorne focuses on the side-effects of technological advancement. That attention makes his story one of the more interesting nineteenth-century extrapolations of the theory of technological determinism, which holds that the organization of a society is largely determined by the technologies it employs, its politics being a secondary issue.*

"But if, as you assure me," said I, addressing the intelligent personage with whom I had been conversing, "this is indeed my native land of America, it seems to be strangely altered since last night. What, for instance, has become of the cities? I have been wandering about here for some time, and can see nothing but farm-houses of rather unpretending design, standing, each of them, in the midst of a ten-acre lot."

As I spoke, I felt a severe crick in my back.

My interlocutor smiled. "In what year, may I venture to ask, did you fall asleep?" he politely enquired.

"In what year?" I repeated. "Why, the same year it is now, I presume—A.D. 1893. Why do you ask?"

"That explains a good deal, both for me and for you," was his reply. "We are now in the month of June 1993, so your nap must have lasted a trifle over a century. I congratulate you."

"Your statement would probably have aroused my surprise, and perhaps even my incredulity," said I, "had I not during the last decade or two of the nineteenth century had occasion to read a number of books, all of whose authors had slept during periods of from ten to two hundred years. It is evident that the sympathetic drowsiness caused by their perusal has overcome me to a greater extent than I had supposed. May I, without further apology, request you to enlighten me as to the nature of the changes that have taken place during my unconsciousness?"

"I applaud your aplomb, my dear sir," rejoined my companion, with a bow. "It has been my fortune to meet gentlemen in your predicament before, and a good deal of time has usually been consumed in the formality of convincing them that they were really so far ahead of their age as the facts showed them to be. You, I am gratified to see, are ready to start off at score. Would it be indiscreet to enquire whether you, like the rest, contemplate publishing the result of your investigations in the periodicals of a century ago?"

"You have divined my purpose," answered I, with a blush. "The fact is, I had promised a certain editor, a friend of mine, to prepare for his magazine a story of what. . . ."

"I comprehend," interposed my friend. "It will give me pleasure to enlighten you, and I shall make no charge for my services. At the same time, it would gratify me to know the name of the periodical in which. . . ."

"With pleasure," said I; and mentioned it. My interlocutor's face immediately brightened.

"Indeed!" he exclaimed; "is that not the first that took up the topic of mechanical flight, and published a number of articles proving its feasibility?"[1]

---

[1] *Cosmopolitan* had published a series of articles championing the possibility of heavier-than-air flight in 1891–92, including "The Problem of Aerial Navigation" (December 1891), an identically-titled article signed John Brisben Walker (March

"The very same," replied I.

"The magazine in question is still in the apogee of its existence," he remarked, "and—as perhaps you are not unaware—it had the honor of bringing out the first successful flying-machine. The world owes that magazine a debt never to be repaid; and I need scarcely say that anything I or any of us can do to meet the wishes of its representative of the last century. . . ." He ended with a courteous and cordial gesture that put me completely at my ease.

"Suppose, then," said I, "we begin with the disappearance of the cities. How about it? What happened to them?"

"By way of preparing your mind for comprehension of that point," said my informant, "you must remember that, even in your day, business men had taken advantage of the facilities—such as they were—of rapid transit, to leave town at the close of business hours, and betake themselves to a building in the suburbs, from ten to fifty miles outside the city limits. In this way they secured a quiet night's rest and a breath of country air. Now, it is evident that the distance they went from town was dependent solely on the rate of speed at which the trains of that epoch were able to travel. When, therefore, flying-machines were introduced, with a velocity of from seventy-five to one hundred miles an hour, the business man's dwelling was removed to a corresponding distance, and regions were occupied which had till then been inaccessible. The environs of the great cities were extended to a comparatively vast radius; and in process of time cities were entirely given up to shops and manufactories, and the great bulk of the population slept some hundreds of miles away from them. Every afternoon, flocks of flying-machines set out in all directions for the country; and since the fare, even to the most remote points, was hardly more than nominal, there were very few who failed to take advantage of the opportunity to escape."

"In short," commented I, "distance, within certain large limits, no longer existed?"

"Precisely! And now came the second step. It was found that the speed of flight rendered the existence of many large towns, comparatively close to one another, superfluous; and it was suggested that all the manufacturing

---

1892), "Mechanical Flight" (May 1892) and "The Aeroplane" (November 1892). Walker was the owner of the magazine at the time, and is presumably the person to whom Hawthorne had promised the present item; he was also a leading manufacturer of automobiles in the 1890s.

and commercial interests of the nation should be concentrated in a certain limited number of places, the geographical situation of which should be fixed to suit the convenience of the majority. Surveys showed that not more than four of these great centers would be required, and sites were accordingly chosen, two on the sea-coast, eat and west, and two in the interior. In no other part of the continent is there so much as a single village. Every family lives on its own lot of land, averaging about ten acres, and all the old crowding of people together is forever done away with. Each family consists of from five to ten members, who do all their own agricultural work, and make a good deal of their own dry goods and clothing."

"You surprise me," said I. "What time have they left to amuse themselves and cultivate their minds?"

"More than they ever had in the old times," was the reply. "You must make allowances for the spread of invention and discovery during the past century, and also for the greater simplicity of the general mode of life, to which I will refer presently. We have long since done away with servants, and with the laboring classes."

"That servants should have been extirpated does not astonish me," I said, "since I find the rest of the human race still in existence; and it was to be expected that the laboring classes would arrive at a point where the working hours would dwindle to nothing, and the pay increase to anything. But I confess I do find it a little incredible that ladies should have given up shopping; and yet that is the inference your words seem to warrant."

"I doubt if you will find a woman in the country who even knows what shopping means," returned the other, confidently. "It all came about naturally. So long as people herded together in cities, in constant view of one another, the imitative instinct of humanity was constantly stimulated, and that strange form of insanity called fashion was in the ascendant. But with the dispersal of the population, we began to act and think more independently, and each of us fell into the way of wearing such garments as suited us individually, instead of following an example set by some deformed or brainless man or woman in some remote part of the world. Though there is, broadly speaking, a certain uniformity in our male and female costumes, it is the result not of apish imitation, but of the gradual evolution of a dress which is proved to be hygienically and aesthetically the best. There is nothing more to it; and the change is due to the abolition of cities, which, again, is the consequence, as I pointed out, of the invention of human flight. And as shopping was occasioned solely by the demands of fashion, you may now understand why our women know and care nothing about it."[2]

"But what has become of the gregarious instincts of humanity?" I demanded. "I can understand that much is gained in the way of health and independence by your present system of life; but there is an electric sympathy in crowds, of which men, as well as women, are conscious. This ten-acre lot arrangement prevents that altogether, and must lead, I should suppose, to an ever-increasing dullness and lethargy, hostile to intellectual and ethical development. What becomes of music, eloquence, and the drama?"

"Your exception is well taken," said my companion. "Human beings do need the occasional excitement of one another's presence in large numbers; the heights of enthusiasm and conviction would be unattainable without it. At the same time, you must have observed that the habitual dwellers in cities were less sensitive to these stimuli than those who were comparatively unused to them. Habit breeds callousness. The nightly lounge at the theater and the opera, the weekly crowd at church, the parade of the fashionable avenues, the annual thronging to summer watering places, these customs only rendered those who indulged in them insensible to the very benefits they were designed to confer.

"So, also, the endless series of dinners, receptions, balls and routs which dominated what was called society, had the final effect of only boring to death the participants in them. Yet they are in themselves excellent things; the trouble was, that owing to the heaping together of people in inextricable masses, they were carried to an unnatural and intolerable excess. Our new plan of existence has not annihilated the principle of human meetings; it has regulated and modified them, and thereby rendered them fully and invariably effective.

"In addition to the great business centers of which I have told you, there is an equal number of places whereon are built theatres, churches, museums, and great pleasure gardens and halls for amusement and for public meetings of all sorts. At these places, at stated intervals—five or six times a year—the people come together in vast numbers, for purposes of mutual entertainment, information and improvement. After a few days spent in this manner, they separate again, and disperse to their homes. In this

---

[2] Given that *Cosmopolitan* in 1993 had been transformed into a glossy women's fashion magazine, there is a certain unintended irony in its publication of this anticipation.

manner they obtain the very best results of association, without running any risk of overdoing it. Of course, it is the flying-machine that makes such gatherings from all parts of the continent practicable."

"And don't the ladies wear bonnets at these gatherings?" I enquired, somewhat anxiously.

"No one wears either hats or bonnets," replied my informant. "It was discovered about sixty years ago that the hair is a sufficient and natural covering for the head, and nothing else is worn by anyone."

"And where are your government headquarters, and your halls of congress?" I asked.

"Nothing of the kind has existed for many years," was the answer. "In the first place, the scattering of the population radically modified the character of the laws needed for our government; and the absence of municipalities and the difficulty of getting officers to carry out the behests of the law over so vast an extent of country, practically brought legislation to a standstill. But, on the other hand, it was soon discovered that laws were scarcely necessary, and were becoming less so every year. The pauper class was rapidly diminishing—it is now non-existent—because land speculation had been put an end to, and the land was free to whomsoever desired to settle on and improve it. Crimes against property ceased; drunkenness died a natural death, owing to the lack of example and provocation which cities had supplied.

"Social vices diminished for the same reason; and, in short, it appeared that there was little or nothing, in the way of pains and penalties, for the law to do. The separate and independent mode of life adopted by the people taught them how to take care of themselves, and to be just to one another; and the fact that immense improvements in the way of telegraphs and telephones had brought every individual of the nation into immediate and effortless communication with every other, gradually made the government of the people, by the people, for the people, a literal instead of merely a figurative truth.

"We are all under one another's moral supervision; a wrong done this morning on the spot on which we stand, for example, would, before sunset, be known to every man and woman in America, and the wrongdoer would be henceforth marked. Matters of supreme public concern are still discussed, at need, at meetings of the delegates of the nation, and the results are disseminated over the continent, not as commands, but as counsel. Really, however, things run themselves nowadays; insomuch that not more than once or twice in my lifetime has it been found necessary to call a consultation of the delegates."

"But how, in case of war," was my next question, "is not the power and concentration afforded by cities severely missed in such emergencies? And are not meetings of the leading citizens then indispensable, to devise measures for defense and to raise armies?"

"If you will reflect for a moment, I think you will perceive that a war would be a difficult thing to start," said the man of the twentieth century, lifting one eyebrow with an arch expression. "Whom are we to fight against?"

"I don't refer to civil war, of course," said I, "but supposing you were attacked from the other side of the Atlantic?"

"The flying-machine is the universal peace-maker," answered he. "It is true that when it was first invented it was recognized as a most formidable war-engine; and I believe that it was employed for that purpose to some extent, before the close of our century. Battles were fought in the air, and bombs were dropped into cities; no doubt there was a general feeling of helplessness and insecurity. It was easy for a single machine to destroy billions of dollars worth of property and innumerable lives. But the consequence was that the fighting soon came to an end.

"It is always governments, and never peoples, who quarrel; and the latter declined to assist in any further destruction. As soon as there was peace, there ensued an era of travel; everybody had his flying-machine, and there was a general interchange of visits all over the world. This continued for a dozen or twenty years. By that time, political geography had been practically obliterated. I am speaking now of Europe; there was never any difficulty in this country. The nations made personal acquaintance with one another through the individuals composing them; free trade had already become universal, since it was found impracticable to maintain custom-houses in the sky.

"Many persons settled down in what had formerly been 'foreign' countries; by and by, there were no longer any foreigners, things got so mixed up that distinct forms of government became, as I told you, impossible and inoperative. The old world became a huge, informal federation; and although

Europe, Asia, Africa and Polynesia are still, in a sense, separate countries, it is only so far as they are geographically divided from one another. The inevitable consequence of this was the gradual adoption of a common language; and today the inhabitants of the planet are rapidly approximating to the state of a homogeneous people, all of whose social, political and commercial interests are identical. Owing to the unlimited facilities of intercommunication, they are almost as closely united as the members of a family; and you might travel round the globe, and find little in the life, manners and even personal appearance of the inhabitants to remind you that you were remote from your own birthplace."

"Personal appearance!" I repeated. "Surely I should find some modifications in Africa or China, for example?"

"Perhaps, if you are an exceptionally keen ethnologist. Of what blood should you take me to be?"

I looked narrowly at my interlocutor. He was a man of little more than middle height, with a square, compact brow and refined, molded features. The face indicated a justly balanced nature, intellectual, yet not to such a degree as to overpower the emotional. His figure was powerful and active and his bearing graceful. In short, I had seldom seen so handsome and manly a man.

"You are a New Englander," said I, after due deliberation, "of English—I think of Welsh—descent."

He laughed heartily.

"My great-grandparents were unadulterated Esquimaux," he replied. "No, we are pretty well disguised even now, and in another hundred years we shall be quite indistinguishable. But it is only fair to admit that the crossing of the races alone is not sufficient to account for the similarity of type. A new element of vitality, a new spirit, has been infused into the human race; and a change has evidently taken place in the interior physical constitution of the dark races, causing them to end both in form and hue towards the Caucasian standard. It would not be in our present line of discourse to explain to you the causes of this; but you must take into consideration the substantial unity of aim and feeling that now exists throughout the world, and remember that the body is formed by the soul, and is its material expression. But the alliance between physical and spiritual science had been scarcely completed in your day, I think, and these hints may therefore not have much significance for you."

"What you say is nevertheless interesting, and I doubt not it may be valuable," said I, with a bow. "Still, as you say, we are here to talk about the consequences of the flying-machine. Now, after making all allowances for your unquestionable improvements and advantages, it still seems to me that life must be rather a dull affair in these last years of the twentieth century. What novelty or change is there to look forward to? What excitement, what uncertainty or peril have you to anticipate, to brace your nerves and rouse your souls withal? You will soon—if you have not already done so—come to a standstill; there will be nothing left to hope for—and not to hope is to despair.

"My apprehension would be that your civilization will presently begin to retrograde; the old passions and follies of mankind will revive; they will deliberately turn their backs on what you call good, and revert to what you call evil; and a century or two hence the world will be once more a barbarism, and the whole march of improvement will have to begin over again. And to tell you the truth, I would rather live in that age than take my place here now and never feel my pulse quicken at an unforeseen emergency, or strive for eminence, or dread disaster."

"And were our condition what you suppose, I should certainly make the choice that you do," replied my companion, "but you have jumped to conclusions which the facts do not support. The main difference between life now and as it was in your day is that ours is comparatively an interior, and therefore a real and absorbing, life. For the first time in history we have a real human society. You had the imitation—the symbol—but not the true thing itself. You will admit that in a perfectly free state man will inevitably select that environment and those companions with which he feels himself most in sympathy—where he finds himself most at home. Now, the power of flight, combined with the modification of the old political conditions that I have mentioned, gave to man the ability to live where and with whom he would.

"The perfect result could not be attained at once, as it might be in a purely spiritual state; but the tendency was present and the issue was only a question of time. By degrees, the individuals throughout the world who by mind and temperament were suited to one another, found one another out, and chose habitations where they might be readily accessible to one another. Thus, each family lives in the midst of a circle of families composing those who are most nearly at one with it in sentiment and quality, and the intercourse of this group is mainly confined to itself. There is between them perfect and intimate friendship and confidence, and you will easily understand that they must realize the true ideal of society.

"There is no loss, no waste, no aimlessness in their communion; there are a constant stimulus and means of elevation to one another, and their advance in goodness and felicity is more rapid than you can perhaps realize; but you know how human peace and happiness can be retarded by the selfish opposition of every man against his brothers, and you my infer what a transformation would ensue upon a reversal of that attitude."

"I recognize your point; but there must still be a certain sort of monotony in this paradoxical existence. Felicity is good as an occasional indulgence, but as a steady diet it is too relaxing. Misfortunes, griefs and disappointments—we need them just as much as we need salt, and cold weather."

The twentieth century man shook his head and smiled. "Since, as I suppose, you are to return to your own historical epoch upon the conclusion of this interview," said he, "we may agree to differ, for the present, as to the objection that you raise. But when you come back to us again for good, I think you will find our life to be not less arduous and full of vicissitudes than your own.

"This earth will never quite be heaven; there will always be struggle, uncertainty and incompleteness. Nor will you find these less poignant because the plane of activity is a more interior and vital one than you have yet known. As your perceptions become more acute, your emotions more sensitive, and your intellect more comprehensive—as your spirit, in short, learns to master your body—you will enter upon an experience compared with which the most stirring career of old times would seem tame and vulgar. But just as your dog or your horse could not be influenced or inspired by the things which mold and agitate your own life, so you—pardon me— are as yet incapable of appreciating the subtle but mighty forces that educate and purify us. This power of flight, on which our present civilization is conditioned, is, like other material phenomena, an emblem. We are lifted to a higher sphere, and thereby to a perception of truths to which the nineteenth century is yet a stranger."

"It strikes me, sir," said I, "that you have intimated that I, and with me the friends and acquaintances whom I have temporarily left behind in the year 1893, are little better than so many asses. I might brook the personal aspersion on myself; but I can do no less than resent it on the part of those whom I have the honor to represent. I fail to see that further intercourse between us is desirable; but, in bidding you good-day, I may remark that I think a more modest attitude on your part would have been becoming; for you must admit that whatever you and your civilization are is due to me—insomuch that if I had not had this dream you would have had no existence whatever. Yet I am willing to be lenient, and the only retaliation I shall permit myself for your discourtesy is simply to wake up, and thereby relegate you to the nothingness out of which you have been evoked."

# THE DANCING PARTNER

## JEROME K. JEROME

*Jerome K. Jerome (1859–1927) was a British journalist and humorist who helped to promote scientific romance in the pages of* The Idler, *an influential periodical he co-edited with Robert Barr. Both editors contributed items of scientific romance to its pages. Jerome's "The New Utopia" (1891) was, like the preceding work, a response to Edward Bellamy, but is more farcically parodic, in keeping with his usual manner.*

*"The Dancing Partner," which appeared in the March 1893 issue of* The Idler *before being reprinted in* Novel Notes *(1893), is part of a long sequence of stories ultimately inspired by the example of the French maker of automata, Jacques de Vaucanson (1709–1782), whose ingenious mechanical simulacra, constructed to amuse Louis XV's court, became legendary following their demolition. Unsurprisingly, that literary tradition is particularly strong in France, where several notable stories in which anthropomorphic automata fail to substitute adequately for real human beings were produced in the nineteenth century, including the Comte de Villiers de L'Isle Adam's phantasmagorical* L'Ève future *(1886; tr. as* Tomorrow's Eve). *Jerome's version shuns the commonplace motif of mistaken identity, but is deftly cynical in developing its cautionary tale.*

"This story," commenced MacShaughnassy, "comes from Furtwangen, a small town in the Black Forest. There lived here a very wonderful old fellow named Nicholaus Geibel. His business was the making of mechanical toys, at which work he had acquired an almost European reputation. He made rabbits that would emerge from the heart of a cabbage, flop their ears, smooth their whiskers, and disappear again; cats that would wash their faces, and mew so naturally that dogs would mistake them for real cats and fly at them; dolls with phonographs concealed within them, that would raise their hats and say, 'Good morning, how do you do?' and some that would even sing a song.

"But he was something more than a mere mechanic; he was an artist. His work was with him a hobby, almost a passion. His shop was filled with all manner of strange things that never would, or could, be sold—things he had made for the pure love of making them. He had contrived a mechanical donkey that would trot for two hours by means of stored electricity, and trot, too, much faster than the live article, and with less need for exertion on the part of the driver; a bird that would shoot up into the air, fly around in a circle, and drop to earth at the exact spot from where it started; a skeleton that, supported by an upright iron bar, would dance a hornpipe, a life-size lady doll that could play the fiddle, and a gentleman with a hollow inside who could smoke a pipe and drink more lager beer than any three average German students put together, which is saying much.

"Indeed, it was the belief of the town that old Geibel could make a man capable of doing everything that a respectable man need want to do. One day he made a man who did too much, and it came about this way.

"Young Doctor Follen had a baby, and the baby had a birthday. Its first birthday put Doctor Follen's household into somewhat of a flurry, but on the occasion of its second birthday, Mrs. Doctor Follen gave a ball in honor of the event. Old Geibel and his daughter Olga were among the guests.

"During the afternoon of the next day some three or four of Olga's bosom friends, who had been present at the ball, dropped in to have a chat about it. They naturally fell to discussing the men, and to criticizing their dancing. Old Geibel was in the room, but he appeared to be absorbed in his newspaper, and the girls took no notice of him.

"'There seem to be fewer men who can dance at every ball you go to,' said one of the girls.

"'Yes, and don't the ones who can give themselves airs,' said another. 'They make quite a favor of asking you.'

"'And how stupidly they talk,' added a third. 'They always say exactly the same things. "How charming you look tonight." "Do you often go to Vienna? Oh, you should, it's delightful." "What a charming dress you have on." "What a warm day it has been." "Do you like Wagner?" I do wish they'd think of something new.'

" 'Oh, I never mind how they talk,' said a fourth. 'If a man dances well he may be a fool for all I care.'

" 'He generally is,' slipped in a thin girl, rather spitefully.

" 'I go to a ball to dance,' continued the previous speaker, not noticing the interruption. 'All I ask is that he should hold me firmly, take me round steadily, and not get tired before I do.'

" 'A clockwork figure would do the thing for you,' said the girl who had interrupted.

" 'Bravo!' cried one of the others, clapping her hands. 'What a capital idea!'

" 'What's a capital idea?' they asked.

" 'Why, a clockwork dancer, or better still, one that would go by electricity and never run down.'

"The girls took up the idea with enthusiasm.

" 'Oh, what a lovely partner he would make,' said one. 'He would never kick you, or tread on your toes.'

" 'Or tear your dress,' said another.

" 'Or get out of step.'

" 'Or get giddy and lean on you.'

" 'And he would never want to mop his face with his handkerchief. I do hate to see a man do that after every dance.'

" 'And he wouldn't want to spend the whole evening in the supper room.'

" 'Why, with a phonograph inside him to grind out all the stock remarks, you wouldn't be able to tell him from a real man,' said the girl who had first suggested the idea.

" 'Oh yes you would,' said the thin girl. 'He would be so much nicer.'

"Old Geibel had laid down his paper, and was listening with both his ears. On one of the girls glancing in his direction, however, he hurriedly hid himself again behind it.

"After the girls were gone, he went into his workshop, where Olga heard him walking up and down, and every now and then chuckling to himself, and that night he talked to her a good deal about dancing and dancing men, asked what dances were most popular, what steps were gone through, with many other questions bearing on the subject.

"Then for a couple of weeks he kept much to his factory, and was very thoughtful and busy, though prone at unexpected moments to break into a quiet low laugh, as if enjoying a joke that nobody else knew of.

"A month later another ball took place at Furtwangen. On this occasion it was given by old Wenzel, the wealthy timber merchant, to celebrate his niece's betrothal, and Geibel and his daughter were again among the invited.

"When the hour arrived to set out, Olga sought her father. Not finding him in the house, she tapped at the door of his workshop. He appeared in his shirt-sleeves, looking hot but radiant.

"'Don't wait for me,' he said. 'You go on. I'll follow you. I've got something to finish.'

"As she turned to obey he called after her: 'Tell them I'm going to bring a young man with me—such a nice young man, and an excellent dancer. All the girls will like him.' Then he laughed and closed the door.

"Her father generally kept his doings secret from everybody, but she had a pretty shrewd suspicion of what he had been planning, and so, to a certain extent, was able to prepare the guests for what was coming. Anticipation ran high, and the arrival of the famous mechanist was eagerly awaited.

"At length the sound of wheels was heard outside, followed by a great commotion in the passage, and old Wenzel himself, his jolly face red with excitement and suppressed laughter, burst into the room and announced in stentorian tones: 'Herr Geibel—and a friend.'

"Herr Geibel and his 'friend' entered, greeted with shouts of laughter and applause, and advanced to the center of the room.

"'Allow me, ladies and gentlemen,' said Herr Geibel, 'to introduce you to my friend, Lieutenant Fritz. Fritz, my dear fellow, bow to the ladies and gentlemen.'

"Geibel placed his hand encouragingly on Fritz's shoulder, and the Lieutenant bowed low, accompanying the action with a harsh clicking noise in his throat, unpleasantly suggestive of a death-rattle. But that was only a detail.

"'He walks a little stiffly'—Old Geibel took his arm and walked him forward a few steps; he certainly did walk stiffly—'but then, walking is not his forte. He is essentially a dancing man. I have only been able to teach him the waltz as yet, but at that he is faultless. Come, which of you ladies may I introduce him to as a partner? He keeps perfect time, he never gets tired, he won't kick you or tread on your toes; he will hold you as firmly as you like, and go as quickly or slowly as you please; he never gets giddy; and he is full of conversation. Come, speak up for yourself, my boy.'

"The old gentleman twisted one of the buttons at the back of his coat, and immediately Fritz opened his mouth, and in thin tones that appeared to proceed from the back of his head, remarked suddenly: 'May I have the pleasure?' and then shut his mouth again with a snap.

"That Lieutenant Fritz had made a strong impression on the company was undoubted, yet none of the girls seemed inclined to dance with him. They looked askance at his waxen face, with its staring eyes and fixed smile, and shuddered. At last Old Geibel came to the girl who had conceived the idea.

"'It is your own suggestion, carried out to the letter,' said Geibel. 'An electric dancer. You owe it to the gentleman to give him a trial.'

"She was a bright saucy little girl, fond of a frolic. Her host added his entreaties, and she consented.

"Herr Geibel fixed the figure to her. Its right arm was screwed round her waist, and held her firmly; its delicately jointed left hand was made to fasten upon her right. The old toymaker showed her how to regulate its speed, and how to stop it, and release herself.

"'It will take you round in a complete circle,' he explained; 'be careful that no one knocks against you, and alters its course.'

"The music struck up. Old Geibel put the current in motion, and Annette and her strange partner began to dance.

"For a while everyone stood watching them. The figure performed its purpose admirably. Keeping perfect time and step, and holding its little partner tight clasped in an unyielding embrace, it revolved steadily, pouring forth at the same time a constant flow of squeaky conversation, broken by brief intervals of grinding silence.

"'How charming you are looking tonight,' it remarked in its thin, faraway voice. 'What a lovely day it has been. Do you like dancing? How well our steps agree. You will give me another, won't you? Oh, don't be so cruel. What a charming gown you have on. Isn't waltzing delightful? I could go on dancing for ever—with you. Have you had supper?'

"As she grew more familiar with the uncanny creature, the girl's nervousness wore off, and she entered into the fun of the thing.

" 'Oh, he's just lovely,' she cried, laughing. 'I could go on dancing with him all my life.'

"Couple after couple now joined them, and soon all the dancers in the room were whirling around behind them. Nicholaus Geibel stood looking on, beaming with childish delight at his success.

"Old Wenzel approached him, and whispered something in his ear. Geibel laughed and nodded, and the two worked their way quietly toward the door.

" 'This is the young people's house tonight,' said Wenzel, as soon as they were outside. 'You and I will have a quiet pipe and a glass of hock over in the counting-house.'

"Meanwhile, the dancing grew more fast and furious. Little Annette loosened the screw regulating her partner's rate of progress, and the figure flew round with her swifter and swifter. Couple after couple dropped out exhausted, but they only went the faster, till at length they remained dancing alone.

"Madder and madder became the waltz. The music lagged behind; the musicians, unable to keep pace, ceased, and sat staring. The younger guests applauded, but the older faces began to grow anxious.

" 'Hadn't you better stop, dear?' said one of the women. 'You'll make yourself so tired.'

"But Annette did not answer.

" 'I believe she's fainted,' cried out a girl who had caught sight of her face as it swept by.

"One of the men sprang forward and clutched at the figure, but its impetus threw him down on the floor, where its steel-cased feet laid bare his cheek. The thing evidently did not intend to part with its prize so easily.

"Had anyone retained a cool head, the figure, one cannot help thinking, might easily have been stopped. Two or three men acting in concert might have lifted it bodily off the floor, or have jammed it into a corner. But few human heads are capable of remaining cool under excitement. Those who are not present think how stupid must have been those who were; those who are reflect afterwards how simple it would have been to do this, that, or the other, if only they had thought of it at the time.

"The women grew hysterical. The men shouted contradictory directions to one another. Two of them made a bungling rush at the figure, which had the result of forcing it out of its orbit at the center of the room and sending it crashing against the walls and furniture. A stream of blood showed itself down the girl's white frock, and followed her along the floor. The affair was becoming horrible. The women rushed screaming from the room. The men followed them.

"One sensible suggestion was made: 'Find Geibel—fetch Geibel!'

"No one had noticed him leave the room; no one knew where he was. A party went in search of him. The others, too unnerved to go back into the ballroom, crowded outside the door and listened. They could hear the steady whir of the wheels upon the polished floor as the thing spun round and round; the dull thud as every now and again it dashed itself and its burden against some opposing object and ricocheted off in a new direction.

"And everlastingly it talked on in that ghostly voice, repeating over and over the same formula. 'How charming you look tonight. What a lovely day it has been. Oh, don't be so cruel. I could go on dancing for ever—with you. Have you had supper?'

"Of course they sought Geibel everywhere but where he was. They looked in every room in the house, then they rushed off in a body to his own place, and spent precious minutes waking up his deaf old housekeeper. At last it occurred to one of the party that Wenzel was missing also, and then the idea of the counting-house across the yard presented itself to them, and there they found him.

"He rose up, very pale, and followed them, and he and old Wenzel forced their way through the crowd of guests gathered outside, and entered the room, and locked the door behind them.

"From within there came the muffled sound of low voices and quick steps, followed by a confused scuffling noise, then silence, then the low voices again.

"After a time the door opened, and those near it pressed forward to enter, but old Wenzel's broad head and shoulders barred the way.

"'I want you—and you, Bekler,' he said addressing a couple of elder men. His voice was calm, but his face was deadly white. 'The rest of you, please go—get the women away as quickly as you can.'

"From that day on, old Nicholaus Geibel confined himself to the making of mechanical rabbits, and cats that mewed and washed their faces."

# THE CONQUEROR OF DEATH

## CAMILLE DEBANS

*Camille Debans (1833–1910) was a French journalist and writer of popular fiction who wrote numerous stories about steam locomotives and natural catastrophes that have marginal elements of scientific romance, but ventured more wholeheartedly into the subgenre in the future war story* Les Malheurs de John Bull *(1884; tr. as* The Misfortunes of John Bull*).* Boissat chimiste *(1892; tr. as* Boissat the Chemist*) is a Berthoudesque study of the scientific mind as well as a crime story.*

*"Le Vainqueur de la mort," published in the popular science magazine* La Science Illustré *in 1895, was the most extravagant of the several stories that Debans contributed to that magazine's feuilleton slot, which used "roman scientifique" as a rubric without succeeding in establishing it more widely as a generic term. It reflects the bad press that hypothetical technologies of longevity generally receive in works of fiction.*

In the early days of January 1999 the Chicago *Tribune* elected to celebrate solemnly the centenary of a discovery that had turned the world upside-down and produced ineradicable benefits, after having nearly brought about the most frightful catastrophes. The article in the American newspaper succinctly recalled the facts. Let us limit ourselves to reproducing the essential details.

You shall see, by virtue of the events that are recalled therein, and especially by virtue of the surprising conclusion, that it is worth the trouble.

\*

The entire world, the *Tribune* said, ought to honor magnificently the man who, having dreamed of substituting himself for God in order to govern at his whim the rain, storms and fine weather, had the glory of finding the formula of his dream and putting it into practice. If statues are raised to the heroes of official massacres, what should be done for a man who endowed humankind with such a fecund prodigy?

It was on 24 June 1899, at four o'clock in the afternoon, that W. Benjamin Smithson created, in a plain on the Mexican frontier where no drop of rain had ever fallen, veritable cataracts in a serene sky, and became by virtue of that fact the dispenser of the abundance of harvests and the regulator of the Earth's wealth.

The enclosure in which the inventor of genius had to operate was in the middle of a plain, at the very place where a considerable city now stands: Smithstown, so named for the glory of Sir Benjamin. In those days, the country was desolate in its aridity. The immense crowd of people that had come to witness the meteorological phenomenon was primarily composed of local inhabitants for whom it represented sudden fortune, and who had never grown any grain at all.

A cannon shot announced the beginning of the experiment. There were as many mockers as believers, and more. Two balloons with a capacity of about 6,000 cubic meters, one filled with oxygen and the other with hydrogen, rose slowly into the air, retained by powerful cables that only allowed them to rise up to a height of eight hundred meters. Beneath each aerostat there was a large gondola as voluminous as the balloon itself, oblong in shape and containing heaped-up bladders full to bursting, also containing hydrogen and oxygen, collected from the clouds of Illinois.

The two taffeta globs were linked together by a metallic device forming part of the apparatus, the principal wire of which unwound as the balloons drew away from the ground and maintained them in communication with a powerful electric pile installed in a vast cavern constructed for the purpose.

Floating with a serene majesty in the placid atmosphere—the sky was an implacable blue—the two aerial monsters rose up slowly. An embryonic sentiment of anxiety gripped bosoms very lightly. Five minutes before, the quips had been raining.

"That's all that'll rain!" said one ferocious joker.

Now that skepticism had evaporated, the imposing allure of the apparatus was intimidating the majority of the spectators.

Suddenly, the balloons stopped rising. The quadruple black mass stood out, bizarrely, against the intense azure of the sky. The chronometers marked four eleven and forty-three seconds—that historic detail is indisputable. W. Benjamin Smithson disappeared into the cavern from which the denouement would depart. There, he took hold of a little wheel, which he subjected to a dozen rapid turns, and then ran out to watch the aerostats. Two seconds went by; an enormous spark flashed, zigzagging between the ripping balloons, and a veritable clap of thunder was heard. Smithson maneuvered a little lever, and the nacelles burst in their turn.

Cruel black vapors formed, in the midst of which electricity raged. Lightning fell on a group of carriages and killed three people. Too bad! Then the cloud that had just formed by virtue of the condensation of the gas thickened so furiously and extended so rapidly toward all the points of the horizon that a fearful panic took hold of the crowd. People started fleeing in all directions, uttering screams of terror and desperate clamors.

"That man is the Devil himself!" howled the most terrorized.

Soon, large raindrops began to moisten the earth. The local inhabitants, ignorant of the use of umbrellas, ran away more rapidly than ever. Only a few fearless Yankees remained, mouths open, looking upwards, marveling at the miracle they were witnessing. And the miracle was completed, for within a few minutes, the rainfall had taken on the proportions of a tropical downpour.

And while the plain drank those benevolent sheets of water, Benjamin Smithson, opening a trap-door contrived in the vault of his cellar, sent into the air, to vertiginous heights, a series of bladders similar to the ones in the nacelles, propelled by powerful helices, which carried them up to the clouds, where they burst in their turn. The rumble of thunder was heard, and the rain increased in intensity.

The sensation that Sir Benjamin's success caused is easily imaginable. In a matter of hours, the entire world had heard the amazing news. Old Europe thought at first that it was a gigantic hoax, but explanatory details and extracts from newspapers were arriving by the minute, and it was necessary to yield to the evidence.

All these things are, of course, familiar to us today, and appear so simple, that it is as if they always existed. We regulate the weather in accordance with the general interest. The sky has no more caprices, and, in consequence, nor has the earth; its fecundity is regulated. At any rate, America went mad for a week. All the most improbable things one can imagine were done from New York to San Francisco and from the St. Lawrence to the Mississippi in honor of Smithson, but still fell short of what that sublime genius deserved. European governments heaped him with honors. The inventor was celebrated in music, painting, sculpture, verse and prose.

Then, there was a sudden urgent alarm. In all the countries that had employed the Smithson method, conflicts of interest, and even of fantasy, were produced. Some people wanted rain and others wanted fine weather for the same day, some having need of water and others of sunshine. Civil wars broke out in weakly-governed countries. But those are no longer anything but memories. A long time ago, the executive powers took charge of the direction of the weather, and there are very few countries in which that management does not function to general satisfaction.

Sir Benjamin Smithson is, therefore, for all humankind, without distinction of races, a unique, incomparable benefactor. We would like the United States to celebrate the hundredth anniversary of his discovery in a fashion that will dazzle the world, and we are expressing the wish that the festivals that we are proposing will be the occasion for new benefits a hundred times more extraordinary, which W. Benjamin Smithson doubtless has in reserve for us after a hundred years.

For W. Benjamin Smithson—this might perhaps stupefy centuries to come or appear to be the most natural thing in the world, according to circumstances—is now a hundred and thirty-one years old. Everyone in the world knows that, but only those of his compatriots who know him personally know that he does not have the appearance of an old man, and that Mrs. Smithson, who became his wife thirty-nine years ago, appears today to be just as youthful, beautiful and as obviously young as on her wedding day.

We therefore dare to say, out loud, what has been repeated for forty years in American drawing rooms. W. Benjamin Smithson, after having discovered fifty secrets that have profited his fellow men, must have found, a long time ago, a means of conquering death and of maintaining himself in a state of eternal youth and virility. It is no longer permissible to doubt it. His worthy companion has, thanks to him, conserved the delightful figure and mental vigor that she had at twenty. Evidently, he knows the great secret. We affirm that with a profound conviction, with an emotion that makes all our muscles quiver and our souls float in the serene regions of a enormous hope. He knows the great secret!

But as he does not have the right to keep it for himself alone, we are convinced that the prodigious scientist wanted to wait for the moment of the centenary to which we have summoned all peoples in order to cause a frisson in human life that will endow it permanently with the most precious gift of all.

It is, therefore, on 24 June 1999 that America will have the immense pride of inaugurating, by virtue of the genius of its most illustrious son, the new era in which people will be able to say: "I shall no longer die."

\*

Needless to say, this article was translated into all languages and commented on in every country. As with the power of making rain or good weather at will, a hundred years before, some people remained skeptical; others, secretly animated by a regrettable desire not to restore their souls to the Creator, did not hesitate to believe the promises of the American journalist.

The centenary, therefore, was awaited with a furious impatience. As the psychological moment approached, the Earth, from pole to pole, was gripped by a divine shiver—for no one was any longer incredulous.

On the eve of the great day, however, at the moment when humankind had nothing more to do than reach out a hand to see the supreme conquest fall into it, the joy, instead of turning to delirium, became anxiety, anguish and fever. What if, at the last moment, the certainty was acquired that the American newspapers were joking at the expense of the two worlds?

But no—W. Benjamin Smithson really was a hundred and thirty-one years old. He had been seen, in person, in Paris and London in 1992. He looked forty-five. His wife was a sexagenarian; nothing was more certain— but ladies who had been her childhood friends, already wrinkled and decrepit, affirmed that Mrs. Smithson had not changed since the third year of her marriage. Thus, the great secret had been found.

"Hosannah!" sang the most convinced. "We shall be immortal!"

But the centenary celebrations, although worthy of the American people and the man they wanted to honor, went by without Sir Benjamin having spoken. Over the entire surface of the globe there was a disappointment that took on all the characteristics of despair.

In Europe, the disillusionment was so rude that the American journalists were held accountable for it; there was talk of making them expiate, by revolutionary means, the fraud of which they appeared to be the impudent inventors. But they defended themselves energetically. The Chicago *Tribune* even took the lead—as they say on racecourses—in crying more loudly than the rest and putting all the blame for what had happened on W. Benjamin Smithson himself. So when, all over the world, it was known that the American was refusing to prolong the lives of his fellows, sheltering his conduct under the pretext of philosophical scruples, an immense clamor of protest rose up from summits and abysms.

"What scandal! What infamy!" came the cry, from all directions. "What! Here's a man who holds our immortality in his hands, and he has the right to dispose of it as he wishes, even to deprive us of it if such is his pleasure? A thousand times no! It's necessary to force him, if you please. Let him be seized. A deep dungeon and, if necessary, torture in his honor, until he talks."

The most illustrious scientists wrote to Benjamin Smithson to demonstrate to him the meanness of his conduct. Some spoke of his duty, others of his glory, some of the rights of humankind, others of the will of God that had chosen him, Smithson, to bring the supreme news to his fellows. . . .

A few, seeing that the objurgations were having absolutely no effect, went as far as insult, and finally, between the two extremes, there were vulgar reasoners who claimed that Smithson, driven by an extravagant ambition, wanted to be alone, with his wife, in possessing eternal youth, in order to hold the nations in a moral domination a hundred times worse than the most ferocious despotism.

In brief, people competed in irrationality. The entire world had lost its head, and yet, in sum, no one even knew whether the American scientist really possessed the talisman of long life.

The majority of European newspapers organized a conference in order to clarify that vital question. In the very first session, someone came forward to observe that a newspaper article is not an article of faith—even if the newspaper was from Chicago. No specific fact proved that Smithson was in possession of the secret that was attributed to him—in consequence of which, the conference ought to address itself to Smithson himself, in order to ask him whether there was any truth in the public rumor.

A letter was drafted in that same session, and three members of the conference were delegated to leave for America.

Smithson received them in the palace by means of which grateful agriculturalists had paid tribute to him a hundred years earlier, which was known as the Red House.

"Gentlemen," he said to them, without the slightest prevarication, "it's true. So, the time has come when it's necessary for me to explain myself. Yes, I have discovered the art of conserving youth—or, to put it better, of arresting the physical disorders produced by time on the human organism and, up to a point, of giving to those who employ my procedure an unalterable health. I was forty-eight years old when I made the discovery, and you can see that I haven't aged since. Mrs. Smithson is over sixty; I shall have the honor of introducing you to her, and you will take her for a young woman. But don't entertain any irrational illusions. I don't boast of having conquered death. In a brawl, in a battle, in consequence of a fall, people can die as before if they fracture their skulls, if they receive a rifle-bullet or a dagger in the heart. . . ."

Smithson was interrupted by one of the three delegates.

"We shall not be so indiscreet as to ask for more details," he said. "Without judging your discovery *a priori*, we assume that it has not modified the economy of the human organism."

"Indeed; it only consolidates it."

"How long do you think that an individual might live by faithfully following your method and prescriptions?"

"I don't know—but I wouldn't be surprised if he could live for ten centuries, if not forever."

A smile slid over the lips of the three delegates, reflecting their interior joy. They had no doubt, after the prodigious Yankee's first declaration, that they would be returning to Europe with the secret of eternal youth.

"Well, Monsieur," said the most eloquent of the three, "we have come respectfully, in the names of the conference assembled in Paris, and, in consequence, on behalf of the City of Light in its entirety—in a word, on behalf of the whole world—to ask you to put the seal on your immense glory by finally unveiling the marvelous secret that will render us the terrestrial paradise. . . ."

Benjamin Smithson replied, very gravely: "I'm flattered, Messieurs, that you have crossed the ocean to take that step, and I've given instructions that your stay should be made as agreeable as poor Americans can contrive—but with regard to my secret, I shall profit from our embassy to inform the world that I have decided never to reveal it."

As the three Frenchmen remained mute with stupefaction, Smithson went on: "After profound meditation, I have acquired the conviction that the indefinite prolongation of human existence would bring about, in a short time, an incomparable disaster more deadly than the benefit would be profitable. I shall therefore say nothing. Not because I want to keep the joy of living for myself alone—for, on the contrary, I have decided to suspend, at a given time, the measures to which I owe my incomparable old age. Whatever his genius might be, a human cannot encroach without folly on the attributions of God."

"What!" cried Pierre Seigreval, the most eminent of the three delegates. "You refuse . . . !"

"Believe that I'm very sorry—but you'll admit that, during my long life, when I have not lost the slightest fraction of my intellectual faculties, I have acquired an experience double that of other humans."

"So?"

"What stands out most clearly from what I have learned," Smithson continued, "is that progress, whatever it might be, does not bring in its development any element of true happiness for humankind. The causes of human happiness: the passions, egotism, vices—in a word, moral maladies—have not changed."

"Oh!" said Seigreval, scandalized. "What you are saying is blasphemy."

"No," the old man replied, smiling. "How can you not see that truth? Evil people would have hundreds of years to wreak harm with the same fury. The good would be subject to their evildoing indefinitely. I tell you that it would be the triumph of malefactors and ingrates."

Having said that, Smithson made the gesture of someone who will not consent to hear further argument; he bowed gently, opening his arms in the fashion of Anglican pastors.

The three journalists protested in vain; he insisted on the unshakability of his resolution. No argument succeeded in influencing him, in making him soften the rigor of his sentence. Soon, he even changed the subject and invited his visitors to dinner.

It was as they were taking their places at the table that he introduced his wife to the delegates. Mrs. Smithson was a petite blonde woman with an amiable face. Her lips were incredibly fresh, her eyes extraordinarily limpid; one might have thought that she was eighteen.

Pierre Seigreval wondered whether he and his companions might be being taken for a ride. Anyone would have been able to believe, like him, that it was all an act, a comedy played for the simple objective of deception. During the meal, however, Mr. and Mrs. Smithson described events that they had witnessed with their own eyes fifty years earlier, and in a tone so sincere that their good faith could not be doubted.

Before leaving to return to France, the delegates made one last attempt.

"At least give us another reason," they said. "Just one."

"Gladly," said Smithson. "Suppose, then, that I deliver my secret to humankind. From that moment on, people no longer die, do they? Now, everyone knows that millions of people are born every year. A simple arithmetical calculation will then suffice to identify the precise moment at which the terrestrial globe would be too small to contain its immortal people. Then what will happen? The strong will do what they can to preserve their place; the weak will band together to defend themselves; there will be war—a universal, internecine war. People will kill one another, and my secret will no longer have any value. All the more reason to renounce it immediately."

What Smithson said was wisdom itself, but it did not succeed in convincing the delegates. They belonged to the species of deaf individuals who do not want to hear. Besides which, all their faculties were concentrated on one unique objective: to extract the divine secret from the American scientist. After that, they would see. . . .

So, when they left the Red House to return to New York, the French journalists were more determined than ever not to abandon the game. At the railway station, a crowd was waiting for them, avid to know the results of their mission. Needless to say, they were all in accord in deploring Sir Benjamin's culpable obstinacy.

"He'll give in eventually, though," said the director of the American *Times*.

"He won't give in," replied Seigreval.

"Well, he has to give in," said a third person, with singular conviction.

There really never was such a burning question for the entire world. Since people had begun to hope for that almost complete attenuation of death, there had been no other topic of conversation, from one end of the Earth to the other. Old people, middle-aged people and the sick could not contain their impatience. They waited hour by hour for the news to arrive. Those who felt themselves close to falling into the great darkness of the tomb, those of whom it was said "He won't last the week," gripped by anguish, sought news incessantly of the state of the negotiations. More than one mother, leaning over the cradle of her doomed child, demanded the miracle of which Smithson was capable—and who can tell whether it might not have been obtained from him by sending five or six desperate mothers as delegates?

When it was learned that Smithson was determinedly refusing to re-veal his secret, there was a perfectly comprehensible explosion of anger. Meetings were organized everywhere; millions of indignant protesters con-demned the conduct of the famous inventor without reserve.

It did not take long for them to be driven to extremes. What! There is a man who can prevent us from dying, and who is refusing to give us the su-preme gift of unscathed life? But he does not have the right to rob us of that part of our heritage! It is necessary to force him, even if we have to inflict torture upon him to do so.

The most furious proposed locking Smithson up until he had responded to the world's demand.

But nothing prevailed against the obstinacy of the Yankee, to such an extent that the nations, in accordance with the customary course of events, became used to that disappointment, which was transformed into a vague hope. People continued to die. Disasters and wars occurred. People occu-pied themselves with other things, and the years went by, slow and exqui-site for the young, rapid and ingrate for the mature and the old.

Smithson was still alive, and his wife too. Neither of them fell into de-crepitude. Even better, the perpetual scientist, as he was now called, em-ployed his genius—the greatest that had ever honored the human race—in performing new miracles, inventing improbable machines or processes.

Thanks to him, aerial transport became commonplace. For the old bal-loons, which no one had ever succeeded in steering, he substituted gigantic aeroplanes in the form of birds, to which electric piles of enormous power but small volume gave movement and life. To those who preferred some-thing more rapid to that still rather slow means of locomotion—it took eight hours to go from Paris to New York—he offered a submarine tunnel, in which the trains traveled at the vertiginous speed of postal communications in pneumatic tubes. In fifteen minutes, passengers who embarked at a station in New York were disembarking in the capital of France, on what was once the site of Les Halles.

Humankind, weary of so many marvels, no longer admired them. The means of production were so powerful that the workers, once so hasty to complain through the mouths of orators at public meetings, only worked for two hours a day. Work had become a distraction, a need, which caused Smithson to reflect, remembering the noisy demands of old, the excessive programs now fallen into profound forgetfulness.

In the year 2073 he departed in a submarine, as a philosopher desirous of clarifying the mystery of the oceans, those of the land being almost entirely known. He admired the vegetation and the fauna of the submarine depths, and, after a few pauses in the most interesting locations, he landed in the vicinity of Bordeaux, where he was welcomed with all the demonstrations of crazed enthusiasm.

But the man was blasé with regard to honors. On the other hand, there was in that triumph, contrived by a slightly intoxicated crowd, something other than recognition. The cunning were trying to daze Smithson, to cover him with garlands, to conquer him so completely, in fact, that he would finally consent to release the secret of long life.

No man was ever subjected to such a diet of flattery and courteous temptation. For more than three months he was not allowed any rest. The Head of State visited him with great ostentation, as if he were the most powerful sovereign in the world. The Académie des Sciences offered him its homage in an extraordinary session, held outside the Institut in the old Galerie des Machines[1] on the Champ-de-Mars, which proved to be too small to contain a crowd avid to learn how death might be defeated. Smithson was proclaimed by acclamation the honorary president of all the scientific societies in the world. He was carried in triumph to his armchair. Then the most eloquent voice in Paris made a speech in which, after having heard himself compared to a god, he was invited to put an end to mortal anguish by revealing the mystery of his life.

---

[1] The Galerie des Machines, a huge pavilion made of iron, steel and glass, was originally constructed as the Palais des Machines for the 1889 Exposition Universelle. When the exhibition ended, however, it was allowed to remain in place; it was used again for the 1900 Exposition, and then became a velodrome, but was eventually demolished in 1910.

He smiled impenetrably.

The orator, doubtless unfamiliar with that smile, which the delegates of the 1999 conference had seen flourish on the Yankee's lips, imagined that he had just caused conviction to enter into the softened spirit of the old man. He thought that by accumulating victorious arguments, he might strike the decisive blow, and launched forth into an admirable oration. Nothing more splendidly persuasive had ever been heard, anywhere, at any time. No one in the audience doubted that the advocate had won humankind's case.

Smithson rose to his feet. A tremor ran through the immense hall like a strange breeze. It was the fever of joy. People held their breath.

The scientist opened his mouth. There was an incredible silence, as if there were not a single one among the forty thousand people there who was not already counting on their relative eternity.

"Messieurs et Mesdames," he said, in excellent French, "I thank you for the welcome that you have given me, which far surpasses my humble merit. . . ."

And, continuing in that fashion, he responded to the compliments and flatteries that had been lavished upon him. He was eloquent, gracious and exquisite in his turn—but about his secret, there was not a word. The session ended without his having made any promise. Anger and disappointment might perhaps have been about to provoke some regrettable manifestation, and disquieting murmurs were already rumbling among certain groups.

Fortunately, skillful clamors of the lower orders circulated the suggestion that Smithson could not decently explain the affair to such an audience. Who could tell how long it might take him? Besides which, it was probably one of the most arduous problems of esoteric science, and no one would understand it. It was necessary to wait.

They did not, however, renounce the quest to make him confess. And as all the maneuvers had proved vain, they took advantage of a further celebration of which he was the hero to put him brutally in the necessity of replying. This time, he consented to do so.

"What you are asking," he said, "would be a hundred times worse than the death from which you want to be liberated. Take the trouble to look around you. By prolonging life you would be perpetuating vice, moral suffering, nameless unhappiness. Believe me, since I am the only man in a position to enlighten you on the matter, indefinite life—which is almost good as it is—would be a cruel torture. I won't tell you that a person would become blasé about everything and would become, after two or three hundred years, a stranger in the midst of younger generations, as old people between ninety and a hundred already are in many cases. That is obvious. But think about what one would become in the midst of unforgiving hatreds. Imagine what ingratitude alone would make of the unfortunate. If I could speak, you would know that I am a frightful example of that—but let's pass on

"Can you see drunkards, gamblers and malefactors renewing their crimes and infamies incessantly, sowing dolor and despair around them for centuries? Imagine certain spouses bound together forever—what am I saying, forever? Where are those who could live together for a hundred and fifty years? Once again, God has made things well. If I had not been frightened by what I foresaw, do you think that I would have hesitated for a moment to make my fellows happy, for whom I have toiled with such courage and obstinacy? Interrogate all those who are listening to me and ask them whether they would be delighted if three-quarters of their friends were immortal, and listen to their reply. And their relatives—that would be something else entirely.

"Oh, you can be sure that I've been on the point of saying everything a hundred times over, for the sake of a little peace—but a hundred times over, too, a secret voice had encouraged me to silence, and I have persisted in it. War, theft, pillage, and internecine massacres are formidable evils. It would not require two centuries, I repeat—and this is perhaps the hundredth time—for humankind, overcrowded, to arrive at those extremities, for want of room on this little round ball that is narrower than perhaps you believe."

He spoke thus for another hour, and concluded by saying: "If I gave in, Messieurs, in a very short time, there would be no maledictions that would not be heaped upon my name and my person."

This time, there was an explosion of fury. The sage Yankee was insulted publicly. Newspapers published abominable diatribes against him. His caricature could be seen at every street-corner, accompanied by wounding captions.

"It's a practical joke," said the most earnest individuals, "and he hasn't lived for as long as people say. The Americans have deceived us in order to poke fun at Europe. If he had the power of which he boasts, would he hesitate? We ought to expel him shamefully."

And they provoked one another to lose their heads. It would not have taken much to pass from insults to acts of violence. Oh, if they had known how near the man, shaken in his resistance, had come to revealing everything! But when he saw that overflow of rage, he contented himself with shrugging his shoulders and murmuring: "There couldn't be any better justification of my resistance."

Before leaving Paris, he had the generosity to make a further gift to humankind, in the form of an inoffensive substance that suppressed almost all pain in all cases of physical suffering. After which he set off for America, and returned to his fatherland, where he was received almost as an enemy.

There, objurgations degenerated into insults. He and his wife were obliged to go into hiding, so to speak. Their dear children and their adorable grandchildren were subjected to base persecution.

Poor Smithson, desolate, sometimes said to his wife: "Who knows whether I might not be wrong. I have a strong temptation to give them what they want, and so much the worse for them."

One day, he saw one of his great-grand-daughters arrive at the Red House, carrying her only son in her arms, devoured by fever. She threw herself down at his knees, in tears, begging him, imploring him to save her child. Eventually she lay down at his feet, affirming that she would not get up again unless he rendered life to the suffering child.

How could he resist such a plea? He gave in. Smithson made the child drink a few drops of a golden liquid—and the mother, mad with joy, saw the fruit of her loins returned to life. . . .

From that moment on, the perpetual scientist became less obstinate in his intransigence. The second centenary of his discovery of weather control drew near. He began to debate with himself as to whether, on that occasion, he ought not to yield.

That did not prevent him from contriving new marvels.

Thanks to the progress he made in telescopy, the great American brought the planets so close that it was possible to confirm the plurality of inhabited worlds. He pushed his irrefutable demonstrations far enough to establish that the worlds nearer to the sun sheltered beings more intelligent and more civilized than those of distant worlds. He was able to boast of establishing communication between Mars, Mercury and Earth.

But all that left people cold; they still wanted to know the great secret. "That's not what we're asking of you."

In the meantime, he imagined a thousand improvements. He made a garden of the entire Earth. Unfortunately, humankind was no better. There were always further demands on the part of the human species. In many places, now, civil discord broke out in the matter of the weather. Some wanted rain, others serene skies. They tore one another limb from limb over that. On the other hand, nations had rapidly transformed aeroplanes into weapons of war. Frightful aerial battles took place in which the victors and the vanquished alike were almost certain to perish. These events caused him to despair. Extreme civilization seemed to be bringing humankind ever closer to black barbarism.

Human beings were scarcely obliged to work, technology having substituted for manual labor almost everywhere, but they were no happier. Everyone had too much time to think, to criticize, to desire enviously. The poor in spirit wanted to rise to the highest rank. The vicious demanded to share out the world to the detriment of the humble and the peaceful.

And yet, Smithson was still waiting for the great celebration that he assumed would be offered him in order to give his fellows the supreme benefit. . . .

This time, however, there was no question of any such thing. The Americans, like everyone else, redoubled their acrimony against the scientist. At the moment when he was counting on a triumphant ovation, there was an upsurge of insults and sarcasm. With bloody unanimity, as if they had been driven by blind destiny, people competed in dragging him into ignominy. It went as far as threats. His house was besieged. Inventions were demanded of him to meet all needs, and the satisfaction of all whims.

"How right I was!" he said, frightened.

And on 24 June 2100, when only three people came to compliment him on his anniversary, Smithson and his wife decided that they would stop drinking the elixir of life.

Within two days they aged through all the time that they had stolen from nature, and died disillusioned, without regret.

# THE STAR

## H. G. WELLS

*H. G. Wells (1866–1946) became, as the general introduction explains and details, the definitive model of British scientific romance, mapping the scope of its themes in the articles, short stories and novels he published between 1893 and 1901; the work in question was also influential in America and France, although writers in both those nations adapted his inspiration to their own context and purposes. Although Wells then focused his efforts on becoming a "serious" writer intent on not only mapping the likely course of the future but tempting to influence it politically, it is for his early scientific romances that he is principally remembered, and in them that his genius principally resides.*

*"The Star," first published in the Christmas number of* The Graphic, *dated 1897, although actually published in December 1896, is not typical of the usual narrative method of Wells's short fiction, adopting a more distanced viewpoint in order to address a theme similar to that of Poe's "The Conversation of Eiros and Charmion." The story is, however, a stylishly laconic tour de force, and one of the key works of the genre.*

It was on the first day of the New Year that the announcement was made, almost simultaneously from three observatories, that the moon of the planet Neptune,[1] the outermost of all the planets that wheel about the sun, had become very erratic. Ogilvy had already called attention to a suspected

---

[1] Triton, the largest satellite of Neptune, was discovered a few days after the planet itself, in 1846, but the second-largest, Nereid, was only discovered in 1949, so Wells only knew of one.

retardation in its velocity in December. Such a piece of news was scarcely calculated to interest a world the greater portion of whose inhabitants were unaware of the existence of the planet Neptune, nor outside the astronomical profession did the subsequent discovery of a faint speck of light in the region of the perturbed planet cause any great excitement. Scientific people, however, found the intelligence remarkable enough, even before it became known that the new body was rapidly growing larger and brighter, that its motion was quite different from the orderly progress of the planets, and that the deflection of Neptune and its satellite was becoming now of an unprecedented kind.

Few people without a training in science can realize the huge isolation of the solar system. The sun with its specks of planets, its dust of planetoids, and its impalpable comets, swims in a vacant immensity that almost defeats the imagination. Beyond the orbit of Neptune there is space, vacant so far as human observation has penetrated, without warmth or light or sound, blank emptiness, for twenty million times a million miles. That is the smallest estimate of the distance to be traversed before the very nearest of the stars is attained. And, saving a few comets more substantial than the thinnest flame, no matter had ever to human knowledge crossed the gulf of space, until early in the twentieth century this strange wanderer appeared. A vast mass of matter it was, bulky, heavy, rushing without warning out of the black mystery of the sky into the radiance of the sun. By the second day it was clearly visible to any decent instrument, as a speck with a barely sensible diameter, in the constellation Leo near Regulus. In a little while an opera glass could attain it.

On the third day of the new year the newspaper readers of two hemispheres were made aware for the first time of the real importance of this unusual apparition in the heavens. "A Planetary Collision," one London paper headed the news, and proclaimed Duhaine's opinion that this strange new planet would probably collide with Neptune. The leader writers enlarged upon the topic; so that in most of the capitals of the world, on January 3rd, there was an expectation, however vague, of some imminent phenomenon in the sky; and as the night followed the sunset round the globe, thousands of men turned their eyes skyward to see—the old familiar stars just as they had always been.

Until it was dawn in London and Pollux setting and the stars overhead grown pale. The Winter's dawn it was, a sickly filtering accumulation of daylight, and the light of gas and candles shone yellow in the windows to show where people were astir. But the yawning policeman saw the thing, the busy crowds in the markets stopped agape, workmen going to their work betimes, milkmen, the drivers of news-carts, dissipation going home jaded and pale, homeless wanderers, sentinels on their beats, and in the country, laborers trudging afield, poachers slinking home, all over the dusky quickening country it could be seen—and out at sea by seamen watching for the day—a great white star, come suddenly into the westward sky!

Brighter it was than any star in our skies; brighter than the evening star at its brightest. It still glowed out white and large, no mere twinkling spot of light, but a small round clear shining disk, an hour after the day had come. And where science had not reached, men stared and feared, telling one another of the wars and pestilences that are foreshadowed by these fiery signs in the Heavens. Sturdy Boers, dusky Hottentots, Gold Coast Negroes, Frenchmen, Spaniards, Portuguese, stood in the warmth of the sunrise watching the setting of this strange new star.

And in a hundred observatories there had been suppressed excitement, rising almost to shouting pitch, as the two remote bodies had rushed together, and a hurrying to and fro, to gather photographic apparatus and spectroscope, and this appliance and that, to record this novel astonishing sight, the destruction of a world. For it was a world, a sister planet of our earth, far greater than our earth indeed, that had so suddenly flashed into flaming death. Neptune, it was, had been struck, fairly and squarely, by the strange planet from outer space and the heat of the concussion had incontinently turned two solid globes into one vast mass of incandescence. Round the world that day, two hours before the dawn, went the pallid great white star, fading only as it sank westward and the sun mounted above it. Everywhere men marveled at it, but of all those who saw it none could have marveled more than those sailors, habitual watchers of the stars, who far away at sea had heard nothing of its advent and saw it now rise like a pygmy moon and climb zenithward and hang overhead and sink westward with the passing of the night.

And when it next rose over Europe everywhere were crowds of watchers on hilly slopes, on house-roofs, in open spaces, staring eastward for the rising of the great new star. It rose with a white glow in front of it, like the glare of a white fire, and those who had seen it come into existence the night before cried out at the sight of it. "It is larger," they cried. "It is brighter!"

And, indeed the moon a quarter full and sinking in the west was in its apparent size beyond comparison, but scarcely in all its breadth had it as much brightness now as the little circle of the strange new star.

"It is brighter!" cried the people clustering in the streets. But in the dim observatories the watchers held their breath and peered at one another. "*It is nearer,*" they said. "*Nearer!*"

And voice after voice repeated, "It is nearer," and the clicking telegraph took that up, and it trembled along telephone wires, and in a thousand cities grimy compositors fingered the type. "It is nearer." Men writing in offices, struck with a strange realization, flung down their pens, men talking in a thousand places suddenly came upon a grotesque possibility in those words, "It is nearer." It hurried along wakening streets, it was shouted down the frost-stilled ways of quiet villages; men who had read these things from the throbbing tape stood in yellow-lit doorways shouting the news to the passers-by. "It is nearer." Pretty women, flushed and glittering, heard the news told jestingly between the dances, and feigned an intelligent interest they did not feel. "Nearer! Indeed. How curious! How very clever people must be to find out things like that!"

Lonely tramps faring through the wintry night murmured those words to comfort themselves—looking skyward: "It has need to be nearer, for the night's as cold as charity. Don't seem much warmth from it if it *is* nearer, all the same."

"What is the new star to me?" cried the weeping woman kneeling beside her dead.

The schoolboy, rising early for his examination work, puzzled it out for himself—with the great white star shining broad and bright through the frost-flower of his window. "Centrifugal, centripetal," he said, with his chin on his fist. "Stop a planet in its flight, rob it of its centrifugal force, what then? Centripetal has it, and down it falls into the sun! And this—!

"Do *we* come in the way? I wonder—"

The light of that day went the way of its brethren, and with the later watchers of the frosty darkness rose the strange star again. And it was now so bright that the waxing moon seemed but a pale yellow ghost of itself, hanging huge in the sunset. In a South African city a great man had married, and the streets were alight to welcome his return with his bride. "Even the skies have illuminated," said the flatterer. Under Capricorn, two negro lovers, daring the wild beasts and evil spirits, for love of one another, crouched together in a cane brake where the fire-flies hovered. "That is our star," they whispered, and felt strangely comforted by the sweet brilliance of its light.

The master mathematician sat in his private room and pushed the papers from him. His calculations were already finished. In a small white phial there still remained a little of the drug that had kept him awake and active for four long nights. Each day, serene, explicit, patient as ever, he had given his lecture to his students, and then had come back at once to this momentous calculation. His face was grave, a little drawn and hectic from his drugged activity. For some time he seemed lost in thought. Then he went to the window, and the blind went up with a click. Half way up the sky, over the clustering roofs, chimneys and steeples of the city, hung the star.

He looked at it as one might look into the eyes of a brave enemy. "You may kill me," he said, after a silence, "but I can hold you—and all the universe for that matter—in the grip of this little brain. I would not change. Even now."

He looked at the little phial. "There will be no need of sleep again," he said.

The next day at noon, punctual to the minute, he entered his lecture theater, put his hat on the end of the table as his habit was, and carefully selected a large piece of chalk. It was a joke among his students that he could not lecture without that piece of chalk to fumble in his fingers, and once he had been stricken to impotence by their hiding his supply. He came and looked under his gray eyebrows at the rising tiers of young fresh faces, and spoke with his accustomed studied commonness of phrasing. "Circumstances have arisen—circumstances beyond my control," he said and paused, "which will debar me from completing the course I had designed. It would seem, gentlemen, if I may put the thing clearly and briefly, that— Man has lived in vain."

The students glanced at one another. Had they heard aright? Mad? Raised eyebrows and grinning lips there were, but one or two faces remained intent upon his calm gray-fringed face. "It will be interesting," he was saying, "to devote this morning to an exposition, so far as I can make it clear to you, of the calculations that have led me to this conclusion. Let us assume—"

He turned towards the blackboard, meditating a diagram in the way that was usual to him.

"What was that about 'lived in vain?'" whispered one student to another.

"Listen," said the other, nodding toward the lecturer.

And presently, they began to understand.

That night the star rose later, for its proper eastward motion had carried it some way across Leo toward Virgo, and its brightness was so great that the sky became a luminous blue as it rose, and every star was hidden in its turn, save only Jupiter near the zenith, Capella, Aldebaran, Sirius and the pointers of the Bear. It was very white and beautiful. In many parts of the world that night a pallid halo encircled it about. It was perceptibly larger; in the clear reflective sky of the tropics it seemed as if it were nearly a quarter the size of the moon. The frost was still on the ground in England, but the world was as brightly as if it were midsummer moonlight. One could see to read quite ordinary print by that cold clear light, and in the cities the lamps burnt yellow and wan.

And everywhere the world was awake that night, and throughout Christendom a somber murmur hung in the keen air over the countryside like the belling of bees in the heather, and this murmurous tumult grew to a clangor in the cities. It was the tolling of the bells in a million belfry towers and steeples, summoning the people to sleep no more, to sin no more, but to gather in their churches and pray. And overhead, growing larger and brighter as the earth rolled on its way and the night passed, rose the dazzling star.

And the streets and houses were alight in all the cities, the shipyards glared, and whatever roads led to high country were lit and crowded all night long. And in all the seas about the civilized lands, ships with throbbing engines, and ships with bellying sails, crowded with men and living creatures, were standing out to ocean and the north. For already the warning of the master mathematician had been telegraphed all over the world, and translated into a hundred tongues. The new planet and Neptune, locked in a fiery embrace, were whirling headlong, ever faster and faster, towards the sun. Already every second this blazing mass flew a few hundred miles, and every second its terrific velocity increased.

As it flew now, indeed, it must pass a hundred million of miles wide of the earth and scarcely affect it. But near its destined path, as yet only slightly perturbed, spun the mighty planet Jupiter and his moons sweeping splendid around the sun. Every moment now the attraction between the fiery star and the greatest of the planets grew stronger. And the result of that attraction? Inevitably Jupiter would be deflected from its orbit into an elliptical path, and the burning star, swung by his attraction wide of its sunward rush, would "describe a curved path" and perhaps collide with, and certainly pass very close to, our Earth. "Earthquakes, volcanic outbreaks, cyclones, sea waves, floods, and a steady rise in temperature to I know not what limit"—so proposed the master mathematician.

And overhead, to carry out his words, lonely and cold and livid, blazed the star of the coming doom.

To many who stared at it that night until their eyes ached, it seemed that it was visibly approaching. And that night, too, the weather changed, and the frost that had gripped all Central Europe and France and England softened towards a thaw.

But you must not imagine because I have spoken of people praying through the night and people going aboard ships and people fleeing toward mountainous country that the whole world was already in a terror because of the star. As a matter of fact, use and wont still ruled the world, and save for the talk of idle moments and the splendor of the night, nine human beings out of ten were still busy at their common occupations.

In all the cities the shops, save one here and there, opened and closed at their proper hours, the doctor and the undertaker plied their trades, the workers gathered in the factories, soldiers drilled, scholars studied. Lovers sought one another, thieves lurked and fled, politicians planned their schemes. The presses of the newspapers roared through the night, and many a priest of this church and that would not open his holy building to further what he considered a foolish panic.

The newspapers insisted on the lesson of the year 1000, for then, too, people had anticipated the end. The star was no star—mere gas—a comet; and if it were a star it could not possibly strike the earth. There was no precedent for such a thing. Common sense was sturdy everywhere, scornful, jesting, a little inclined to persecute the obdurate fearful.

That night, at seven-fifteen by Greenwich time, the star would be at its nearest to Jupiter. Then the world would see the turn things would take. The master mathematician's grim warnings were treated by many as so much mere elaborate self-advertisement. Common sense at last, a little heated by argument, signified its unalterable convictions by going to bed. So, too, barbarism and savagery, already tired of the novelty, went about their nightly business, and save for a howling dog here and there, the beast world left the star unheeded.

And yet, when at last the watchers in the European States saw the star rise, an hour later it is true, but no larger than it had been the night before, there were still plenty awake to laugh at the master mathematician—to take the danger as if it had passed.

But hereafter the laughter ceased. The star grew—it grew with a terrible steadfastness hour after hour, a little larger each hour, a little nearer the midnight zenith, and brighter and brighter, until it had turned night into a second day. Had it come straight to earth instead of in a curved path, had it lost no velocity to Jupiter, it must have leapt the intervening gulf in a day, but as it was it took five days altogether to come by our planet. The next night it had become a third the size of the moon before it set to English eyes, and the thaw was assured. It rose over America near the size of the moon, but blinding white to look at, and *hot*; and a breath of hot wind blew now with its rising and gathering strength, and in Virginia, and Brazil, and down the St. Lawrence valley, it shone intermittently through a driving reek of thunder-clouds, flickering violet lightning, and hail unprecedented. In Manitoba was a thaw and devastating floods. And upon all the mountains of the earth the snow and ice began to melt that night, and all the rivers coming out of the high country flowed thick and turbid, and soon—in their upper reaches—with swirling trees and the bodies of beasts and men. They rose steadily, steadily, in ghostly brilliance, and came trickling over their banks at last, behind the flying population of their valleys.

And along the coast of Argentina and up the South Atlantic the tides were higher than had ever been in the memory of man, and the storms drove the waters in many cases scores of miles inland, drowning whole cities. And so great grew the heat during the night that the rising of the sun was like the coming of a shadow. The earthquakes began and grew until all down America from the Arctic Circle to Cape Horn, hillsides were sliding, fissures were opening, and houses and walls crumbling to destruction. The whole side of Cotopaxi slipped out in one vast convulsion, and a tumult of lava poured out so high and broad and swift and liquid that in one day it reached the sea.

So the star, with the wan moon in its wake, marched across the Pacific, trailed the thunderstorms like the hem of a robe, and the growing tidal wave that toiled behind it, frothing and eager, poured over island and island and swept them clear of men. Until that wave came at last—in a blinding light and with the breath of a furnace, swift and terrible it came—a wall of water, fifty feet high, roaring hungrily, upon the long coasts of Asia, and swept inland across the plains of China. For a space the star, hotter now and larger and brighter than the sun in its strength, showed with pitiless brilliance the wide and populous country: towns and villages with their pagodas and trees, roads, wide cultivated fields, millions of sleepless people staring in helpless terror at the incandescent sky; and then, low and growling, came the murmur of the flood. And thus it was with millions of men that night; a flight nowhither, with limbs heavy with heat and breath fierce and scant, and the flood like a wall swift and white behind. And then death.

China was lit glowing white, but over Japan and Java and all the islands of Eastern Asia the great star was a ball of dull red fire because of the steam and smoke and ashes the volcanoes were spouting forth to salute its coming. Above was the lava, hot gases and ash, and below the seething floods, and the whole earth swayed and rumbled with the earthquake shocks. Soon the immemorial snows of Thibet and the Himalaya were melting and pouring down by ten million deepening converging channels upon the plains of Burmah and Hindostan. The tangled summits of the Indian jungles were aflame in a thousand places, and below the hurrying waters around the stems were dark objects that still struggled feebly and reflected the blood-red tongues of fire. And in a rudderless confusion a multitude of men and women fled down the broad river-ways to that one last hope of men—the open sea.

Larger grew the star, and larger, hotter, and brighter with a terrible swiftness now. The tropical ocean had lost its phosphorescence, and the whirling steam rose in ghostly wreaths from the black waves that plunged incessantly, speckled with storm-tossed ships.

And then came a wonder. It seemed to those who in Europe watched for the rising of the star that the world must have ceased its rotation. In a thousand open spaces of down and upland the people who had fled thither from the floods and the falling houses and sliding slopes of hill watched for that rising in vain. Hour followed hour through a terrible suspense, and the star rose not. Once again men set their eyes upon the old constellations they had counted lost to them forever. In England it was hot and clear overhead, though the ground quivered perpetually, but in the tropics, Sirius and

Capella and Aldebaran showed through a veil of steam. And when at last the great star rose near ten hours late, the sun rose close upon it, and in the center of its white heat was a disk of black.

Over Asia it was the star had begun to fall behind the movement of the sky, and then suddenly, as it hung over India, its light had been veiled. All the plain of India from the mouth of the Indus to the mouths of the Ganges was a shallow waste of shining water that night, out of which rose temples and palaces, mounds and hills, black with people. Every minaret was a clustering mass of people, who fell one by one into the turbid waters, as heat and terror overcame them. The whole land seemed a-wailing and suddenly there swept a shadow across that furnace of despair, and a breath of cold wind, and a gathering of clouds, out of the cooling air. Men looking up, near blinded, at the star, saw that a black disk was creeping across the light. It was the moon, coming between the star and the earth. And even as men cried to God at this respite, out of the East with a strange inexplicable swiftness sprang the sun. And then star, sun and moon rushed together across the heavens.

So it was that presently, to the European watchers, star and sun rose close upon each other, drove headlong for a space and then slower, and at last came to rest, star and sun merged into one glare of flame at the zenith of the sky. The moon no longer eclipsed the star but was lost to sight in the brilliance of the sky. And though those who were still alive regarded it for the most part with the dull stupidity that hunger, fatigue, heat and despair engender, there were still men who could perceive the meaning of these signs. Star and earth had been at their nearest, had swung about one another, and the star had passed. Already it was receding, swifter and swifter, in the last stage of its headlong journey downward into the sun.

And then the clouds gathered, blotting out the vision of the sky, the thunder and lightning wove a garment round the world; all over the earth was such a downpour of rain as men had never before seen, and where the volcanoes flared red against the cloud canopy there descended torrents of mud. Everywhere the waters were pouring off the land, leaving mud-silted ruins, and the earth littered like a storm-worn beach with all that had floated, and the dead bodies of the men and brutes, its children. For days the water streamed off the land, sweeping away soil and trees and houses in the way, and piling huge dykes and scooping out Titanic gullies over the countryside. Those were the days of darkness that followed the star and the heat. All through them, and for many weeks and months, the earthquakes continued.

But the star had passed, and men, hunger-driven and gathering courage only slowly, might creep back to their ruined cities, buried granaries, and sodden fields. Such few ships as had escaped the storms of that time came stunned and shattered and sounding their way cautiously through the new marks and shoals of once familiar ports. And as the storms subsided men perceived that everywhere the days were hotter than of yore, and the sun larger, and the moon, shrunk to a third of its former size, took now four-score days between its new and new.

But of the new brotherhood that grew presently among men, of the saving of laws and books and machines, of the strange change that had come over Iceland and Greenland and the shores of Baffin's Bay, so that the sailors coming there presently found them green and gracious, and could scarce believe their eyes, this story does not tell. Nor of the movement of mankind now that the earth was hotter, northward and southward towards the poles of the earth. It concerns itself only with the coming and passing of the Star.

The Martian astronomers—for there are astronomers on Mars, although they are very different beings from men—were naturally profoundly interested by these things. They saw them from their own standpoint of course. "Considering the mass and temperature of the missile that was flung through our solar system into the sun," one wrote, "it is astonishing what a little damage the earth, which it missed so narrowly, has sustained. All the familiar continental markings and the masses of the seas remain intact, and indeed the only difference seems to be a shrinkage of the white discoloration (supposed to be frozen water) round either pole." Which only shows how small the vastest of human catastrophes may seem, at a distance of a few million miles.

# A CORNER IN LIGHTNING

## GEORGE GRIFFITH

*George Griffith was the abbreviated form of his name, employed as a signa-
ture by the British journalist George Chetwynd Griffith-Jones (1857–1906),
who was commissioned by his employer, the newspaper entrepreneur C.
Arthur Pearson, to produce a more exciting future war story than one running in a rival periodical. He responded with the wonderfully extravagant*
The Angel of the Revolution, *which ran as a serial in* Pearson's Weekly
*for most of 1893, in which a band of revolutionary socialists calling them-
selves Terrorists employ airships, submarines and new explosives to bomb
the world's tyrannies into submission and establish their own benevolent
dictatorship. It was followed almost immediately by a sequel, "The Syren of
the Skies" (1894;* Olga Romanoff *in book form), which could only exceed its
scope by crashing a comet into the Earth. The two serials established Griffith
as the second major exemplar of scientific romance after H. G. Wells, and
he spent the remainder of his career repeating himself endlessly, with rapidly
diminishing energy and a marked swing away from the political left, as he
sank increasingly into alcoholism.*

*Griffith's shorter works retained their coherency better than his longer
ones, and "A Corner in Lightning," published in the March 1898 issue of*
Pearson's Magazine, *before being reprinted in the collection* Gambles with
Destiny *(1899), is the most clearly focused of them all, being also the shortest.
Although by no means as radical as* The Angel of the Revolution, *it retains
a political edge that contributes to its narrative energy and facilitates the development of its central motif. As the twentieth century progressed, stories of
drastic technological interruption inevitably became more commonplace, but
"A Corner in Lightning" was ground-breaking in its day. Extant versions of*

231

*the story differ slightly, though not substantially; the version reproduced here
is taken from* Gambles with Destiny.

They had been dining for once in a way *tête-à-tête*, and she—that is to say,
Mrs. Sidney Calvert, a bride of eighteen months' standing—was half lying,
half sitting in the depths of a big, cozy, saddle-bag armchair on one side of
a bright fire of mixed wood and coal that was burning in one of the most
improved imitations of the medieval fireplace. Her feet—very pretty little
feet they were, too, and very daintily shod—were crossed, and poised on
the heel of the right one at the corner of the black marble curb.

Dinner was over. The coffee service and the liqueur case were on the
table, and Mr. Sidney Calvert, a well set-up young fellow of about thirty,
with a handsome, good-humored face, which a close observer would have
found curiously marred by a chilly glitter in the eyes and a hardness that
was something more than firmness about the mouth, was walking up and
down on the opposite side of the table smoking a cigarette.

Mrs. Calvert had just emptied her coffee cup, and as she put it down
on a little three-legged console table by her side, she looked around at her
husband and said: "Really Sid, I must say that I can't see why you should
do it. Of course it's a very splendid scheme and all that sort of thing, but,
surely you, one of the richest men in London, are rich enough to do without it. I'm sure it's wrong, too. What should we think if somebody managed
to bottle up the atmosphere and made us pay for every breath we drew?
Besides, there must surely be a good deal of risk in deliberately disturbing
the economy of Nature in such a way. How are you going to get to the Pole,
too, to put up your works?"

"Well," he said, stopping for a moment in his walk and looking thoughtfully at the lighted end of his cigarette, "in the first place, as to the geography, I must remind you that the Magnetic Pole is not the North Pole. It is in
Boothia Land, British North America, some 1500 miles south of the North
Pole.[1] Then, as to the risk, of course one can't do big things like this without

---

[1] The north magnetic pole was, indeed, in the Boothia peninsula of Canada when James
Clark Ross first reached it in 1831. It has shifted over time, but had not moved very far
when the present story was written.

taking a certain amount of it, but still, I think it will be mostly other people that will have to take it in this case.

"Their risk, you see, will come in when they find that cables and telephones and telegraphs won't work, and that no amount of steam-engine grinding can get up a respectable amount of electric light—when, in short, all the electric plant of the world loses its value, and can't be set going without buying supplies from the Magnetic Polar Storage Company, or, in other words, from your humble servant and the few friends that he will be graciously pleased to let in on the ground floor. But that is a risk that they can easily overcome just by paying for it. Besides, there's no reason why we shouldn't improve the quality of the commodity. 'Our Extra-Special Refined Lightning!' 'Our Triple-Concentrated Essence of Electric Fluid' and 'Competent Thunderstorms delivered at the Shortest Notice' would look very nice in advertisements, wouldn't they?"

"Don't you think that's rather a frivolous way of talking about a scheme which might end in ruining one of the most important industries in the world?" she said, laughing in spite of herself at the idea of delivering thunderstorms like pounds of butter or skeins of Berlin wool.

"Well, I'm afraid I can't argue that point with you because, you see, you will keep looking at me when you talk, and that isn't fair. Anyhow, I'm equally sure that it would be quite impossible to run any business and make money out of it on the lines of the Sermon on the Mount. But come, here's a convenient digression for both of us. That's the Professor, I expect."

"Shall I go?" she said, taking her feet off the fender.

"Certainly not, unless you wish to," he said, "or unless the scientific details are going to bore you."

"Oh, no, they won't do that," she said. "The Professor has such a perfectly charming way of putting them, and, besides, I want to know all that I can about it."

"Professor Kenyon, sir."

"Ah, good evening, Professor! So sorry you could not come to dinner." They both said this simultaneously as the man of science walked in.

"My wife and I were just discussing the ethics of this storage scheme when you came in," he went on. "Have you anything fresh to tell us about the practical aspects of it? I'm afraid she doesn't altogether approve of it, but as she is very anxious to hear all about it, I thought you wouldn't mind her making one of the audience."

"On the contrary, I shall be delighted," replied the Professor, "the more so as it will give me a sympathizer."

"I'm very glad to hear it," said Mrs. Calvert approvingly. "I think it will be a very wicked scheme if it succeeds, and a very foolish and expensive one if it fails."

"After which there is of course nothing more to be said," laughed her husband, "except for the Professor to give his dispassionate opinion."

"Oh, it shall be dispassionate, I can assure you," he replied, noticing a little emphasis on the word. "The ethics of the matter are no business of mine, nor have I anything to do with its commercial bearings. You have asked me merely to look at technical possibilities and scientific probabilities, and of course I don't propose to go beyond these."

He took another sip at a cup of coffee that Mrs. Calvert had handed him, and went on.

"I've had a long talk with Markovitch this afternoon, and I must confess that I never met a more ingenious man or one who knew as much about magnetism and electricity as he does. His theory that they are the celestial and terrestrial manifestations of the same force, and that what is popularly called electric fluid is developed only at the stage where they become one, is itself quite a stroke of genius, or, at least, it will be if the theory stands the test of experience. His idea of locating the storage works over the Magnetic Pole of the Earth is another, and I am bound to confess that, after a very careful examination of his plans and designs, I am distinctly of opinion that, subject to one or two reservations, he will be able to do what he contemplates."

"And the reservations, what are they?" asked Calvert, a trifle eagerly.

"The first is one that it is absolutely necessary to make with regard to all untried schemes, and especially to such a gigantic one as this. Nature, you know, has a way of playing most unexpected pranks with people who take liberties with her. Just at the last moment, when you are on the verge of success, something that you confidently expect to happen doesn't happen, and there you are, left in the lurch. It is utterly impossible to foresee anything of this kind, but you must clearly understand that if such a thing did happen it would ruin the enterprise just when you have spent the greatest part of the money on it—that is to say, at the end and not at the beginning."

"All right," said Calvert, "we'll take that risk. Now, what's the other reservation?"

"I was going to say something about the immense cost, but that I presume you are prepared for." Calvert nodded, and he went on. "Well, that point being disposed of, it remains to be said that it may be very dangerous—I mean to those who live on the spot, and will be actually engaged in the work."

"Then I hope you won't think of going near the place, Sid!" interrupted Mrs. Calvert, with a very pretty assumption of wifely authority.

"We'll see about that later, little woman. It's early days yet to get frightened about possibilities. Well, Professor, what was it you were going to say? Any more warnings?"

The Professor's manner stiffened a little as he replied. "Yes, it is a warning, Mr. Calvert. The fact is I feel bound to tell you that you propose to interfere very seriously with the distribution of one of the subtlest and least-known forces of Nature, and that the consequences of such an interference might be most disastrous, not only for those engaged in the work, but even the whole hemisphere, and possibly the whole planet.

"On the other hand, I think it is only fair to say that nothing more than a temporary disturbance may take place. You may, for instance, give us a series of very violent thunderstorms, with very heavy rains; or you may abolish thunderstorms and rain together until you get to work. Both prospects are within the bounds of possibility, and, at the same time, neither may come to anything."

"Well, I think that quite good enough to gamble on, Professor," said Calvert, who was thoroughly fascinated by the grandeur and magnitude, to say nothing of the dazzling financial aspects of the scheme. "I am very much obliged to you for putting it so clearly and so nicely. Unless something unexpected happens, we shall get to work on it at once. Just fancy what a glorious thing it will be to play Jove to the nations of the earth, and dole out lightning to them at so much a flash!"

"Well, I don't want to be ill-natured," said Mrs. Calvert, "but I must say that I hope the unexpected will happen. I think the whole thing is very wrong to begin with, and I shouldn't be at all surprised if you blew us all up, or struck us all dead with lightning, or even brought on the Day of Judgment before its time. I think I shall go to Australia while you're doing it."

*

A little more than a year had passed since this after-dinner conversation in the dining room of Mr. Sidney Calvert's London house. During that time the preparations for the great experiment had been swiftly but secretly carried out. Ship after ship laden with machinery, fuel, and provisions, and carrying laborers and artificers to the number of some hundreds, had sailed away into the Atlantic, and had come back in ballast and with bare working crews aboard them. Mr. Calvert himself had disappeared and reappeared two or three times, and on his return he had neither admitted nor denied any of the various rumors which gradually got into circulation in the city and in the Press.

Some said that it was an expedition to the Pole, and that the machinery consisted partly of improved ice-breakers and newly-invented steam-sledges, which were to attack the ice-hummocks after the fashion of battering rams, and so gradually smooth a road to the Pole. To these little details others added flying machines and navigable balloons.

Others again declared that the object was to plow out the North-West passage and keep a waterway clear from Hudson's Bay to the Pacific all the year round, and yet others, somewhat less imaginative, pinned their faith to the founding of a great astronomical and meteorological observatory at the nearest possible point to the Pole, one of the objects of which was to be the determination of the true nature of the Aurora Borealis and the Zodiacal Light.

It was this last hypothesis that Mr. Calvert favored as far as he could be said to favor any. There was a vagueness, and, at the same time, a distinction about a great scientific expedition which made it possible for him to give a sort of qualified countenance to the rumors without committing himself to anything, but so well had all his precautions been taken that not even a suspicion of the true object of the expedition to Boothia Land had got outside the little circle of those who were in his confidence.

So far everything had gone as Orloff Markovitch, the Russian Pole to whose extraordinary genius the inception and working out of the gigantic project were due, had expected and predicted. He himself was in supreme control of the unique and costly works which had grown up under his constant supervision on that lonely and desolate spot in the far North where the magnetic needle points straight down to the center of the planet.

Professor Kenyon had paid a couple of visits with Calvert, once at the beginning of the work and once when it was nearing completion. So far not the slightest hitch or accident had occurred, and nothing abnormal had been noticed in connection with the earth's electrical phenomena save unusually frequent appearances of the Aurora Borealis, and a singular decrease in the deviation of the mariner's compass. Nevertheless, the Professor had firmly but politely refused to remain until the gigantic apparatus was set to work, and Calvert, too, had, with extreme reluctance, yielded to his wife's entreaties, and had come back to England about a month before the initial experiment was to be begun.

The twentieth of March, which was the day fixed for the commencement of operations, came and went, to Mrs. Calvert's intense relief, without anything out of the common happening. Though she knew that over a hundred thousand pounds of her husband's money had been sunk, she found it impossible not to feel a thrill of satisfaction in the hope that Markovitch had made his experiment and failed.

She knew that the great Calvert Company, which was practically himself, could very well afford it, and she would not have regretted the loss of three times the sum in exchange for the knowledge that Nature was to be allowed to dispose of her electrical forces as seemed good to her. As for her husband, he went about his business as usual, only displaying slight signs of suppressed excitement and anticipation now and then, as the weeks went by and nothing happened.

She had not carried out her threat of going to Australia. She had, however, escaped from the rigors of the English spring to a villa near Nice, where she was awaiting the arrival of her second baby, an event which she had found very useful in persuading her husband to stop away from the Magnetic Pole. Calvert himself was so busy with what might be called the home details of the scheme that he had to spend the greater part of his time in London, and could only run over to Nice now and then.

It so happened that Miss Calvert put in an appearance a few days before she was expected, and therefore while her father was still in London. Her mother very naturally sent her maid with a telegram to inform him of the fact and ask him to come over at once. In about half a hour the maid came back with the form in her hand bringing a message from the telegraph office that, in consequence of some extraordinary accident, the wires had almost ceased to work properly and that no messages could be got through distinctly.

In the rapture of her new motherhood Kate Calvert had forgotten all about the great Storage Scheme, so she sent the maid back again with the request that the message should be sent off as soon as possible. Two hours later she sent again to ask whether it had gone, and the reply came back that the wires had ceased working altogether and that no electrical communication by telegraph or telephone was for the present possible.

Then a terrible fear came to her. The experiment had been a success after all, and Markovitch's mysterious engines had been all this time draining the earth of its electric fluid and storing it up in the vast accumulators, which would only yield it back again at the bidding of the Trust which was controlled by her husband!

Still she was a sensible little woman, and after the first shock she managed, for her baby's sake, to put the fear out of her mind, at any rate until her husband came. He would be with her in a day or two, and, perhaps, after all, it was only some strange but perfectly natural occurrence which Nature herself would set right in a few hours.

When it got dusk that night, and the electric lights were turned on, it was noticed that they gave an unusually dim and wavering light. The engines were worked to their highest power, and the lines were carefully examined. Nothing could be found wrong with them, but the lights refused to behave as usual, and the most extraordinary feature of the phenomenon was that exactly the same thing was happening in all the electrically lighted cities and towns in the northern hemisphere.

By midnight, too, telegraphic and telephonic communication north of the Equator had practically ceased, and the electricians of Europe and America were at their wits' end to discover any reason for this unheard of disaster, for such in sober truth it would be unless the apparently suspended force quickly resumed action on its own account. The next morning it was found that, so far as all the marvels of electrical science were concerned, the world had gone back a hundred years.

Then people began to awake to the magnitude of the catastrophe that had befallen the world. Civilized mankind had been suddenly deprived of the services of an obedient slave which it had come to look upon as indispensable.

But there was something even more serious than this to come. Observers in various parts of the hemisphere remembered that there hadn't been a thunderstorm anywhere for some weeks. Even the regions most frequently visited by them had had none. A most remarkable drought had also set in almost universally. A strange sickness, beginning with physical lassitude and depression of spirits which confounded the best medical science of the world was manifesting itself far and wide, and rapidly assuming the proportions of a gigantic epidemic.

In the physical world too, metals were found to be afflicted with the same incomprehensible disease. Machinery of all sorts got "sick," to use a technical expression, and absolutely refused to act, and forges and foundries everywhere came to a standstill for the simple reason that metals seemed to have lost their best properties, and could no longer be utilized as they had been. Railway accidents and breakdowns on steamers, too, became matters of everyday occurrence, for metals and driving-wheels, piston-rods and propeller-shafts, had acquired an incomprehensible brittleness which only began to be understood when it was discovered that the electrical properties which iron and steel had formerly possessed had almost entirely disappeared.

So far Calvert had not wavered in his determination to make, as he thought, a colossal amount of money by his usurpation of one of the functions of Nature. To him the calamities which, it must be confessed, he had deliberately brought upon the world were only so many arguments for the ultimate success of the stupendous scheme. They were proof positive to the world, or at least they very soon would be, that the Calvert Storage Trust really did control the electricity of the Northern Hemisphere. From the Southern nothing had yet been heard beyond the news that the cables had ceased working.

Hence, as soon as he had demonstrated his power to restore matters to their normal condition, it was obvious that the world would have to pay his price under penalty of having the supply cut off again.

It was now getting towards the end of May. On the 1st of June, according to the arrangement, Markovitch would stop his engines and permit the vast accumulation of electric fluid in his storage batteries to flow back into the accustomed channels. Then the Trust would issue its prospectus, setting forth the terms on which it was prepared to permit the nations to enjoy the gift of Nature whose pricelessness the Trust had proved by demonstrating its own ability to corner it.

On the evening of May 25<sup>th</sup> Calvert was sitting in his sumptuous office in Victoria Street, writing by the light of a dozen wax candles in silver candelabra. He had just finished a letter to his wife, telling her to keep her spirits up and fear nothing; that in a few days the experiment would be over and everything restored to its former condition, shortly after which she would be the wife of a man who would soon be able to buy up all the other millionaires in the world.

As he put the letter into the envelope there was a knock at the door, and Professor Kenyon was announced. Calvert greeted him stiffly and coldly, for he more than half guessed the errand he had come on. There had been two or three heated discussions between them of late, and Calvert knew before the Professor opened his lips that he had come to tell him that he was about to fulfill a threat that he had made a few days before. And this the Professor did tell him in a few dry, quiet words.

"It's no use, Professor," he replied, "you know yourself that I am powerless, as powerless as you are. I have no means of communicating with Markovitch, and the work cannot be stopped until the appointed time. Of course I am very sorry that the effects of the experiment have been so much more serious than I anticipated. . . ."

"But you were warned, sir!" the Professor interrupted warmly. "You were warned, and when you saw the effects coming you might have stopped. I wish to goodness that I had had nothing to do with this infernal business, for infernal it really is. You have not only sacrificed the industries and convenience of nations to your lust of wealth and power. Thousands of deaths already lie at your door. This mysterious epidemic, which is neither more nor less than electrical starvation, is spreading every day, and human science has no remedy for it. You alone hold the remedy, and yet you confess that you are powerless to apply it before a given date!

"Who are you that you should usurp one of the functions of the Almighty?—for that is really what you are doing? I have kept your criminal secret too long, and I will keep it no longer. You have made yourself the enemy of Society, and Society still has the power to deal with you. . . ."

"My dear Professor, that's all nonsense, and you know it!" said Calvert, interrupting him with a contemptuous gesture. "If Society were to lock me up, it should do without electricity till I were free. If it hung me it would get none, except on Markovitch's terms, which would be higher than mine. So you can tell your story whenever you please. Meanwhile, you'll excuse me if I remind you that I am rather busy."

Just as the Professor was about to take his leave the door opened and a boy brought in an envelope deeply edged with black. Calvert turned white to the lips and his hand trembled as he took it and opened it. It was in his wife's handwriting, and was dated five days before. He read it through with fixed, staring eyes; then he crushed it into his pocket and strode toward the telephone. He rang the bell furiously, and then started back with an oath on his lips, remembering that he had made it useless. The sound of a bell brought a clerk into the room immediately.

"Get me a hansom at once!" he almost shouted, and the clerk vanished.

"What is the matter? Where are you going?" asked the Professor.

"Matter? Read that!" he said, thrusting the crumpled letter into his hand. "My little girl is dead—dead of that accursed sickness which, as you justly say, I have brought on the world, and my wife is down with it too, and may be dead by this time. This letter is five days old. My God, what have I done? What can I do? I'd give fifty thousand pounds to get a telegram to Markovitch. Curse him and his infernal scheme! If she dies I'll go to Boothia Land and kill him! Hullo! What's that? Lightning—by the living God—and thunder!"

As he spoke such a flash of lightning as had never split the skies of London before flared in a huge ragged stream of flame across the zenith, and a roar of thunder such as London's ears had never heard shook every house in the vast city to its foundation. Another and another followed in rapid succession, and all through the night and well into the next day there raged, as it was afterwards found, almost all over the Northern Hemisphere, such a thunderstorm as had never been known in the world before and never would be again.

With it, too, came hurricanes and cyclones and deluges of rain, and when, after raging for nearly twenty-four hours, it at length ceased convulsing the atmosphere and growled itself away into silence, the first fact that came out of the chaos and desolation that it had left behind it was that the normal electrical conditions of the world had been restored—after which mankind set itself to repair the damage done by the cataclysm and went about its business in the usual way.

The epidemic vanished instantly and Mrs. Calvert did not die.

Nearly six months later a white-haired wreck of a man crawled into her husband's office and said, feebly: "Don't you know me, Mr. Calvert? I'm Markovitch, or what there is left of him."

"Good God, so you are!" said Calvert. "What happened to you? Sit down and tell me all about it."

"It's not a long story," said Markovitch, sitting down and beginning to speak in a thin, trembling voice. "It isn't long but it is very bad. Everything went well at first. All succeeded as I said it would, and then, I think it was just four days before we should have stopped, it happened."

"What happened?"

"I don't know. We must have gone too far, or by some means an accidental discharge must have taken place. The whole works suddenly burst into white flame. Everything made of metal melted like tallow. Every man in the works died instantly—burnt, you know, to a cinder. I was four or five miles away, with some others, seal shooting. We were all struck down insensible. When I came to myself I found I was the only one alive.

"Yes, Mr. Calvert, I am the only man that has got back from Boothia alive. The works are gone. There are only some heaps of melted metal lying about on the ice. After that I don't know what happened. I must have gone mad. It was enough to make a man mad, you know. But some Indians and Eskimos, who used to trade with us, found me wandering about, so they told me, starving and out of my mind, and they took me to the coast. There I got better and then was picked up by a whaler, and so I got home. That's all. It was very awful, wasn't it?"

Then his face fell forward into his trembling hands, and Calvert saw the tears trickling between his fingers. Suddenly his body slipped gently out of the chair and on to the floor; and when Calvert tried to pick him up he was dead.

And so the secret of the Great Experiment, so far as the world at large was concerned, never got beyond the walls of Mr. Sidney Calvert's cozy dining room after all.

# THE MEMORY CELL

## WALTER BESANT

*Walter Besant (1836–1901) was, like Grant Allen, a journalist, historian, and social reformer who helped set the literary stage for the works of H. G. Wells and George Griffith. His futuristic fantasy* The Revolt of Man *(1882) is a satire of sex-role reversal whose rhetoric was misunderstood as misogynistic by many readers, while* The Inner House *(1888) is an interesting philosophical fantasy about the possible long-term effects of a technology of longevity.*

*"The Memory Cell," first published in an anthology* For Britain's Soldiers [in the Boer War] *in 1900 and reprinted in the collection* A Five Years' Tryst and Other Stories *(1902), is a further philosophical meditation on a hypothetical question, which could doubtless have been extrapolated to much greater length and complexity, but benefits from the deftly challenging terseness of its conclusion.*

When the Professor first talked to me about the thing, I confess that I paid little or no attention to his words. This was partly because he was perpetually inventing new projects, and, of course, burning to tell somebody; partly because the apparent sympathy which made me the favorite receptacle of his ideas was really assumed in order to hide a natural indolence of mind, so that I only pretended to listen; and partly because, at this time when scientific research is so constantly discovering new things any new theory seems no more impossible than, say, talking to a man at twenty miles' distance, or hearing the living voice of a dead man, or sending letters along a wire.

We called him the Professor, not because he lectured, or professed, or taught anything, but because he thought and talked of nothing in the world but his kind of science. Other fellows, he knew, cared about trifles—art—music—letters. For him there was but one subject worthy of a man's attention, and it was his own. He attended to it all day long in his laboratory; and, as he was a wealthy creature, he had a very noble laboratory, with machines of gruesome cunning. Anyone who would sit there and listen while he talked he rewarded with cigars quite beyond the reach of ordinary man.

One day—it was in early summer, and a flowery spray of Gloire de Dijon was lying along the open window—I sat with him in the largest armchair procurable, lighting the best cigar in the world, mind and body perfectly at rest, and ready to let him talk for an hour.

"There is a disease," he began—I always heard the beginning, and sometimes the end, just the same as a sermon—"a disease—call it if you will—perhaps you prefer to call it. . . ."

"Anything you like, Professor."

"A natural function of the brain, which only becomes a disease when it causes pain; a disease which has been hitherto most strangely neglected."

"Now you become practical, Professor. Cure diseases, if you can."

It was his habit never to take the slightest notice of any remark, question or criticism. He just went on. Some men didn't like the habit. With such a cigar, however, I felt that I had no right to be affronted. Besides, he was always so full of his subject that he only wanted to relieve his mind by pouring out some of the contents. He wanted neither advice, nor criticism, nor opinion. His own judgment was enough for him.

"The disease is universal; it is common to humanity. Everybody has it—Kaiser to scavenger. As we grow old it grows troublesome. Many quite young people suffer horribly from it. I know a man—a young man of five-and-twenty—in whom it is like a flame burning night and day within. The agony which men and women endure from this disease. . . ."

"Is it gout?" I asked.

". . . Is beyond all belief. Of all diseases this is the worst, because there has been hitherto no cure for it. None has ever been attempted. Oddly enough, no one has ever thought of attempting its cure."

"Asthma, perhaps."

"And we have looked upon it as one of the Inevitables, like death or decay. Yet while we fight against these, we have never taken up arms against the other. Why? Why? It belongs to the brain. We have had some success with other functions of the brain; we can deal with cells of other kinds; why not with this? Youth is spent in mistakes; old age, for most of us, in regrets, in rages, in self-accusation. Man! there is no more terrible disaster than Memory in the whole long list."

He paused, looking through me but not at me. I understood that it would no longer be necessary for me to listen. Therefore I allowed my attention to wander while the Professor went on.

"Therefore"—towards the end my thoughts always returned—"I shall not yet give my method to the world. Not, in fact, until I have demonstrated to my own complete satisfaction the fact that it is not an experiment or a theory, but a great, a practical discovery with permanent results. In other words, when I have proved that I can so deaden the Memory Cell as to produce oblivion over any proposed period, and even substitute for that period a false Memory causing happiness to the patient, then—and not till then—will I give my method to the world. We have seen already too much disappointment in premature announcements of certain methods and certain cures. Mine shall be a solid discovery or nothing."

Now, at these words I was more than a little startled, and repented me of wandering attention.

"I have already," the Professor concluded, "made certain experiments which are at least hopeful. I must tell somebody, and I have chosen you, as one whom I have already tried and proved"—he knew nothing about the wandering thoughts. "It helps one to talk over a thing, and this is, if you come to think of it, a really big thing, isn't it now?"

"Big thing? Man, it's colossal! But—I say—what about Repentance? If you destroy Memory you destroy Repentance. You confirm the sinner in his sin."

He replied, with the simplicity which belongs to everything truly great: "I shall only render Repentance unnecessary, by destroying the only stimulus to Repentance. Nobody wants to get better who feels no pain. Now come with me."

He led me out of his laboratory, which stood apart from the house at one end of a long garden. At the other end stood the house: an old manor-house, partly Elizabethan, with a stone terrace running along the front, and overlooking a lawn. On the terrace stood an old man, leaning on a stick. He was poorly clad in rusty black; his face was pinched; he looked what he was—the man who had failed in life.

"One of my experiments," said the Professor. "He is that most hopeless of creatures, the poet whom the world will not read. I found him in poverty—which troubled him little—and tortured by the memory of a ruined life. You shall see what I have done for him."

He walked across the lawn and laid his hand gently on the old man's shoulder. "So!" he said, "lost in thought, my Poet? Do you remember old triumphs—or do you dream of new?"

"I was living in the past," the Poet replied. "We who are old live mostly in the past. It is our chief happiness. We cease to work; the chambers of imagery are darkened; but the past remains. We do not cease to live while our name still lingers in men's hearts."

We left him standing in the sunshine, his eyes limpid, and wrapt in the happiness of his false Memory.

"Is that illusion permanent?" I asked.

"I know not. The man is old; he has a disease which will kill him soon. I hope that he will retain the happiness I have conferred upon him to the end. You shall see, however, other cases. The first is a woman whom I found in agonies unspeakable. After a madness of years, she awoke to an understanding of what it meant: the ruin of the husband and the children deserted by her."

At this moment there were no signs of agonies or of any self-reproach. The lady as sitting at an open window, her hands folded, in peaceful resignation. She wore widow's weeds, and was a lovely woman still, though no longer young, despite her stormy past.

"Isabel," said the Professor, "you should be in the garden this sunny day, not sitting alone with your thoughts."

"Oh," she replied, with a sad smile, "how can I be alone, dear friend? I have always with me my dear children and my husband. Death cannot part us—nor can it deprive me of past happiness. I have no present; my mind is in the past or the future, with my dear ones."

We passed on. "And that illusion?" I asked.

"I believe it will endure. She is at peace now. Her Memory for a period of twenty years is entirely destroyed. A false Memory takes its place. I have done this for her."

We entered the house. He took me into his library, a large room containing many thousands of books, wherein a young man of twenty or so was at work. He lifted a bright, intelligent face and smiled greeting.

"Getting on, Harry?" asked the Professor. "Go on—we are not come to disturb you."

"I am doing very well," he replied. "The only thing that troubles me is that I shall finish before long."

"Then we will find something more for you. Don't hurry. Don't hurry." He pretended to consult a book, and we went out.

"That boy," said the Professor, "has been imprisoned for a year for embezzling his employer's money. As usual, for the sake of a worthless girl. His life is ruined. What have I done for him? He has forgotten the girl and his employer, and the crime and the prison. He thinks he came to me from school; he is quite happy."

"Will his illusion last?" I asked.

"I do not know. Perhaps. If it does not, I must find another. I shall now show you a case on which I have expended all my skill. If this case succeeds, then I shall have no doubt whatever as to my discovery."

He led the way along the corridor and stopped before a closed door. "This," he said, "is a case of rescue. The three you have seen are cases of disappointment or of remorse. This is one in which an innocent child has been cursed for the sins of his father. Think of everything that is abominable; exhaust your experience of human wickedness; picture all the shame and infamy that can disgrace a name, and you will still be far below the truth. With this story behind him—public property, mind—it would be impossible for the boy to enter upon any career, to belong to any profession, or even to live among respectable people; every avenue would be closed to him. It would be necessary to live in the depths. His name must be purged for three generations at least before it can hope to rise and begin again. Well, I bought the boy of his villainous father, who does not know the name of the purchaser. I have begun by destroying in his brain the whole memory of his life from the very beginning. He remembers nothing. So far we have got. I have now to reconstruct the past for him. This had to be done very carefully. He will be an orphan, and my ward; he will have no relations; his parents are dead; his father was, if you like, a traveler, who died—where?—in Patagonia, perhaps. His mother was, if you like, a Brazilian—eh?—relations unknown. His cousins—why has he no cousins? Family quarrels, I suppose. And he is my ward. You can just look in, but he must not be disturbed."

He opened the door. A boy of fourteen or so sat upright in a chair, his hands hanging listlessly at his side, his eyes absolutely vacant; there was *nothing* behind those eyes—no memory, no understanding. One shuddered at the vacancy of mind indicated by those eyes.

With him sat a nurse, waiting upon him. "There is no change," she said. "He sits all day like this; he never speaks, he only murmurs. I have to feed him; he knows nothing."

"So far," said the Professor, "we have done very well. Look at the child, my friend. Is there any Memory there? It is gone, I hope, for good. Better to have no Memory at all than the Memory that was within him when I got hold of him. Poor lad! You shall never know that your father was the notorious Edward Algernon Stevedore, who was expelled from the Army for cheating at cards; that he is a common rogue and swindler; that he drove your mother mad with his villainies; and that he sold you, his only son, for a five-pound note. You shall have brighter recollections than these."

"I suppose," said the nurse, "that he will have to recollect things whatever you do."

"You think so, do you? Very well—very well. I will ask you what you think in a week or two. Give him a week or two, and you shall see a new light in those fishy eyes; you shall find such a boy as you never expected. Look at the shape of his head. There is intellect in the brow, resolution in the chin, tenacity in the jaw, the power of ruling in the nose. The boy, nurse, is born for courage and for success."

"Poor lad!" said the nurse hopelessly. "He doesn't look like it, just at present. To be sure, I have never seen such an idiot, yet with such a head."

"Now," said the Professor, outside the room, "I have shown you what I am doing. Forget, if you can, my secret. Let me be the first to divulge it, as soon as I am satisfied with my results. If you yourself," he looked at me with the wistfulness of one who wants to perform another skilful operation, "have anything on your mind—any little murder, robbery of trust money, forgery, betrayal of innocence, lost opportunities, chances thrown away— don't hesitate to come to me. Immediate relief I can promise, at least."

At that period of my life Memory had few reproaches. I thanked him, and went away pondering on his strange experience.

This talk took place in the month of June and the year 1884. After the summer holiday, in October, I called again upon the Professor. His housekeeper received me. Her master, she said, was gone. There had been death in the house. The old gentleman who wrote such beautiful verses had died, making a truly edifying end; and the lady whom the master called Isabel was also dead—gone to rejoin her children, she said; and then the master went away, taking with him his private secretary and his ward. I asked about the latter. He had come through his illness bravely, and now there wasn't a livelier young gentleman anywhere.

\*

Ten years passed before I saw the Professor again. When a man goes abroad and stays there for a few years, he drops out of the groove, and his place is filled up. Most of the old set were married, and marriages separate the company of those who start together. I had quite forgotten the Professor's secret; if I ever thought of it at all, it was as part of his general crankiness. I met him at a metropolitan station; he greeted me warmly as if we had parted the day before. I reminded him that it was ten years since we had last met. Then I remembered the occasion. "And how," I asked, "has the great Experiment on the Memory Cell succeeded?"

"There's my train," he replied, abruptly. "Meet me tomorrow morning, at ten, at the entrance of the High Courts of Justice, and you shall see."

We sat in the gallery of a Court, whether of Queen's Bench or Chancery, I know not; nor does it matter. Down below, the Court was filling up rapidly. The barristers sat in a row; below them the solicitors; at the side stood the clerks with bags; the jury waited to be called; the witnesses already trembled in their seats. Presently the judge appeared; the barristers rose, and the business of the day began.

"He's among them," murmured the Professor. "He is Junior in a case set down for hearing today. There he is, talking with the solicitor, I suppose. That's my ward."

Truly a handsome young man, tall and brave of aspect.

"Does he look as if a dreadful past weighed him down?" the Professor went on. "Not a bit. He's a Fellow of his college, first class in classics and in law, he has been called six months, and he has already made a beginning. Ten years since I showed you the case, and in all that time not a glimmer— mind! not a glimmer—of the truth has reached his brain."

"And now will you give your discovery to the world?"

"Now, I believe, I may." He heaved a deep sigh. "One is not worthy—no one is worthy—of such honor as will be mine."

The case began. It was one of a disputed will. Fifteen years ago, as our Junior opened the history, there was a profligate youth who had a considerable fortune, which he was spending, after the manner of his kind, among sharps and drabs. This young man, while yet the bulk of his fortune re-mained, fell sick unto death, and was, in fact, expected to die. While he was at the worst, in the middle of the night, and when the end was looked for every moment, the man with whom he mostly consorted, a very notorious person who passed by the name of "The Colonel," or Colonel Tracy, called upon the landlord of the house in order to witness himself the signing of the sick man's will. Next day, however, contrary to expectation, the patient began to mend, and in a short time he was taken away by his friends; he mended his morals as well as his health, and returned no more to his for-mer companions, but lived soberly until his death, which had happened quite recently. And then an unexpected will was produced. It bequeathed the whole of the testator's property absolutely to a certain woman whose character, like that of the man known as "The Colonel," was of the worst kind possible. No later will could be found. Investigations showed that the circumstances attending the drawing up and the signing and the witness-ing of the will were highly suspicious, and this action was brought in order to set it aside.

The case was one of those in which the story came out quite plain and clear. The young drunkard; the man who encouraged him, egged him on, and plundered him; the sudden illness; the crafty attempt to secure the dy-ing man's fortune—all this was easy to understand. But there was the sig-nature, strong and unmistakable; there were two witnesses to the signature. Undue influence is not an easy thing to establish. And plain forgery, in such a case, may be suspected, but cannot well be proved.

For reasons which you will understand immediately, I do not know how the case ended. I believe they generally compromise such cases.

So far as I assisted at the hearing, they called four witnesses. The first of these was the lady to whom the estate had been devised. She was quite a common person, about forty years of age, dressed with some smartness. As to her own part in the business, there was nothing that she desired to conceal. Colonel Tracy gave her the will, telling her that the young fellow hadn't died after all, but was fetched away by his friends, which was a piece of terrible bad luck; that she must keep the will, because the young Juggins was sure to drink himself to death before long, and it might be useful. She had kept the will, therefore; she found out also where the young man lived and used secretly to watch him; when, after fifteen years, he died, she went to a lawyer and gave him the will. She was never, so to speak, a friend of the deceased, but she had seen him in the Colonel's company. The Colonel was a sporting man. She knew very well that the Colonel was sharping the young man; she did not know why the estate was left to her. The Colonel told her about it when he gave her the paper. If the thing had come off, probably the Colonel would have had most of the money, because at that period the Colonel could have had everything that belonged to her, so noble an opinion had she formed of him.

The lady's evidence, of which this is only a portion, revealed an interesting glimpse of life where there are no foolish restraints of honor or self-respect.

When she retired, the medical man who had attended the young gentleman was called. He said that as appeared in his notebook, the patient was apparently dropping into a comatose condition on the evening in question; that he himself expected to learn that he had died in the night; that he did not think it likely, from the patient's condition, both in the evening and the morning, that he could collect his thoughts sufficiently to make a will. He would not, however, say that it was impossible.

The third witness was the landlord of the house. He said that he remembered the incident perfectly; he was called up in the dead of night; the Colonel placed the pen in the sick man's hand; to the best of his recollection the man signed his name; could not say if the Colonel guided his fingers; then he and the Colonel witnessed the will.

The fourth witness was called by the name of Herbert Shelley. His appearance caused some interest, because he wore the garb of a convict.

At this point the Professor began to show signs of great emotion. He started; he changed color; his hands trembled; he gazed hard at the window; he looked anxiously at his ward—signs at which I vaguely wondered.

The man was tall, and had a look of distinction even in that grisly uniform. His features were sharp and clear: a pointed chin; thin, firm lips, keen eyes, and the nose of the soldier. He showed neither shame nor bravado as he stood up before all; he might have been standing on the hearthrug of a club, so easy and self-possessed was his bearing.

Our Junior conducted the examination, armed with his papers.

"You were tried and sentenced," he began, "under the name, I believe, of Herbert Shelley?"

"I was using that name at the time," he replied calmly. "I was sentenced, if the statement will save you a question, for obtaining money under false pretences."

"Quite so. At an earlier period—fifteen years ago—you called yourself sometimes Colonel Tracy."

"Herbert Tracy, I called myself. My friends called me Colonel."

"I did not know that name," murmured the Professor. "It is the man. It is the man."

The witness then proceeded to narrate the circumstances of the will. The man thought he was dying; he requested witness to draw his will; witness found a form of Will in Letts's *Diary*, and copied it out; he asked the testator to whom he left his estate; testator replied to Susan Cheriton; witness inserted the name; called up the landlord, and the testator signed. Next day he began to get better; a few days afterwards his friends took him away; then witness gave the girl the will, told her what a near thing it had been, and advised her to keep the paper. That was all he knew of the matter. Why had the testator bequeathed his whole estate to the girl? Witness did not know; it was not a time for asking questions. Was naturally pleased at the choice, as the lady's friend.

"You have passed under other names, I believe?"

"Under many names. I have lived by my wits. The profession necessitates a change of names."

"The trouble to which you referred was connected with a bogus company, was it not?"

"It was. I had fifteen months' imprisonment for it."

"You have been a betting-man, a card-sharper, a billiard-player, a writer of begging letters?"

"I live by my wits," he repeated. "That means that I use my wits."

"Quite so, Quite so. You were Mr. Herbert Shelley, alias Colonel Tracy, alias other things. You were once, even, a gentleman, I believe?"

The man winced—but only for a moment.

"I was," he replied.

"And you held the rank of captain in a regiment of the line? You sent in your papers by request of the colonel on account of a charge of cheating at cards."

"There was such a charge. I resigned my commission and my clubs."

"You were married to a lady of fortune, whose estate you squandered?"

"Say, rather, enjoyed, I enjoyed it very much as long as it lasted."

"What was your name at the time?"

"My name was Edward Algernon Stevedore."

Then a most extraordinary thing happened. Counsel suddenly started, stared at the witness, and then—I understand it now, though at the moment I wondered—a look of recognition or recollection flashed in his eyes. He dropped his papers; he clutched at the desk before him. His face became livid; horror, shame, loathing, terror—as I now understand the effect of those emotions—appeared in swift succession before him; the people, staring, thought he was seized with violent pains. He swayed this way and that, and spoke in a changed, husky voice.

"You are the notorious Edward Algernon Stevedore," he said slowly. "You were expelled from the Army for cheating at cards, you have become a common rogue and swindler, you drove your wife mad with your villainies, you sold your son for a five-pound note, and you are there—and I. . . ." he fell forward in a fit.

"It is his own father," said the Professor, "and his Memory has come back to him."

He rushed down the stairs and met the people in the corridor carrying out the unfortunate Junior, still unconscious.

They carried him to King's College Hospital at the back of the Courts. Here he presently recovered consciousness; but he looked dazed and miserable when the Professor put him into a conveyance and carried him away.

The incident was noted in the evening papers and on the bills. *Sudden Illness of a Barrister in Court.* No one knew, and no one guessed, the cause. In the evening, thinking on this strange affair, I remembered that the last words spoken by the young man in Court were the very words used by his guardian ten years before, when he showed me the boy and told me something of his history. He had succeeded, at that time, in destroying his boy's Memory. Were the first, new impressions on that white sheet which had contained the memories of fourteen years—those plain and unmistakable words?

The Professor, a few days afterwards, called upon me. He was much dejected. "I have had a most terrible time," he told me. "I have been loaded with reproaches. The boy has been driven nearly mad with shame and loathing; he threatened suicide; he said he could never return to his work.

I told him all. He heard it and asked for more—seemed as if he wanted to pile up the disgrace."

"Well?"

"Nobody knows the truth, except you and me. Nobody suspects it; nobody can ever find it out. My ward doesn't know it either. He has now gone back to chambers."

"He accepts his lot?"

"Such a lot can never be accepted. No, sir. I have removed a patch or two from his Memory. That is all. His recollection of the Court ends with the first part of that abominable villain's evidence; he thinks he was seized with a fainting fit; all that followed, including his shame and misery, has been expunged. He has since, by my advice, consulted a physician, who says—ah!—yes—that it was overwork. He knows nothing; and I hope will have no recurrence of his late attack.

"Meantime, I think I shall not divulge my discovery until I am better satisfied. I want to make such a recurrence of the past impossible. Give me ten years more."

# THE SHADOW AND THE FLASH

## JACK LONDON

*Jack London (1876–1916) was enormously successful as a writer of popular fiction in the first decade of the twentieth century, and established a world-wide reputation, using his popularity to promote his idiosyncratic but fervent socialist ideas, notably in the futuristic dystopian novel* The Iron Heel *(1908) and the revolutionary melodrama "Goliah" (1908). His short scientific romances include the classic novella "The Scarlet Plague" (1912) and "The Red One" (1918), an adventure story featuring a crashed alien spaceship. The latter was published posthumously, following his suicide.*

*"The Shadow and the Flash," first published in the June 1903 issue of* The Bookman *and reprinted in the collection* Moon-Face and Other Stories *(1906), is an ironic account of invention driven by obsession, reminiscent of H. G. Wells in its narrative strategy, and probably inspired by his example. It is one of the central texts of American scientific romance.*

When I look back, I realize what a peculiar friendship it was. First, there was Lloyd Inwood, tall, slender, and finely knit, nervous and dark. And then Paul Tichlorne, tall, slender, and finely knit, nervous and blond. Each was the replica of the other in everything except color. Lloyd's eyes were black; Paul's were blue. Under stress of excitement, the blood coursed olive in the face of Lloyd, crimson in the face of Paul. But outside this matter of coloring they were as alike as two peas. Both were high-strung, prone to excessive tension and endurance, and they lived at concert pitch.

But there was a trio involved in this remarkable friendship, and the third was short, and fat and chunky, and lazy, and, loath to say, it was I. Paul and Lloyd seemed born to rivalry with each other, and I to be peacemaker between them. We grew up together, the three of us, and full often have I received the angry blows each intended for the other. They were always competing, striving to outdo each other, and when entered upon some such struggle there was no limit either to their endeavors or passions.

This intense spirit of rivalry obtained in their studies and their games. If Paul memorized one canto of "Marmion," Lloyd memorized two cantos, Paul came back with three, and Lloyd again with four, till each knew the whole poem by heart. I remember an incident that occurred at the swimming hole—an incident tragically significant of the life-struggle between them. The boys had a game of diving to the bottom of a ten-foot pool and holding on by submerged roots to see who could stay under the longest. Paul and Lloyd allowed themselves to be bantered into making the descent together. When I saw their faces, set and determined, disappear in the water as they sank swiftly down, I felt a foreboding of something dreadful. The moments sped, the ripples died away, the face of the pool grew placid and untroubled, and neither black nor golden head broke the surface in quest of air. We above grew anxious. The longest record of the longest-winded boy had been exceeded, and still there was no sign. Air bubbles trickled slowly upward, showing that the breath had been expelled from their lungs, and after that the bubbles ceased to trickle upward. Each second became interminable, and, unable longer to endure the suspense, I plunged into the water.

I found them down at the bottom, clutching tight to the roots, their heads not a foot apart, their eyes wide open, each glaring fixedly at the other. They were suffering frightful torment, writhing and twisting in the pangs of voluntary suffocation; for neither would let go and acknowledge himself beaten. I tried to break Paul's hold on the root, but he resisted me fiercely. Then I lost my breath and came to the surface, badly scared. I quickly explained the situation, and half a dozen of us went down and by main strength tore them loose. By the time we got them out, both were unconscious, and it was only after much barrel-rolling and rubbing and pounding that they finally came to their senses. They would have drowned there, had no one rescued them.

When Paul Tichlorne entered college, he let it be generally understood that he was going in for the social sciences. Lloyd Inwood, entering at the same time, elected to take the same course. But Paul had had it secretly in mind all the time to study the natural sciences, specializing in chemistry, and at the last moment he switched over. Though Lloyd had already arranged his year's work and attended the first lectures, he at once followed Paul's lead and went in for the natural sciences and especially for chemistry.

Their rivalry soon became a noted thing throughout the university. Each was a spur to the other, and they went into chemistry deeper than did ever students before—so deep, in fact, that ere they took their sheepskins they could have stumped any chemistry or "cow college" professor in the institution, save "old" Moss, head of the department, and even him they puzzled and edified more than once. Lloyd's discovery of the "death bacillus" of the sea toad, and his experiments on it with potassium cyanide, sent his name and that of his university ringing around the world; nor was Paul a whit behind when he succeeded in producing laboratory colloids exhibiting amoeba-like activities, and when he cast new light upon the processes of fertilization through his startling experiments with simple sodium chlorides and magnesium solutions on low forms of marine life.

It was in their undergraduate days, however, in the midst of their profoundest plunges into the mysteries of organic chemistry, that Doris Van Benschoten entered into their lives. Lloyd met her first, but within twenty-four hours Paul saw to it that he also made her acquaintance. Of course, they fell in love with her, and she became the only thing in life worth living for. They wooed her with equal ardor and fire, and so intense became their struggle for her that half the student body took to wagering wildly on the result. Even "old" Moss, one day, after an astounding demonstration in his private laboratory by Paul, was guilty to the extent of a month's salary of backing him to become the bridegroom of Doris Van Benschoten.

In the end she solved the problem in her own way, to everybody's satisfaction except Paul's and Lloyd's. Getting them together, she said that she really could not choose between them because she loved them both equally well, and that, unfortunately, since polyandry was not permitted in the United States, she would be compelled to forego the honor and happiness of marrying either of them. Each blamed the other for this lamentable outcome, and the bitterness between them grew more bitter.

But things came to a head soon enough. It was at my home, after they had taken their degrees and dropped out of the world's sight, that the beginning of the end came to pass. Both were men of means, with little inclination and no necessity for professional life. My friendship and their mutual animosity were the two things that linked them in any way together.

While they were very often at my place, they made it a fastidious point to avoid each other on such visits, though it was inevitable, under the circumstances, that they should come upon each other occasionally.

On the day I have in recollection, Paul Tichlorne had been mooning all morning in my study over a current scientific review. This left me free to my own affairs, and I was out among my roses when Lloyd Inwood arrived. Clipping and pruning and tacking the climbers on the porch, with my mouth full of nails, and Lloyd following me about and lending a hand now and again, we fell to discussing the mythical race of invisible people, that strange and vagrant people the traditions of which have come down to us. Lloyd warmed to the talk in his nervous, jerky fashion, and was soon interrogating the physical properties and possibilities of invisibility. A perfectly black object, he contended, would elude and defy the acutest vision.

"Color is a sensation," he was saying. "It has no objective reality. Without light, we can see neither colors nor objects themselves. All objects are black in the dark, and in the dark it is impossible to see them. If no light strikes upon them, then no light is flung back from them to the eye, and so we have no vision-evidence of their being."

"But we see black objects in daylight," I objected.

"Very true," he went on warmly, "and that is because they're not perfectly black. Were they perfectly black, absolutely black, as it were, we could not see them—nay, not in the blaze of a thousand suns could we see them! And so I say, with the right pigments, properly compounded, an absolutely black paint could be produced which would render invisible whatever it was applied to."

"It would be a remarkable discovery," I said, noncommittally, for the whole thing seemed too fantastic for aught but speculative purposes.

"Remarkable!" Lloyd slapped me on the shoulder. "I should say so. Why, old chap, to coat myself with such a paint would be to put the world at my feet. The secrets of kings and courts would be mine, the machinations of diplomats and politicians, the play of stock-gamblers, the plans of trusts and corporations. I could keep my hand on the inner pulse of things and become the greatest power in the world. And I. . . ." He broke off shortly, then added, "Well, I have begun my experiments, and I don't mind telling you that I'm right in line for it."

A laugh from the doorway startled us. Paul Tichlorne was standing there, a smile of mockery on his lips.

"You forget, my dear Lloyd," he said.

"Forget what?"

"You forget," Paul went on—"ah, you forget the shadow."

I saw Lloyd's face drop, but he answered sneeringly, "I can carry a sunshade, you know. Then he turned suddenly and fiercely upon him. "Look here, Paul, you'll keep out of this if you know what's good for you."

A rupture seemed imminent, but Paul laughed good-naturedly. "I wouldn't lay fingers on your dirty pigments. Succeed beyond your most sanguine expectations, yet you will always fetch up against the shadow. You can't get away from it. Now I shall go on the very opposite tack. In the very nature of my proposition the shadow will be eliminated. . . ."

"Transparency!" ejaculated Lloyd, instantly. "But it can't be achieved."

"Oh, no; of course not." And Paul shrugged his shoulders and strolled off down the briar-rose path.

That was the beginning of it. Both men attacked the problem with all the tremendous energy for which they were noted, and with a rancor and bitterness that made me tremble for the success of either. Each trusted me to the utmost, and in the long weeks of experimentation that followed I was made a party to both sides, listening to their theorizings and witnessing their demonstrations. Never, by word or sign, did I convey to either the slightest hint of the other's progress, and they respected me for the seal I put upon my lips.

Lloyd Inwood, after prolonged and unintermittent application, when the tension upon mind and body became too great to bear, had a strange way of obtaining relief. He attended prize fights. It was at one of those brutal exhibitions, whither he had dragged me in order to tell his latest results, that his theory received striking confirmation.

"Do you see that red-whiskered man?" he asked, pointing across the ring to the fifth tier of seats on the opposite side. "And do you see the next man to him, the one in the white hat? Well, there is quite a gap between them, is there not?"

"Certainly," I answered. "They are a seat apart. The gap is the unoccupied seat."

He leaned over to me and spoke seriously. "Between the red-whiskered man and the white-hated man sits Ben Wasson. You have heard me speak of him. He is the cleverest pugilist of his weight in the country. He is also a Caribbean negro, full-blooded, and the blackest in the United States. He has on a black overcoat buttoned up. I saw him when he came in and took that seat. As soon as he sat down he disappeared. Watch closely; he may smile."

I was for crossing over to verify Lloyd's statement, but he restrained me. "Wait," he said.

I waited and watched, till the red-whiskered man turned his head as though addressing the unoccupied seat; and then, in the empty space, I saw the rolling whites of a pair of eyes and the white double crescent of two rows of teeth, and for the instant I could make out a negro's face. But with the passing of the smile his visibility passed, and the chair seemed vacant as before.

"Were he perfectly black, you could sit alongside him and not see him," Lloyd said; and I confess the illustration was apt enough to make me well-nigh convinced.

I visited Lloyd's laboratory a number of times after that, and found him always deep in his search after the absolute black. His experiments covered all sorts of pigments, such as lamp-blacks, tars, carbonized vegetable matters, soots of oils and fats, and the various carbonized animal substances.

"White light is composed of the seven primary colors," he argued to me, "but it is itself, of itself, invisible. Only by being reflected from objects do it and the objects become visible. But only that portion of it that is reflected becomes visible. For instance, here is a blue tobacco-box. The white light strikes against it, and, with one exception, all its component colors—violet, indigo, green, yellow, orange and red—are absorbed. The one exception is blue. It is not absorbed, but reflected. Therefore the tobacco-box gives us a sensation of blueness. We do not see the other colors because they are absorbed. We only see the blue. For the same reason, grass is green. The green waves of white light are thrown upon our eyes."

"When we paint our houses, we do not apply color to them," he said at another time. "What we do is to apply certain substances that have the property of absorbing from white light all the colors except those that we would have our houses appear. When a substance reflects all the colors to the eye, it seems to us white. When it absorbs all the colors, it is black. But, as I said before, we have as yet no perfect black. All the colors are not absorbed. The perfect black, guarding against high lights, will be utterly and absolutely invisible. Look at that, for example."

He pointed to the palette lying on his work table. Different shades of black pigments were brushed on it. One, in particular, I could hardly see. It gave my eyes a blurring sensation, and I rubbed them and looked again.

"That," he said, impressively, "is the blackest black you or any mortal eye ever looked upon. But just you wait, and I'll have a black so black that no mortal man will be able to look upon it—and see it!"

On the other hand, I used to find Paul Tichlorne plunged as deeply into the study of light polarization, diffraction, and interference, single and double refraction, and all manner of strange organic compounds.

"Transparency: a state or quality of body which permits all rays of light to pass through," he defined for me. "That is what I am seeking. Lloyd blunders up against the shadow with his perfect opaqueness, but I escape it. A transparent body casts no shadow; neither does it reflect light-waves—that is, the perfectly transparent does not. So, avoiding high lights, not only will such a body cast no shadow, but, since it reflects no light, it will also be invisible."

We were standing by the window at another time. Paul was engaged in polishing a number of lenses, which were ranged along the sill. Suddenly, after a pause in the conversation, he said: "Oh, I've dropped a lens. Stick your head out, old man, and see where it went to."

Out I started to thrust my head, but a sharp blow on the forehead caused me to recoil. I rubbed my bruised brow and gazed with reproachful inquiry at Paul, who was laughing in gleeful, boyish fashion.

"Well?" he said.

"Well?" I echoed.

"Why don't you investigate?" he demanded. And investigate I did. Before thrusting out my head, my senses, automatically active, had told me there was nothing there, that nothing intervened between me and out-of-doors, that the aperture of the window opening was utterly empty. I stretched forth my hand and felt a hard object, smooth and cool and flat, which my touch, out of its experience, told me to be glass. I looked again, but could see positively nothing.

"White quartzose sand," Paul rattled off, "sodic carbonate, slaked lime, cullet, manganese peroxide—there you have it, the finest French plate glass, made by the great St. Gobain company, who made the finest plate glass in the world, and this is the finest piece they ever made. It cost a king's ransom. But look at it! You can't see it. You don't know it's there till you run your head against it.

"Eh, old boy! That's merely an object-lesson—certain elements, in themselves opaque, yet so compounded as to give a resultant body which is transparent. But that is a matter of inorganic chemistry, you say. Very true. But I dare to assert, standing here on my two feet, that in the organic, I can duplicate whatever occurs in the inorganic.

"Here!" he held a test-tube between me and the light, and I noted the cloudy or muddy liquid it contained. He emptied the contents of another test-tube into it, and almost instantly it became clear and sparkling.

"Or here!" With quick, nervous movements among his array of test-tubes, he turned a white solution to a wine color, and a light yellow solution to a dark brown. He dropped a piece of litmus paper into an acid, when it changed instantly to red, and on floating it in an alkali it turned as quickly to blue.

"The litmus paper is still the litmus paper," he enunciated in the formal manner of the lecturer. "I have not changed it into something else. Then what did I do? I merely changed the arrangement of its molecules. Where, at first, it absorbed all colors from the light but red, its molecular structure was so changed that it absorbed red and all colors except blue. And so it goes, *ad infinitum*. Now, what I purpose to do is this." He paused for a space. "I purpose to seek—ay, and to find—the proper reagents, which, acting upon the living organism, will bring about molecular changes analogous to those you have just witnessed. But those reagents, which I shall find, and for that matter, upon which I already have my hands, will not turn the human body to blue or red or black, but they will turn it to transparency. All light will pass through it. It will be invisible. It will cast no shadow."

A few weeks later I went hunting with Paul. He had been promising me for some time that I should have the pleasure of shooting over a wonderful dog—the most wonderful dog, in fact, that ever a man shot over, so he averred, and continued to aver till my curiosity was aroused. But on the morning in question I was disappointed, for there was no dog in evidence.

"Don't see him about," Paul remarked, unconcernedly, and we set off across the fields.

I could not imagine, at the time, what was ailing me, but I had a feeling of some impending and deadly illness. My nerves were all awry, and, from the astounding tricks they played me, my senses seemed to have run riot.

Strange sounds disturbed me. At times I heard the swish-swish of grass being shoved aside, and once the patter of feet across a patch of stony ground.

"Did you hear anything Paul?" I asked once.

But he shook his head and thrust his feet steadily forward.

While climbing a fence, I heard the low, eager whine of a dog, apparently from within a couple of feet of me; but on looking about me I saw nothing.

I dropped to the ground, limp and trembling.

"Paul," I said, "we had best return to the house. I am afraid I am going to be sick."

"Nonsense, old man," he answered. "The sunshine has gone to your head like wine. You'll be all right. It's famous weather."

But, passing along a narrow path through a clump of cottonwoods, some object brushed against my legs and I stumbled and nearly fell. I looked with sudden anxiety at Paul.

"What's the matter?" he asked. "Tripping over your own feet?"

I kept my tongue between my teeth and plodded on, though sore perplexed and thoroughly satisfied that some acute and mysterious malady had attacked my nerves. So far my eyes had escaped; but, when we got to the open fields again, even my vision went back on me. Strange flashes of varicolored, rainbow light began to appear and disappear on the path before me. Still, I managed to keep myself in hand, till the varicolored lights persisted for a space of fully twenty seconds, dancing and flashing in continuous play. Then I sat down, weak and shaky.

"It's all up with me," I gasped, covering my eyes with my hands. "It has attacked my eyes. Paul, take me home."

But Paul laughed long and loud. "What did I tell you? The most wonderful dog, eh? Well, what do you think?"

He turned partly from me and began to whistle. I heard the patter of feet, the panting of a heated animal, and the unmistakable yelp of a dog. Then Paul stooped down and apparently fondled the empty air.

"Here, give me your fist."

And he rubbed my hand over the cold nose and jowls of a dog. A dog it certainly was, with the shape and the smooth, short coat of a pointer.

Suffice to say, I speedily recovered my spirits and control. Paul put a collar about the animal's neck and tied his handkerchief to its tail. And then was vouchsafed us the remarkable sight of an empty collar and a waving handkerchief cavorting over the fields. It was something to see that collar and handkerchief pin a bevy of quail in a clump of locusts and remain rigid and immovable till we had flushed the birds.

Now and again the dog emitted the varicolored flashes I had mentioned: the one thing, Paul explained, which he had not anticipated and which he doubted could be overcome.

"They're a large family," he said, "these sun dogs, wind dogs, rainbows, halos, and, parhelia. They are produced by refraction of light from mineral and ice crystals, from mist, rain, spray, and no end of things; and I am afraid they are the penalty I must pay for the transparency. I escaped Lloyd's shadow only to fetch up against the rainbow flash."

A couple of days later, before the entrance to Paul's laboratory, I encountered a terrible stench. So overpowering was it that it was easy to discover the source: a mass of putrescent matter on the doorstep which in general outlines resembled a dog.

Paul was startled when he investigated my find. It was his invisible dog, or, rather, what had been his invisible dog, for it was now plainly visible. It had been plying about but a few minutes before in all health and strength. Closer examination revealed that the skull had been crushed by some heavy blow. While it was strange that the animal should have been killed, the inexplicable thing was that it should so quickly decay.

"The reagents I injected into its system were harmless," Paul explained. "Yet they were powerful, and it appears that when death comes they force practically instantaneous disintegration. Remarkable! Most remarkable! Well, the only thing is not to die. They do no harm so long as one lives. But I do wonder who smashed in that dog's head."

Light, however, was thrown upon this when a frightened housemaid brought the news that Gaffer Bedshaw had that very morning, not more than an hour back, gone violently insane, and was strapped down at home, in the huntsman's lodge, where he raved of a battle with a ferocious and gigantic beast that he had encountered in the Tichlorne pasture. He claimed that the thing, whatever it was, was invisible, wherefore his tearful wife and daughters shook their heads, and wherefore he but waxed the more violent, and the gardener and the coachman tightened the straps by another hole.

Nor, while Paul Tichlorne was thus successfully mastering the problem of invisibility, was Lloyd Inwood a whit behind. I went over in answer to a message of his to come and see how he was getting on. Now, his laboratory occupied an isolated situation in the midst of his vast grounds. It was built in a pleasant little glade, surrounded on all sides by a dense forest growth, and was to be gained by way of a winding and erratic path. But I have traveled that path so often as to know every foot of it, and conceive my surprise when I came upon the glade and found no laboratory. The quaint shed structure with its red sandstone chimney was not. Nor did it look as if it ever had been. There were no signs of ruin, no debris, nothing.

I started to walk across what had once been its site. "This," I said to myself, should be where the step went up to the door." Barely were the words out of my mouth when I stubbed my toe on some obstacle, pitched forward, and butted my head into something that felt very much like a door. I reached out my hand. It was a door. I found the knob and turned it; and at once, as the door swung inward on its hinges, the whole interior of the laboratory impinged upon my vision. Greeting Lloyd, I closed the door and backed up the path a few paces. I could see nothing of the building. Returning and opening the door, at once all the furniture and every detail of the interior were visible. It was indeed startling, the sudden transition from void to light and form and color.

"What do you think of it, eh?" Lloyd asked, wringing my hand. "I slapped a couple of coats of absolute black on the outside yesterday to see how it worked. How's your head? You bumped it pretty solidly, I imagine.

"Never mind that," he interrupted my congratulations. "I've something better for you to do."

While he talked he began to strip, and when he stood naked before me he thrust a pot and brush into my hand and said, "Here, give me a coat of this."

It was an oily, shellac-like stuff, which spread quickly and easily over the skin and dried immediately.

"Merely preliminary and precautionary," he explained when I had finished; "but now for the real stuff."

I picked up another pot he indicated, and glanced inside, but could see nothing.

"It's empty," I said.

"Stick your finger in it."

I obeyed, and was aware of a sensation of cool moisture. On withdrawing my hand I glanced at the forefinger, the one I had immersed, but it had disappeared. I moved and knew from the alternate tension and relaxation of the muscles that I moved it, but it defied my sense of sight. To all appearances I had been shorn of a finger; nor could I get any visual impression of it till I extended it under the skylight and saw its shadow plainly blotted on the floor.

Lloyd chuckled. "Now spread it on, and keep your eyes open."

I dipped the brush into the seemingly empty pot, and gave him a long stroke across his chest. With the passage of the brush the living flesh disappeared from beneath. I covered his right leg, and he was a one-legged man defying all laws of gravitation. And so, stroke by stroke, member by member, I painted Lloyd into nothingness. It was a creepy experience, and I was glad when naught remained in sight but his burning black eyes, poised apparently unsupported in mid-air.

"I have a refined and harmless solution for them," he said. "A fine spray with an air-brush, and presto! I am not."

This deftly accomplished, he said, "Now I shall move about, and do tell me what sensations you experience."

"In the first place, I cannot see you," I said, and I could hear his gleeful laugh from the midst of the emptiness. "Of course," I continued, "you cannot escape your shadow, but that was to be expected. When you pass between my eye and an object, the object disappears, but so unusual and incomprehensible is its disappearance that it seems to me as though my eyes had blurred. When you move rapidly, I experience a bewildering succession of blurs. The blurring sensation makes my eyes ache and my brain tired."

"Have you any other warnings of my presence?" he asked.

"No, and yes," I answered. "When you are near me I have feelings similar to those produced by dank warehouses, gloomy crypts, and deep mines. And as sailors feel the loom of the land on dark nights, so I think I feel the loom of your body. But it is all very vague and intangible."

Long we talked that last morning in his laboratory and when I turned to go, he put his unseen hand in mine with nervous grip, and said, "Now I shall conquer the world!" And I could not dare to tell him of Paul Tichlorne's equal success.

At home I found a note from Paul, asking me to come up immediately, and it was high noon when I came spinning up the driveway on my wheel. Paul called me from the tennis court, and I dismounted and went over. But the court was empty. As I stood there, gaping open-mouthed, a tennis ball struck me on the arm, and as I turned about, another whizzed past my ear. For aught I could see of my assailant, they came whirling at me from out of space, and right well was I peppered with them. But when the balls already flung at me began to come back for a second whack, I realized the situation. Seizing a racket and keeping my eyes open, I quickly saw a rainbow flash appearing and disappearing and darting over the ground. I took out after it, and when I laid the racquet upon it for a half-dozen stout blows, Paul's voice rang out:

"Enough! Enough! Oh! Ouch! You're landing on my naked skin, you know! Ow! O-w-w! I'll be good! I'll be good! I only wanted you to see my metamorphosis," he said, ruefully, and I imagined he was rubbing his hurts.

A few minutes later we were playing tennis—a handicap on my part, for I could have no knowledge of his position save when all the angles between himself, the sun, and me, were in proper conjunction. Then he flashed, and only then. But the flashes were more brilliant than the rainbow—purest blue, most delicate violet, brightest yellow, and all the intermediary shades, with the scintillating brilliancy of the diamond, dazzling, blinding, iridescent.

But in the midst of our play I felt a sudden cold chill, reminding me of deep mines and gloomy crypts, such a chill as I had experienced that very morning. The next moment, close to the net, I saw a ball rebound in mid-air and empty space, and at the same instant, a score of feet away, Paul Tichlorne emitted a rainbow flash. It could not be he from whom the ball had rebounded, and with sickening dread I realized that Lloyd Inwood had come upon the scene. To make sure, I looked for his shadow, and there it was, a shapeless blotch the girth of his body—the sun was overhead—moving along the ground. I remembered his threat, and felt sure that all the long years of rivalry were about to culminate in uncanny battle.

I cried a warning to Paul, and heard a snarl as of a wild beast, and an answering snarl. I saw the dark blotch move swiftly across the court, and a brilliant burst of varicolored light moving with equal swiftness to meet it; and then shadow and flash came together and there was the sound of unseen blows. The net went down before my frightened eyes. I sprang toward the fighters, crying:

"For God's sake!"

But their locked bodies smote against my knees, and I was overthrown.

"You keep out of this, old man!" I heard the voice of Lloyd Inwood from out of the emptiness; and then Paul's voice crying, "Yes, we've had enough of peacemaking!"

From the sound of their voices I knew they had separated. I could not locate Paul, and so approached the shadow that represented Lloyd. But from the other side came a stunning blow on the point of my jaw, and I heard Paul scream angrily, "Now will you keep away?"

Then they came together, the impact of their blows, their groans and gasps, and the swift flashings and shadow-movings telling plainly of the deadliness of the struggle.

I shouted for help, and Gaffer Bedshaw came running into the court. I could see, as he approached, that he was looking at me strangely, but he collided with the combatants and was hurled headlong to the ground. With a despairing shriek and a cry of "O Lord, I've got 'em!" he sprang to his feet and tore madly out of the court.

I could do nothing, so I sat up, fascinated and powerless, and watched the struggle. The noonday sun beat down with dazzling brightness on the naked tennis court. And it was naked. All I could see was the blotch of shadow and the rainbow flashes, the dust rising from the invisible feet, the earth tearing up from beneath the straining foot-grips, and the wire screen bulge once or twice as their bodies hurled against it. That was all, and after a time, even that ceased. There were no more flashes, and the shadow had become long and stationary; and I remembered their set boyish faces when they clung to the roots in the deep coolness of the pool.

They found me an hour afterward. Some inkling of what had happened got to the servants and they quitted the Tichlorne service in a body. Gaffer Bedshaw never recovered from the second shock he received, and is confined in a madhouse, hopelessly incurable. The secrets of their marvelous discoveries died with Paul and Lloyd, both laboratories being destroyed by grief-stricken relatives. As for myself, I no longer care for chemical research, and science is a tabooed topic in my household. I have returned to my roses. Nature's colors are good enough for me.

# THE GORILLOID

## EDMOND HARAUCOURT

*Edmond Haraucourt (1856–1941) was an avant garde poet, songwriter and playwright at the center of the Parisian literary community of the 1880s, who found a vocation that would allow him to make a steady living when he became a museum curator. After making a spectacular debut as a writer of prose fiction with* Immortalité *(1888; tr. as "Immortality"), the ultimate skeptical extrapolation of the notion of a paradisal afterlife, his short fiction became remarkable for seeking unexplored extremes; he wrote several other far-futuristic fantasies in addition to the one below, all of which are available in English in the Black Coat Press collection* Illusions of Immortality *(2012). Most of his scientific romances were published as short serials in the feuilleton slot of* Le Journal, *which also accommodated a long story sequence detailing the origins of conscious thought and technological adaptation in a Neanderthal horde, collected as* Daâh, le premier homme *(1914; tr. as* Daâh, The First Human).*

*"Le Gorilloïde," which was published in* Le Journal *in January 1904 before appearing as a booklet in 1906, is typical of Haraucourt's tendency to venture into previously unexplored regions of the imagination, usually endeavoring to find novel narrative strategies that would allow him to do so. It is a masterpiece of the French genre.*

I

Of Others

> *The first day of the new year incites
> our minds to look into the future.*
> Guy de l'Estang (1413)

Four thousand centuries have passed. The face of the world has changed. Our continent has been swallowed up by new seas; the glacial waters of the Pole descend as far as the shores of Africa. The only inhabitable regions girdle the globe between the two tropics. All our animal and vegetable species have been transformed during the Quinary period and the majority have ceased to exist. Humankind no longer exists.

On the other hand, several races of apes have been perfected, and among them, the Gorillas, having reached the highest degree of development, constitute the superior being. They live in societies, and their civilization, like their science, is highly advanced.

Now, on the 26.3 of the year 71.9.37, an extraordinary item of news spread, and for two lunes—the day then being thirty-six hours long—the newspapers everywhere were discussing Professor Sffaty's discovery.

On an exploratory voyage to the North Pole, the illustrious scientist ventured into previously unknown regions. Having reached a latitude of 46°[1] he encountered a rocky archipelago of Secondary origin, where he wintered. On those islets he collected the fossil bones of vanished species, notably several skeletons of a previously unknown antediluvian ape, which presented strange resemblances to the Gorillas.

The professor even succeeded in capturing a live specimen of one of these "humans"—as he called the prehistoric animal in question.

The news of this event, initially treated with great suspicion, did not take long to spread, and immediately impassioned public opinion in spite of its scientific character. Violent polemics appeared in the newspapers, the question at stake being: *Are Apes descended from Humans?*

Politics and religion envenomed the debate, which promptly ceased to remain zoological.

A lecture by Professor Sffaty, advertised as being due to take place in the large lecture-hall of the Museum of Karysk, has brought together an enormous and select crowd. People have fought over tickets. Five hundred Gorillas of the noblest birth, the most illustrious apes in politics, finance and the various institutes have assembled in the hall, which has been crowded since the doors opened.

The building's surroundings are cluttered with a popular multitude, and one might believe that all Gorillakind is taking an interest, in its conscience

---

[1] 46° is the approximate latitude of Mont Blanc, the highest peak in the Alps.

and in its dignity, in the questions that are about to be treated in that solemn session.

The auditorium is unsettled; the adverse opinions of materialism and idealism are already manifest with a latent acrimony that the severity of the location is only just retaining within the bounds of decency. The police, affecting to fear a riot, have taken exceptional measures to ensure order in the hall and its surroundings.

While waiting for the lecture to begin, opera glasses are aimed at two twin tables that have been laden with bones.

The moment is approaching; the room is warming up.

Professor Sffaty finally appears.

Prolonged applause and a hostile tumult greet his entrance simultaneously.

He is rather pale but quite calm. His fine bearing and the dignity of his attitude end up holding sway. After only a quarter of an hour, silence is almost reestablished, and the doctor can finally make himself heard.

He speaks.

*

Messieurs,

Whatever humility imposes itself on the pioneers of Science, who habitually live in confrontation with the most sublime problems and incessantly observe the impotence of effort, I have the conviction today of seeing my tribulations and fatigues recompensed by a discovery of the most fundamental importance, and of presenting to you a document of the greatest possible interest to the history of our race, its origins and its future.

*Sensation.*

The newspapers of the entire world have already spoken to you about it, perhaps a little too hastily. Perhaps they have also been too hasty, and too categorical, in evaluating the character of this scientific revelation. Is it true as they claim, that I am bringing you our ancestor? In other words, is it true that Gorillas are descended from Humans? Messieurs, let us proceed less rapidly. Such a question is serious, and requires only to be resolved as calmly as possible, by means of a very careful examination, with a precise method. That is why, before presenting the strange animal that will be the object of our study to you, it is first appropriate to look back, in order better to explain the conditions of its existence and the environment in which it has been able to manifest itself.

*Various movements.*

Have no fear, Mesdames; I shall keep this necessary preamble as brief as possible, in order not to irritate you by abusing your patience.

*Smiles.*

Messieurs, everything leads us to believe that the boreal regions, presently covered by an immense Ocean, were not always sunk beneath the glacial waters. We know, and no one any longer disputes it, that the polar zone was once much less extensive, and that in the first ages of the world, when the terrestrial globe knew no seasons, the average temperature at the poles was equal to that of the tropics, and certainly far superior to that which we enjoy today in our equatorial climes. That certainty has been acquired by Science.

However, the hypothesis, more contestable and more contested, of a vanished continent which occupied that portion of our planet, in the epoch when the zone of polar ice scarcely descended below the forty-second degree of north latitude, is another matter. Those problematic lands, which legend calls Europides or Europe, would have spread out in the place where the ice of the Europic Ocean now extends, and the rare islands that we see, scattered over that vast sea, would simply be the summits of its highest mountains, still emerging to attest the previous existence of a continent that is no more.

Let us hasten to say that the existence of a continent is still no more than a hypothesis—a logical hypothesis, corroborated by all the notions of geology, but which has not, to date, been scientifically demonstrated by authentic vestiges, the only evidence that we can admit. For you can easily understand that it is permissible to say: "The sea once covered the continent on which we reside, and has built us this fatherland—here are its traces!"—but it is less easy to go to study, at enormously profound submarine depths, the vestiges of an ancient terrestrial life. And although we observe experimentally that everywhere the land is, the sea was, we cannot establish by the same method that land surged forth where the sea hollows out—but we can at least suppose it, by analogy. Continents have their vicissitudes. No one is unaware that, since the creation of the globe, all the land presently visible and known, was by turns abandoned and repossessed, left once again by the sea that subsequently came to reoccupy it, and the successive layers of the terrestrial crust are here to certify this perpetual alternation.

*A commencement of lassitude appears to be boring the audience, whose members are utterly uninterested in geological considerations, and want to hear something else. Estimating that the preamble is long, several ladies are shifting in their seats and fanning themselves. The explorer pays no heed. He continues calmly.*

That a Europe, or Europides, existed is therefore probable. One can even assert that, to some extent, the discovery of the Gorilloid that we have brought back is a further argument in favor of the thesis.

In fact, Messieurs, a constant harmony reigns in nature between all the various manifestations of life; animals and vegetables alike exist in a direct relationship with the environment they inhabit. You know that, and every one of you has been able to observe it many times over while taking walks. Species, in the animal kingdom as well as the vegetable, corresponding to the climates of their respective regions, are appropriated by them, in a sense denouncing them. Regions that are damp or dry, cold or hot, elevated or low-lying, have their particular flora and fauna.

Now, that law of appropriation is manifest in many other effects, less familiar but no less logical; what is true for temperatures, altitudes or hygrometric conditions is also true for space: the proportions of extent exercise their influence on forms of life, and that influence imposes itself like that of any other ambient condition. The population of islands cannot and does not resemble that of continents; they have their own inhabitants and always will. Large herbivores correspond to abundant pasture; fast-moving animals such as deer, reindeer or horses suppose the deployment of large surfaces, without which they would not be able to live or develop normally—and, let us also say, without which they could not be born. A bird with a large wingspan is conclusive evidence of distance, as a fish is conclusive evidence of water.

If, therefore, we encounter, in insular points, the fossils of species that I shall call continental, we can affirm without hesitation that the islands were formerly an integral part of a continent, from which they were separated by some cataclysm.

Such is precisely the case with the Alpians that we have just explored. Our collection of fossils, gathered among the rocks of the boreal region, attests to the existence in those desolate regions of a once-prosperous continent. You can, at your leisure, examine these specimens of fossil bones, which the ice has conserved for us over several thousand centuries, and which will subsequently be classified at the Museum. But henceforth, and most of all, the strange simian that you will shortly contemplate, the last survivor of a world, will appear to you and cannot fail to appear to you, as the witness of a lost continent, and perhaps of a level of culture that seems to have been quite advanced, not only physically but also intellectually.

*Movements. The explorer addresses a few whispered words to his assistant, who steps back. Prolonged agitation in the auditorium.*

Before then. . . .

*Various movements. Murmurs.*

Messieurs, I understand your legitimate impatience, and it flatters me, as a proof of the powerful interest that you are kind enough to attach to my discovery, but the presentation of the Human cannot usefully be made if it is not preceded by an osteological examination of earlier specimens: the skeletons of yesterday, rather than the living specimen of today, will permit us to judge the degree of advancement reached by the race in the times of its prosperity. I shall pass over that study as rapidly as possible, in order to return to it in a future lecture, but it is impossible for me to omit it, however anxious I am to please you!

*The professor steps back to the tables on which the fossil bones are placed.*

Messieurs I tell you that the Gorilloid, to which we have given the name Human, was not an unconscious brute. The dimensions of his skull prove it, no less than the opening of his facial angle. Among all the animal species that are or have been alive, only one facial angle is as widely open: ours.

*Various sensations. The scientist, his arm outstretched, lifts up a human skull and displays its profile triumphantly. His attitude, a trifle over-theatrical, is emphatic, and some people seem inclined to consider it provocative; that impression is accentuated when the lecturer, turning to a blackboard standing behind him, shows thereon the human angle and the gorillan angle, which are identical. Pointing to them each in turn he says:*

Theirs, then; ours, now. It's the same.

*Prolonged movements.*

The dentition, analogous to ours, attests an omnivore; this mammal held itself, as we do, in a vertical position, only utilizing its hind limbs for walking; it was a bimane!

*Sensations.*

Finally, the presence of certain osseous apophyses, the detailed study of which I shall not impose upon you, undeniably proves the progressive atrophy of organs once possessed by the first specimens of the species, but which gradually disappeared as the race was refined—such as, for example, the vestige of a caudal appendage, which the Human skeleton presents, as ours does.

*Murmurs, protests. The professor affects not to hear them, pauses briefly, and continues:*

We therefore find ourselves, without a doubt, in the presence of an advanced, civilized, albeit degenerate, species, which occupied, before ours, continents anterior to ours: a superior species like our own, perhaps capable of abstract thought, and perhaps having had arts and sciences like ours!

I shall have said everything about this point, Messieurs, when I have added to these summary remarks the assertion of one fact, and one only, which doubtless seems to you rich in possible deductions: these bones have now been collected in a native state in the soul of the Quinary epoch, as were those of the animals we found; they were buried in tombs of carved stone. Humans buried their dead!

*Prolonged sensation.*

Thus, Messieurs, Humans lived in society. Furthermore, they built. An agglomeration of sand and calcareous matter, compressed between the stones of tombs, which serves to hold them together, clearly appears to be, not a natural product, but the work of an intentional fabrication. Thus, Humans possessed industries. Living in society—as proved by the association of the tombs—they were able to group their houses like their tombs, and constitute cities . . . don't laugh, Messieurs, I'm not affirming it yet, but I say that they could: the hypothesis, although not demonstrated, is at least plausible, and logic authorizes it! When we have searched the sea-bed—and we will search it, the Europic Sea, where the cities are submerged, as I am convinced they are, for want of proof to the contrary—and have brought back into the light those miserable remains of a vanished epoch, of a doomed species, then, doubtless, you will no longer be laughing. The irony of incredulity—which is to say, of ignorance—will be forced to admit, with us, with reason, and with common sense, the one art that supposes all the arts, that the possibility of one renders all the others possible and necessary, if there is time enough to attain them, and that it is evidence of a retrograde mind, in no way noble but merely closed, in no way proud but simply vain, to refuse to conceive the possibility of races that are, or once were, equal to ours.

*Enthusiastic applause from some benches. Whistles. Protests. The applause is redoubled. Tumult.*

The honor of Gorillakind. . . .

*New interruption. Animal cries. The professor makes as if to withdraw. In the face of that threat, calm is gradually reestablished.*

Messieurs, I am not polemicizing here; I am practicing science. There are some who are scornful of my thinking, who have been able momentarily to attribute to me the malevolent intention of offending the susceptibilities of others. I respect all beliefs, in the desire to see mine respected in return, and I do not consider that the verities acquired regarding the evolution of animal species are incompatible with any notion of the divinity, or that they cast a slur on legally recognized religions. I repeat that I am not making a political point here. . . .

*Applause.*

. . . and I deem that the honor of the gorillan species cannot reside in a jealous exclusivism, but, on the contrary, in the glory of thinking and seeking the truth, whatever it may be, on any subject whatsoever.

Dogmas inform us that the World was created for us and for us alone. Let us leave the dogmas there, I shall not dispute them; but let us at least recognize that, if such a conviction has been able to arise in our minds, analogous minds might have had it before us, and might have it after us. Who knows what the Alpian Bimanes of whom these are the relics, the Humans, might have thought about these matters? Who knows whether this Gorilloid species had not arrived at its full development, while our ancestors, still primitive, were living in the caves of the prehistoric age, and who can tell whether its members might have professed, in our regard, an exclusivism analogous to the one on which we now pride ourselves in our turn? Who can tell whether they might not have had, like us, dogmas and gods, faith in their immortal souls?

Gentlemen, let us not pass judgment on things unknown, for fear of making temeritous judgments. The beings I am showing you might have believed themselves to be great. They are no longer. Respect their ashes! A few thousand centuries ago, the creatures that I have discovered thought, loved, suffered and desired, but it now requires the science of another race merely to establish that they existed!

These beings, superior to all known animals, reigned over themselves and over the globe, in the distant epochs when the habitable portion of our planet had not yet been reduced to the intertropical zone. Their domain was vaster than ours, but perhaps their notion of good and evil was identical to ours. How did they disappear? The law of evolution that had fashioned them logically, degenerated them logically, and when environmental conditions ceased to be in harmony with the species' organism, they logically died out.

When, shortly, we compare these two skeletons with the survivor that you are going to see, you will comprehend the slow regression of a grandeur that has attenuated, a strength that is exhausted, a race that is on the brink of extinction.

*Applause. The professor turns and makes a sign to his assistant, who receives his instructions and leaves the room. The session is suspended briefly. Animated dialogues in the hall.*

*The assistants return, carrying a sort of cubic cage on a stretcher, covered with a sheet; they deposit it on a large table next to the podium and hang a placard on it: DO NOT TOUCH.*

*Lively movement of curiosity. Silence is completely reestablished. Opera-glasses are aimed at the veiled cage. The professor approaches and slowly lifts the edge of the sheet. He leans toward the cage, shaking his head in an amicable manner, as if to reassure the captive beast.*

*He opens the door of the cage.*

*The Human appears.*

*On the invitation of the professor, who encourages it with a hand gesture, the Human crosses the threshold and advances across the table.*

*Cries of surprise, followed by words rapidly exchanged in low voices.*

*The Human is clad in an ample bearskin cloak. It measures about one meter ten. Its head, enormous and pale, is speckled—its face as well as his head—with sparse hairs, dirty white in color. The blinking eyes, which seem to be those of an albino, are protected by long white lashes. Its expression is one of fright. Its torso and limbs are invisible beneath the draped cloak.*

*The professor leans toward the specimen and gently, by means of gestures, invites it to take off its cloak. The animal is visibly reluctant. In spite of the specimen's resistance, the professor proceeds to undress it himself.*

*A further cry of astonishment goes up in the auditorium.*

*The Human is completely naked; its upper body is weak and flat, as if crushed, but the abdomen is swollen and sticks out. The arms, extraordinarily short, terminate in minuscule hands with spatulate fingers. The short and knock-kneed limbs have enormous attachments. The entire body, dull gray in color, is striated with white hairs similar to those on the face.*

*The Human, embarrassed under the gazes of the crowd, turns its head to the right and the left, anxiously, as if seeking a refuge.*

*The opera-glasses study it; the dialogues become more animated. In many places a scarcely-scientific laughter shakes the powerful shoulders of aristocratic Gorillas. The ladies, keenly amused by the examination of the grotesque little male, whisper among themselves. A few scientists, who have come on to the stage, touch the Human, open its mouth, tap it on the back, work its joints, and examine the texture of its skin and the nuances of its hair with magnifying glasses.*

*

## II.
### The Last Couple

*When it is reckoned that scientific and worldly curiosity has had time to satisfy itself, Professor Sffaty asks for the stage to be cleared, and returns to the table on which the two fossilized human skeletons are laid. He stands behind it.*

*By his attitude, he makes it understood that he is going to speak. Calm is gradually reestablished in the audience. The assistants shout: "Silence, please!"*

*People cough. They settle down.*

*The professor drinks some water.*

*The silence is complete.*

*The professor speaks:*

A first glance was sufficient, Mesdames and Messieurs, for you to observe the evident kinship between this small creature and our race, and I ask for no more proof for that than your cry of surprise—but we shall return to that delicate question later.

The second observation that imposes itself is that of a singularly notable difference between this ultimate specimen of a species and the two fossil skeletons that you are about to see, and which are themselves fundamentally different from one another.

Three individuals, three epochs! The first, four thousand centuries old. . . . *Sensations.*

. . . goes back to the Quaternary period, in the course of which Humans seem to have been the veritable monarchs of the globe. The second skeleton, much more recent, dates from the Quinary epoch; it is a specimen of degeneration, which marks an intermediate stage between the glorious human here to my right and the rebrutalized human here to my left, the last survivor.

I shall spare you, Mesdames, the eminently instructive comparative study of these three types. Merely note the fundamental uniformity of the three modes: the animal is one, always the same, but gulfs of time separate the three individuals; between them, the work of degeneration has taken effect. In the same way that the species, in the course of centuries, and by virtue of an uninterrupted series of transformations, was able to obtain the full development of its organs and faculties, and to raise itself to a highly advanced state of culture, so it was able—I will gladly say that it was obliged—in continuing along the same path, to overshoot the target, while it still believed itself to be following it; having already reached the summit, it was necessary for it to complete its journey and descend again, while it imagined itself to be still climbing because it never stopped marching!

Every organism has a limit of development, which it cannot surpass; when it has completed the sequence of its schema, it stops, and from then on, any further effort only accelerates the fatal and inevitable disorganization. The force that developed it becomes the force that disaggregates it; stone, subjected to too much pressure, crumbles; metal evaporates; a planet dissolves; a plant becomes etiolated; a species degenerates; a kingdom falls apart; a rope breaks! All power has an end; all expansion a term. That extreme of possible resistance is called the critical point.

Messieurs, the weakness of species is not being able to stop at the critical point; minerals cling to it better than plants, which transgress it less than animals; of all the last-named, the most intelligent are the most injurious to themselves, because the notion of their capability incites them to employ their latent strength in a way that exceeds the norm; in attempting to live more, to live to excess, they kill themselves. Perhaps we should be led to conclude that the viability of races is in inverse proportion to the consciousness they have of themselves, and that consciousness of strength is a mortal peril for any being that possesses it.

What we can, at least, affirm as certain is that the state of perfection resides in Harmony; that alone regulates the world and engenders life; the equilibrium of forces constitutes perfect beauty, the only beauty, and also the indispensable condition of all existence. When one of the forces becomes excessive, the equilibrium is broken, and the work belongs henceforth to death. To desire to go beyond is to aspire to destruction; to surpass natural limits is to return to oblivion.

Where are the limits? Our Reason searches for them but does not know them; Art sometimes divines them, and Science sometimes defines them, but our certainties are restricted. We go on nevertheless, and effort towards the better sometimes leads us toward the worse, with the result that we often deteriorate that which was worth more before our coming, and history informs us that in many reforms, our confidence in the hope of edifying that which might be merely ends up degrading that which was.

*Repeated applause.*

I am only speaking here, Messieurs, from an abstract point of view, and I beg you not to see allusions in my discourse that are not there. We are not examining, at present, the burning social questions of the gorilla species, but the past conditions of the human species, and I say that this bimane, once arrived at its most noble development—which is to say, the perfect equilibrium between its psychic strengths and its physical strengths, was able to aspire to an exaggerated development thereof, and sought it to its own detriment.

An abuse of its thinking faculties, insufficiently equilibrated by the use of its muscular faculties, produced a cerebral hypertrophy concomitant with the atrophy of its limbs. Is it not permissible to suppose that this superior species, in the momentum of intellectual labor and nervous vibration, was unable to stop, and that it has deliberately killed itself, without wishing to comprehend, intoxicated as it was by the conquering power of its genius?

Such a conjecture, Messieurs, makes you smile in the face of this monster—and yet, comparative anatomy proposes this hypothesis to us, and even imposes it upon us. In fact, let us return to the skeleton of the Quaternary Human.

*Professor Sffaty turns a handle, and the black velvet-topped table that bears the various parts of a human skeleton, fixed to it by metal supports, slowly tilts and presents it face to the audience.*

Consider this being, its skull—what do we see? A large, solid case in exact proportion to the thoracic cage, with the limbs of locomotion and prehension. The human species is here in full bloom: it is Quaternary Humankind, the Human-King! To produce this majestic performance required centuries of selection, thousands of centuries. Now, let us compare it with this descendant of the penultimate hour, the child of the death-throes.

*Turning another handle, he tilts the second table and presents the reconstituted bones of the Quinary Human.*

This is the Quinary Human. Look: the skull has become ridiculously vast; the dorsal spine, crushed beneath that weight, which it can no longer hold high and straight, is bent. The ribs, which it draws backwards, retreat, and the torso becomes hollow. That retreat will naturally occasion a preeminence of the abdomen, which, no longer being maintained, swells and sags. But what it is necessary to note above all, Messieurs, is the condition of the upper and lower limbs, for they will furnish us with a precious indication, and will allow us an induction of a higher order.

The limbs, under that strengthless body, have weakened, become bowed, while we see the joints acquiring an excessive importance, still trying to maintain in equilibrium the fragile edifice of a animal on the brink of collapse—which is to say, ready to fall upon the ground from which it has progressively raised itself up. The arms are perhaps more significant still; their vigor and utility being no longer entertained by any exercise, they have become cachexic, reduced from one age to the next—and a gradual diminution of the muscles very probably preceded that shrinkage of the bones.

But what should we conclude from that, Messieurs, if not that the atrophy of the organs was consecutive to the disuse of their functions? The arms that are being lost, the legs that are becoming twisted, are limbs that are no longer being used, or are being used less and less. By contrast, the fingers, long, slender and nimble, give evidence of the frequent and subtle employment of the hand, exclusively devoted to delicate work and rapid gestures.

It is at this point, Messieurs, that I require all your attention. Two organs have developed to the detriment of the others: the brain and the hand. I shall be more precise: the brain and the fingers. Is it the case, therefore, that they alone were employed, all the rest having become useless? Is it the case that Humans, in their final period, were all thought and digitation? Is it the case that they had no need of anything else, and had begun to restrict the expenditure of their effort to a minimum? Is it the case that they had been able, by virtue of a long series of conquests, to tame natural forces, reducing them to the servitude of their slightest need, no longer having from then on, in order to produce movement, light, heat and death, to displace themselves on land or water and perhaps through the air, to move anything except their fingertips?

*Sensation.*

Messieurs, that power is frightening. Our scientists have not yet attained it, fortunately for us and our children, since it precedes the end of everything. But it was logical, just as the denouement was. For what could become of such a being, after such an ascension?

At this point, Messieurs, I hear an objection that you have every right to make: the decline of Humankind, you will say, must have been slowed down for a long time by the profusion of imbeciles that doubtless existed in the human species and who prevented it from perishing. I confess, Messieurs, that the great utility of imbeciles to a race is incontestable, for they maintain a level of mediocrity that is opposed to the excess of mental development, and holds back its fatal consequences. I also agree that perhaps they might have saved the society, but the gods did not permit it; a terrible event undermined their beneficial endeavor.

What?

Geology provides us with the answer.

While animals are alive and modifying themselves, the Earth, an enormous macrobe, has a life of its own, knowing nothing of the species pullulating on its surface. It too has its slow or abrupt transformations, for worlds, like us and more than us, are subject to the law of perpetual becoming.

Suppose, therefore, that at the end of the Quinary Period—which is to say, when Humans reigned over everything, but only reigned by means of the brain and the fingers—a cataclysm similar to those produced many times before, changed the face of our planet once again. Imagine the peoples—for we must believe in the existences of human peoples, human nations, human fatherlands—violently dispossessed of their empires, decimated and exiled, scattered in the wilderness of a new world. What then becomes of that series of groups which escaped the disaster? What will be the situation of those creatures delivered henceforth solely to the resources of individual capability, deprived of their science and their technology, their hands empty in the face of formidable nature, their arms disarmed before the laws of eternal life? Such beings, artificially constituted, capable of prospering by means of the mutual aid of the Society that they have organized artificially but incapable of existing by themselves, must perish.

Messieurs, that is exactly what happened; the supposition I requested of you is an established fact of the history of the heavenly body we inhabit: geology informs us of the upheaval that occurred at the end of the Quinary Epoch and brought it to a close. Human societies were abolished at a stroke. In effect, humans became extinct. The disappearance of that superb race thus presents itself as a normal consequence of its excessive development, and the marvel is not in seeing so much ability collapse in a single moment into a conclusive inability to live; on the contrary, it would have been astonishing if it had been able to prolong its existence and survive the shock that reduced it to primitive existence and its necessities.

That is why, Messieurs, the only surprising thing is seeing that some specimens, admittedly very rare, have been able to continue the species. The prodigy would seem inconceivable to us, in fact, if paleontology did not provide example of analogous survivals; indeed, the large cetaceans and the large pachyderms, not to mention the large reptiles—the whale, the elephant, the rhinoceros, the crocodile—had not completely disappeared in the time that we will call, if you will permit, the Reign of Humankind. We possess their fossils; those degenerate witnesses of the Quaternary and Tertiary epochs had therefore persisted for millions of years beyond their normal age, and humans were able to see those vestiges of another time, to marvel at their proportions and their unusual forms, and to be as astonished by them as we are by this human! In the same way, a few humans persisted in living when they had no right to do so, and have been able to survive into our era.

Evidently, the humans that survive no longer furnish us with an exact image of what humans were at the supreme moment of their cerebral hypertrophy—far from it! For you can easily understand that those degenerates, thrust back into the midst of natural forces and constrained by them to sustain a precarious struggle, had, by adaptation, to recover a few armaments and sensibly attenuate the vices of their deformation. That is the probability indicated to us by reason; it is also a reality that anatomy demonstrates to us.

The individual that you see here, compared to the skeletons of its ancestors, is sufficient to prove that humankind, following the world's upheaval, was reanimalized. We have brought back another document that will make this comparative study easier, and permit us conclusions more clearly categorical. I am talking about a third skeleton: a modern skeleton, that of the female counterpart of the male you can see.

*Sensation.*

It was for us a capital regret that we were unable to collect in the living state this last human female. Its presence in our collections would doubtless have permitted us to obtain products whose rearing and consequent study would have been very curious. Unfortunately, in spite of our efforts to spare it, the poor beast was killed during the hunt.

*Marked sensation.*

We have dissected it with great care, and if I abstain from presenting that anatomical specimen to you, so precious for the demonstration of the hypothesis that I announced to you just now, it is, firstly, to avoid extending inordinately a lecture that is already long, and also out of a sense of compassion—for one day when, by chance, the male you see here perceived the bones of its companion in our laboratory, it showed us evidence of the most violent despair, uttering sobs that were almost gorillan, and I would reproach myself, Mesdames, for repeating that dolorous scene in front of you.

*Disapproving murmurs. The professor pretends not to hear them. He drinks some water.*

*The murmurs accentuate, however; the crowd demands the spectacle of that dolor, about which they have been told while refusing to let them see it. The protests become increasingly violent, and Professor Sffaty resigns himself to having the skull, at least, of the female brought out.*

*The sign that he addresses to his assistants, understood by everyone, reestablishes calm; applause resounds.*

*The Human contemplates this frantic clamor with bewilderment. Solitary for centuries, it no longer has any notion of assemblies, and the noise frightens it. It turns its head, looking to the right and the left, seeking a means of escape.*

Suddenly, it perceives the skull in the hands of an assistant. It recognizes it and, mad with fury, it runs to grab it. But the Gorilla raises its long arms above its head and the gnome, impotent, falls to its knees, extends its joined hands toward the skull of the last female human, and weeps.

Smiling, the Gorilla lowers its arms again. The Human takes possession of the cherished head and covers it with kisses. Its little shoulders are seen heaving with each sob.

An assistant takes the skull back and carries it away. The Human extends its arms toward the retreating relic.

The crowd applauds.

*

### III.
### The Gorilloid

That moving scene, in exciting the nervous tension of the auditorium, had been well-designed to prepare a feverish welcome for Professor Sffaty's conclusions: anticipated conclusions, discounted by some, revolting to others, impatiently awaited by the combativeness of all.

Suddenly, a relative tranquility emerges throughout the hall; silence is gradually reestablished, and that very silence resembles an injunction finally to formulate those subversive conclusions, against which some are waiting to protest indignantly.

The lecturer, who senses that public preoccupation and is not at all apprehensive about it, collects himself momentarily before he resumes speaking. Then he extends his right hand, and in a firm but unprovocative voice, he says:

I would have finished, Messieurs, if it were not still necessary for me to touch upon, if only briefly, the thorniest part of this study, and to reach the conclusion you expect of us. I indicated it at the beginning of this talk, and public opinion, with adverse passions, has already asked the question. Are Gorillas descended from Humans?

Movements.

I am only too well aware that the hypothesis alone has raised indignant protests, and that we have been accused of attacking the self-respect of our race, which God created and fashioned in his own image. I am only too well aware of how difficult and scabrous the question is from social, religious and mundane viewpoints. Messieurs, from the scientific viewpoint, it is not; we study life in its multiform aspects, we study it without preconceptions and without fury, in order to extract, insofar as it is possible, the great laws that preside over the progression of beings. In any case, in order to reassure the most legitimate scruples, I will immediately tell you my personal and categorical response to the question posed:

No! Gorillas are not descended from Humans.

*Various movements.*

The reason is simple. Humans have disappeared, and we have just contemplated their ruination. Now, if they were truly our ancestors, they would still exist, since they would exist in us, by means of us, who would represent their perpetual life down here. So, since it pleases some people to consider that descendancy as a humiliation for us and an abasement of our dignity, let us discard the hypothesis, Messieurs. I consent to that, and I assert it.

But if we are not descended from Humans, does that mean that they and we are not descended from a common ancestor? If they are not our ancestors, does that mean that they are not our kin—elder brethren of a sort?

*Agitation. Ironic laughter.*

You would laugh even louder if I told you that once, in the Quaternary centuries, the human species was able to smile as you are doing, and become indignant, too, at the mere idea of a kinship with us! Then, it was radiant in all its glory, while we were still struggling in the limbo of animality, striving with great difficulty to bring forth our consciousness. It was doubtless scornful of us, refusing to recognize any link between itself and us, seeing us as nothing but beasts, and—who knows?—perhaps putting us in cages. . . .

*Laughter.*

I'm joking, Messieurs. But if Humans were once able to contest the fraternity of the two races, and deny us because they doubted our perfectibility, we are able in our turn to reason in the same way, since intellectual ability presents itself to us as an accomplished fact. We have less right than them to deny the evident similarities, and the necessity of confessing that common characteristics engender common possibilities imposes itself even more forcefully upon us. Among the myriad species that exist or have existed, none is closer to ours. Time alone separates us. Like us, they have passed through the phases of their normal evolution, in parallel with us, but before us. They ascended more rapidly; they descended again sooner.

That ascent, Messieurs, we know about today; that branch of Simians, themselves the issue of Prosimians, which were born of Marsupials, eventually goes back, via the Protomammals all the way to the Dipneumona and the Gastraeads,[2] and the inferior Mollusks connect them with the Zoophytes, the Algae and the original Protoplasma.

Undoubtedly, Messieurs, Humans protested, in their time, against such a humble origin, and did not want to admit that it was also the most noble, since the baseness of the extraction procures the laborious climb, and honors the climber. That they would be no more inclined than we are to consent to recognize that verity, is also probable. The pride of that advanced race must have been equal to ours, if not even more foolish, and we are entitled to credit any presumptuousness to beings whose skulls were able to acquire a form like this!

*He takes the enormous skull of the Quinary Human in both hands, and holds it up before the crowd.*

Who among us can say what dreams were hatched in there? Perhaps humans considered themselves, as we do, to be angelic, supraterrestrial creatures, who had nothing in common with the rest of life! Humans, before us, might perhaps have been able to believe that the world had been created for them, that a God was watching over them, that the stars shone in order to embellish their nights, and that their existence was the ultimate reason for everything! Perhaps they believed, like us, that they possessed within them the principle of an immortal soul!

*Laughter.*

That opinion amuses us today, Messieurs, and yet, grotesque as it appears to us when it is professed by others, we do not hesitate to renew it for our own usage.

---

[2] I have substituted the Latin *Dipneumona* for the text's *Dipneusties*; implying possession of two sets or kinds of breathing apparatus, it has been applied to various animal groups, the one intended here probably being lungfishes, imagined as the ancestors of all land vertebrates. The obsolete term *Gastraead* referred to a hypothetical primitive organism similar in form to an embryonic gastrula: an aggregation of cells whose components have begun to differentiate, but still seems capable of assuming any mature form. It was a derivative of Ernst Haeckel's assertion that "ontogeny recapitulates phylogeny," which is only true in a very vague, quasi-metaphorical sense.

*Protests. Several ladies get up and leave.*

Forgive me, I beg you, if it is impossible for me not to point out the fundamental vice of the reasoning that opposes us. When we observe, for two branches of the same family, the same progress, is it not illogical to admit it for one and deny it for the other?

*Animated protests. Tumult.*

I see nothing diminishing for us in being the relatives of Humans, who were majestic in their epoch as we are in ours! I cannot see anything humiliating in the honor of having, like them, followed the route of progress.

*Laughter and shouting. Violent protests. Someone whistles.*

It is Pride that is manifest here, and I am addressing myself to Reason!

*Applause from several benches.*

Pride doomed Humankind! Pride is the force that creates at the outset, and kills in the end! It drives those who pursue a task, and leads them astray when the task is finished! Pride in the work accomplished is called vanity!

*Increasing tumult.*

Is it certain that the highest are also the greatest, and that we are able to measure our work accurately? In the ages when Humans were infatuated with their power, building the cities and knowledge that have disappeared with them, modest corals were building a world and empires, which have triumphed over the sea and on which we live!

*Bravo! Bravo!*

*Enough!*

*Bravo!*

Why become irritated, Messieurs? Let us look around us more widely! Everything moves and works in fraternal nature! Nothing is stationary, and progress is incessant for all.

For progress is not, as some think, the exclusive prerogative of intelligent creatures; it is applicable to everything that lives; it is life in motion, and that is why nothing can slow it down or stop it. It moves, and must move; it is irreducible and necessary, incessant in the divine order, like the great laws of universal gravitation, from which it follows and results, Messieurs, and it continues in us and around us, everywhere and simultaneously!

That is what traces the thread connecting groups and individuals, and we can follow it back, following with it, through the ages, through the species, the curve of unbreakable linkages by which the infinitely small and the infinitely great are connected! If you consent to comprehend the divine labor of Progress, follow it and trace it back, the curve that it has traced since the dawn of time, and you will see how it took hold of matter in order to extract from it, little by little, life in its innumerable forms, which it diversified and ramified, which it specialized and focused, separating each from the rest without ever detaching it! Follow it, and by means of the chain of evident filiations it will lead you without interruption to a conception of the common origin of the unique family!

*Movement.*

Brethren of aphids, but brethren also of stars, you will perceive the infinitesimal in relation to the immense, borne away together by the Law that regulates everything!

Then, Messieurs, the immense and the infinitesimal will seem to you to be equals, with regard to the infinite in which they move obediently. Then, too, you will conceive that the unanimous ascension of beings is identified with the circle of total movement, and that it is, if I might put it thus, the orbit of existence.

Then, finally, by virtue of having contemplated here the Humankind that Progress raised so high to drag down so low, we shall obtain a great enlightenment, and you will emerge from this enclosure, Messieurs, with the notion and the proof of an exceedingly important truth; for you will know that Progress is not a goal, in the narrow sense that our moralists understand, but, on the contrary, the very Force that raises us all from oblivion and leads us all back to it, with the same gentleness, the same certainty and the same means, in order to maintain universal, eternal, infinite life!

*Repeated applause. Lively animation.*

*The professor, surrounded, receives congratulations. Groups press around the platform on which the Human is standing.*

*In the middle of that crowd, the animal shows signs of great nervous distress; its face is grimacing with tics and its eyes, rolling in their orbits, frequently turn toward the professor, from whom it seems to be imploring help.*

*In spite of the prohibition on the blackboard, hands reach out toward it, to stroke it. It utters shrill cries, and becomes more and more distressed.*

*At a signal from the professor, the assistants open the cage, in which the Human hurriedly takes refuge. It is seen crouching down at the back.*

*The keepers take it away.*

# THE VOICE IN THE NIGHT

## WILLIAM HOPE HODGSON

*William Hope Hodgson (1877–1918), the son of an Anglican clergyman, did not get along with his father and ran away to sea in his teens; he developed his physical strength in order to resist bullying. When he eventually qualified as a mate he developed a strong interest in photography, recording the various phenomena he encountered in his travels. His early writings were poetry and non-fiction, but when he settled on land he opened a school of physical culture and began selling fiction to the American pulp magazines, much of it consisting of horror stories set at sea, frequently featuring bizarre life-forms, tacitly or explicitly set within a distinctive metaphysical context that placed them in a unique sector of scientific romance. The Boats of the "Glen-Carrig" (1907) runs together two of the several stories he set in the Sargasso Sea but his second patchwork novel,* The House on the Borderland *(1908) is a more extravagant metaphysical fantasy including a spectacular cosmic vision. His last-published novel,* The Night Land *(1912), is a phantasmagorical far-futuristic fantasy. He was killed in action during the Great War.*

*"The Voice in the Night," first published in the November 1907 issue of* Blue Book *and reprinted in* Men of the Deep Waters *(1914), is typical in its substance of the tales of exotic biological menace set in remote parts of the world that Hodgson wrote during the first phase of his career; it is the most poignantly harrowing of them all.*

It was a dark starless night. We were becalmed in the Northern Pacific. Our exact position I do not know; for the sun had been hidden during the course of a weary, breathless week, by a thin haze which had seemed to float above us, about the height of our mastheads, at whiles descending and shrouding the surrounding sea.

With there being no wind, we had steadied the tiller, and I was the only man on deck. The crew, consisting of two men and a boy, were sleeping for'ard in their den; while Will—my friend and the master of our little craft—was aft in his bunk on the port side of the little cabin.

Suddenly, from out of the surrounding darkness, there came a hail:

"Schooner, ahoy!"

The cry was so unexpected that I gave no immediate answer, because of my surprise.

It came again—a voice curiously throaty and inhuman, calling from somewhere upon the sea on our port broadside:

"Schooner, ahoy!"

"Hullo!" I sung out, having gathered my wits somewhat. "Who are you? What do you want?"

"You need not be afraid," answered the queer voice, having probably noticed some trace of confusion in my tone. "I am only an old man."

The pause sounded oddly; but it was only afterwards that it came back to me with any significance.

"Why don't you come alongside, then?" I queried somewhat snappishly; for I liked not his hinting at my having been a trifle shaken.

"I . . . I . . . can't. It wouldn't be safe. I. . . ." The voice broke off, and there was silence.

"What do you mean?" I asked, growing more and more astonished. "Why not safe? Where are you?"

I listened for a moment; but there came no answer. And then, a sudden indefinite suspicion, of I know not what, coming to me, I stepped swiftly to the binnacle, and took out the lighted lamp. At the same time, I knocked on the deck with my heel to waken Will. Then I was back at the side, throwing the yellow funnel of light out into the silent immensity beyond our rail. As I did so, I heard a slight, muffled cry, and then the sound of a splash as though someone had dipped oars abruptly. Yet I cannot say that I saw anything with certainty; save, it seemed to me, that with the first flash of the light, there had been something in the waters, where there was now nothing.

"Hullo, there!" I called. "What foolery is this?"

But there came only the indistinct sounds of a boat being pulled away into the night.

Then I heard Will's voice, from the direction of the after scuttle: "What's up, George?"

"Come here, Will," I said.

"What is it?" he asked, coming across the deck.

I told him the queer thing which had happened. He put several questions; then, after a moment's silence, he raised his hands to his lips, and hailed: "Boat, ahoy!"

From a long distance away there came back to us a faint reply, and my companion repeated his call. Presently, after a short period of silence, there grew in our hearing the muffled sound of oars; at which Will hailed again.

This time there was a reply.

"Put away the light."

"I'm damned if I will," I muttered; but Will told me to do as the voice bade, and I shoved it down under the bulwarks.

"Come nearer," he said, and the oar-strokes continued. Then, when apparently some half-dozen fathoms distant, they again ceased.

"Come alongside," exclaimed Will. "There's nothing to be frightened of aboard here!"

"Promise that you will not show the light?"

"What's to do with you," I burst out, "that you're so infernally afraid of the light?"

"Because . . ." began the voice, and stopped short.

"Because what?" I asked quickly.

Will put his hand on my shoulder. "Shut up a minute, old man," he said, in a low voice. "Let me tackle him."

He leant more over the rail.

"See here, Mister," he said, "this is a pretty queer business, you coming upon us like this, right out in the middle of the blessed Pacific. How are we to know what sort of a hanky-panky trick you're up to? You say there's only one of you. How are we to know, unless we get a squint at you—eh? What's your objection to the light, anyway?"

As he finished, I heard the noise of the oars again, and then the voice came; but now from a greater distance, and sounding extremely hopeless and pathetic.

"I'm sorry . . . sorry! I would not have troubled you, only I am hungry, and . . . so is she."

The voice died away, and the sound of the oars, dipping irregularly, was borne to us.

"Stop!" sung out Will. "I don't want to drive you away. Come back! We'll keep the light hidden, if you don't like it." He turned to me. "It's a damned queer rig, this; but I think there's nothing to be afraid of?"

There was a question in his tone, and I replied. "No, I think the poor devil's been wrecked around here, and gone crazy."

The sound of the oars drew nearer.

"Shove that lamp back in the binnacle," said Will; then he leaned over the rail and listened.

I replaced the lamp, and came back to his side. The dipping of the oars ceased some dozen yards distant.

"Won't you come alongside now?" asked Will in an even voice. "I have had the lamp put back in the binnacle."

"I . . . I cannot," replied the voice. "I dare not come nearer. I dare not even pay you for the . . . the provisions."

"That's all right," said Will, and hesitated. "You're welcome to as much grub as you can take. . . ." Again he hesitated.

"You are very good," exclaimed the voice. "May God, who understands everything, reward you. . . ." It broke off huskily.

"The . . . the lady?" said Will, abruptly. "Is she . . . ?"

"I have left her behind upon the island," came the voice.

"What island?" I cut in.

"I know not its name," returned the voice. "I would to God . . . !" it began, and checked itself as suddenly.

"Could we not send a boat for her?" asked Will at this point.

"No!" said the voice, with extraordinary emphasis. "My God! No!" There was a moment's pause; then it added, in a tone which seemed a merited reproach: "It was because of our want I ventured . . . because her agony tortured me."

"I am a forgetful brute," exclaimed Will. "Just wait a minute, whoever you are, and I will bring you something at once."

In a couple of minutes he was back again, and his arms were full of various edibles. He paused at the rail.

"Can't you come alongside for them?"

"No . . . I *dare not*," replied the voice, and it seemed to me that in its tones I detected a note of stifled craving—as though the owner hushed a mortal desire. It came to me then in a flash, that the poor old creature out here in the darkness was *suffering* for actual need of that which Will held in his arms; and yet, because of some unintelligible dread, refraining from dashing to the side of our little schooner, and receiving it. And with the lightning-like conviction, there came the knowledge that the Invisible was not mad, but sanely facing some intolerable horror.

"Damn it, Will!" I said, full of many feelings, over which predominated a vast sympathy. "Get a box. We must float off the stuff to him in it."

This we did, propelling it away from the vessel, out into the darkness, by means of a boathook. In a minute, a slight cry from the Invisible came to us, and we knew that he had secured the box.

A little later, he called out a farewell to us, and so heartful a blessing that I am sure we were the better for it. Then, without more ado, we heard the ply of the oars across the darkness.

"Pretty soon off," remarked Will, with perhaps just a little sense of injury.

"Wait," I replied. "I think somehow he'll come back. He must have been badly needing that food."

"And the lady," said Will. For a moment he was silent; then he continued: "It's the queerest thing I've ever tumbled across, since I've been fishing."

"Yes," I said, and fell to pondering.

And so the time slipped away . . . an hour, another and still Will stayed with me; for the queer adventure had knocked all desire for sleep out of him.

The third hour was three parts through, when we heard again the sound of oars across the silent ocean.

"Listen!" said Will, a low note of excitement in his voice.

"He's coming, just as I thought," I muttered.

The dipping of the oars grew nearer, and I noted that the strokes were firmer and longer. The food had been needed.

They came to a stop a little distance off the broadside, and the queer voice came again to us through the darkness: "Schooner, ahoy!"

"That you?" asked Will.

"Yes," replied the voice. "I left you suddenly, but . . . but there was great need."

"The lady?" questioned Will.

"The . . . lady is grateful now on earth. She will be more grateful soon in . . . in heaven."

Will began to make some reply, in a puzzled voice, but became confused, and broke off short. I said nothing. I was wondering at the curious pauses, and, apart from my wonder, I was full of a great sympathy.

The voice continued: "We . . . she and I, have talked, as we shared the result of God's tenderness and yours. . . ."

Will interposed, but without coherence.

"I beg of you not to . . . to belittle your deed of Christian charity this night," said the voice. "Be sure that it has not escaped His notice." It stopped, and there was a full minute's silence. Then it came again: "We have spoken together upon that which . . . which has befallen us. We had thought to go out, without telling any, of the terror which has come into our . . . lives. She is with me in believing that tonight's happenings are under a special ruling, and that it is God's wish that we should tell to you all that we have suffered since . . . since. . . ."

"Yes?" said Will softly.

"Since the sinking of the *Albatross*."

"Ah!" I exclaimed, involuntarily. "She left Newcastle for 'Frisco some six months ago, and hasn't been heard of since."

"Yes," answered the voice, "but some few degrees to the north of the line she was caught in a terrible storm, and dismasted. When the day came, it was found that she was leaking badly, and, presently, it falling to a calm, the sailors took to the boats, leaving . . . leaving a young lady—my fiancée—and myself upon the wreck.

"We were below, gathering together a few of our possessions, when they left. They were entirely callous, through fear, and when we came up on the deck, we saw them only as small shapes afar off upon the horizon. Yet we did not despair, but set to work and constructed a small raft. Upon this we put such few matters as it would hold, including a quantity of water and some ship's biscuit. Then, the vessel being very deep in the water, we got ourselves on to the raft, and pushed off.

"It was later, when I observed that we seemed to be in the way of some tide or current, which bore us from the ship at an angle; so that in the course of three hours, by my watch, her hull became invisible to our sight, her broken masts remaining in view for a somewhat longer period. Then, towards evening, it grew misty, and so through the night. The next day we were still encompassed by the mist, the weather remaining quiet.

"For four days we drifted through this strange haze, until, on the evening of the fourth day, there grew upon our ears the murmur of breakers at a distance. Gradually it became plainer, and, somewhat after midnight, it appeared to sound upon either hand at no very great space. The raft was raised upon a swell several times, and then we were in smooth water, and the noise of the breakers was behind.

"When the morning came, we found that we were in a sort of great lagoon; but of this we noticed little at the time; for close before us, through the enshrouding mist, loomed the hull of a large sailing vessel. With one accord we fell upon our knees and thanked God; for we thought that here was an end to our perils. We had much to learn.

"The raft drew near to the ship, and we shouted on them to take us aboard; but none answered. Presently the raft touched against the side of the vessel, and, seeing a rope hanging downwards, I seized it and began to climb. Yet I had much ado to make my way up, because of a kind of gray, lichenous fungus which had seized upon the rope, and which blotched the side of the ship lividly.

"I reached the rail and clambered over it, on to the deck. Here I saw that the decks were covered, in great patches, with gray masses, some of them rising into nodules several feet in height; but at the time I thought less of this matter than of the possibility of there being people aboard the ship. I shouted; but none answered. Then I went to the door below the poop deck. I opened it, and peered in. There was a great smell of staleness, so that I knew in a moment that nothing living was within, and with the knowledge, I shut the door quickly, for I felt suddenly lonely.

"I went back to the side where I had scrambled up. My . . . my sweetheart was still sitting quietly upon the raft. Seeing me look down she called up to know whether there were any aboard the ship. I replied that the vessel had the appearance of having been long deserted, but that if she would wait a little I would see whether there was anything in the shape of a ladder by which she could ascend to the deck. Then we would make a search through the vessel together. A little later, on the opposite side of the decks, I found a rope-ladder. This I carried across, and a minute afterwards she was beside me.

"Together we explored the cabins and apartments in the after part of the ship; but nowhere was there any sign of life. Here and there within the cabins themselves, we came across odd patches of that queer fungus; but this, as my sweetheart said, could be cleansed away.

"In the end, having assured ourselves that the after portion of the vessel was empty, we picked our ways to the bow, between the ugly gray nodules of that strange growth; and here we made a further search, which told us that there was indeed none aboard but ourselves.

"This being now beyond any doubt, we returned to the stern of the ship and proceeded to make ourselves as comfortable as possible. Together we cleared out and cleaned two of the cabins; and after that I made examination whether there was anything eatable in the ship. This I soon found was so, and thanked God in my heart for His goodness. In addition to this I discovered the whereabouts of the fresh-water pump, and having fixed it, I found the water drinkable, though somewhat unpleasant to the taste.

"For several days we stayed aboard the ship, without attempting to get to the shore. We were busily engaged in making the place habitable. Yet even thus early we became aware that our lot was even less to be desired than might have been imagined; for though, as a first step, we scraped away the odd patches of growth that studded the floors and walls of the cabins and saloon, yet they returned almost to their original size within the space of twenty-four hours, which not only discouraged us, but gave us a feeling of vague unease.

"Still we would not admit ourselves beaten, so set to work afresh, and not only scraped away the fungus, but soaked the places where it had been with carbolic, a can full of which I had found in the pantry. Yet, by the end of the week the growth had returned in full strength, and, in addition, it had spread to other places, as though our touching it had allowed germs from it to travel elsewhere.

"On the seventh morning, my sweetheart woke to find a small patch of it growing on her pillow, close to her face. At that, she came to me, so soon as she could get her garments upon her. I was in the galley at the time lighting the fire for breakfast.

"'Come here, John,' she said, and led me aft. When I saw the thing upon her pillow I shuddered, and then and there we agreed to go right out of the ship and see whether we could not fare to make ourselves more comfortable ashore.

"Hurriedly, we gathered together our few belongings, and even among these I found that the fungus had been at work, for one of her shawls had a little lump of it growing near one edge. I threw the whole thing over the side, without saying anything to her.

"The raft was still alongside, but it was too clumsy to guide, and I lowered down a small boat that hung across the stern, and in this we made our way to the shore. Yet, as we drew near to it, I became gradually aware that here the vile fungus which had driven us from the ship was growing riot. In places it rose into horrible, fantastic mounds, which seemed almost to quiver, as with a quiet life, when the wind blew across them. Here and there it took on the form of vast fingers, and in others it just spread out flat and smooth and treacherous. In places, it appeared as grotesque stunted trees, seeming extraordinarily kinked and gnarled—the whole quaking vilely at times.

"At first, it seemed to us that there was no single portion of the surrounding shore which was not hidden beneath the masses of the hideous lichen; yet, in this, I found we were mistaken, for somewhat later, coasting along the shore at a little distance, we descried a smooth white patch of what appeared to be sand, and there we landed.

"It was not sand. What it was I do not know. All that I have learned is that upon it the fungus will not grow; while everywhere else, save where the sand-like earth wanders oddly, path-wise, amid the gray desolation of the lichen, there is nothing but that loathsome grayness.

"It is difficult to make you understand how cheered we were to find one place that was absolutely free from the growth, and here we deposited our belongings. Then we went back to the ship for such things as it seemed to us we should need. Among other matters, I managed to bring ashore with me one of the ship's sails, with which I constructed two small tents, which, though exceedingly rough-shaped, served the purpose for which they were intended. In these we lived and stored our various necessities, and thus in a matter of some four weeks all went smoothly and without particular unhappiness. Indeed, I may say with much of happiness, for . . . for we were together.

"It was on the thumb of her right hand that the growth first showed. It was only a small circular spot, much like a little gray mole. My God, how the fear leapt to my heart when she showed me the place! We cleansed it, between us, washing it with carbolic and water. In the morning of the following day she showed her hand to me again. The gray warty thing had returned. For a little while, we looked at one another in silence. Then, still wordless, we started again to remove it.

"In the midst of the operation she spoke suddenly. 'What's that on the side of your face, dear?' Her voice was sharp with anxiety. I put my hand up to feel.

"'There! Under the hair by your ear. A little to the front a bit.' My finger rested upon the place, and then I knew.

"'Let us get your thumb done first,' I said. And she submitted, only because she was afraid to touch me until it was cleansed. I finished washing and disinfecting her thumb, and then she turned to my face. After it was finished we sat together and talked awhile of many things, for there had come into our lives sudden, very terrible thoughts. We were, all at once, afraid of something worse than death.

"We spoke of loading the boat with provisions and water and making our way out on to the sea; yet we were helpless, for many causes, and . . . and the growth had attacked us already. We decided to stay. God would do with us what was His will. We would wait.

"A month, two months, three months passed and the places grew somewhat, and there had come others. Yet we fought so strenuously with the fear that its headway was but slow, comparatively speaking.

"Occasionally we ventured off to the ship for such stores as we needed. There we found that the fungus grew persistently. One of the nodules on the maindeck became soon as high as my head.

"We had now given up all thought or hope of leaving the island. We had realized that it would be unallowable to go among healthy humans, with the things from which we were suffering.

"With this determination and knowledge in our minds we knew that we should have to husband our food and water; for we did not know, at that time, but that we should possibly live for many years.

"This reminds me that I have told you that I am an old man. Judged by the years this is not so, but . . . but. . . ."

He broke off, then continued somewhat abruptly: "As I was saying, we knew that we should have to use care in the matter of food. But we had no idea how little food there was left of which to take care. It was a week later that I made the discovery that all the other bread tanks—which I had supposed full—were empty, and that, beyond odd tins of vegetables and meat, and some other matters, we had nothing on which to depend but the bread in the tank which I had already opened.

"After learning this I bestirred myself to do what I could, and set to work at fishing in the lagoon, but with no success. At this I was somewhat inclined to feel desperate until the thought came to me to try outside the lagoon, in the open sea.

"Here, at times, I caught odd fish, but so infrequently that they proved of but little help in keeping us from the hunger which threatened.

"It seemed to me that our deaths were likely to come by hunger, and not by the growth of the thing which had seized upon our bodies.

"We were in this state of mind when the fourth month wore out, when I made a very horrible discovery. One morning, a little before midday, I came off the ship with a portion of the biscuits which were left. In the mouth of her tent I saw my sweetheart sitting, eating something.

"'What is it, my dear?' I called out as I leapt ashore. Yet, on hearing my voice, she seemed confused, and, turning, slyly threw something towards the edge of a little clearing. It fell short, and a vague suspicion having arisen within me, I walked across and picked it up. It was a piece of the gray fungus.

"As I went to her with it in my hand, she turned deadly pale, then rose red.

"I felt strangely dazed and frightened. 'My dear! My dear!' I said, and could say no more. Yet at my words she broke down and cried bitterly.

"Gradually, as she calmed, I got from her the news that she had tried it the preceding day, and . . . and liked it. I got her to promise on her knees not to touch it again, however great our hunger. After she had promised she told me that the desire for it had come suddenly, and that, until the moment of desire, she had experienced nothing towards it but the most extreme repulsion.

"Later in the day, feeling strangely restless, and much shaken with the thing which I had discovered, I made my way along one of the twisted paths formed by the white, sand-like substance which led among the fungoid growth. I had, once before, ventured along there, but not to any great distance. This time, being involved in perplexing thought, I went much further than hitherto.

"Suddenly I was called to myself by a queer hoarse sound on my left. Turning quickly I saw that there was movement among an extraordinarily shaped mass of fungus close to my elbow. It was swaying uneasily, as though it possessed life of its own. Abruptly, as I stared, the thought came to me that the thing had a grotesque resemblance to the figure of a distorted human creature. Even as the fancy flashed into my brain, there was a slight, sickening noise of tearing, and I saw that one of the branch-like arms was detaching itself from the surrounding gray masses, and coming toward me. The head of the thing, a shapeless gray ball, inclined in my direction.

"I stood stupidly, and the vile arm brushed across my face. I gave out a frightened cry, and ran back a few paces. There was a sweetish taste upon my lips where the thing had touched me. I licked them, and was immediately filled with an inhuman desire. I turned and seized a mass of the fungus. Then more . . . and more. I was insatiable. In the midst of devouring, the remembrance of the morning's discovery swept into my mazed head. It was sent by God. I dashed the fragment I held to the ground. Then, utterly wretched and feeling a dreadful guiltiness, I made my way back to the little encampment.

"I think she knew, by the marvelous intuition which love must have given, as soon as she set eyes on me. Her quiet sympathy made it easier for me, and I told her of my sudden weakness, yet omitted to mention the extraordinary thing which had gone before. I desired to spare her all unnecessary terror.

"But, for myself, I had added an intolerable knowledge, to breed an incessant terror in my brain; for I doubted not but that I had seen the end of one of those men who had come to the island in the ship in the lagoon; and in that monstrous ending I had seen our own.

"Thereafter we kept from the abominable food, though the desire for it had entered into our blood. Yet our drear punishment was upon us, for, day by day, with monstrous rapidity, the fungoid growth took hold of our poor bodies. Nothing we could do would check it materially, and so . . . and so . . . we who had been human, became . . . well, it matters less each day. Only . . . only we had been man and maid!

"And day by day the fight is more dreadful, to withstand the hungerlust for the terrible lichen.

"A week ago we ate the last of the biscuit, and since that time I have caught three fish. I was out here fishing tonight when your schooner drifted upon me out of the mist. I hailed you. You know the rest, and may God, out of His great heart, bless you for your goodness to a . . . a couple of outcast souls."

There was the dip of an oar . . . another. Then the voice came again, and for the last time, sung through the slight surrounding mist, ghostly and mournful.

"God bless you! Goodbye!"

"Goodbye," we shouted together, hoarsely, our hearts full of many emotions.

I glanced about me. I became aware that dawn was upon us.

The sun flung a stray beam across the hidden sea, pierced the mist dully, and lit up the receding boat with a gloomy fire.

Indistinctly, I saw something nodding between the oars. I thought of a sponge . . . a great gray nodding sponge. . . .

The oars continued to ply. They were gray—as was the boat—and my eyes searched a moment vainly for the conjunction of hand and oar. My gaze flashed back to the . . . head. It nodded forward as the oars went backward for the stroke. Then the oars were dipped, the boat shot out of the patch of light, and the . . . the thing went nodding into the mist.

# THE SINGULAR FATE OF BOUVANCOURT

## MAURICE RENARD

*Maurice Renard (1875–1939) was the French writer most enthusiastically inspired by translations of H. G. Wells; he became an ardent propagandist for "scientific marvel fiction," which he distinguished from the relatively staid French tradition of Vernian fiction. His first novel,* Docteur Lerne, sous-dieu *(1908; tr. as* Dr. Lerne, Subgod*) is a melodramatic account of extraordinary surgical transformation, but the novel with which he followed it up, the satirical microcosmic romance* Un Homme chez les microbes *(tr. as* A Man Among the Microbes*), proved difficult to place, and he rewrote it several times, eventually advertising the version he published in 1928 as the "fifth edition." He fared much better with the classic mystery story* Le Péril bleu *(1911; tr. as* The Blue Peril*).*

*Renard had several more works in progress when the Great War broke out, but when he was released from the army five years later, his family's property having been destroyed by the German invasion, he was obliged to move into the more popular field of crime fiction in order to make a living, although he did reprocess one of his abandoned works in that context as* Le Maître de lumière *(1933; tr. as* The Master of Light*). All of his generic work is available in English in five volumes published by Black Coat Press in 2010.*

*"La Singular destinée de Bouvancourt," first published in his second collection,* Le Voyage immobile suivi d'autres histoires singulières *(1909; tr. as* The Motionless Voyage and Other Singular Stories*) was one of two stories Renard produced featuring the adventurous physicist in question, the other being "L'Homme au corps subtil" (1913; tr. as "The Man with the Rarefied Body"). Like much of the French scientific romance of the era, it develops its central idea flamboyantly, while maintaining an interest in the particular*

*psychology of scientific endeavor, reminiscent of S. Henry Berthoud's pioneering endeavors.*

During my absence from Pontargis, Bouvancourt had got a new housekeeper. The new servant insisted that her master had gone out, but she was deceiving me, inasmuch as I could hear my friend's voice trumpeting in the laboratory at the end of the corridor, so I took the liberty of shouting: "Bouvancourt! Hey, Bouvancourt! It's me, Sambreuil. Can I come in, in spite of your orders?"

"Ah, my dear doctor, what a pleasure it is to see you again!" the scientist replied, from off-stage. "I've never had such a keen desire to shake your hand, Sambreuil, but there's a snag. I'll be shut up in here for half an hour. It's impossible for me to open the door just now. So go through the drawing-room into my study, I beg you; we can chat through the door, as we can here, and you'll be more comfortable there than in the hallway."

I had been familiar with the layout of the little apartment for a long time. The residence was dear to me because of the resident, and, as the Louis XV drawing-room was the usual venue of our conversations, I took pleasure in seeing it briefly once again, even though the furniture was singularly pretentious in its banality. Bouvancourt, in fact, believed himself—quite mistakenly—to be first and foremost a master decorator. He spent his leisure time nailing, sawing and hanging things, and it was not, in the eyes of the great physicist, his slenderest entitlement to glory to have designed and constructed those chairs and bracket-tables "to complement a set of authentic fire-irons."

With an affectionate glance, therefore, I honored the horrible imitation furniture, the woodwork sculpted with a stamp, and the specious tapestry cynically pretending to be an Aubusson—and it never even occurred to me to be shocked, so familiar had that ugliness become. Bouvancourt's ridiculous pretension, however, was vividly recalled to my mind once I was in his study. He had brought the most frightful embellishment thereto.

In order to make the room seem larger by means of a *trompe-l'oeil*, he had set a large mirror against the wall separating the study from the Louis XV drawing-room. It was a simulacrum of a door, and matched the actual door; it was a mirage of sorts, reminiscent of the booby-traps that one finds in the Musée Grévin.[1] The large mirror was supported by the floor itself and, in order better to deceive the eye, it was framed by large claret-colored plush curtains similar to those at the widows and other doorways. Oh, those curtains! I knew immediately whose hands had molded them into pleats, inflated them in billows, precipitated them in torrents, and which infernal upholsterer had tied them up with those tasseled cords! And I stood in front of that terrible lambrequin, whose cords twisted its fabric in a ferociously ingenious embrace, quite speechless.

"Well, doctor," said the laboratory door, in Bouvancourt's muffled voice, "are you there yet?"

"Yes—but I was admiring your sense of decoration. You've got a mirror here—magnificent!"

"Isn't it? How do you like the drapery? It's my own work, you know. The study seems enormous, doesn't it? It's very fashionable just now. Isn't my study chic?"

In truth, the room did not lack "chic," certainly not because of the objects designed to furnish it, but for the reason that it served as an annex to the juxtaposed laboratory, and concealed a chaotic crowd of astonishing machines of all shapes, sizes and materials, for practical work and demonstration. Two windows, one looking out on the boulevard and the other on the street, illuminated the corner room, sprinkling glitters, gleams and flashes over the ebonite, the glass and the copper. Thus more-or-less lit up, various balance-pans, disks and cylinders were visible. Manuscripts were heaped up on the desks, as if thrown there in a glorious fever of genius. An algebraic problem whitened the blackboard. Science exhaled its chemical aroma. In all sincerity, I exclaimed: "Yes, Bouvancourt, old chap—yes, it's chic, your study!"

"Excuse me for receiving you in this fashion," he went on. "It's Saturday today. My laboratory assistant. . . ."

"Still Felix?"

"Yes, of course."

"Hello, Felix!"

---

[1] The Musée Grévin at 10 Boulevard Montmartre, founded in 1882 and named after its first artistic director, Alfred Grévin, is a wax museum, the Parisian equivalent of London's Madame Tussaud's.

"Good day, Monsieur Sambreuil."

"My laboratory assistant," Bouvancourt went on, "asked if he could finish early. He's going away tomorrow, and I can't put this experiment off."

"Is it very interesting, then?"

"Extremely, my dear chap. It's the final one of a series; it ought to be conclusive. I'll doubtless make a nice discovery. . . ."

"What?"

"The free penetration, by invisible light, of substances that the Röntgen rays still have difficulty traversing: glass, bones and others. We're working in the dark. I'm trying to take a photograph. Permit me to remain silent for a few minutes—it won't take long. Come on Felix!"

Then I heard the insectile hum that induction coils make. There were several of them going; the buzzers, according to their tightness, imitated the sonorous flight of bees or that of hornets, and their swarm sang in passable cacophonic harmony. That infernal pedal-note, humming amid the calm of a provincial town, encouraged drowsiness, and I would probably have dozed off if it were not for the trams, whose passage along the boulevard filled the first floor with a periodic racket. Their electrical wires ran close to the house at the level of the windows; there was even a bracket supporting the cables attached to the facade between the laboratory window and the study windows. Every time they made contact with this suture, the trolleys produced a spark. My idle waiting was enlivened thereby. The coils, meanwhile, continued their parody of a beehive.

Several trolley-shafts rattled past in succession. Ever-inclined to calculation, I counted them.

"Will you be finished soon, Bouvancourt?"

"Have a little patience, Monsieur Sambreuil," Felix replied, vaguely.

"Is it going well?"

"Marvelously. We're almost there."

These words gave me a furious desire to get to the other side of the door, in order to see the new phenomenon occur for the first time and contemplate the inventor at the moment of his invention. By means of his discoveries, Bouvancourt had already inscribed several dates in the calendar of Renown.

A clock chimed. I shivered. The moment was historic.

"Can't I come in now, Felix?" I lamented. "I'm getting bored. That's the twentieth tram going past, my lad, and. . . ."

I said no more. As it touched the suture, the twentieth tram emitted a spark as crackly and as dazzling as a bolt of lightning. Then behind the laboratory door, there was a sequence of explosions, simultaneous with a series of assorted anodyne blasphemies.

Puff!

"Oh thunder!"

Piff!

"Dash it!"

Paff!

"A thousand million curses!"

Et cetera. Bouvancourt's anger was banal, but not sacrilegious. When the fusillade had ceased, he cried: "We'll have to do it all over again! What a disaster! What bad luck, my poor Felix!"

"What's happened, then?" I said.

"My Crookes tubes[2] have blown up, of course! That's what's happened! It's not difficult to guess!"

Prudently, I shut up. A few seconds later, I heard Felix opening the door to the hallway and going out.

Finally, Bouvancourt appeared.

"Hello!" I said to him. "What have you done? What a state you're in!"

At first, I was nonplussed by his appearance. The cause of my astonishment gradually became clearer. The physician gave the impression of being surrounded by a very thin fog—a sort of violet tint, visually analogous to mildew, enveloped his entire body with a vaporous and transparent film. There was a strong odor of ozone.

Bouvancourt was quite unmoved. "Right!" he said, simply. "Most curious, indeed. It must be a residue of the accursed experiment. It'll go away, gradually."

He offered me his hand. The colored aura that enveloped him in mauve was intangible, but I was astonished to find that the hand was extremely

---

[2] A Crookes tube was a primitive discharge tube developed by William Crookes in the 1870s, consisting of a partly-evacuated glass cylinder with an electrode at either end; it differed from subsequent cathode ray tubes in that the electrodes were not heated, so they did not emit electrons directly. Crookes tubes were usually operated, as Bouvancourt's are, by Ruhmkorff induction coils; it was this kind of apparatus that permitted Röntgen's accidental discovery of X-rays in 1895.

flaccid. Suddenly, the scientist snatched it away from mine and pressed it to his torso, under the evident influence of a palpitation.

"You're not well, my dear chap—you need to rest. Shall I examine you?"

"Come, come—no childishness, doctor! It will pass. In an hour, it'll no longer be visible, I swear. Then again, to the Devil with the disappointment, since here you are, back again! Let's talk about something else, if you please. What do you think of this novelty? Isn't it fine work, that lambrequin? And the mirror! A Saint-Gobain, old chap!"

And while Ingres' violin[3] whined away in my memory, he led me to his masterpiece.

Suddenly, however, stupefaction immobilized us. We looked at one another interrogatively, not daring to say anything. Finally, Bouvancourt asked me, in a tremulous voice: "There's no doubt, is there? You can see it too—there's nothing there!"

"Perfectly," I stammered. "Nothing . . . nothing at all. . . ."

There, indeed, the miracle commenced. I don't actually know which of us perceived it first. The certain fact is that, although we were both facing the mirror, *my image alone was reflected therein.* Bouvancourt had lost his. In the place which it should have occupied all that could be seen was the very distinct reflection of the desk and the more distant one of the blackboard.

I was bewildered. Bouvancourt started uttering cries of joy. Gradually, he calmed down. "Well, old chap," he said, "this is, I think, a discovery of the first magnitude . . . and one that I scarcely expected. Oh, how fine it is, my friend! There's nothing there! How fine that is, my dear doctor! I confess that I don't understand it, though. The cause escapes me. . . ."

"Your mauve aureole. . . ." I suggested.

"Shh!" said Bouvancourt. "Shut up."

He sat down in front of the glass, empty of his effigy, and began debating the issue, although that did not require him to stop laughing and gesticulating. "You see, doctor, I understand in part. For reasons that I won't confide to you—for fear of being roundly scolded—I've impregnated myself with

---

[3] The great French painter Ingres played the violin for pleasure relaxation, so the phrase "le violon d'Ingres" became a popular nineteenth-century nickname for any such secondary pastime. Renard could not know when he wrote the story that Man Ray would transform the significance of the phrase by producing a classic surrealist visual representation of it in 1924.

a certain fluid, the tenacity of which I was far from suspecting. I'm presumably saturated with it, for that nimbus seems to me to be an excess of fluid, superabundant to that within me, which is leaking out.

"We recently discovered that this gas—that light, if you prefer—has an unexpected property. I only expected it to have the faculty of traversing substances already permeable to ultra-violet radiation—flesh, wood, etc.—plus bone and glass. A vague relationship is certainly discernible between the property that I supposed it to have and the unexpected quality that has just been manifest . . . all the same, I can't explain it. X-rays, it's true, are unreflectable, but. . . ."

"Optical science has not yet unveiled the secret of reflection, has it?" I asked.

"No. In reflection, optical science studies a set of results whose cause is not well-understood. It observes facts, without knowing the exact nature of their source, and pronounces the rules according to which they are routinely produced—then names these rules "laws" because, until today, there has been nothing to falsify them. Light, the agent of optical phenomena, is a mystery. Now, this mystery is all the more difficult to solve because half of its manifestations, ascertained and studied intently for some years, are not directly perceptible, being not only impalpable, silent, odorless and tasteless like the others, but also cold and dark.

"Yes, only ten years ago, it was imagined that light was reflected by objects, more or less totally, but that it never penetrated into them." Bouvancourt raised his voice. "What magic! All these bodies, transpierced!" He tapped the mahogany of his armchair with his curved index-finger. Then, seized by a sudden idea, he leaned toward the mirror and tapped it in the same fashion.

That drew a fearful exclamation from me. His finger perforated the crystal as easily as the surface of a placid wave! Circles were born at the point of entry and radiated one by one, their concentric ripples disturbing the limpidity of the vertical lake as they were propagated.

Bouvancourt shuddered and looked at me. Then, getting up and stepping resolutely toward the mirror, he buried himself entirely within it, with a slight sound like rustling paper. An eddy made the deforming images dance. When everything calmed down, I saw the violet man *on the other side of the glass*. He looked me up and down and laughed soundlessly, comfortably installed in the reflection of the armchair.

Beneath my own finger, the product of Saint-Gobain resounded solidly and impassively.

In the environment of the reflected study, Bouvancourt's lips moved, but no words reached me. Then he put his head through the bizarre partition that separated us, upsetting the vision again. "What a strange place!" he said to me. "I can't hear my own voice there."

"I couldn't distinguish it either—but couldn't you select another means of communication? Your immersions and emersions prevent me from seeing for some time."

"They stop me too; I perceive you in the study as you see me in its reflection, with the difference that I'm keeping company with your image."

His head plunged back into the extraordinary world. He moved about there without any apparent difficulty, touching objects and feeling them. As he displaced a flask on a shelf, a ringing sound made me turn my eyes toward the actual room, and I saw the actual flask rise up into the air momentarily and replace itself on the shelf. By this means, Bouvancourt provoked several movements in the actual study symmetrical with those he initiated in the apparent study. When he passed close to my double, he took care to go around him. Once, deliberately, he pushed him lightly, and I felt myself moved sideways by an invisible individual.

After a few experiments of this sort, Bouvancourt stopped next to the reflected blackboard. He seemed to look for something to his right, then slapped his forehead, and discovered the sponge to his left. Having rubbed out the equations and formulas, he made his own impressions with a nimble piece of chalk. He wrote in large characters, in order that I could read them easily from the threshold of the mirrored room that was forbidden to me. He often left the slate, hazarded an exploration, verified a suspicion or tested some conjecture, then returned to write the result of the experiment. Behind me, the actual piece of chalk tapped away at the real slate with a noise like that of a telegraph, extending indecipherable gibberish from right to left, in inverted letters.

Bouvancourt wrote the following account. I copied it out in my notebook, for the dimension of the characters quickly covered the board and necessitated frequent erasures.

*I'm in a strange region. One can breathe here without difficulty. Where can it be situated? We'll think about that later. For now, it's appropriate to observe.*

*All these doubles of reality are flaccid to a supreme extent—almost incon-*
*sistent. The room in which I'm located ends suddenly where the visual field of*
*the mirror finishes. On my side, the wall against which the mirror is set is a*
*dark field pierced with a rectangle of light . . . a dark and impenetrable plane.*
*It's distressing to look at, even more so to touch. It's neither rough, nor hard,*
*nor warm, but simply impenetrable; I don't know how to express it.*

*If I open the window, the same opaque night extends to either side of the*
*reflected landscape. It's that too, which constitutes the unreflected sides of*
*images, including the back of your own copy, doctor. Your phantom is divided*
*into two zones—the one facing the glass is similar to one of your halves; the*
*other is a silhouette composed of that frightful obscurity. The line that divides*
*them is very precise and when you turn round, the line remains immobile, as*
*if you were turning in front of a luminous hearth at night, always half-illumi-*
*nated and half in shadow.*

*The ammonia has no odor. Liquids have no taste. The Ramsden machine*
*is letting off apparent sparks, devoid of energy, in the direction of the Leyden*
*jar.*[4]

We were in the course of our correspondence when I wanted to trans-
mit to Bouvancourt my uncertainties regarding what would happen in inclined mirrors, or those in the ceiling—or, even better, on the floor, and
my opinion regarding investigations of the weight imposed in these various
hypotheses and even in the present case. With that end in view, I sponged
the slate myself. It took a few seconds.

I had just begun to write my proposal when the chalk leapt violently
from my hand. In awkward, tremulous characters, *going from left to right,*
*as normal*—an indication that the scientist was writing backwards himself,
and wanted to make me understand without delay, at whatever cost—it
traced: HELP! At the same time, a misty human form appeared next to me,
holding the white chalk.

I ran to the mirror. Bouvancourt ran within it to meet me. His forehead was bloody. He crashed into the glass with all his force, as if to break
it—but a block of granite could not have put up more resistance. It had
become impenetrable, with an incomprehensible solidity, with respect to

---

[4] A Ramsden machine employs a rotating disk to produce static electricity by means
of friction; a Leyden jar—a bottle equipped with two electrodes, one internal and the
other external—is a device for storing static electricity.

powers retained from the world beyond it. The scientist's head reddened from another wound, and I understood that, during my brief absence, he had attempted to escape. The mauve aura had dissipated, and the unfortunate man, abandoned by the fluid—doubtless vital in that unknown atmosphere—was giving increasing signs of asphyxia.

Several more times he charged, crashed into and bruised himself on the inflexible separation. The most frightful thing of all was seeing *his image* gradually reappear *on my side*, becoming a second bloody Bouvancourt, maddened and monstrous, with his dark half—and to see those two prisoners face to face, their lips silently twisting in howls and cries for help, continually throwing themselves at one another—hand to hand, forehead to forehead, blood to blood—and continually crashing into one another with the same savage gestures and the same impotent blows.

I tried—with what objective and by what intuition?—to drag the reflection into the laboratory. Having reached the limit of the mirror's visual field, though, the inconsistent being was arrested there, as if by the most immovable object. That frontier cut obliquely through the wide-open door, blocking it more solidly than a rampart of rubble with respect to the scientist's specter. With all my strength, I pulled him and pushed him against that immaterial barrier—which evaded my perception—without succeeding in getting him through it. He depended intimately on Bouvancourt's actual body, and that, as I had forgotten, was a prisoner in the fabulous region.

It was necessary to do something, though. The reflection was gasping for breath in my arms. What could I do? I lay him down on the floor—and there, in the depths of the mirror, Bouvancourt lay down spontaneously, red in the face, with his eyes closed.

I took a decision. In the drawing-room hearth there were those heavy eighteenth-century fire-irons: I went to fetch one of them.

At the first blow, the mirror cracked from side to side. It was soon reduced to smithereens. The wall appeared, and the fire-iron scraped the thick wall.

I turned round. Bouvancourt's reflection was no longer there. Then a woman's scream resounded in the drawing-room. I found the housekeeper there, attracted by the din.

"Well? What?" I said to her, going back in. To my profound amazement, she pointed to her inanimate master lying on the parquet floor. The leg of a bracket-table, still in place, transfixed his thigh.

I declare here and now that a minute before, when I had gone into it to grab the fire-iron, that room had been absolutely deserted.

The physicist was alive, and he recovered consciousness after a few rhythmic tractions of the tongue and a few maneuvers of artificial respiration—but it was necessary for me to loosen the bracket-table and haul with all my muscular strength on the piece of wood before I succeeded in drawing it out. Its extraction left a singularly neat wound, piercing the flesh clean through and grazing the femur—a wound that, to tell the truth, did not really merit that name; it was more like a hole, whose edges manifested no sign of contusion. The weight of the table had not, therefore, been driven into the thigh. Besides, the fastening immobilized it. One might have thought—and perhaps it's the truth—that the limb had re-formed around the table-leg, sealing it in like a mold.

I did not have time, though, to dwell on that subject; Bouvancourt's condition demanded all my attention. It was not his leg-wound that threatened his life, however, but the ulcers that covered him, and strange internal burns, from which he might never recover. It was the worst dermatitis that I have ever treated, accompanied by hair-loss and a malady of the finger- and toe-nails. In brief, he showed all the notorious symptoms of prolonged exposure to invisible light, which I had observed many a time in X-rayed patients before the introduction of instantaneous photographs.

In addition, Bouvancourt admitted to me that he had attempted to photograph an iron candelabrum through his own body and a sheet of glass—an experiment aborted in the manner I have related, which was the origin of this adventure. "I've composed the metal of my electrodes from a mixture of radium and platinum," he told me. He talked to me continually from his bed, directing innocent curses against the misfortune that had taken him away from his experiments, and hence from the solution of the enigma.

To calm him down, I informed him of the observations I had made, showing him the necessity of combining all our certainties in order to build logical suppositions thereon that would permit us to work more adequately. I devoted myself to an investigation of the relevant locations, in the hope that their examination might reinforce our documentation with further observations. I only discovered one thing: the bracket-table in the drawing-room was fixed, relative to the plane of the shattered mirror, at a point symmetrical with the one where I had set down Bouvancourt's image in the study.

I imparted this information to the scientist.

"Are you familiar," he asked me, "with the trick employed by makers of magic lanterns known as *melting views*?"

"Yes," I replied. "It consists of replacing one image projected on a screen by another. It's worked by means of two projectors; the first is slowly darkened while the second is gradually unmasked."

"There is, therefore, if I'm not mistaken," the physicist went on, "a moment when both images are visible together on the canvas, mingling their different subjects—the masts of a ship emerge, for instance, in the midst of a group of friends. . . ."

"Well?" I said. "What does that have to do with . . .?"

"Imagine," the scientist cut in, "that the first view projected were my portrait, and that the second represented a Louis XV bracket-table. It seems to me that it gives a good enough idea of what happened to me at the moment when you broke the mirror . . . especially if the table had been photographed in my drawing-room and your humble servant in his study. . . ."

"It doesn't explain anything."

"Indeed. On the other hand, however, everything that happened to us tends, in spite of reason, to justify a way of seeing that encourages belief in a space hidden behind mirrors. . . ."

"But where do you imagine your—how can I put it—*temporary*[5] space to be located?" I retorted. "In the present case, the reflected study would have occupied the same space as the drawing-room."

"That's it—that's exactly it," said the professor.

"But at the end of the day, Bouvancourt, the drawing-room is the drawing-room! Two things can't be in the same place at the same time—that's crazy!"

"Ahem!" he said, pulling a face. "Crazy! First, there are melting views. Then again, we merely live in space and time, and do not know them. Immensity and eternity are inconceivable. Can you claim to know in detail the part of a whole that you do not know? Are you *certain* that two things can't exist in the same time? Are you *sure* that they can't exist in the same place,

---

[5] The French *temporaire* can also be translated as "provisional," which might make more apparent sense in this instance, but as the word is subsequently contrasted with "permanent" I have used the direct transcription. There is an inevitable temptation, given the customs of modern usage, to substitute "virtual" and "real," but that would be stretching permissible translation too far.

simultaneously?" In a mocking voice, he added: "After all, the space of my body is, at the same time, that of an invalid and that of an elector of equal volume, not to mention other individuals. . . ."

I was relieved to see that he was clearly joking, and the subject of the conversation changed. Besides, only experiments could satisfy us with regard to so extraordinary an event—which, I sometimes suspect, might not have happened as I thought I observed.

Scarcely convalescent, pale and limping, Bouvancourt began his research. Fearing indiscretions, he sent Felix away—whom I replaced, as best I could—and set to work.

Let us state right away that *temporary space*—as we shall call it henceforth, by contrast with *permanent space*—never re-opened. The guinea-pigs that our prudence led us to utilize died of various afflictions, some of them hairless, others corroded by ulcers, some without claws, several of some unknown sort of fit. Three were struck down when, after many deceptions, Bouvancourt attempted to reproduce the trolley-spark artificially; one was killed by the scientist, who, in a rage, persisted in introducing it by force into a mirror. None, however, ever went to prance around in the world of reflections. Nothing could engender the famous violet transparency within them.

I gave up on the project. Bouvancourt continued it. "You're wrong," he told me. "I have a theory. There aren't just mirrors of glass . . . there are other substances endowed with reflective power, but more permeable. . . ."

Poor old Bouvancourt! How stubbornly he pursued his chimera! What endurance and temerity! I had prescribed a strict program of treatment for him, under pain of death. Far from following it, he exposed himself continually to the terrible influences that had already nearly killed him. Every day, I saw his complexion become more jaundiced and his bald head slump further. The pathological symptoms reappeared. He became hideous, and he knew it.

After a little while, he told me that on the day of his discovery, he would probably be less delighted with the triumph than with not having to pore over mirrors any more.

"Patience, though!" he added. "Another week or two, and the Academy of Sciences shall learn something new!"

\*

Yesterday, at dawn, a canal boatman noticed some unusual items of apparatus on the towpath. Taken to the police station, they were recognized by a sagacious inspector as "chemistry equipment." He went to Bouvancourt's house, in order to obtain fuller information. There, he learned that the scientist had disappeared the previous evening.

He was fished out of the canal.

"There are other substances more permeable than glass endowed with reflective power...."

Some people say that he drowned after having been electrocuted, in an excess of precaution. Others add, delicately, that "perhaps his housekeeper knows something about it."

"He committed suicide," affirmed the *Echo de Pontargis*, "suffering from an incurable malady occasioned by his perilous studies."

Someone once said to me, with a charming smile: "The cold light had burned his brain, eh!"

Only I know the truth.

I can see Bouvancourt on the edge of the nocturnal canal. He dips the zinc electrodes of his battery into the bichromate. Immediately, the Ruhmkorff coil emits its bee-like or hornet-like buzz; the bulb becomes phosphorescent. The scientist believes himself to be impregnated with mysterious clarity.

He looks into the liquid depths, at the inverted image of the restful landscape, snowy in the moonlight. He looks at that temporary space, into which the incorporated fluid ought to authorize him to descend into an even paler moonlight, an even brighter landscape....

And he descends, not knowing what laws of gravity govern that universe, at the risk of sinking into the gulf of the firmament open at his feet.

And he descends ... but he finds nothing but permanent space—which is to say, in actuality, water: the weighty water in which human beings cannot live; the water of epilogues, whose silence is that which follows so many stories; the water of finality.

# THE HORROR OF THE HEIGHTS

## Sir Arthur Conan Doyle

*Sir Arthur Conan Doyle (1859–1930) trained and practiced as a physician before his sideline writing popular fiction brought him enormous success and fame, primarily as the creator of the archetypal detective Sherlock Holmes. Although he wrote a handful of early short stories in the scientific romance genre he devoted no particular effort to it until he produced the classic novel* The Lost World *(1912), featuring the charismatic scientist and explorer Professor Challenger. He followed it up rapidly with a sequel, the near-apocalyptic disaster story* The Poison Belt *(1913). The Great War interrupted his career, and the death of his son in action prompted him to develop a strong interest in spiritualism, which deflected the third and last novel featuring Professor Challenger in a very different direction.*

*"The Horror of the Heights" was written between* The Lost World *and* The Poison Belt, *when Doyle's interest in scientific romance was at its peak. It was written at a moment when the dream of flight featured in the earliest stories in the present anthology had been realized, but the conquest of the air had only just begun, leaving imaginative scope for the envisaging of exotic challenges. It has something in common with William Hope Hodgson's tales of exotic life-forms lurking in the margins of the unknown, and marks the end of the era when such margins could still be located on earth. After the Great War of 1914–18, the world seemed smaller, and more familiar, and the fringe of the unknown, which could still be located above Wiltshire in "The Horror of the Heights," was forced into a more distant exile, eventually finding a refuge in the greater wilderness of outer space, the literary colonization of which American science fiction soon began.*

The idea that the extraordinary narrative which has been called the Joyce-Armstrong fragment is an elaborate practical joke evolved by some unknown person, cursed by a perverted and sinister sense of humor, has now been abandoned by all who have examined the matter. The most macabre and imaginative of plotters would hesitate before linking his morbid fancies with the unquestioned and tragic facts which reinforce the statement. Though the assertions contained in it are amazing and even monstrous, it is none the less forcing itself upon the general intelligence that they are true, and that we must readjust our ideas to the new situation. This world of ours appears to be separated by a slight and precarious margin of safety from a most singular and unexpected danger. I will endeavor in this narrative, which reproduces the original document in its necessarily somewhat fragmentary form, to lay before the reader the whole of the facts up to date, prefacing my statement by saying that, if there be any who doubt the narrative of Joyce-Armstrong, there can be no question at all as to the facts concerning Lieutenant Myrtle, R.N., and Mr. Hay Connor, who undoubtedly met their end in the manner described.

The Joyce-Armstrong fragment was found in the field which is called Lower Haycock, lying one mile to the westward of the village of Withyham, upon the Kent and Sussex border. It was on the fifteenth of September last that an agricultural laborer, James Flynn, in the employment of Matthew Dodd, farmer, of the Chauntry Farm, Withyham, perceived a briar pipe lying near the footpath which skirts the hedge in Lower Haycock. A few paces farther on he picked up a pair of broken binocular glasses. Finally, among some nettles in the ditch, he caught sight of a flat, canvas-backed book, which proved to be a note-book with detachable leaves, some of which had come loose and were fluttering along the base of the hedge. These he collected, but some, including the first, were never recovered, and leave a deplorable hiatus in this all-important statement. The notebook was taken by the laborer to his master, who in turn showed it to Dr. J. H. Atherton, of Hartfield. This gentleman at once recognized the need for an expert examination, and the manuscript was forwarded to the Aero Club in London, where it now lies.

The first two pages of the manuscript are missing. There is also one torn away at the end of the narrative, though none of these affect the general coherence of the story. It is conjectured that the missing opening is concerned with the record of Mr. Joyce-Armstrong's qualifications as an aeronaut, which can be gathered from other sources and are admitted to be unsurpassed among the air pilots of England. For many years he has been looked upon as among the most daring and the most intellectual of flying men, a combination which has enabled him to both invent and test several new devices, including the common gyroscopic attachment which is known by his name. The main body of the manuscript is written neatly in ink, but the last few pages are in pencil and are so ragged as to be hardly legible, exactly, in fact, as they might be expected to appear if they were scribbled off hurriedly from the seat of a moving aeroplane. There are, it may be added, several stains, both on the last page and on the outside cover which have been pronounced by the Home Office experts to be blood—probably human and certainly mammalian. The fact that something closely resembling the organism of malaria was discovered in this blood, and that Joyce-Armstrong is known to have suffered from intermittent fever, is a remarkable example of the new weapons which modern science has placed in the hands of our detectives.

And now a word as to the personality of the author of this epoch-making statement. Joyce-Armstrong, according to the few friends who really knew something of the man, was a poet and a dreamer, as well as a mechanic and an inventor. He was a man of considerable wealth, much of which he had spent in the pursuit of his aeronautical hobby. He had four private aeroplanes in his hangars near Devizes, and is said to have made no fewer than one hundred and seventy ascents in the course of last year. He was a retiring man with dark moods, in which he would avoid the society of his fellows.

Captain Dangerfield, who knew him better than anyone, says that there were times when his eccentricity threatened to develop into something more serious. His habit of carrying a shotgun with him in his aeroplane was one manifestation of it. Another was the morbid effect which the fall of Lieutenant Myrtle had upon his mind. Myrtle, who was attempting the height record, fell from an altitude of something over thirty thousand feet. Horrible to narrate, his head was entirely obliterated, though his body and limbs preserved their configuration. At every gathering of airmen, Joyce-Armstrong according to Dangerfield, would ask, with an enigmatic smile: "And where, pray, is Myrtle's head?"

On another occasion, after dinner, at the mess of the Flying School on Salisbury Plain, he started a debate as to what will be the most permanent danger which airmen will have to encounter. Having listened to successive opinions as to air-pockets, faulty construction, and over-banking, he ended up by shrugging his shoulders and refusing to put forward his own views, though he gave the impression that they differed from any advanced by his companions.

It is worth remarking that after his own complete disappearance it was found that his private affairs were arranged with a precision which may show that he had a strong premonition of disaster. With these essential explanations I will now give the narrative exactly as it stands, beginning at page three of the blood-soaked notebook.

*

Nevertheless, when I dined at Rheims with Coselli and Gustav Raymond I found that neither of them was aware of any particular danger in the higher layers of the atmosphere. I did not actually say what was in my thoughts, but I got so near to it that if they had any corresponding idea they could not have failed to express it. But then they are two empty, vainglorious fellows with no thought beyond seeing their silly names in the newspaper. It is interesting to note that neither of them had ever been much beyond the twenty-thousand-foot level. Of course, men have been higher than this both in balloons and in the ascent of mountains. It must be well above that point that the aeroplane enters the danger zone—always presuming that my premonitions are correct.[1]

Aeroplaning has been with us now for more than twenty years, and one might well ask: Why should this peril be only revealing itself in our day? The answer is obvious. In the old days of weak engines, when a hundred horse-power Gnome or Green was considered ample for every need, the flights were very restricted. Now that three hundred horse-power is the rule rather than the exception, visits to the upper layers have become easier

---

[1] When this story was written, the altitude record for an aircraft—set, as subsequently noted in the history, by Roland Garros, in September 1912—was 18,405 feet. In our history thirty thousand feet was first attained in June 1919 by Jean Casale. As the story also notes further on, Henry Coxwell and James Glaisher had ascended higher than thirty thousand feet in a balloon in 1862, but the latter lost consciousness due to the low air pressure and intense cold, deterring anyone else from attempting to break their record until 1927, when Hawthorne Gray succeeded, but died when his oxygen supply ran out.

and more common. Some of us can remember how, in our youth, Garros made a world-wide reputation by attaining nineteen thousand feet, and it was considered a remarkable achievement to fly over the Alps.

Our standard now has been immeasurably raised, and there are twenty high flights for one in former years. Many of them have been undertaken with impunity. The thirty-thousand-foot level has been reached time after time with no discomfort beyond cold and asthma. What does that prove? A visitor might descend upon this planet a thousand times and never see a tiger. Yet tigers exist, and if he chanced to come down in the jungle he might be devoured.

There are jungles of the upper air, and there are worse things than tigers which inhabit them. I believe in time they will map these jungles accurately out. Even at the present moment I could name two of them. One of them lies over the Pau-Biarritz district of France. Another is just over my head as I write here in my house in Wiltshire. I rather think there is a third in the Hamburg-Wiesbaden district.

It was the disappearance of the airmen that first set me thinking. Of course, everyone said that they had fallen into the sea, but that did not satisfy me at all. First, there was Verrier in France; his machine was found near Bayonne, but they never got his body.

There was the case of Baxter also, who vanished, though his engine and some of the iron fixings were found in a wood in Leicestershire. In that case, Dr. Middleton, of Amesbury, who was watching the flight with a tele-scope, declares that just before the clouds obscured the view he saw the machine, which was at an enormous height, suddenly rise perpendicularly upwards in a succession of jerks in a manner that he would have thought to be impossible. That was the last seen of Baxter. There was a correspondence in the papers, but it never led to anything.

There were several other similar cases, and then there was the death of Hay Connor. What a cackle there was about an unsolved mystery of the air, and what columns in the halfpenny papers, and yet how little was ever done to get to the bottom of the business! He came down in a tremendous vol-plané from an unknown height. He never got off his machine and died in his pilot's seat. Died of what? "Heart disease," said the doctors. Rubbish! Hay Connor's heart was as sound as mine is. What did Venables say? Ven-ables was the only man who was at his side when he died. He said that he was shivering and looked like a man who had been badly scared. "Died of fright," said Venables, but could not imagine what he was frightened about. Only said one word to Venables, which sounded like "Monstrous." They could make nothing of that at the inquest. But I could make something of it. Monsters! That was the last word of poor Harry Hay Connor. And he *did* die of fright, just as Venables thought.

And then there was Myrtle's head. Do you really believe—does anyone really believe—that a man's head could be driven clean into his body by the force of a fall? Well, perhaps it may be possible, but I, for one, have never believed that it was so with Myrtle. And the grease upon his clothes—"all slimy with grease," said somebody at the inquest. Queer that nobody got thinking after that! I did—but then, I had been thinking for a good long time.

I've made three ascents—how Dangerfield used to chafe me about my shotgun!—but I've never been high enough. Now, with this new light Paul Veroner machine and its one hundred and seventy-five Robur, I should easily touch the thirty thousand tomorrow. I'll have a shot at the record. Maybe I shall have a shot at something else as well. Of course, it's dangerous. If a fellow wants to avoid danger he had best keep out of flying altogether and subside into flannel slippers and a dressing-gown. But I'll visit the air-jungle tomorrow—and if there's anything there I shall know it. If I return, I'll find myself a bit of a celebrity. If I don't, this notebook of mine may explain what I am trying to do, and how I lost my life in doing it. But no drivel about accidents or mysteries, if you please.

*

I chose my Paul Veroner monoplane for the job. There's nothing like a monoplane when real work is to be done. Beaumont[2] found that out in the very early days. For one thing, it doesn't mind damp, and the weather looks as if we should be in the clouds all the time. It's a bonny little model and answers my hand like a tender-mouthed horse. The engine is a ten-cylinder rotary Robur working up to one hundred and seventy-five. It has all the modern improvements: enclosed fuselage, high-curling land-

---

[2] André Beaumont was the pseudonym of the French aviation pioneer Jean Louis Conneau (1880–1937), who won several air races in 1911 and co-founded Franco-British Aviation in London and Paris in 1913.

ing skids, brakes, gyroscopic steadiers, and three speeds, worked by an alteration of the angle of the planes upon the Venetian blind principle. I took a shotgun with me and a dozen cartridges filled with buckshot. You should have seen the face of Perkins, my old mechanic, when I directed them to put them in.

I was dressed like an Arctic explorer, with two jerseys under my overalls, thick socks inside my padded boots, a storm-cap with flaps, and my talc goggles. It was stifling outside the hangars, but I was going for the summit of the Himalayas, and had to dress for the part. Perkins knew there was something on and implored me to take him with me. Perhaps I should if I were using the biplane, but a monoplane is a one-man show, if you want to get the last foot of lift out of it. Of course, I took an oxygen bag; the man who goes for the altitude record without one will either be frozen or smothered—or both.

I had a good look at the planes, the rudder-bar, and the elevating lever before I got in. Everything was in order so far as I could see. Then I switched on my engine and found that she was running sweetly. When they let her go she rose almost at once upon the lowest speed. I circled my home field once or twice just to warm her up, and then, with a wave to Perkins and the others, I flattened out my planes and put her on her highest. She skimmed like a swallow down wind for eight or ten miles until I turned her nose up a little and she began to climb in a great spiral for the cloud bank above me. It's all-important to rise slowly and adapt yourself to the pressure as you go.

It was a close, warm day for an English September, and there was the hush and heaviness of impending rain. Now and then there came sudden puffs of wind from the south-west—one of them so gusty and unexpected that it caught me napping and turned me half-round for an instant. I remember the time when gusts and whirls and air-pockets used to be things of danger before we learned to put an overmastering power into our engines.

Just as I reached the cloud-banks, with the altimeter marking three thousand, down came the rain. My word, how it poured! It drummed upon my wings and lashed against my face, blurring my glasses so that I could hardly see. I got down to a low speed, for it was painful to travel against it. As I got higher it became hail, and I had to turn tail to it. One of my cylinders was out of action—a dirty plug, I should imagine—but still I was rising steadily with plenty of power.

After a bit the trouble passed, whatever it was, and I heard the full deep-throated purr—then ten singing as one. That's where the beauty of our modern silencers comes in. We can at last control our engines by ear. How they squeal and squeak and sob when they are is trouble! All those cries for help were wasted in the old days, when every sound was swallowed up by the monstrous racket of the machine. If only the early aviators could come back to see the beauty and perfection of the mechanisms which have been bought at the cost of their lives!

About nine-thirty I was nearing the clouds. Down below me, all blurred and shadowed with rain, lay the vast expanse of Salisbury Plain. Half a dozen flying machines were doing hackwork at the thousand foot level, looking like little black swallows against the green background. I dare say they were wondering what I was doing up in cloud-land. Suddenly a gray curtain drew across beneath me and the wet folds of vapor were swirling round my face. It was clammily cold and miserable. But I was above the hail-storm, and that was something gained.

The cloud was as dark and thick as a London fog. In my anxiety to get clear, I cocked her nose up until the automatic alarm-bell rang, and I actually began to slide backwards. My sopped and dripping wings had made me heavier than I thought, but presently I was in a lighter cloud, and soon had cleared the layer. There was a second—opal-colored and fleecy—at a great height above my head, a white unbroken ceiling above, and a dark unbroken floor below, with the monoplane laboring upwards upon a vast spiral between them.

It is deadly lonely in these cloud-spaces. Once a great flight of some small water-birds went past me, flying very fast to the westwards. The quick whirr of their wings and their musical cry were cheery to my ear. I fancy they were teal, but I am a wretched zoologist. Now that we humans have become birds we must really learn to know our brethren by sight.

The wind down beneath me whirled and swayed the broad cloud-plain. Once a great eddy formed in it, a whirlpool of vapor, and through it, as down a funnel, I caught sight of the distant world. A large white biplane was passing at a vast depth beneath me. I fancy it was the morning mail service betwixt Bristol and London. Then the drift swirled inwards again and the great solitude was unbroken.

Just after ten I touched the lower edge of the upper cloud-stratum. It consisted of the diaphanous vapor drifting swiftly from the westward.

The wind had been steadily rising all this time and it was now blowing a sharp breeze—twenty-eight an hour by my gauge. Already it was very cold, though my altimeter only marked nine thousand. The engines were working beautifully and we went droning steadily upwards.

The cloud-bank was thicker than I had expected, but at last it thinned out into a golden mist before me, and then in an instant I had shot out from it, and there was an unclouded sky and a brilliant sun above my head—all blue and gold above, all shining silver below, one vast glimmering plain as far as my eyes could reach. It was a quarter past ten o'clock, and the barograph needle pointed to twelve thousand eight hundred.

Up I went and up, my ears concentrated upon the deep purring of my motor, my eyes busy always with the watch, the revolution indicator, the petrol lever, and the oil pump. No wonder aviators are said to be a fearless race. With so many things to think of there is no time to trouble about oneself. About this time I noticed how unreliable is the compass when above a certain height from earth. At fifteen thousand feet mine was pointing east and a point south. The sun and wind gave me my true bearings.

I had hoped to reach an eternal stillness in these high altitudes, but with every thousand feet of ascent the gale grew stronger. My machine groaned and trembled in every joint and rivet as she faced it, and swept away like a sheet of paper when I banked her on the turn, skimming down the wind at a greater pace, perhaps, than ever mortal man has moved. Yet I always had to turn again and tack into the wind's eye, for it was not merely a height record that I was after. By all my calculations it was above little Wiltshire that my air-jungle lay, and all my labor might be lost if I struck the outer layers at some further point.

When I reached the nineteen-thousand foot level, which was about midday, the wind was so severe that I looked with some anxiety to the stays of my wings, expecting momentarily to see them snap or slacken. I even cast loose the parachute behind me, and fastened its hook into the ring of my leathern belt, so as to be ready for the worst. Now was the time when a bit of scamped work by the mechanic is paid for by the life of the aeronaut. But she held together bravely. Every cord and strut was hanging and vibrating like so many harp strings, but it was glorious to see how, for all the beating and buffeting, she was still the conqueror of Nature and the mistress of the sky.

There is surely something divine in man himself that he should rise so superior to the limitations which Creation seemed to impose—rise, too, by such unselfish heroic devotion as his air-conquest has shown. Talk of human degeneration! When has such a story as this been written in the annals of our race?

These were the thoughts in my head as I climbed that monstrous inclined plane with the wind sometimes beating in my face and sometimes whistling behind my ears, while the cloud-land beneath me fell away to such a distance that the folds and hummocks of silver had all smoothed out into one flat, shining plain.

But suddenly I had a horrible and unprecedented experience. I have known before what it is to be in what our neighbors have called a *tourbillon*, but never on such a scale as this. That huge, sweeping river of wind of which I have spoken had, as it appears, whirlpools within it which were as monstrous as itself. Without a moment's warning I was dragged suddenly into the heart of one. I spun round for a minute or two with such velocity that I almost lost my senses, and then fell suddenly, left wing foremost, down the vacuum funnel in the center.

I dropped like a stone, and lost nearly a thousand feet. It was only my belt that kept me in my seat, and the shock and breathlessness left me hanging half-insensible over the side of the fuselage. But I am always capable of a supreme effort—it is my one great merit as an aviator. I was conscious that the descent was slower. The whirlpool was a cone rather than a funnel, and I had come to the apex. With a terrific wrench, throwing my weight all to one side, I leveled my planes and brought her head away from the wind.

In an instant I had shot out of the eddies and was skimming down the sky. Then, shaken but victorious, I turned her nose up and began once more my steady grind on the upward spiral. I took a large sweep to avoid the danger-spot of the whirlpool, and soon I was safely above it. Just after one o'clock I was twenty-one thousand feet above the sea-level. To my great joy I had topped the gale, and with every hundred feet of ascent the air grew stiller.

On the other hand, it was very cold, and I was conscious of that particular nausea which goes with rarefaction of the air. For the first time I unscrewed the mouth of my oxygen bag and took an occasional whiff of the glorious gas. I could feel it running like a cordial through my veins, and

I was exhilarated almost to the point of drunkenness. I shouted and sang as I soared upwards into the cold, still outer world.

It is very clear to me that the insensibility which came upon Glaisher, and in a lesser degree upon Coxwell, when, in 1862, they ascended in a balloon to the height of thirty thousand feet, was due to the extreme speed with which a perpendicular ascent is made. Doing it at an easy gradient and accustoming oneself to the lessened barometric pressure by slow degrees, there are no such dreadful symptoms. At the same great height I found that even without my oxygen inhaler I could breathe without undue distress. It was bitterly cold, however, and my thermometer was at zero, Fahrenheit.

At one-thirty I was nearly seven miles above the surface of the earth, and still ascending steadily. I found, however, that the rarefied air was giving markedly less support to my planes, and that my angle of ascent had to be considerably lowered in consequence. It was already clear that even with my light weight and strong engine-power there was a point in front of me where I should be held. To make matters worse, one of my sparking-plugs was in trouble again and there was intermittent misfiring in the engine. My heart was heavy with the fear of failure.

It was about that time that I had a most extraordinary experience. Something whizzed past me in a trail of smoke and exploded with a loud, hissing sound, sending forth a cloud of steam. For the instant I could not imagine what had happened. Then I remembered that the earth is for ever being bombarded by meteor stone, and would be hardly inhabitable were they not in nearly every case turned to vapor in the outer layers of the atmosphere. Here is a new danger for the high-altitude man, for two others passed me when I was nearing the forty-thousand-foot mark. I cannot doubt that at the edge of the earth's envelope the risk would be a very real one.

My barograph needle marked forty-one thousand three hundred when I became aware that I could go no further. Physically, the strain was not yet greater than I could bear, but my machine had reached its limit. The attenuated air gave no firm support to the wings, and the least tilt developed into side-slip, while she seemed sluggish on her controls. Possibly, had the engine been at its best, another thousand feet might have been within our capacity, but it was still misfiring, and two out of the ten cylinders appeared to be out of action. If I had not already reached the zone for which I was searching then I should never see it upon this journey. But was it not possible that I had attained it?

Soaring in circles like a monstrous hawk upon the forty-thousand-foot level I let the monoplane guide herself, and with my Mannheim glass I made a careful observation of my surroundings. The heavens were perfectly clear; there was no indication of those dangers which I had imagined.

I have said that I was soaring in circles. It struck me suddenly that I would do well to take a wider sweep and open up a new air-tract. If the hunter entered an earth-jungle he would drive through it if he wished to find his game. My reasoning had led me to believe that the air-jungle which I had imagined lay somewhere over Wiltshire. This should be to the south and west of me. I took my bearings from the sun, for the compass was hopeless and no trace of earth was to be seen—nothing but the distant silver cloud-plain. However, I got my direction as best I might and kept her head straight to the mark. I reckoned that my petrol supply would not last for more than another hour or so, but I could afford to use it to the last drop, since a single magnificent vol-plané could at any time take me to the earth.

Suddenly I was aware of something new. The air in front of me had lost its crystal clearness. It was full of long, ragged wisps of something which I can only compare to very fine cigarette-smoke. It hung about in wreaths and coils, turning and twisting slowly in the sunlight. As the monoplane shot through it, I was aware of a faint taste of oil upon my lips, and there was a greasy scum upon the woodwork of the machine. Some infinitely fine organic matter appeared to be suspended in the atmosphere. There was no life there. It was inchoate and diffuse, extending for many square acres and then fringing off into the void.

No, it was not life. But might it not be the remains of life? Above all, might it not be the food of life, of monstrous life, even as the humble grease of the ocean is the food for the mighty whale? The thought was in my mind when my eyes looked upwards and I saw the most wonderful vision that ever man has seen. Can I hope to convey it to you even as I saw it myself last Thursday?

Conceive a jelly-fish such as sails in our summer seas, bell-shaped and of enormous size, far larger, I should judge, than the dome of St. Paul's. It was of a light pink color with a delicate green, but the whole huge fabric so tenuous that it was but a fairy outline against the dark blue sky. It pulsated with a delicate and regular rhythm. From there depended two long, drooping green tentacles, which swayed slowly backwards and forwards.

This gorgeous vision passed gently with noiseless dignity over my head, as light and fragile as a soap bubble, and drifted upon its stately way.

I had half-turned my monoplane, that I might look at this beautiful creature, when, in a moment, I found myself amidst a perfect fleet of them, of all sizes, but none so large as the first. Some were quite small, but the majority about as big as an average balloon, and with much the same curvature at the top. There was in them a delicacy of texture and coloring which reminded me of the finest Venetian glass. Pale shades of pink and green were the prevailing tints, but all had a lovely iridescence where the sunlight shimmered through their dainty form. Some hundred of them drifted past me, a wonderful fairy squadron of strange, unknown argosies of the sky—creatures whose forms and substance were so attuned to these pure heights that one could not conceive anything so delicate within actual sight or sound of earth.

But soon my attention was drawn to a new phenomenon—the serpents of the outer air. These were long, thin, fantastic coils of vapor-like material, which turned and twisted with great speed, flying round and round at such a pace that the eyes could hardly follow them. Some of these ghost-like creatures were twenty or thirty feet long, but it was difficult to tell their girth, for their outline was so hazy that it seemed to fade away into the air round them.

These air-snakes were of a very light gray or smoke color, with some darker lines within, which gave the impression of a definite organism. One of them whisked past my very face, and I was conscious of a cold, clumsy contact, but their composition was so unsubstantial that I could not connect them with any thought of physical danger, any more than the beautiful bell-like creatures which had preceded them. There was no more solidity in their frames than in the floating spume from a broken wave.

But a more terrible experience was in store for me. Floating downwards from a great height there came a purplish patch of vapor, small as I saw it first, but rapidly enlarging as it approached me, until it appeared to be hundreds of square feet in size. Though fashioned of some transparent, jelly-like substance, it was none the less of a much more definite outline and solid consistence than anything which I had seen before. There were more traces, too, of a physical organization, especially two vast shadowy, circular planes upon either side, which may have been eyes, and a perfectly solid white projection between them which was as curved and cruel as the beak of a vulture.

The whole aspect of this monster was formidable and threatening, and it kept changing its color from a very light mauve to a dark, angry purple so thick that it cast a shadow as it drifted between my monoplane and the sun.

On the upper curve of its huge body there were three great projections which I can only describe as enormous bubbles, and I was convinced as I looked at them that they were charged with some extremely light gas which served to buoy up the misshapen and semi-solid mass in the rarefied air. The creature moved swiftly along, keeping pace readily with the monoplane, and for twenty miles or more it formed my horrible escort, hovering over me like a bird of prey which is waiting to pounce. Its method, its progression—done so swiftly that it was not easy to follow—was to throw out a long, glutinous streamer in front of it, which in turn seemed to draw forward the rest of the writhing body. So elastic and gelatinous was it that never for two successive minutes was it the same shape, and yet each change made it more threatening and loathsome than the last.

I knew that it meant mischief. Every purplish flush of its hideous body told me so. The vague, goggling eyes which were turned always upon me were cold and merciless in their viscid hatred. I dipped the nose of my monoplane downwards to escape it. As I did so, as quick as a flash, there shot out a long tentacle from this mass of floating blubber, and it fell as light and sinuous as a whip-lash across the front of my machine.

There was a loud hiss as it lay for a moment across the hot engine, and it whisked itself into the air again, while the huge flat body drew itself together as if in sudden pain. I dipped in a vol-piqué, but again a tentacle fell over the monoplane and was shorn off by the propeller as easily as it might have cut through a smoke-wreath.

A long, gliding, sticky, serpent-like coil came from behind and caught me round the waist, dragging me out of the fuselage. I tore at it, my fingers sinking into the smooth, glue-like surface, and for an instant I disengaged myself, but only to be caught round the boot by another coil, which gave me a jerk that tilted me almost on to my back.

As I fell I blazed off both barrels of my gun, though indeed, it was like attacking an elephant with a pea-shooter to imagine that any human weapon could cripple that mighty bulk. And yet I aimed better than I knew, for, with a loud report, one of the great blisters upon the creature's back exploded with the puncture of the buckshot.

It was very clear that my conjecture was right, and that these vast clear bladders were distended with some lifting gas, for in an instant the huge cloud-like body turned sideways, writhing desperately to find its balance, while the white beak snapped and gaped in horrible fury. But already I had shot away on the steepest glide that I dared to attempt, my engine still full on, the flying propeller and the force of gravity shooting me downwards like an aerolite. Far behind me I saw a dull, purplish smudge growing swiftly smaller and merging into the blue sky behind it. I was safe out of the deadly jungle of the outer air.

Once out of danger I throttled my engine, for nothing tears a machine to pieces quicker than running on full power from a height. It was a glorious spiral vol-plané from nearly eight miles of altitude—first, to the level of the silver cloud-bank, then to that of the storm-clouds beneath it, and finally, in beating rain, to the surface of the earth.

I saw the Bristol Channel beneath me as I broke from the clouds, but, having still some petrol in my tank, I got twenty miles inland before I found myself stranded in a field half a mile from the village of Ashcombe. Then I got three tins of petrol from a passing motor-car, and at ten minutes past six that evening I alighted gently in my own home meadow at Devizes, after such a journey as no mortal on earth has ever yet taken and lived to tell the tale.

I have seen the beauty and I have seen the horror of the heights—and greater beauty or horror than that is not within the ken of man.

And now it is my plan to go once again before I give my results to the world. My reason for this is that I must surely have something to show by way of proof before I lay such a tale before my fellow men. It is true that others will soon follow and will confirm what I have said, and yet I should wish to carry conviction from the first.

Those lovely iridescent bubbles of the air should not be hard to capture. They drift slowly upon their way, and the swift monoplane could intercept their leisurely course. It is likely enough that they would dissolve in the heavier layers of the atmosphere, and that some small heap of amorphous jelly might be all that I should bring back to earth with me. And yet something there would surely be by which I could substantiate my story.

Yes, I will go, even if I run a risk by doing so. These purple horrors would not seem to be numerous. It is probable that I shall not see one. If I do I shall dive at once. At the worst there is always the shotgun and my knowledge of

*Here a page of the manuscript is unfortunately missing. On the next page is written, in large, straggling writing:*

Forty thousand feet. I shall never see earth again. They are beneath me, three of them. God help me; it is a dreadful death to die!

*

Such, in its entirety, is the Joyce-Armstrong Statement.

Of the man nothing has since been seen. Pieces of his shattered monoplane have been picked up on the preserves of Mr. Budd-Lushington, upon the borders of Kent and Sussex, within a few miles of the spot where the notebook was discovered. If the unfortunate aviator's theory is correct that this air-jungle, as he called it, existed only over the south-west of England, then it would seem that he had fled from it at the full speed of his monoplane, but had been overtaken and devoured by these horrible creatures at some spot in the outer atmosphere above the place where the grim relics were found.

The picture of that monoplane skimming down the sky, with the nameless terrors flying as swiftly beneath it and cutting it off always from the earth while they gradually closed in upon their victim, is one upon which a man who valued his sanity would prefer not to dwell. There are many, as I am aware, who still jeer at the facts which I have here set down, but even they must admit that Joyce-Armstrong has disappeared, and I would commend to them his own words:

"This notebook may explain what I am trying to do, and how I lost my life in doing it. But no drivel about accidents or mysteries, if you please."

# Appendix

A Chronology of the Most Important Longer Works of Scientific
Romance Published between 1830 and August 1914

1833 Charles Nodier "Hurlubeu" & "Léviathan le Long" (Fr, tr. as "Perfectibility")

1835 Edgar Allan Poe "The Unparalleled Adventure of One Hans Pfaall" (U.S.)

1836 Louis-Napoléon Geoffroy *Napoléon et la conquête du monde* (Fr, tr. as *The Apocryphal Napoleon*)

1846 Émile Souvestre *Le Monde tel qu'il sera* (Fr, tr. as *The World as It Shall Be*)

1848 Edgar Allan Poe *Eureka: A Prose Poem* (U.S.)

1859 Herrmann Lang *The Air Battle* (UK)

1862 Edmond About *L'Homme à l'oreille cassée* (Fr, tr. as *The Man with the Broken Ear*)

1863 Jules Verne *Cinq semaines en ballon* (Fr, tr. as *Five Weeks in a Balloon*)

1864 Jules Verne *Voyage au centre de la terre* (Fr, tr. as *Journey to the Centre of the Earth*)

1865 Jules Verne *De la terre à la lune* (Fr, tr. as *From the Earth to the Moon*)

1869 Edward Everett Hale "The Brick Moon" (U.S.)
Jules Verne *Autour de la lune* (Fr, tr. as *Around the Moon*)

1870 Jules Verne *Vingt mille lieues sous les mers* (Fr, tr. as *Twenty Thousand Leagues Under the Sea*)

1871 Edward Bulwer-Lytton *The Coming Race* (UK)
George T. Chesney "The Battle of Dorking" (UK)

1872 Samuel Butler *Erewhon; or, Over the Range* (UK)

1874 Andrew Blair *Annals of the Twenty-Ninth Century* (UK)

1877 Jules Verne *Hector Servadac* (Fr, tr. as *Hector Servadac*)

1879 Jules Verne (and Paschal Grousset) *Les Cinq cent millions de la Bégum* (Fr, tr. as *The Begum's Fortune*)

1880 Edward Bellamy *Dr. Heidenhoff's Process* (U.S.)
Percy Greg *Across the Zodiac* (UK)

1883 Didier de Chousy *Ignis* (Fr, tr. as *Ignis: The Central Fire*)
Albert Robida *Le Vingtième siècle* (Fr, tr. as *The Twentieth Century*)

1884 Edwin Abbott (as "A Square") *Flatland* (UK)

1885 Richard Jefferies *After London* (UK)

1886 Villiers de l'Isle-Adam *L'Ève future* (Fr, tr. as *The Future Eve*)
Jules Verne *Robur le conquérant* (Fr, tr. as *The Clipper of the Clouds*)

1887 W. H. Hudson *A Crystal Age* (UK)
J.-H. Rosny "Les Xipéhuz" (Fr, tr. as "The Xipehuz)

1888 Edward Bellamy *Looking Backward 2000–1887* (U.S.)
Walter Besant *The Inner House* (UK)

1889 Louis Boussenard *Dix mille ans dans un bloc de glace* (Fr, tr. as *Ten Thousand Years in a Block of Ice*)
Edgar Fawcett "Solarion" (US)
Hugh MacColl *Mr. Stranger's Sealed Packet* (UK)
John Ames Mitchell *The Last American* (US)
Mark Twain *A Connecticut Yankee in King Arthur's Court* (US)

1890 Robert Cromie *A Plunge into Space* (UK)
Ignatius Donnelly *Caesar's Column* (US)
William Morris *News from Nowhere* (UK)

1892 Ignatius Donnelly *The Golden Bottle* (US)
Albert Robida *La Vie électrique* (Fr, tr. as *Electric Life*)

1893 Camille Flammarion *La Fin du Monde* (Fr, tr. as *Omega: The End of the World*)
George Griffith *The Angel of the Revolution* (UK)

1894 George Griffith *Olga Romanoff* (UK)
Gustavus W. Pope *Journey to Mars* (US)

1895 Grant Allen *The British Barbarians* (UK)
Robert Cromie *The Crack of Doom* (UK)
John Davidson *A Full and True Account of the Wonderful Mission of Earl Lavender* (UK)
Edgar Fawcett *The Ghost of Guy Thyrle* (US)
George Griffith *The Outlaws of the Air* (UK)
C. H. Hinton *Stella and An Unfinished Communication* (UK)
Jules Verne *L'Île à hélice* (Fr, tr. as *Propellor Island*)
H. G. Wells *The Time Machine* (UK)

1896 H. G. Wells *The Island of Dr Moreau* (UK)

1897 Fred T. Jane *To Venus in Five Seconds* (UK)
H. G. Wells *The Invisible Man* (UK)

1898 Paul Adam *Lettres de Malaisie* (Fr, tr. as "Letters from Malaisie")
Clement Fézandie *Through the Earth* (US)

M. P. Shiel *The Yellow Danger* (UK)
Frank R. Stockton *The Great Stone of Sardis* (US)
Stanley Waterloo *Armageddon* (US)
H. G. Wells *The War of the Worlds* (UK)

1899 Fred T. Jane *The Violet Flame* (UK)
H. G. Wells "A Story of the Days to Come" (UK)
———*When the Sleeper Wakes* (UK)

1900 Robert William Cole *The Struggle for Empire* (UK)
Garrett P. Serviss *The Moon Metal* (US)

1901 Joseph Conrad & Ford Maddox Hueffer *The Inheritors* (UK)
George Griffith *A Honeymoon in Space* (UK)
M. P. Shiel *The Lord of the Sea* (UK)
———*The Purple Cloud* (UK)
H. G. Wells *The First Men in the Moon* (UK)

1902 Alfred Jarry *Le Surmâle* (Fr, tr. as *The Supermale*)

1904 Robert W. Chambers *In Search of the Unknown* (US)
G. K. Chesterton *The Napoleon of Notting Hill* (UK)
André Couvreur *Caresco surhomme* (Fr, tr. as *Caresco, Superman*)
H. G. Wells *The Food of the Gods and How it Came to Earth* (UK)

1905 Edwin Lester Arnold *Lieut. Gullivar Jones: His Vacation* (UK)
Vincent Harper *The Mortgage on the Brain* (US)
Rudyard Kipling *With the Night Mail* (UK)

1906 Jules Hoche *Le Faiseur d'hommes et sa formule* (Fr, tr. as *The Maker of Men and His Formula*)
V. T. Sutphen *The Doomsman* (US)

1907 Charles Derennes *Le Peuple du pôle* (Fr, tr. as *The People of the Pole*)
C. H. Hinton *An Episode of Flatland* (UK)
William Hope Hodgson *The Boats of the "Glen Carrig"* (UK)
Jack London *The Iron Heel* (US)

1908 John Davidson *The Testament of John Davidson* (UK)
    James Elroy Flecker *The Last Generation* (UK)
    William Hope Hodgson *The House on the Borderland* (UK)
    Maurice Renard *Le Docteur Lerne, sous-dieu* (Fr, tr. as *Doctor Lerne, Subgod*)
    H. G. Wells *The War in the Air* (UK)

1909 E. M. Forster "The Machine Stops" (UK)
    Garrett P. Serviss *A Columbus of Space* (US)

1910 J.-H. Rosny "La Mort de la terre" (Fr, tr. as "The Death of the Earth")

1911 J. D. Beresford *The Hampdenshire Wonder* (UK)
    Maurice Renard *Le Péril bleu* (Fr, tr. as *The Blue Peril*)
    Garrett P. Serviss *The Second Deluge* (US)

1912 Edgar Rice Burroughs "Under the Moons of Mars" (US)
    Arthur Conan Doyle *The Lost World* (UK)
    George Allan England "Darkness and Dawn" (US)
    William Hope Hodgson *The Night Land* (UK)
    Jack London "The Scarlet Plague" (US)
    Gaston de Pawlowski *Voyage au pays de la quatrième dimension* (Fr, tr. as *Journey to the Land of the Fourth Dimension*)

1913 J. D. Beresford *Goslings* (UK)
    Arthur Conan Doyle *The Poison Belt* (UK)
    J.-H. Rosny *La Force Mystérieuse* (Fr, tr. as "The Mysterious Force")

1914 Edmond Haraucourt *Daâh, le premier homme* (Fr, tr. as *Daâh, the First Human*)
    Han Ryner *Les Pacifiques* (Fr, tr. as "The Pacifists")